Diamond in the Rough

Books by Jen Turano

Gentleman of Her Dreams: A LADIES OF DISTINCTION *Novella*
from *With All My Heart Romance Collection*

A Change of Fortune

A Most Peculiar Circumstance

A Talent for Trouble

A Match of Wits

After a Fashion

In Good Company

Playing the Part

At Your Request: An APART FROM THE CROWD *Novella*
from *All For Love Romance Collection*

Behind the Scenes

Out of the Ordinary

Caught by Surprise

Flights of Fancy

Diamond in the Rough

AMERICAN HEIRESSES · 2

Diamond in the Rough

JEN TURANO

BETHANYHOUSE
a division of Baker Publishing Group
Minneapolis, Minnesota

© 2019 by Jennifer L. Turano

Published by Bethany House Publishers
11400 Hampshire Avenue South
Bloomington, Minnesota 55438
www.bethanyhouse.com

Bethany House Publishers is a division of
Baker Publishing Group, Grand Rapids, Michigan

Printed in the United States of America

Library of Congress Cataloging in Publication Data
Names: Turano, Jen, author.
Title: Diamond in the rough / Jen Turano.
Description: Minneapolis : Bethany House Publishers, [2019] | Series: American
   heiresses ; 2
Identifiers: LCCN 2019016545 | ISBN 9780764231681 (trade paper) | ISBN
   9780764234880 (hardcover) | ISBN 9781493420292 (e-book)
Subjects: | GSAFD: Christian fiction. | Love stories.
Classification: LCC PS3620.U7455 D53 2019 | DDC 813/.6—dc23
LC record available at https://lccn.loc.gov/2019016545

This is a work of fiction. Names, characters, incidents, and dialogues are products of the author's imagination and are not to be construed as real. Any resemblance to actual events or persons, living or dead, is entirely coincidental.

Scripture quotations are from the King James Version of the Bible.

Cover design by Dan Thornberg, Design Source Creative Services

Author is represented by Natasha Kern Literary Agency.

19 20 21 22 23 24 25   7 6 5 4 3 2 1

For Barb Petrozzi

*You've always been one of my dearest friends, no matter
how many miles separate us. Thank you for all the support
you've given me, and for reading all of my books, no matter
that historical romances really aren't your thing.*

Love you!
Jen

CHAPTER 1

Any smidgen of hope that her entrance into New York high society would be deemed a rousing success died the moment Miss
Poppy Garrison's tiara became firmly attached to the sleeve of
her dance partner.

Wincing when Mr. Murray Middleton began turning her around
in a circle, a step that would have certainly been easier to execute
if her head wasn't stuck to his sleeve, Poppy listed to the left but
came to a rapid halt when Mr. Middleton abruptly stopped moving.

"Miss Garrison, what in the world are you about?" he asked in
a voice no louder than a whisper. "If you're unaware, the Gypsy
Quadrille does not require any manner of peculiar posturing. Your
deviation from the tried and true steps is drawing notice." He bent
closer to her, an easy feat since she was still attached to his sleeve.
"I realize you're not overly familiar with the ways of the New York
Four Hundred, but take it from someone in the know, it's not quite
the thing to diverge from the expected steps. That could very well
see you excluded from the smart set forever."

Mr. Middleton then attempted to take a step away from her,
a move that left her convinced she'd just become parted from a

great deal of blond hair that had once been styled in a most elegant manner but now must be looking nothing less than frightful.

"I'm not posturing," she managed to whisper back, even though she felt the distinct urge to release a howl of pain since her head was now stinging dreadfully. "I'm stuck."

"Stuck?"

"Indeed. To your jacket. Or at least my tiara is."

"A curious circumstance to be sure, but perhaps if I give you a twirl, you'll become unstuck."

Before Poppy could utter a single protest to what was certainly a horrible idea, Mr. Middleton surged into motion, giving her a very enthusiastic twirl. Fire raced over her scalp as the tiara was yanked from her head, taking numerous strands of her hair with it in the process, even as the tiara remained firmly attached to Mr. Middleton's sleeve. Then, for some unfathomable reason, Mr. Middleton gave her another twirl, sending her careening away from him and into the crowd of guests assembled on the edge of the dance floor located on the top floor of Delmonico's.

With her arms flailing about, she pitched forward, her plunge toward the ground interrupted when strong hands grabbed hold of her, pulling her directly against what felt like a rock-solid chest.

Lifting her head, Poppy felt a tingle creep up her neck as her gaze settled on the face of the gentleman who'd saved her from a nasty spill.

He wasn't who one would consider the handsomest gentleman in the room, but he had a presence about him that drew and held her attention. His hair was dark, as were his eyes, and he had a sharp blade of a nose, which didn't hold her attention long, not after she caught a glimpse of his lips—lips that weren't curving in the least and . . .

"Are you all right, miss?"

The moment that question left the gentleman's mouth, Poppy found herself going noticeably weak at the knees, a direct result of the distinct English accent that flowed over her like rich honey being drizzled over a hot biscuit.

Blinking out of those thoughts when she realized she'd curled her hands into the lapels of the gentleman's jacket, causing him to arch a dark brow at her, Poppy released her hold on him and stepped back, willing knees that were still a tad wobbly to cooperate.

She smiled. "You're English."

"British."

"Isn't that the same thing?"

"Not at all."

Poppy's smile dimmed. "I suppose I should now beg your pardon, sir, although I wasn't attempting to insult you, merely—"

"Miss Garrison, what, pray tell, are you doing?"

Dread was immediate as she recognized the voice behind her as belonging to the esteemed Mr. Ward McAllister, a gentleman her grandmother had told her had the power to see her accepted into society—or not.

Forcing herself to turn, Poppy winced when she discovered Mr. McAllister scowling at her, his moustache twitching in a most concerning manner.

"Well?" Mr. McAllister demanded. "Explain yourself."

Her mind, unfortunately, took that moment to go completely blank. "Forgive me, but what was the question?"

Mr. McAllister's moustache twitched again. "I asked you to explain why you've disrupted the Gypsy Quadrille, one I personally chose to open up the first Family Circle Dancing Class of the Season." He puffed out his chest. "I hope you're aware that only two hundred and twenty-five guests are invited to this affair, and only a select few, yourself included, are presented with the supreme honor of participating in the quadrille. There were more than a few young ladies who were sorely disappointed to find themselves not included in the opening dance. I have to believe none of those disappointed young ladies would have ever contemplated causing the type of ruckus you have."

Poppy wrinkled her nose. "Perhaps one of those young ladies is currently lingering on the sidelines and would be more than happy to take over for me, something I would appreciate since I'm woefully inept at the intricacies of this particular dance."

Mr. McAllister's eyes flashed in a less-than-encouraging way. "Do not toy with me, Miss Garrison. You will not enjoy the consequences." He crossed his arms over his chest. "I demand an explanation, and without further delay, if you please. If you've neglected to notice, the entire ballroom is waiting with bated breath to learn why the opening quadrille has come to a screeching halt."

Poppy glanced past Mr. McAllister and found that the dancers who'd been given the honor of participating in the Gypsy Quadrille, all of whom were garbed in brightly colored costumes similar to the one she was wearing, were standing still as statues. She then directed her attention to the guests who'd been observing the quadrille, finding them watching her closely, their gazes alive with speculation.

"I do seem to have drawn an unusual amount of interest," she said weakly before she summoned up another smile, one that Mr. McAllister didn't return. "I had no idea my mishap would cause such mayhem." She craned her neck. "How curious that the musicians appear to have frozen in place as well, quite as if they're figurines in a music box that needs a few good whirls to get them into motion again."

Mr. McAllister stepped closer to her. "Not that this is the moment to descend into such unusual observations, Miss Garrison, but the musicians froze on my command, and the dancers stopped dancing because they know they cannot successfully continue on with this quadrille until you resume your place with Mr. Middleton." Mr. McAllister released a sniff. "What *could* you have been thinking to cause such a disruption?"

"I wasn't thinking much of anything beyond trying to puzzle out how best to get my tiara unattached from Mr. Middleton's jacket."

Mr. McAllister swung his attention to Mr. Middleton, who was still trying to tug the tiara in question from his sleeve. Mr. McAllister snapped his attention back to Poppy. "How is it possible your tiara became attached to Mr. Middleton's sleeve in the first place?"

Poppy shot a look to Mr. Middleton, noticing that his cheeks were stained a telltale shade of red, which stood out vividly against a complexion that was unusually pale and in stark contrast to the lightness of his blond hair.

She did not know Mr. Middleton well, having only made his acquaintance the week prior, after her grandmother had received a last-minute invitation from Mr. McAllister inviting Poppy to participate in the Gypsy Quadrille.

Her grandmother, Mrs. George Van Rensselaer, known to her closest confidants as Viola, had been beside herself with glee over that coveted invitation. Poppy, on the other hand, had accepted the invitation with a great deal of wariness because she'd never danced a quadrille before in her life.

That wariness had only increased after she'd been shown the intricate steps of the dance at a Family Circle Dancing Class practice session. When she'd voiced her concerns to her grandmother after that session, claiming there was little hope she'd be able to master the steps on such short notice, her grandmother had dismissed the concerns out of hand, stating that Van Rensselaers were known for their ability to adapt to any situation.

Viola, from that point forward, could not be persuaded to change her mind. She'd insisted Poppy practice the steps with Mr. Parsons, the family butler, every evening for hours, but even with that practice, Poppy had known she was ill prepared to perform in front of New York high society.

She had a feeling her dance partner, Mr. Murray Middleton, had come to that very same conclusion and must now be bemoaning that his original dance partner, Miss Susan Welles, had turned an ankle a week and a half before.

After meeting Mr. Middleton, Poppy had been left questioning whether Miss Welles had truly suffered a great injury or if she'd used a turned ankle as an excuse to avoid taking to the floor with Mr. Middleton.

Mr. Middleton, being all of twenty-one years of age, a year younger than Poppy's twenty-two, was what one could only call a nervous sort. He was constantly in motion, fiddling with his sleeve, his necktie, and even his hair, and because he did not possess much height to speak of, he seemed much younger than his years.

Poppy had tried her best to put the poor gentleman at ease while they'd been practicing their quadrille steps, but after Mr. Middleton had gotten a glimpse of them in the mirror and realized that Poppy was a good three inches taller than he was, he'd descended in what could almost be considered a fit of the vapors, convinced that society would mock them because of their discrepancy in height.

Frankly, his lack of height might have been directly responsible for the tiara mishap. When she'd been about to glide underneath his arm in a difficult move, he'd not raised his arm high enough— or perhaps it had gone as high as he was capable of raising it— which had resulted in her getting a bit of a wallop from him as she'd begun to turn, and that walloping evidently left her tiara attached to his sleeve.

"We don't have all night, Miss Garrison," Mr. McAllister growled.

Blinking from her thoughts, Poppy looked back to Mr. Middleton, saw the panic in his eyes, and knew there was only one thing to do, even if it might see her banished from fashionable New York forever.

Squaring her shoulders, she turned back to Mr. McAllister. "The only explanation I have is this: I fear I must have turned at the wrong time, which was how I became attached to Mr. Middleton's sleeve."

"How do you explain almost knocking over Mr. Reginald Blackburn?"

"Who?"

"Mr. Blackburn, the gentleman who saved you from sprawling to the ground."

Turning, she glanced at the gentleman who'd caught her and saw him watching her closely, as if he found her to be a most curious creature. Not caring to be watched in such a manner, she turned back to Mr. McAllister and inclined her head. "It certainly was not my intention to mow over Mr. Blackburn, sir, although given the size of the man, I doubt I would have been successful even if that *had* been my intention."

Mr. McAllister looked as if he'd gotten a whiff of something unpleasant. "One would hope a young lady would never contemplate the unlikely scenario of mowing a gentleman over."

Poppy nodded. "I'm sure you're right, although I have, unintentionally of course, knocked down more than my fair share of gentlemen—but not on a dance floor," she hurried to add. "Not that this paints me in a favorable light, but the oddest things happen to me when I least expect them to, and—"

"I don't believe this is exactly the time for us to delve into what sounds like unusual happenstances," Mr. McAllister interrupted. "You've a quadrille to finish, and if you don't want to see yourself banned from future society events, I suggest you return to Mr. Middleton and allow us to get on with matters."

"I would think you've already decided to ban me from future events."

Mr. McAllister closed his eyes and seemed to be counting under his breath. Opening his eyes after ten seconds had passed, he took hold of her arm and began marching her toward Mr. Middleton. "I'm not casting you out of society *yet*, but do know that I'll be keeping a sharp eye on you from this point forward. One more incident and you might very well find yourself back on the family horse farm, no matter the high esteem I hold for your grandmother." He drew her to a stop next to Mr. Middleton. Plucking the tiara from Mr. Middleton's jacket and ignoring the tearing sound of Mr. Middleton's sleeve, Mr. McAllister plopped the tiara onto Poppy's head, then gave it a good shove onto her head, pulling her hair in the process. After sending her a significant look, he turned smartly on his heel and strode away. Clapping his hands a second later, music filled the room, and a second after that, everyone swept back into motion.

Mr. Middleton grabbed hold of her arm and steered her forcefully across the dance floor, weaving in and out of their fellow dancers, tightening his grip when she stumbled.

"If this is a sign of how the rest of the season is going to unfold, I should consider taking a tour of the Continent," Mr. Middleton muttered, pulling her to the right even as he dashed a gloved hand over a forehead that glistened with perspiration. "I thought both of us were doomed, but . . ." His steps slowed. "What were you thinking, taking the blame? You should have said it was my fault. That's what any other lady would have said."

Poppy winced when she realized she'd just stepped on Mr. Middleton's foot. "I hardly believe it would have been fair to cast blame your way. If anything, you should be given a medal for agreeing to take the floor with me."

Mr. Middleton, gentleman that he apparently was, didn't respond to that as he settled into the daunting feat of leading her through the remainder of the quadrille. He whispered to her that she needed to exchange places with the young lady directly beside her, and after she wobbled past that lady and moved around that lady's dance partner, Mr. Middleton took her arm, looking resigned when she stumbled over his foot again.

Poppy tucked a strand of loose hair behind her ear, not allowing herself to dwell on the disaster she was certainly sporting on her head. "I must say that you make a most impressive figure on the dance floor, Mr. Middleton. I must also add that it shows a great deal of character on your part that you haven't abandoned me yet, even though I'm certain you've been tempted to do exactly that."

Mr. Middleton turned her smartly around, then took hold of her arm as they moved in a circular motion with the rest of the dancers. "You're very kind, Miss Garrison, and I must say that your perseverance is to be commended. There aren't many young ladies who'd have continued with this quadrille after suffering such an unforeseen incident. I expected you to flee from the ball the moment you got free from my sleeve."

"I'm not the type of lady who flees from unpleasantness, Mr. Middleton," Poppy said. "Besides, my grandmother went on and on about the importance of this particular event, and I know she'd be more than displeased if I made what would surely be seen by society as a dramatic exit." She stumbled over Mr. Middleton's foot and sent him a smile when he helped her regain her balance. "I am curious, though, about what sets this Family Circle Dancing Class apart from all the other frivolities offered this week."

A hefty dose of horror flickered through Mr. Middleton's eyes. "Have a care, Miss Garrison. Society takes their frivolities very seriously and expects its members to understand the importance of every event." He leaned closer to her. "I trust you've heard of the Patriarch Balls?"

"My grandmother has assured me I'll be attending every one of those this Season, beginning with the first Patriarch Ball held in January, sponsored by none other than *the* Mrs. Astor."

"I would expect nothing less, given that your grandfather is well acquainted with the original patriarchs who have the honor of choosing the guests for each of those balls." He nodded to the crowd surrounding them. "Invitations to the Patriarch Balls are most sought after, but what society leaders began to realize was this: Those balls draw attention, not to the many eligible young ladies within society, but to the established society matrons, whom everyone fawns over to shore up their own society positions. Because of that, it was decided that a venue to draw notice to the *young* ladies was needed, hence the creation of the Family Circle Dancing Class, and hence the reason behind it being one of the first important events of the social season."

Moving with Mr. Middleton to join the line of dancers in what would be their final promenade of the Gypsy Quadrille, Poppy ignored the many whispers of the guests lining the ballroom floor as she and Mr. Middleton swept past them. "So there *is* a waiting list to be invited to this ball?"

"There is, as well as waiting lists to join many other societal functions this season."

"I imagine I'll now find my name on the very bottom of all those lists."

Mr. Middleton shook his head. "Your grandmother wields considerable power within the New York Four Hundred, as does your grandfather, even though he's rarely in town. Mr. McAllister may bluster and threaten banishment, but I doubt he'll dare follow through with those threats. He might, however, make it next to impossible for you to become a diamond of the first water, so you will need to tread carefully with your behavior from this point forward."

As they reached the edge of the dance floor, Mr. Middleton whispered a reminder that she would be expected to curtsy before the grand society dame who was their sponsor that evening, a formidable woman by the name of Mrs. Eugene Kruger.

Hoping she wouldn't fall over while curtsying, since she was unaccustomed to wearing the large bustles that were all the fashion this season, Poppy sank into a curtsy after Mr. Middleton brought her to a stop in front of Mrs. Kruger, relief slipping over her when she managed to rise with ease, even though she thought her bustle might have shifted to the right.

Stepping out of the way to allow the couple behind them to be acknowledged, Poppy exchanged a smile with Mr. Middleton.

"I imagine you're glad that's over," she said.

"I must admit you're right about that, although I'll be even more relieved after I've delivered you back to your grandmother." He gave a bit of a shudder. "She is certain to be put out over our performance."

"She won't be put out with us," Poppy countered. "We did, after all, manage to make it through to the end, and what grandmother wouldn't be pleased about that?"

"While completing the quadrille was an impressive feat if there ever was one, I don't believe your grandmother is going to see that in the same light we do."

Poppy swallowed the argument that was on the tip of her tongue because Mr. Middleton had just made an excellent point.

Her grandmother, who insisted Poppy address her as Viola, was a difficult woman to say the least, and over the two months Poppy had been living under her roof, she'd come to realize that Viola was nothing like the other grandmothers Poppy had encountered over the years.

Being in her early sixties, although she could easily pass for fifty, Viola was a lady who only dressed in the first state of fashion. She never stepped foot out of her dressing room without every blond hair in place, her nails buffed, and her face looking radiant, which was a direct result of the numerous creams she bought from Paris. Her posture was always perfect, her bearing regal, and she wrapped the extreme wealth she'd been born into around her like a cloak, one that brought to mind images of snobbery at its finest.

"Shall we get this over with?" Mr. Middleton asked as he gave her a tug in Viola's direction.

She fought a grin when Mr. Middleton began dragging his feet the closer they got to her grandmother. Her urge to grin disappeared when they stopped in front of Viola, who, even though she was smiling, had temper flashing out of her blue eyes.

"I do hope, Poppy," Viola began in a voice that was downright frigid, "that the debacle I just watched you participate in was not some curious ruse on your part to get released from the agreement you and I have. If it was, I assure you, it was all for naught because I have no intention of releasing you from your promise that easily."

Chapter 2

"Who in their right mind would come up with a ruse that would see a person's tiara stuck to a gentleman's jacket?" Poppy asked.

Viola's nostrils flared. "You've not made it a secret that you find New York society vexing. Frankly, I've been expecting you to devise a plan to get released from our agreement, no matter if the means to achieve that may have you resorting to unlikely scenarios."

"You're giving me far too much credit for creativity," Poppy returned. "If you neglected to notice, I was having difficulty simply remembering all the steps to the quadrille. I certainly didn't have time to compose some elaborate ruse, even though that might not have been a bad idea *if* I had any intention of trying to get released from our agreement, which I *don't*."

Viola glanced around, narrowed her eyes on a gathering of young ladies standing near them, all of whom immediately dashed away in a rustle of silk, then returned her attention to Poppy. "We'll continue this discussion later when we have more privacy." She turned her attention to Mr. Middleton, who immediately seemed to shrink in size. "How was it, Mr. Middleton, that you allowed my granddaughter to become such fodder for the gossips? Did it not occur to you to step in and accept full blame for the disaster everyone observed?"

"Ah . . . well . . ." Mr. Middleton began as he turned concerningly pale and simply stopped speaking.

Poppy released a breath and caught her grandmother's eye. "It is not well done of you, Grandmother—"

"Viola," her grandmother interrupted.

"It is not well done of you, *Viola*," Poppy amended, "to take Mr. Middleton to task for a situation that was *not* of his making. Not that you could be aware of this, what with our limited contact over the years, but I'm occasionally prone to clumsiness, which was directly responsible for the mayhem Mr. Middleton and I recently experienced."

Viola held up a pair of opera glasses she always kept at the ready. "I was watching your progress during the quadrille, and from what I observed, Mr. Middleton was at fault, but . . ." Her eyes flashed. "You didn't admit to Mr. McAllister that you have a propensity for clumsiness, did you?"

"He seems to be a rather astute gentleman, so he probably came to that conclusion on his own."

Viola settled a glare on Mr. Middleton. "And you didn't feel the need to step in and disabuse Mr. McAllister of the notion my granddaughter is a clumsy sort?"

"Do you know that I once got knocked straight off a horse because a duck flew into me?" Poppy asked when Mr. Middleton seemed at a complete loss for words.

Viola pulled her glare from Mr. Middleton and settled it on Poppy. "Why would you take this particular moment to share such an outlandish tale?"

"Because that tale lends credence to the idea that I often find myself in the most ridiculous situations. I mean, it's not a frequent occurrence for people to lose their seat on a horse because of a duck, even if the stallion I'd taken out that day was possessed of a questionable temperament."

"You willingly chose to ride a stallion with a questionable temperament?"

"I grew up on a horse farm. I rode horses all the time with

19

questionable temperaments, especially the ones that were unaccustomed to wearing a saddle."

"You've taken part in breaking horses?" Mr. Middleton asked, his voice rising a good octave as his eyes turned wide as dinner plates.

"I have, although—"

"This is hardly the place to discuss such matters," Viola interrupted. "We're at Delmonico's, for goodness' sake. Talk of breaking horses is not proper fodder for polite conversation."

"Too right you are, Mrs. Van Rensselaer," Mr. Middleton hurried to agree. "And because it's almost time to repair to the first floor for dinner, if you'll excuse me, I need to retrieve the name of the lady I'm to escort in to dine."

"I thought you'd be escorting me to dinner," Poppy said.

"While that would be . . . *delightful* to be sure, Miss Garrison, I normally find myself relegated to escorting society matrons into dinner over the younger set." He shook his head. "My mother has made it known that I'm a gentleman always available to step in when men are scarce, but I'm not warmly embraced by the fashionable set. That's why it's highly doubtful I'll find your name on the card I'm off to retrieve from Mr. McAllister."

"I find you to be most fashionable, Mr. Middleton," Poppy argued. "And that right there is exactly why you won't find *my* name on your card, not with how annoyed Mr. McAllister seems to be with me."

Mr. Middleton's cheeks turned pink. "No one has ever called me fashionable."

"Then you're not associating with the right people," Poppy returned before she frowned. "I thought seating assignments for society dinners were given out at the beginning of an event."

Mr. Middleton nodded. "They usually are, but because the Earl of Lonsdale is in attendance this evening, Mr. McAllister has decided to add a bit of suspense to tonight's event, leaving everyone on tenterhooks as to whom they'll be dining with this evening." He leaned closer to her. "Perhaps you'll be fortunate enough to find the earl as *your* dinner partner."

Viola leveled a cool look on Mr. Middleton. "The Earl of Lons-dale is the honored guest this evening, which means he'll be escorting Mrs. Kruger into dinner because she is the sponsor of this event, a rule of etiquette I would have thought you'd remember, Mr. Middleton."

Mr. Middleton gave a bob of his head. "Quite right, Mrs. Van Rensselaer. I seem to have lost my head there for a moment. And on that note, I believe I'll take my leave and seek out my dinner partner."

Poppy smiled. "I hope that partner will be someone possessed of a charming nature. That might go far in turning your evening from a horrifying experience to something more along the lines of pleasant."

Mr. Middleton bowed over Poppy's hand. "Taking the floor with you was not a horrifying experience—or at least not a *completely* horrifying experience." He raised her hand to his lips, pressed a kiss on it, then smiled. "You're a most unconventional lady, Miss Garrison, refreshingly so, and I hope you won't be opposed to me paying you a call later this week. You might enjoy a brisk buggy ride in Central Park. I have access to a smashing set of bays I believe you'll find most impressive."

"That sounds lovely, Mr. Middleton. I'll look forward to it."

Mr. Middleton smiled and released her hand. He turned to Viola and began to bow but stopped mid-bow when Viola quirked a brow in return. Straightening, and without speaking another word, he bolted away.

Waiting until he disappeared into the crowd, Poppy turned to her grandmother. "You really shouldn't glower so at poor Mr. Middleton. You just scared the stuffing out of him."

"I'm not above using intimidation to dissuade a most unsuitable gentleman from pursuing you."

"I don't believe Mr. Middleton is intent on pursuing me, merely accompanying me around Central Park for an excursion. Still, if he did have an interest, why would you take issue with that? He comes from a reputable family, and he's a lovely dancer."

Viola took hold of Poppy's arm. "He lacks ambition. But further talk of his other deficiencies will need to wait. You're looking frightful, which means we need to make haste to the retiring room and get you and your hair set to rights before we go down to dinner."

"You're going to restyle my hair?" Poppy asked as they began moving through the crowd.

"Don't be ridiculous. We'll have the woman attending the retiring room fix your hair. Delmonico's always keeps such women available to assist the guests, but there's no telling how competent this woman will be. Don't expect your hair to look as lovely as it did when you started out this evening."

"I'll be satisfied simply to have it out of my face so I won't risk dipping it into whatever soups may be served this evening."

"A charming thought to be sure," Viola muttered as they reached the retiring room.

Stepping into the room behind her grandmother, Poppy discovered three young ladies standing before the mirror, two of whom were pinching their cheeks, while the other was accepting a hand towel from a woman dressed in a severe black outfit, with the only relief being the starched white apron she was wearing.

"Ladies, we need the room," Viola said, and just like that, the ladies abandoned their cheek pinching and hand drying and all but raced out the door.

"Did you notice the looks of terror that immediately crossed their faces when they caught sight of you?" Poppy asked, walking over to a stool that was in front of the mirror and taking a seat. "It's an unusual talent you possess, and I can't help wondering if being able to terrify young ladies with a single glance is an accomplishment you intentionally perfected over the years."

"I don't purposely set out to terrify the young ladies of society." Viola nodded to the woman left in the room with them, one who also seemed to have a trace of terror on her face. "Miss Garrison needs her hair restyled, but we don't have much time, so do hurry."

Eyeing the curling tong that was resting on the counter, Poppy frowned. "I'm not certain it's wise to demand haste of a woman who is soon to apply a hot tong to my head." She smiled at the woman. "Take whatever time you need, Miss . . . ?"

"I'm Alice, miss. Alice Burns," the woman mumbled as Viola let out a huff.

"This is not the time to exchange pleasantries with the help, Poppy. We have pressing matters to discuss, and now that we're alone, I'm free to broach topics that are somewhat delicate without anyone overhearing me."

Knowing there was little benefit in pointing out that they weren't alone since Alice was standing directly beside them, Poppy folded her hands in her lap while Alice began untangling the tiara from her hair.

"Returning to the problem of Mr. Middleton," Viola said a moment later. "As I mentioned earlier, he lacks ambition, but worse than that, he's completely under his mother's thumb."

"Mr. Middleton is very young, and from what I understand, he's the baby of the Middleton family," Poppy countered. "It's little wonder his mother still has sway over him."

Viola caught Poppy's eye in the reflection of the mirror. "While I understand that your upbringing has been unconventional to say the least, what you need to grasp more than anything is this: Your acceptance into high society all comes down to the connections you form. An association with Mr. Middleton will do nothing to elevate your status. And given what just transpired with Mr. McAllister, you're in a tenuous position as it is."

"Mr. Middleton is of the belief that your influence will spare me from whatever repercussions Mr. McAllister may wish to level against me."

"My influence will guarantee invitations to future events, but it will not guarantee you acceptance into the fashionable set. That means you do not have the luxury of forming friendships with people I can only describe as misfits."

"I've always felt that misfits are far more interesting than normal folks."

"*Folks* is not a word I ever want to hear out of your mouth again, not if you don't want to see your time in New York ending in failure *and* without securing the affections of a suitable gentleman."

Waiting until Alice had secured her hair with a few strategically placed hairpins, Poppy turned to her grandmother. "I did not come to New York for the explicit purpose of finding a husband."

"There's absolutely no reason for you to not make the most of this Season and look for a prospective groom. You'll need one eventually, especially if, heaven forbid, you decide to return to your father's horse farm and take up with the work you evidently do there."

"While it does appear that everyone assumes my lifelong ambition is to continue with the work I've always done at Garrison Farms, that's not written in stone. If you've forgotten, I have two younger brothers, both of whom will be more than capable of taking over for my father in what I hope is the very distant future."

Viola's eyes began to gleam. "Does that mean you might entertain the thought of enjoying the summer Season with me in Newport?"

"I might, although it's far too soon to say for certain, what with how daunting this New York Season is shaping up to be." She smiled. "Newport does sound inviting, though, and before I left Pennsylvania, I had a lovely talk with Reverend Thomas Cameron, who lent me some invaluable advice about how I should view my time away from Garrison Farms."

"Who, pray tell, is Reverend Thomas Cameron?"

"He's been the minister at the church I've attended for years, and he's a man whose counsel I respect."

The gleam in Viola's eyes turned to wariness. "What type of counsel could this small-town reverend lend you?"

"Well, as you must know, Mother was adamant that I refuse your offer of a Season, but Reverend Cameron thought I should accept, convincing me that time away from the farm would be a wonderful way for me to broaden my horizons and see more of what the world has to offer."

Viola's brows knit together. "Your mother told me that I was ruining your life by taking you away from your beloved farm, and also that I was certain to cause you irreparable harm by bringing you out in high society." She caught Poppy's eye. "Why would Elizabeth have told me that if you'd willingly decided, after seeking the counsel of this Reverend Cameron, to travel to New York?"

"Surely you haven't forgotten how Mother seems to extract a great deal of enjoyment out of annoying you."

Viola's lips thinned. "There is that, but tell me this. Did your Reverend Cameron not mention anything about looking for a suitable husband while you're in New York? I would think that even a rural man of the cloth would want to encourage a lady who is rapidly approaching spinsterhood to take advantage of such a wonderful opportunity to become acquainted with so many eligible gentlemen."

"We never discussed that particular subject because, if you'll recall, the *main* reason I agreed to this Season in New York was because that was *your* condition before you would agree to assist my parents out of their unexpected financial difficulties."

Viola lifted her chin. "I don't know how their financial difficulties could have been *unexpected* when they were foolish enough to take out a large loan to expand the Garrison enterprise."

Poppy shifted on the seat, stilling when Alice suddenly came closer to her with the hot curling tong. "My parents had no way of knowing that the bank would suffer a financial setback and call in the loan a good two years before it was supposed to be due."

"They shouldn't have taken out a loan in the first place. Elizabeth could have simply contacted me and asked for the money needed for the expansion of the stables into Kentucky."

"You and Mother have been mostly estranged from each other ever since she ran off with my father twenty-four years ago."

"Elizabeth and I still have a small amount of contact."

"You speak once a year when my mother travels to New York in December to bid you a Merry Christmas and do a bit of shopping."

"That's still contact."

"Barely, and it's not as if either of you enjoy an emotional reunion."

"The Van Rensselaers are not known to be overly emotional."

"Mother is a Van Rensselaer and she can be downright sentimental at times."

"There's always an odd duck in every family."

"I've been known to become quite emotional, especially if I'm reading a novel that has a less-than-happy ending," Poppy said as Alice abandoned the curling tong and began gathering the newly created curls onto the top of Poppy's head. "I have fond memories of Mother stealing into my room to spirit away books she was convinced would cause me to become morose for days."

Clear horror flashed through Viola's eyes. "I've always been of the firm belief that novels were to blame for Elizabeth's disgraceful abandonment of New York. I highly doubt she'd have thought about running away with your father if she hadn't been privy to tales of forbidden love."

"Perhaps if you hadn't been so determined to see her married to a man of your choosing, you would have seen that my father was perfect for her."

"Mr. William Daft, the man I'd selected for Elizabeth, was a charming young gentleman. He would have most assuredly provided your mother with a fine home and whatever else she may have desired."

"Mother once told me Mr. Daft was like Mr. Collins from *Pride and Prejudice*."

"Which proves my point about her being overly influenced through novels, although I've never read *Pride and Prejudice* so I'm not at liberty to comment on whether Mr. Daft shared characteristics with a certain Mr. Collins."

"How is it possible you've never read *Pride and Prejudice*?"

"I don't read novels, nor can I be persuaded to change my mind about that after I experienced Elizabeth running off with Harold." Viola pursed her lips. "Your father, if you didn't know, was only in New York all those years ago to deliver horses that your grandfather bought from Garrison Farms. The next thing I know, your mother was inviting him into our house for tea, and then, after I insisted she discontinue her budding friendship with Harold, she ran off with him. I'm convinced that Jane Austen's insipid novels were directly responsible for leaving Elizabeth with an unrealistic view of the world, one where romance ruled the day and everyone got their own happily-ever-after."

"But Mother *did* get her very own happily-ever-after. She's still wildly in love with my father."

"*Wildly in love* is most unseemly." Viola's eyes turned chilly. "I do not intend to go through such nonsense again with you, which is why I'm going to expect you to discontinue with your novel reading and pursue something more practical, such as painting. I'm also going to demand that you discontinue associations with questionable sorts, and—"

"I'm not particularly fond of demands."

Viola ignored her, although she seemed to begin counting under her breath, quite like Mr. McAllister had done earlier. After a good twenty seconds passed, Viola cleared her throat. "As I was saying, I will not tolerate you surrounding yourself with misfits or questionable sorts. The dowry I've settled on you is quite sizable and might even have to be increased after tonight's debacle. But because of the fortune I'm prepared to give away to the suitable gentleman I know is out there for you somewhere, I won't stand back and watch you squander what should be a brilliant opportunity simply because you seem to possess the same willful and stubborn attitude as—"

"You've settled a dowry on me?" Poppy interrupted, leaning forward on the stool, even though doing so left her head stinging because Alice had been trying to press the tiara back into her curls.

Viola waved that aside with a flick of a diamond-encrusted wrist. "I've no idea why you would be surprised to learn that. Surely you didn't think I would bring you out for a New York Season without taking proper steps to assure you'd enjoy some type of success, did you?"

"You never mentioned anything about a dowry."

"Well, now you know, although I'm surprised you never considered the matter before since it's a common practice for young ladies of good standing to have their families settle a dowry on them to guarantee a most splendid match."

Poppy tilted her head. "Father has every intention of giving me a large portion of the land that surrounds Garrison Farms in Pennsylvania, now that he's moving the bulk of our business to Kentucky. We own thousands of acres in Pennsylvania, and those acres can certainly be considered a dowry of sorts. That means I have no need of the dowry you're evidently keen to settle on me—one that will assuredly have all the fortune hunters pursuing me in earnest."

Viola brushed that aside. "An aging horse farm or the land that encompasses that farm is not a proper dowry, and I wouldn't worry about fortune hunters, Poppy. The type of wealth I'm willing to give to a future husband of yours is enough to intimidate men incapable of earning their own fortunes, although . . ." Her gaze turned rather distant. "I do have high hopes that your dowry might entice a few gentlemen in possession of aristocratic titles. I've always longed to enjoy a Season in London, and if you were to capture the attention of an aristocrat, that would be quite the feather in both of our caps."

Poppy resisted the urge to rub her suddenly aching forehead. "How is an aristocrat intent on procuring himself a fortune to shore up his estates any different than an American fortune hunter?"

"He's in possession of a title, of course, and then, well, British aristocrats do have that most delicious manner of speaking."

"You have a proclivity for British accents?"

"I must admit that I do." Viola's gaze sharpened on Poppy's face. "You seem surprised by that, dear."

Knowing better than to admit to a determined grandmother that she too enjoyed British accents, Poppy shrugged. "I suppose there is something charming about the manner in which Englishmen speak, although I have no desire to set my sights on an aristocrat." She shuddered. "I hate to think about all the rules that I would be expected to obey if I married one of those. You must have realized by now that I'm not always keen to follow rules."

Viola's lips pursed. "That hasn't slipped my notice. But returning to what we were discussing before—that being getting you firmly ensconced within the fashionable set."

"Was that what we were discussing before?"

"You'll need to form proper friendships with the right members of the New York Four Hundred," Viola continued as if Poppy hadn't spoken. "To assist you with that, I've already arranged a lovely tea for you. You'll be joined with ladies I feel are above reproach: Miss Adele Tooker, Miss Edith Iselin, and Miss Cynthia Roche."

"Miss Roche barely spoke to me the other day while we were practicing the Gypsy Quadrille, and Miss Tooker was rude to Mr. Middleton when he merely inquired if her family had any special plans for the holiday season."

Viola opened her mouth but was interrupted from replying when a brisk knock sounded on the retiring room door. A second later, the door opened and Miss Beatrix Waterbury stepped into the room, looking lovely in an ivory gown, her vivid red hair arranged in a most charming fashion, although the tiara she was wearing was half the size of the one Viola had insisted Poppy wear.

Beatrix Waterbury was considered one of the great American heiresses of the day, but she was not a lady who put on airs. She was also fast friends with Miss Isadora Delafield, or rather Mrs. Ian MacKenzie since she'd recently married. That was a mark in her favor since Poppy was acquainted with Isadora as well. That acquaintance was what had led Beatrix to immediately seek out Poppy after she'd learned Poppy was residing in New York, and her warm air and genuine offer of friendship had been greatly appreciated.

"Do forgive me for interrupting," Beatrix began, nodding in Viola's direction. "Mrs. Kruger asked me to seek you out because the Earl of Lonsdale is eager to become introduced to Poppy."

Viola's eyes immediately began to sparkle. "How encouraging. He's eager to meet my Poppy, is he?"

Beatrix smiled. "He didn't state that to me when I was introduced to him, but I don't imagine Mrs. Kruger would have told me that if it weren't true."

"You've already been introduced to Lord Lonsdale?" Viola asked, the sparkle in her eyes dimming ever so slightly.

"I have, although there's no reason for you to look disgruntled about that, Mrs. Van Rensselaer." Beatrix's smile turned into a grin. "Once the earl discovered I'm somewhat spoken for, he wasn't as keen to pursue a conversation with me, evidently determining that would be a clear waste of his time in New York."

Viola frowned. "Did I miss a formal announcement regarding you being spoken for, Miss Waterbury?"

Beatrix gave an airy wave of her hand. "It's no secret that Mr. Thomas Hamersley and I have been friends since he was in short pants and I was in short dresses. And while there's not been a formal announcement, nor will there be for the foreseeable future, I find it prudent to allow gentlemen to know that I'm not actively seeking a husband. It tends to help negate any troublesome misunderstandings with gentlemen who *are* searching for brides."

Poppy rose to her feet, thanked Alice for setting her hair to rights, then turned to Beatrix. "May I assume Lord Lonsdale has come to America in order to secure himself a wife?"

"Of course he has—or rather to secure himself an heiress," Beatrix amended. "But don't let that discourage you from becoming acquainted with him. He seems to be a charming man."

"Then we mustn't keep him waiting," Viola said firmly, rising from her chair to take Poppy's arm. "Remember to smile, dear, and for goodness' sake, don't tell him the story about the duck."

In a blink of an eye, Poppy was steered rather forcefully out the door, Beatrix following behind. Viola paused for the briefest second after they entered the ballroom, but then she pulled Poppy forward, muttering instructions out of the side of her mouth that Poppy couldn't understand.

Bringing her to a stop next to a gathering of young ladies, Viola gave Poppy's arm a squeeze right as Mrs. Kruger stepped in front of them, a gentleman on either side of her.

To Poppy's concern, one of the gentlemen turned out to be Mr. Blackburn. He was once again watching her closely, the intensity of his gaze leaving her flustered and causing her to miss half of the introduction Mrs. Kruger was already performing.

Not appreciating the subtle shove her grandmother suddenly gave her, Poppy took two steps forward but found herself stumbling over something that felt remarkably like a stick. With a bit of a shriek, she went plummeting toward the floor again, saved from yet another nasty tumble by none other than the rather brooding Mr. Blackburn.

CHAPTER 3

"I don't expect you were anticipating a lady stumbling into your arms twice in one evening, but I do appreciate your quick reflexes, sir."

As Mr. Reginald Blackburn set the seemingly mishap-prone Miss Poppy Garrison away from him, then helped her find her balance when she immediately began to wobble, he struggled for some manner of polite response, although what type of response he could possibly give was quite beyond him at the moment.

He thought he'd been prepared to deal with American ladies, whom Bertie, the Prince of Wales, had told him were overly exuberant at times, but nothing could have prepared him for the unusual experience of dealing with a young lady like Miss Garrison.

To his relief, Miss Garrison did not seem to expect a response from him because she suddenly seemed to realize her bustle was askew. Reaching behind her, she began trying to tug the bustle back into place, evidently unconcerned that trying to set herself to rights in the middle of a society event was not something guests were accustomed to seeing.

Poor Mrs. Kruger, the sponsor of the Family Circle Dancing Class, seemed to have been rendered speechless as she gaped at Miss Garrison, a concerning circumstance since Reginald had been hoping that lady would step forward and break the uncomfortable silence that had settled around them.

Glancing to his cousin, Charles Wynn, the Ninth Earl of Lonsdale, who could normally be counted on to save a situation when it turned uncomfortable, Reginald noticed that Charles was currently gazing at Miss Garrison with a dazed expression in his eyes. That expression suggested it was highly unlikely his cousin would be the one to break the awkward silence.

It wasn't that Reginald could say he blamed Charles for sporting a dazed expression because Miss Garrison, even with her propensity for unusual mishaps, was a lady who drew a man's notice.

She was above average height, but instead of being overly thin and willowy, she possessed a most impressive figure—something he could personally attest to since that figure had been pressed up against him twice in the past hour. Her delightful curves were displayed to perfection in the brightly colored gypsy costume she was wearing, the unusual colors of her costume complementing skin that was not the pale white he was accustomed to seeing. Instead, her skin appeared to be sun-kissed, lending one the impression that Miss Garrison was a lady who spent more than the average time outdoors. Her hair was a rich shade of gold, mixed with lighter strands that suggested she often went without a hat, but it was her face that held a person's attention.

She wasn't what one would consider a classic beauty since she did not possess the delicate features that were currently in fashion, but there was something almost mesmerizing about the way the features she did possess were arranged on her face.

Her eyes, a peculiar shade of cobalt blue, were unusually large and rimmed with dark lashes that were at distinct odds with her golden hair. Her brows were finely sculpted, as were her cheekbones, and her nose was slim and had just a hint of a tilt to it. Her lips were a perfectly normal shade of pink, but there was something about the fullness of her lips that lent her an air of mystery, while the creases at the very corner of those lips gave one the impression she smiled often and enjoyed life to the fullest.

"It looks to me, Miss Garrison, as if you could use some assistance, which I am only *too* happy to provide. May I suggest we repair to the retiring room in order to afford you the privacy I'm sure you've simply neglected to realize you need?"

Pulling his attention from Miss Garrison, who was now emitting what sounded like grunts as she struggled to beat her bustle back into place, Reginald settled his gaze on the young lady who'd just stepped up to join them, Miss Adele Tooker.

Miss Tooker had been one of the first ladies presented to his cousin, an introduction Charles had certainly enjoyed because Miss Tooker, from what Mr. McAllister had whispered to Reginald as Charles had been kissing the lady's hand, was most sought after this season. She was a lovely lady, possessed a classically beautiful face, and, more importantly, possessed a sizable fortune. She was also, according to Mr. McAllister, enthralled with the aristocracy, and given the way she'd fluttered her lashes at Charles, it had been clear that Miss Tooker would not be opposed to becoming better acquainted with an honest-to-goodness earl.

Ladies such as Miss Tooker, those overly anxious to acquire titles in exchange for the large dowries their fathers settled on them, were exactly why Reginald's father had insisted Reginald accompany his cousin to America.

Charles, although a jovial and charming gentleman, was not what one would consider an overly intellectual sort. He'd only recently inherited his title, along with numerous estates from his father, who, sadly enough, had not been an intellectual either and had woefully neglected the family finances and estates. Because of that neglect, Charles was in desperate need of funds and had decided that to save his family from certain ruin, he'd have to marry extremely well.

No amount of arguing from Reginald had been enough to dissuade Charles from deciding his only hope lay in acquiring an American heiress. Charles was convinced those heiresses were dripping in money their industrious fathers had made, and he was only too willing to accept that money—no matter that he would have to marry an American in the process.

34

The problem with that decision, though, was that Charles was susceptible to pretty faces and could very well forget he needed a vast fortune if a particularly pretty face struck his fancy.

Reginald's father, having promised Charles's father on his deathbed that he would look after Charles to the best of his abilities, had convinced Reginald that he'd have to accompany his cousin to America to make certain the heiress Charles set his sights on truly possessed an impressive fortune. His father also wanted Reginald to convince Charles to choose a lady in possession of at least a semblance of proper decorum. That meant that Miss Poppy Garrison, no matter her pretty face, was probably not going to be an appropriate choice for Charles, although Miss Tooker, on the other hand, might be.

"There," Miss Garrison suddenly exclaimed, straightening as she shoved her tiara, which she only just seemed to realize was slipping over her forehead, back into place. "No need to revisit the retiring room now, however . . ." Miss Garrison shook out the folds of her skirt right before she began striding toward the chair that was closest to where she'd stumbled, bending down and looking under that chair before she straightened and moved on to the next chair.

"What are you doing now?" Miss Tooker asked, raising a hand to a lily-white throat that was encircled with a diamond choker.

"I'm looking for what tripped me up," Miss Garrison said right before she suddenly dropped to all fours, shimmied underneath a small table covered in fine linen, then shimmied her way out again, brandishing a cane. "Aha," she declared, getting to her feet and holding out the cane. "Here's the culprit, although why someone left it behind is a mystery since people usually don't neglect to remember to take their canes with them when they quit a room."

Miss Tooker stepped closer to Miss Garrison and frowned. "There's no mystery here, Miss Garrison," she began. "That looks like Mr. Phalen's cane. He's a dear elderly man who often misplaces his cane." She turned and nodded to an older gentleman sitting in a chair a few feet away, his chin resting on his chest, taking a bit of a snooze. "I'm sure he'd be mortified to learn his cane was responsible for your accident."

As Miss Garrison glanced to Mr. Phalen, her lips curved for all of a second, but then her brows drew together when she returned her attention to Miss Tooker. "Bit odd that his cane got so far away from him, don't you think?"

"Why would you find that odd?"

Miss Garrison darted another look to Mr. Phalen. "I find it odd that you *don't* find it odd, what with how feeble Mr. Phalen appears to be. But to spell it out for you, what do you think the chances are that someone purposefully used his cane to trip me?"

Miss Tooker blinked. "I would think that's slim to none because I don't know anyone who'd purposefully trip anyone since that would be quite beyond the pale." She shot a glance to Charles, smiled a lovely smile at him, then took the cane from Miss Garrison. "However, unlikely intrigues aside, I do believe you were in the midst of becoming introduced to Lord Lonsdale. Allow me to return this to Mr. Phalen for you so that Mrs. Kruger may proceed." Sending Charles one last smile, Miss Tooker glided away as Mrs. Kruger launched into another formal introduction, one Miss Garrison had completely missed the first time around, although given the circumstances, he could understand that particular lapse.

What Reginald was having difficulty understanding, though, was her blatant disregard for expected behavior, because after she'd recovered from her fall, instead of being sufficiently mortified, she had gone about readjusting her bustle as if it were an everyday occurrence for a lady to adjust her feminine accessories in the presence of numerous gentlemen.

He'd grown up in a household that demanded the strictest adherence to the rules of decorum, and while some might call him snobbish, Reginald was of the firm belief that always maintaining the proprieties was exactly what separated true ladies and gentlemen from the masses.

Gentlemen, of which he considered himself to be a member, were expected to follow certain requirements ranging from being well-versed in matters of politics, estate business, and classical literature, to treating ladies as delicate objects with tender feelings that must never be injured.

Ladies, on the other hand, were expected to be proficient in all the feminine arts, such as music, needlepoint, and penning charming letters to their many correspondents. They were also expected to dress with style, glide across a room, and certainly never draw attention to themselves through theatrical mishaps or a brazen disregard for the tried-and-true rules of decorum.

He was rapidly concluding that Miss Poppy Garrison was severely lacking when it came to the basics of true femininity, which meant she was not remotely suitable to become a candidate for Charles's interest, let alone become a candidate for the role of countess.

". . . great honor to present Lord Lonsdale," Mrs. Kruger was saying, drawing Reginald's attention. "Lord Lonsdale, this is Mrs. George Van Rensselaer and her lovely granddaughter, Miss Poppy Garrison, who I do believe I mentioned has only *very* recently come to the city."

As Charles stepped forward to take Mrs. Van Rensselaer's hand and place the expected kiss upon it, Reginald braced himself when Charles turned his attention to Miss Garrison. To his surprise, however, after Charles kissed her hand, she sent him a pretty smile and dipped into a curtsy, although she didn't dip very low to the ground, but that might have been because it looked as if her bustle were beginning to shift again. After she straightened and retrieved her hand from Charles, she turned to Reginald.

"And you are, of course, Mr. Blackburn, unless I'm mistaken and you're actually a member of the aristocracy as well, in which case I'll apologize in advance for not using your proper title, such as Your Grace or Your Majesty," she said before Mrs. Kruger could introduce the two of them properly.

Reginald chanced a glance at Charles, who was smiling indulgently at Miss Garrison as if she'd just said something incredibly witty instead of showing herself to be woefully unfamiliar with the intricacies of British aristocracy. Summoning up a smile, Reginald took a step toward Mrs. Van Rensselaer and took her hand even as he nodded to Miss Garrison. "I'm afraid I'm a mere Mr. Blackburn, although it would be delightful to have people address me as Your Majesty." He placed a kiss on Mrs. Van Rensselaer's hand, then turned to Miss Garrison, who was watching him with a great deal of curiosity in her vivid blue eyes.

"Are there many people who go by the title of Your Majesty in Britain?" she asked as he took her hand and kissed it.

"Only the queen at the moment."

Miss Garrison's eyes began to twinkle. "Which explains why you'd be delighted if people addressed you as such. But tell me, even though you're not in possession of a title, do you have any of those lofty ancestral estates I've heard so much about—ones that have a ghoul in the dungeon and a ghost in the attic?"

Unable to help but wonder if the brash young lady standing before him was attempting to decipher if he was a gentleman of means or not—or a gentleman worth pursuing if she had her sights on gracing the hallways of an English estate as its mistress—Reginald took a second to consider his answer.

Being the second son of a duke, he lived in many lofty ancestral estates throughout the year, but he didn't actually *own* any of those homes—all of them were entailed and would go to his older brother someday. Because of that, and because he certainly didn't want to encourage Miss Garrison in any way if she did have him in her sights, he didn't have a single qualm about what came out of his mouth next. "I'm afraid I don't own a single ancestral estate, Miss Garrison."

"Oh, that's too bad. I was hoping to question you further on—"

"Whether I've traveled to America to secure myself a bride because my ancestral estates are in need of shoring up?" he finished for her, earning a wrinkle of a nose in return.

"Of course not," Miss Garrison surprised him by saying. "I wanted to ask you whether or not you feel ghosts really exist or if you'd seen any floating around. Since you just admitted you don't own an ancestral estate, I assume you wouldn't have much knowledge about ancestral ghosts, which is why I'm disappointed." She frowned. "I'm curious, though, as to why you thought I was about to question you on a subject that even I, having only recently arrived in town, know is quite beyond the pale—broaching the topic of marrying for money."

An unexpected wave of heat began traveling up Reginald's neck. "Forgive me, Miss Garrison. That *was* beyond the pale for me to say."

Miss Garrison inclined her head. "Apology accepted, and forgive me if you find what I'm going to ask next offensive as well, but since *you* broached the topic . . . *have* you come to America to secure an heiress?"

Glancing around, Reginald found that while he'd been speaking with Miss Garrison, a crowd of young ladies had begun pressing closer, anticipation on their faces as they waited for his response.

He suppressed a groan even as he realized there was nothing left to do now except make it perfectly clear he was not in the market for an heiress, although how he was going to do that without offending any of them, which would then reflect poorly on Charles, was beyond him.

"So you *are* here to find yourself an heiress," Miss Garrison proclaimed, drawing his immediate attention along with a good deal of annoyance.

"No I'm not," he argued. "But since you seem to be a most determined sort, allow me to expand on exactly what I'm doing here." He nodded to Charles. "I've come to America as Lord Lonsdale's traveling companion. But more importantly, I'm here to advise him on any important decisions he may need to make."

Miss Garrison's eyes narrowed. "Decisions that revolve around eligible young ladies who may be interested in procuring his . . . affections?"

"Indeed."

CHAPTER 4

The moment that bit of ridiculousness left his mouth, Reginald wanted to call it back. Glancing to Charles, he found his cousin looking at him as if he'd lost his mind, and frankly, he couldn't say he blamed the man. Horror immediately chugged through his veins as reality set in about what he'd just been responsible for doing.

He'd not had any intention of letting New York society learn he was aiding Charles in his quest for a bride, but something about the manner in which Miss Poppy Garrison had been questioning him had apparently caused him to speak impulsively, uncharacteristically so, and disclose information that might now have him becoming in much demand with the heiresses who wanted to garner Charles's affections.

The reason he'd originally decided to introduce himself as Mr. Blackburn instead of Lord Blackburn, second son of a duke, was because he'd not wanted to draw attention away from his cousin. Now, however, he was certain to garner more than his fair share of notice, but at least that notice would be given because young ladies were interested in earning Charles's favor, not because they were interested in pursuing him.

Wincing when he realized that the young ladies who'd been inching his way were now smiling and fluttering their lashes, he sent them a nod before he turned back to Miss Garrison. She was not fluttering her lashes at him, but was instead watching him closely with what seemed to be an entire storm brewing in her unusual eyes.

"What a daunting task you've set for yourself, Mr. Blackburn," she began coolly. "Proclaiming yourself the gatekeeper for Lord Lonsdale's affections will assuredly be trying, although, given your arrogant and unpleasant nature, I'm—*ouch*." She stopped talking and looked at her grandmother. "Did you just pinch me?"

Mrs. Van Rensselaer arched a brow. "Don't be absurd." She turned a smile on Charles. "How are you finding the weather in New York, Lord Lonsdale?"

Charles returned the smile, relief flickering through his eyes. "It's lovely, Mrs. Van Rensselaer, although I've been given to understand that it's been unusually warm in New York for this time of year—not that I'm complaining about that, mind you."

"And will you be staying through the holidays to enjoy the Season when it truly begins in earnest, and by that I mean after the first Patriarch Ball in January?" Mrs. Van Rensselaer asked.

Charles's smile faltered ever so slightly. "I'm hoping to return to London before Christmas."

Miss Garrison shot Reginald a significant look. "That's not going to give you much time to advise him, and if I were offering *my* friend advice, I'd suggest he resist the urge to hurry through a process that's going to affect him for the rest of his life, and—" Miss Garrison stopped talking, sent her grandmother a glare, then began rubbing her arm, quite as if she'd just suffered another pinch.

Clearly seeking a distraction from the topic at hand, Charles turned to Mrs. Kruger, who seemed to have been rendered speechless again. "I've just noticed that guests are moving toward the staircase, which must signify dinner is about to be served. Shall we begin making our way downstairs? I understand you and I are to make a grand entrance when all the guests have been seated, but I would hazard a guess that Mr. McAllister is waiting for us downstairs to make certain it goes off without a hitch." With that, Charles took Mrs. Kruger's arm and hurried away, leaving Reginald behind.

"And wasn't that just an illuminating conversation?" Miss Beatrix Waterbury, a young lady Reginald had met at the beginning of the evening, commented as she stepped up to join them, beaming an impish smile all around.

"I'm not certain I'd go so far as to claim it was illuminating," a nervous-looking man said as stepped up to join them. "Poor Lord Lonsdale all but fled from you, Miss Garrison, which will certainly be remarked upon often tonight."

"I thought you went off to find the name of your dinner partner, Mr. Middleton," Mrs. Van Rensselaer barked at the man, who Reginald only then realized was the poor soul who'd been partnered with Miss Garrison for the disastrous Gypsy Quadrille.

"That's why I'm back. I discovered that my partner for dinner is—"

"Do not tell me Mr. McAllister paired you up with Poppy again."

Mr. Middleton raked a hand through his hair. "He . . . ah . . . well . . ."

"How marvelous that we'll get to share the meal together," Poppy interrupted. "I was hoping you'd be chosen for me."

"I wasn't given your name, Miss Garrison," Mr. Middleton said in a rush. "I'm here to take Miss Waterbury down to dinner."

"Wonderful," Miss Waterbury exclaimed as she took the arm Mr. Middleton suddenly thrust out to her. "I don't believe we've ever had an opportunity to dine together, which means we'll have much to discuss over the courses."

Mr. Middleton immediately looked wary. "What do you normally enjoy discussing over the courses?"

Miss Waterbury patted his arm. "Oh, the usual social intrigues . . . or perhaps we'll forgo the tried-and-true topics of conversation and delve into something meaningful, such as the plight of the suffragists or what new inventions have shown up in the city of late."

"I'm more of a tried-and-true conversationalist," Mr. Middleton muttered.

"Of course you are," Miss Waterbury said with another pat to Mr. Middleton's arm before she turned a smile on Poppy. "Care to share a table with Mr. Middleton and me after you find your escort?"

"How kind of you to invite me. Of course I'll join you," Poppy said, even though her grandmother seemed to be trying to catch her eye as she shook her head ever so discreetly. "But speaking of my escort, I wonder if he's gotten lost since he's not shown up to claim me."

Reginald cleared his throat. "He's not lost, Miss Garrison."

"How do you know?"

He was not encouraged when her eyes began flashing again. "Because *I've* been given the supreme honor of escorting you to dine this evening. Do forgive me for not mentioning that sooner. I fear I allowed other matters to distract me."

"Why would Mr. McAllister ask you to dine with *me*?" she demanded, crossing her arms over her chest. "Is he unaware that you've apparently been tasked with the daunting feat of vetting ladies for that oh-so-desirous position of Lady Lonsdale, a position for which I'm undoubtedly not qualified?"

"I never specifically claimed to be *vetting* ladies for Lord Lonsdale. If you'll recall, I said I was here to offer him my advice."

"It's the same thing," she shot back.

Having nothing of worth to say to that because Miss Garrison had just voiced a most valid point, Reginald settled for offering her his arm, which she took, albeit reluctantly. He then offered his other arm to Mrs. Van Rensselaer, which she didn't hesitate to accept.

"I overheard Mr. McAllister telling Miss Tooker that Lord Lonsdale asked to have Mr. Blackburn seated next to you at dinner," Mr. Middleton said as he and Miss Waterbury fell into step beside them.

Miss Garrison stopped walking. "Why would he have done that?"

"Because you've obviously caught his eye," Mrs. Van Rensselaer said, satisfaction in her voice.

"I wouldn't get your hopes up, Viola," Miss Garrison said with a wave of a gloved hand, which sent her bracelets jingling. "Mr. Blackburn will most assuredly be taking notes as we dine, jotting down all of the many faux pas I'm sure to commit, which will effectively take me out of the running as a potential heiress for Lord Lonsdale." She smiled rather grimly. "However, since it's highly unlikely Mr. McAllister will allow a change in seating assignments, we'll simply need to make the best of the matter, although to be clear"—she pinned Reginald under a stormy gaze—"I'm not happy about this. Not happy about this at all."

Forty minutes later, Reginald discovered that Miss Garrison was not a lady who embraced an unhappy attitude for long. She'd been chatting pleasantly with Mr. Middleton and Miss Waterbury throughout the few courses that had already been served, although she'd been blatantly ignoring Reginald, something he'd never experienced before in his life and couldn't claim to enjoy.

Mrs. Van Rensselaer, on the other hand, along with her dinner partner, the elderly Mr. Phalen, who turned out to be rather hard of hearing because he demanded snippets of conversation be repeated every other minute, had been more than attentive. Mrs. Van Rensselaer had clearly grasped the importance of Reginald proclaiming himself an advisor to Lord Lonsdale, and had been questioning him almost nonstop about Lord Lonsdale and what exactly he was searching for in a countess.

"You say Lord Lampton enjoys fishing?" Mr. Phalen suddenly shouted, drawing attention from guests seated at a nearby table.

"I said he enjoys snails, a dish I just noticed the servers bringing out," Reginald corrected, pitching his voice louder than normal so Mr. Phalen could hear him. "And it's Lord Lonsdale, not Lampton."

"Lionsburg?" Mr. Phalen shot back.

"Lonsdale," Miss Garrison said, leaning over the table and smiling at Mr. Phalen. "It's Lord Lonsdale, Mr. Phalen."

Mr. Phalen glanced at Reginald. "Why didn't you say so in the first place?"

"Don't know what I was thinking," Reginald returned as Miss Garrison picked up a pair of tongs that was lying by her charger plate and frowned.

"What are these for?"

"Those are for the snails Mr. Blackburn just mentioned," Mr. Middleton said from two seats away as he leaned over Miss Waterbury. He held up a tiny two-pronged fork. "You'll need to use these as well after you capture a snail with the tong."

Miss Garrison's eyes widened. "When you say *capture* . . . does that mean the snails are still alive?"

Mr. Middleton smiled. "Perhaps *captured* is not the right word. They'll be well cooked, and breaded if I'm not mistaken, but they'll be served in their original shells, which is why you have the tongs because the shells can be slippery."

"That doesn't sound very appetizing," Miss Garrison said weakly, right as a server placed a small plate with four snails in front of her.

"Snails taste exactly like chicken," Mr. Middleton said. "Or . . . somewhat like chicken," he amended when Reginald quirked a brow.

"I suppose I could give them a try, although we've already been served so much food that I'm not certain I'm going to have room to sample anything else, not with how tightly I've been laced into this—"

"Poppy," Mrs. Van Rensselaer interrupted. "You will think before you speak, which means we'll redirect the conversation now to something more suitable, such as the weather."

Miss Garrison frowned at her grandmother before she turned to Reginald and smiled a smile that was so sweet it took him by complete surprise and left him feeling decidedly off-kilter.

"Please add that to my list of etiquette transgressions—bringing unmentionables into the conversation—which will allow you to present a more sound argument when you and Lord Lonsdale sit down to discuss whether or not I meet the undoubtedly stringent requirements to become an honest-to-goodness countess."

Reginald's feeling of being off-kilter disappeared in a thrice. Tapping his finger against the side of his head, he smiled. "There's no need for me to comprise a physical list, Miss Garrison. I'm perfectly capable of keeping a mental list right here in my head."

To his annoyance, her smile widened. "That sounds like a challenge if I've ever heard one, and I *do* so enjoy a good challenge."

He blinked. "Does that mean you're soon to wage war on proper etiquette?"

Miss Garrison glanced to her grandmother, blew out a breath, then returned her attention to him. "An intriguing notion to be sure, but no, I'm not going to *intentionally* wage war on etiquette."

When she didn't expand further on that, he leaned toward her. "I should tell you that I too enjoy a good challenge, and I am more than up for rising to whatever challenge comes my way."

"How delightful," she exclaimed. "With that settled, allow us to return to our snails."

Feeling that the situation was anything but settled but having no idea where to take the conversation from there, Reginald watched as Miss Garrison picked up her tongs, squeezed the handle a few times, then aimed them toward the snails on her plate. She then went about what was apparently the tricky business of trying to pick one of them up.

"Would you look at that, captured at last," she finally said, her eyes twinkling as she considered the snail she'd managed to catch. She turned the tongs side to side before she gave them a small shake. "They do seem to hold fast to the shell."

Reaching for the small fork next to her plate, she picked it up and began looking rather determined. Before she could wield the fork, though, she, for some unknown reason, gave the tongs another flick right as she seemed to squeeze the handle.

Reginald winced as he watched the snail suddenly go hurtling through the air, over the table, and then . . .

Everyone at the table seemed to hold their breath as the snail continued its flight right before it smacked some poor gentleman in the back of the head. Splatters of snail flew from the shell, gasps rang out from numerous guests, and then utter silence descended.

As if in slow motion, the gentleman turned in his chair. Two servers rushed forward, one scrambling after the shell that was now rolling over the floor, while the other began plucking snail out of the gentleman's hair. A moment later, the servers retreated, leaving the gentleman leveling a glare on Reginald's table, or more specifically, Miss Garrison, who was turning a lovely shade of pink.

Anticipation seemed to settle over the tables situated near them as the gentleman rose to his feet and took a single step forward. But, to Reginald's surprise, the gentleman blinked, and then smiled at Miss Garrison.

"Miss Garrison," the gentleman exclaimed as he began walking toward Poppy. "I had no idea you were currently in the city."

Miss Garrison's eyes widened as the gentleman stopped directly before her and took hold of her hand. "Mr. Flaherty," she began. "Thank goodness it's you. I mean, not thank goodness you were the victim of my runaway snail, but thank goodness I know you, and thank goodness you seem to be in an understanding frame of mind."

Mr. Flaherty brought Miss Garrison's hand to his lips and kissed it, releasing it a second later. "There's no need for you to fret about the snail. I'm certain runaway snails happen frequently, which means we'll simply put the incident behind us. What are you doing in the city? The last time we spoke, you didn't mention that you were going to be traveling here."

"I didn't know at that time I'd be enjoying a Season, but allow me to introduce you to my grandmother." Miss Garrison nodded to Viola. "This is Mr. Nigel Flaherty, Viola. Mr. Flaherty, this is Mrs. George Van Rensselaer, my grandmother."

Mr. Flaherty moved to stand in front of Mrs. Van Rensselaer, taking the hand she offered him. "It's a pleasure to make your acquaintance, Mrs. Van Rensselaer."

Speculation immediately flickered through Mrs. Van Rensselaer's eyes as Mr. Flaherty placed the expected kiss on her hand. "It's a pleasure to meet you as well, Mr. Flaherty, but how are you acquainted with my granddaughter, and how is it that you and I have never met before?"

"I've only recently arrived in the city, having lived most of my life in Pittsburgh," Mr. Flaherty said. "And I became acquainted with Miss Garrison after I traveled to Garrison Farms to purchase a new horse because Garrison Farms has the reputation of having the best horses in the country." He turned a smile upon Miss Garrison. "You'll be pleased to learn that Cyrus, the horse you chose for me, is working out very well indeed. In fact, I've brought him to New York and would welcome an opportunity to take him out riding with you."

"I would enjoy that, Mr. Flaherty, and, forgive me, but I'm forgetting my manners. Allow me to introduce you to the rest of my table."

Taking a second to do just that, Miss Garrison performed the introductions without a single misstep. Miss Waterbury, however, instead of presenting Mr. Flaherty with a smile and her hand as they were introduced, picked up her wineglass and leveled cool eyes on the man.

"You mentioned you only recently arrived in the city from Pittsburgh," Miss Waterbury began, earning a nod from Mr. Flaherty in return.

"I did."

Miss Waterbury tapped a finger against her wineglass. "Then that would make you the Mr. Nigel Flaherty my very dear friend, Isadora Delafield, now Mrs. Ian MacKenzie, mentioned to me a time or two."

A rueful smile flickered across Mr. Flaherty's face. "One and the same, Miss Waterbury, and from the wariness in your eyes, you've heard tales that show me in a less-than-favorable light."

"Are you about to deny the validity of those tales?" Miss Waterbury asked.

"Not at all," Mr. Flaherty surprised Reginald by saying. "I'm guilty as charged and have taken full responsibility for the actions of a man I came to find out was nothing less than a rogue employee. That employee, I'm sad to say, took it upon himself to try to win my company concessions, no matter that his attempts to do so caused irreparable harm and anguish to people living in a small Pennsylvania community." Mr. Flaherty shook his head. "I never intended for the man to take matters so far, but his actions are a direct reflection on me and my company, which is exactly why I've owned up to the transgressions done."

"Become a changed man, have you?" Miss Waterbury asked, skepticism dripping from her every word.

Mr. Flaherty nodded. "I have, although because you're apparently fast friends with Mrs. MacKenzie, I understand why you'd doubt my intentions and know that I have much work to do to convince everyone I'm determined to make amends."

Miss Waterbury took a sip of her wine. "I suppose time will tell on that, Mr. Flaherty."

"Indeed it will," he said before he returned his attention to Miss Garrison. "But now I must return to my table." He nodded to an older woman sitting at his table, who was turned in her seat, smiling pleasantly. "I'm currently enjoying the hospitality of a very dear friend of mine, Mrs. Ridgeway, who has invited me to enjoy the New York social Season with her."

Reginald glanced to Mrs. Ridgeway, who seemed to be around Mrs. Van Rensselaer's age. Inclining his head when he noticed she was looking at him, she inclined her head in return, sent a fond smile to Mr. Flaherty, then turned back around, immediately rejoining the conversation at her table.

". . . perhaps a trip to Central Park might be in order, Miss Garrison," Mr. Flaherty was saying, drawing Reginald's attention. "I'd welcome an opportunity to get your opinion on how Cyrus is doing. He's a spirited stallion and still gives me a few difficulties if I take him on an overly crowded street."

"I'd be more than happy to lend you my opinion," Miss Garrison said, earning a smile from Mr. Flaherty before he excused himself and returned to his table.

The second he took his seat, Mrs. Van Rensselaer cleared her throat and leaned forward, her gaze settled on Miss Waterbury. "Was it necessary to put poor Mr. Flaherty through that interrogation?"

Miss Waterbury didn't so much as flinch. "From what Isadora told me about the man, he's not to be trusted."

Mrs. Van Rensselaer frowned. "Is he a fortune hunter?"

Miss Waterbury shook her head. "Rumor has it he has scads and scads of money, but possessing incredible wealth doesn't mean one possesses great moral character." She nodded to Poppy. "There's every chance he's truly attempting to change his ways, but you should have a care if he calls on you to go riding."

"Sound advice for—" Whatever else Miss Garrison was going to say got lost when Mr. Phalen suddenly released a snort and sat bolt upright in his chair, looking a bit confused to find himself still in the middle of a meal.

"Looks like we've been served snails," he shouted, nodding to the plates still sitting in front of them.

Miss Garrison exchanged a grin with Miss Waterbury before she picked up the tongs again and looked them over. Turning to Reginald, she sent him what seemed to be a genuine smile. "I'm certain what I'm about to do next will need to go on that list you're composing in your head, but for the safety of everyone around us, it's necessary." With that, she set aside the tongs and plucked a snail up in her hand, nodding to Mr. Middleton. "You're certain this tastes like chicken?"

"Relatively certain, although it's not chicken, it's snail, so you're simply going to have to decide for yourself," Mr. Middleton returned.

"That's hardly reassuring," Miss Garrison said before she dug the contents of the shell out with her small fork, popped it into her mouth, chewed it for all of a second, then snatched the linen napkin off her lap and proceeded to spit the contents of her mouth into the napkin.

Reginald felt the distinct need to rub his eyes because he was not exactly certain he'd truly seen what he thought he did. "I may very well need to concede the challenge and begin making a physical list," he muttered as Miss Garrison blotted her lips, sent him a scowl, then snatched up a glass filled with Apollinaris water and took a hefty gulp. Setting aside the glass, she leveled a glare on Mr. Middleton.

"That in no way tasted like chicken," she said before she picked up the engraved menu in front of her place setting and began perusing it. "Thank goodness," she said a moment later. "I'm familiar with everything else that's left to be served and must say I'm looking forward to the bonbons and ices that are soon to come."

"I'm looking forward to the *Soufflé macarons*," Miss Waterbury said, picking up her menu. "As well as the *Paté de gibier aux truffes*."

"Oh, those do sound delicious, although I'm not certain, what with how tightly I've been laced into this torture device known as a corset that I'll have enough . . ." Miss Garrison stopped talking, probably because her grandmother had begun tapping her knife against a crystal glass.

Miss Garrison smiled far too innocently right before she rose from her chair, that unexpected action having Reginald, along with Mr. Middleton, jumping to their feet, although Mr. Phalen stayed put in his chair, having nodded off again.

"Do not even think about trundling off to the retiring room," Mrs. Van Rensselaer hissed in a rather ominous tone.

"I'll be right back," Miss Garrison said as if she'd not heard her grandmother's warning as Miss Waterbury jumped to her feet.

"I'll go with you," Miss Waterbury said, and a mere second later, the two ladies had linked their arms together and strolled away at a remarkably rapid clip.

Mrs. Van Rensselaer suddenly rose from her chair and began marching his way. After assisting her into the seat Miss Garrison had just vacated, Reginald sat down beside her, bracing himself since she clearly had something on her mind.

"You claimed you enjoy a good challenge," Mrs. Van Rensselaer began.

"I did," he said, wincing when he detected the slightest trace of wariness in his tone.

"Wonderful. Allow me to be frank."

"Does George know you've decided to change your name, Viola?" Mr. Phalen suddenly asked, leaning forward and shaking his head, his nap apparently over. "Don't think he'll enjoy calling you Frank, not when he's been calling you Viola all these years. But speaking of George, where is he?"

Mrs. Van Rensselaer frowned. "He's out of town on business, but he'll be back for Christmas. And I haven't changed my name to Frank."

Mr. Phalen returned the frown. "You said, and I quote, 'Allow me to be Frank.'"

Reginald would have laughed if Mrs. Van Rensselaer had not taken that moment to send him a look of clear exasperation. Pressing his lips firmly together, he swallowed his amusement while she sent a scowl Mr. Phalen's way.

"It was a figure of speech, and with that said, do feel free to return to your nap."

Mr. Phalen's lips twitched before he dutifully closed his eyes, a bit of a snort escaping his mouth a moment later.

"Now then, where was I?" Mrs. Van Rensselaer asked.

"You were going to be frank, and apparently not Frank as in the name."

"Indeed." She caught Reginald's eye. "You've clearly noticed that my granddaughter is new to the ways of society and currently seems to be floundering."

"I can't argue with that."

"Too right you can't, which brings me back to that challenge I mentioned." She smiled. "It has not escaped my notice that Lord Lonsdale has been keeping a sharp eye on my granddaughter throughout this meal."

Reginald glanced to where Charles was sitting. Unfortunately,

Charles was currently gazing somewhat longingly after Miss Garrison as she and Miss Waterbury wove their way through the many tables scattered about the room. He returned his attention to Mrs. Van Rensselaer. "That does seem to be a valid observation."

"And is it also a valid observation that you seem determined to find a young lady for Lord Lonsdale who possesses impeccable manners and will do justice to the title of countess?"

"I don't see a reason to dispute that."

Mrs. Van Rensselaer inclined her head. "Lovely, which brings me to a proposition."

"What type of proposition?"

"You and I both know that Lord Lonsdale is already on the road to being smitten with my Poppy, and smitten gentlemen can rarely be deterred from pursuing the lady of their affection. With that said, I doubt you want Lord Lonsdale to take a bride back to England who lacks the basics of social graces." She raised an expectant brow his way.

"I *would* prefer he settle his sights on a young lady who won't frequently embarrass him."

"Of course you would, and because Lord Lonsdale does seem to have already become enamored with my granddaughter, I'm hopeful you'll agree to accept the challenge I'm about to extend to you."

"I'm listening."

Mrs. Van Rensselaer leaned toward him. "My granddaughter, Mr. Blackburn, is in desperate need of someone taking her in hand when it comes to the proprieties and expected behavior of a young lady. Unfortunately, I've not seen much success with any attempts I've made to get her on the path to social success. I'm now convinced that you are exactly the type of gentleman who would be up for what can only be described as a most intimidating challenge—that of turning my Poppy, who is currently a diamond in the rough, into a diamond of the first water."

CHAPTER 5

"You're fidgeting again."

Poppy pulled her attention from the carriage window where she'd been watching the hustle and bustle on Broadway and settled it on Reginald. That irritating gentleman was sitting opposite her on the carriage seat, apparently in full instructor mode as they trundled toward the Metropolitan Opera House.

Over the three days since the Family Circle Dancing Class, she'd been forced to spend hours with the gentleman, encouraged by her grandmother to soak in every morsel of information he'd be dispensing through the lessons Viola had somehow cajoled him into teaching her. And even though Poppy admitted he was more than proficient with instructing her on everything proper, his propensity for pointing out the smallest infraction on her part rankled.

She was also, much to her surprise, finding herself not as susceptible to a British accent as she'd once been, especially not when it was paired with reprimands and suggestions every other minute.

"You're still fidgeting."

Deliberately wriggling on the seat, which earned her a sigh from Viola, who was sitting directly beside her, Poppy smiled. "You'd be fidgeting as well, Reginald, if you'd been stuffed into a corset that is at least a size too small and then forced to wear a bustle that barely allows my bottom any room on this seat. Why, I'm fortunate I haven't pitched forward yet and found myself traveling the rest of the way to the opera on the floor of this carriage."

Reginald turned to Viola. "I'm beginning to reconsider my refusal to allow you to pay me for the instructions you've asked me to give your granddaughter."

Viola didn't so much as blink. "I had a feeling you'd eventually regret that decision. Do know that I'm perfectly willing to offer you compensation; you only need to tell me how much it's going to take to get Poppy up to snuff."

"Even with how large your fortune is rumored to be, I'm not certain that it'll be enough to accomplish that particular feat."

"She does seem to be challenging you quite dreadfully." Viola arched a brow Poppy's way. "And why are you addressing Mr. Blackburn by his given name?"

"She knows it annoys me," Reginald said before Poppy could answer, which left her nodding even as she reached into her reticule and pulled out a folded piece of notepaper she'd tucked inside. She handed it to Reginald.

"I've taken the liberty of providing you with a list of what I feel are my transgressions thus far, since I've yet to be convinced your mind is capable of handling so many of them in such a short period of time. And"—she held up her hand when he opened his mouth to argue with her—"I've titled it *Reasons Why Poppy Will Never Become a Diamond of the First Water*. You'll notice I've included my insistence on using your given name as the number one lapse from proper manners."

Reginald unfolded the paper, glanced it over, then lifted his head. "You neglected to write down that bit about you spitting out the snail a few nights ago."

"Because that wasn't a lapse on my part, but simply a way to avoid tossing up my accounts in the middle of a most formal atmosphere, which you must admit would have been far worse."

"Can't argue with that," Reginald muttered before he tucked the notepaper into his pocket and began studying her far too closely.

Not caring to be considered in such a manner by a gentleman who was turning into one of the most exasperating people she'd ever met, Poppy turned and looked out the window again.

Wiping away the fog her breath was making against the glass, she ignored the immediate admonishment from her grandmother and leaned forward to enjoy the sight of a New York evening.

The road was clogged with gleaming carriages heading to their respective society events, most of those carriages heading toward the Metropolitan Opera House where there was soon to be a performance of *Die Königin von Saba*, or *The Queen of Sheba* as Reginald had translated for her, by the esteemed composer Karl Goldmark. As the carriages trundling around her passed beneath the eerie halos of streetlamps that burned against the darkness of the night, Poppy imagined the occupants of *those* carriages were enjoying frivolous conversations and a great deal of laughter. She certainly would have preferred that over the lectures she'd been experiencing ever since Reginald had arrived at her grandmother's brownstone to escort her and Viola that evening.

It wasn't that she didn't appreciate the efforts on her grandmother's part to see her accepted into high society, but spending two hours that afternoon with Reginald as he'd tolled on and on about what wines were expected to be served with what course had sent her into an almost catatonic state.

"I quite enjoyed the opera we're about to see when it was performed in London," Reginald said, drawing her attention. "It was held in the Royal Italian Opera house in Covent Garden, and the costumes and scene settings were spectacular."

"Then I'm certain you'll enjoy this evening's entertainment," Viola said. "The Metropolitan Opera House is most impressive, although it doesn't boast the history of the Royal Italian Opera house because the Metropolitan has only been open for three years."

"Where did you go for opera before the Metropolitan opened?" Reginald asked.

"The Academy of Music, but it closed earlier this year, forced out of business because of the Metropolitan." Viola released a breath. "The Academy was an exclusive venture—perhaps *too* exclusive, if the truth be known. I told Caroline Astor that she should have a care with excluding men such as William H. Vanderbilt from purchasing private boxes there, but she didn't heed my advice. Because of that, Mr. Vanderbilt, along with a few other industrialists, commissioned to have the Metropolitan built. No expense was spared, and the Academy was doomed from the first day the Metropolitan opened for business, with a performance from Christine Nilsson, singing the role of Marguerite in Charles Gounod's *Faust*."

As the carriage began to slow, Poppy glanced out the window again, frowning when they passed the main entrance to the Metropolitan. "Should we notify the driver that he's missed the front door?"

"For those fortunate enough to own private boxes," Viola began, "comes the privilege of having private entrances, located on Thirty-ninth and Fortieth Street."

"But then you miss seeing the grandeur of what I'm sure must be an impressive entranceway," Poppy argued.

"Have you not been to the opera since you've been in the city?" Reginald asked.

"I'm afraid not, because the wardrobe Viola ordered for me from the House of Worth only got delivered a few weeks ago." Poppy turned from the window, smoothing a hand over the velvet cloak that covered a blush-colored gown made of the finest silk. "Since I was not able to travel to Paris to have my measurements taken, Mr. Charles Worth was forced to use the measurements we sent him through a transatlantic telegram. Unfortunately, given the tightness of some of the selections he sent, I've concluded the ink must have smudged on the telegram, which would explain the less-than-perfect fit of some of my gowns, which, much to Viola's dismay, had to be altered." She shook her head again. "I'm sure that after one adds in the cost of the alterations along with the original fortune spent on the gowns, I'm currently in possession of the costliest wardrobe of the Season."

Reginald retrieved the list she'd given him from his pocket, scanned it, then retrieved a pen from another pocket and scribbled something down.

"What could I possibly have done wrong now?" she demanded as he tucked the pen away. "And because you just wrote down whatever I did do, does that mean you concede defeat in regard to our challenge that you couldn't possibly commit to memory all of my social missteps?"

He looked up from the list. "I suppose I am conceding defeat with that, but only because I'm determined to succeed with the challenge your grandmother has laid before me, and a list may aid in achieving that success. As for your question about what you did wrong, I've mentioned, more than once now, that ladies are never to bring the cost of their clothing into polite conversation."

"We're not currently in a polite setting."

"You should approach every situation as a polite situation."

"Where's the fun in that?" she asked, ignoring what sounded like a grunt from Reginald right as the carriage pulled to a stop. A moment later, the door opened, and a now-muttering Reginald stepped out. Poppy overheard something about "what was I thinking" before he straightened, helped Viola from the carriage, then extended his hand to her.

Wincing as she stepped to the ground because her corset didn't seem to want to allow her any movement at all, she sucked in a short breath of air, blowing that breath out when she got her first good look at the Metropolitan.

It was an imposing building, built in a palazzo style, its façade glowing from the bright light streaming out of the many windows. Before Poppy could fully appreciate the sight, though, Reginald took her arm, and with Viola on his other arm, walked with them to a door that was being held open by a formally attired usher.

As she made her way up crimson-carpeted stairs to the first parterre toward the "Diamond Horseshoe," the prestigious tier of private boxes where the Van Rensselaer box was located, Poppy gazed around, unable to help but gawk at her opulent surroundings.

Following another usher dressed in burgundy livery into the Van Rensselaer box, Poppy found herself in a room papered in green. Beautiful paintings of different landscapes dotted the walls, the colors in those paintings picking up the colors of the settee and matching chairs that were artfully arranged around the small room. A crystal chandelier hung in the very center of the room, its many-faceted crystals showering the room with soft light.

Unbuttoning her cloak, she handed it to the usher with a smile, who returned the smile, although rather discreetly, before he turned and took the overcoat Reginald handed him, bowing himself out of the room a moment later.

"This is the sitting room," Viola said, gesturing around. "It's where, if your grandfather were ever in the city for a Season, he could retreat to enjoy a cigar and whiskey if the boredom of watching an opera became too much."

"Who would ever find an opera boring?" Poppy asked.

Viola and Reginald exchanged a glance before Reginald took a step closer to her. "Have you not had the opportunity to attend many operas?"

"By the question, I'm going to assume you're asking me that because operas can apparently turn tedious, but no, I've never been to an opera." She smiled. "We don't have an opera house in the small town where I grew up. We do, however, enjoy plays and the like in a barn that Mr. Walter Lewis, the gentleman who owns the large farm directly adjacent to Garrison Farms, allows us to use for entertainment purposes."

Reginald blinked. "You really grew up on a farm?"

"I did, although Garrison Farms isn't a true farm these days. We raise horses, but my paternal great-grandparents did start off as farmers, until my great-grandfather decided to pursue his love of horses."

"May I dare hope you traveled to New York often to see your maternal grandparents?"

"I'm afraid not. Viola and my mother are estranged, which made coming to New York a bit tricky."

"There's no need to disclose personal matters to Mr. Blackburn," Viola said with a flick of her wrist. "As I'm sure he'll agree, sharing such information is frowned upon and will only draw censure."

"It's not as if all of New York doesn't know you and Mother had a falling-out years ago," Poppy argued before she nodded to Reginald. "My mother ran off with my father, turning her back on what I've been told was a splendid start to her debut season."

"Again, not information Mr. Blackburn needs to know."

Reginald exchanged another telling look with Viola before he took a step toward red velvet curtains that were currently drawn. "May I assume the loge is to be found behind these?"

"The loge *is* behind the curtain," Viola said, hurrying to join him, clearly relieved at the change of topic. "But it's a little early yet to be taking our seats." She turned to Poppy. "The general audience will be seated by eight thirty, but members of society never take their seats until the middle of the first act."

"Why would anyone want to miss the beginning of the first act?"

"Because no one comes to the opera for the opera," Viola said. "We come to be seen, which is why all the ladies of society will be dressed in Parisian splendor, wearing jewels that are meant to impress." She nodded to Poppy's head. "That's why I chose one of my favorite tiaras for you to wear tonight, because the rubies in that tiara look lovely under the lights between acts."

Poppy didn't bother to mention that the tiara in question felt like she had a bushel of apples on her head because it was so heavy. Moving across the sitting room, she opened the red velvet curtain the slightest bit, finding most of the general audience seats filled, while the curtains on all the private boxes remained staunchly shut. Turning back to her grandmother, she squared her shoulders.

"I would like to watch the opera from the very beginning."

Viola lifted her chin. "It isn't done."

"But how will I keep up with the story of the Queen of Sheba if I don't see it from the beginning?"

"It's in Italian. There's every chance you won't be able to keep up even if you do see it from the beginning."

Poppy crossed her arms over her chest. "But you're one of the most esteemed matrons of society. Surely your influence is enough to stave off any outrage if I went out and took my seat right now. I've never seen an opera before and would like to experience the full event."

Viola considered her for a very long moment, and then, to Poppy's surprise, her grandmother was gliding across the room, taking hold of the gilded rope that was attached to the curtains, and pulling it.

The loud gasp from the audience that accompanied the action left Poppy questioning her desire to see everything, especially when she followed her grandmother through the open curtains and realized they'd drawn everyone's attention.

People were gawking at her, some even going so far as to train their opera glasses on her. Poppy smoothed her hands down the front of her gown and then took the arm Reginald suddenly thrust her way, thankful for his support as he led her to her seat because her legs felt decidedly unsteady.

After helping her into one of the two front chairs, he stepped back, taking a seat on one of the four chairs that were in the second row.

"Wouldn't it be more pleasant if you were to pull your chair up next to us?" she asked.

"Gentlemen often prefer to take a seat in the second row."

"So you can catch a nap without drawing as much notice?"

His lips twitched. "Indeed, although I doubt I'll feel inclined to nap this evening since I'm here to watch how you comport yourself, which will allow me to structure future lessons in areas where you may be somewhat deficient."

"You do know how to put a damper on an event, don't you?" Poppy said, earning another surprising twitch of Reginald's lips right as the lights dimmed. Turning to the stage, Poppy felt a shiver of excitement slide over her as the first note sounded.

It took a mere five minutes for her to become completely enthralled with opera. There was something mesmerizing about the scene unfolding below her, what with the splendid costumes the cast was wearing and the incredible pureness of the voices raised in song. She didn't even allow the entrance of Mrs. Astor and her entourage during the middle of the first act to distract her from the story unfolding on the stage, nor did she turn when people entered her box, not until the last note rang out on the first act and the lights came up.

"Come greet everyone, Poppy," Viola said from behind her, her grandmother's request having her rising from her chair and turning from the now curtained stage.

Summoning up a smile, she soon found her hand taken by Lord Lonsdale, who'd stepped up directly beside her and was sending her a charming smile.

"You're looking lovely this evening, Miss Garrison," Lord Lonsdale said after he'd kissed her hand, his eyes traveling the length of her. "What a beautiful frock you're wearing. Worth, is it?"

"Yes, and I thank you for your compliment." She turned to Miss Adele Tooker, who'd suddenly materialized beside Lord Lonsdale, looking lovely in a gown of palest pink, the intricate lacework suggesting her gown was from Worth as well. "Miss Tooker."

"Miss Garrison," Miss Tooker returned. "Enjoying the opera?"

"It's a wonderful production, but were you not afraid you'd miss something of importance regarding the plot by joining us before the first act ended?"

Miss Tooker gave an airy wave of her gloved hand. "I'm afraid I missed all of the first act. We arrived halfway through it, and then, well, Lord Lonsdale and I were enjoying a game of bean bags in my parents' box."

Poppy frowned. "You'd rather play bean bags than watch the opera?"

"I find opera to be very boring indeed, as does Lord Lonsdale," Miss Tooker said, sharing a smile with Lord Lonsdale. "How charming, though, and a touch provincial, that you actually seem to be enjoying the production."

Catching the pointed look Reginald was sending her, Poppy swallowed the retort that was on the very tip of her tongue and forced a smile. "I imagine I *must* seem provincial to you, Miss

Tooker. After all, I did spend most of my twenty-two years residing in what you would certainly consider the country."

Miss Tooker's eyes widened. "You're twenty-two?"

Inclining her head, Poppy smiled. "Positively ancient, I know, but I'm afraid there's not much I can do about my age."

Miss Tooker stepped closer to her and lowered her voice. "You should have a care, Miss Garrison, about such disclosures. Twenty-two almost has you firmly on the spinster shelf. You should own to only twenty."

"Being almost a spinster doesn't concern me in the least."

"That's what most spinsters say," Miss Tooker shot back. "But everyone knows they're trying to save face over the notion they've never secured the interest of a gentleman."

"I've secured the interest of a gentleman before, although—"

"The second act is about to begin," Reginald said, scaring her half to death when he appeared directly at her side. "Shall I see you back to your seat?"

"I was hoping Miss Garrison would agree to join Miss Tooker and me in a game of bean bags," Lord Lonsdale said.

Glancing to Viola, Poppy found her grandmother sending her a discreet nod, but because she didn't want to miss the second act, she ignored it and shook her head. "Perhaps another time, Lord Lonsdale. I'm anxious to see how the rest of the opera unfolds."

"Perhaps during intermission, then," he said right as the lights flickered. Sending Lord Lonsdale the barest hint of a curtsy because the musicians were already beginning to play, Poppy practically dragged Reginald back to her chair, surprised when he took the seat next to her.

"Your grandmother asked me to sit beside you during the second act. She is chatting with Mrs. Augustus Newbold," Reginald said.

"She doesn't trust me to behave myself if I sit here on my own?"

She couldn't be certain, but she thought Reginald might have grinned, his grin hidden because the lights had dimmed again. "I'm sure that was one of her reasons, but she also didn't want you to sit by yourself."

Allowing herself the luxury of rolling her eyes since Reginald couldn't see her, Poppy soon found herself pulled back into the opera.

Before she knew it, the second act came to an end, and when the lights came back on, she found that Lord Lonsdale and Miss Tooker had rejoined them, along with Mr. Nigel Flaherty and his dear friend, Mrs. Ridgeway.

"Miss Garrison," Nigel exclaimed as he headed her way, coming to a stop directly in front of her as she got to her feet. "How delightful you look this evening."

"Ah, she does look delightful," Mrs. Ridgeway exclaimed before she could respond, surprising Poppy when she took hold of her arm and beamed a bright smile. "Why, you quite put all the other young ladies to shame, and . . ."

As Mrs. Ridgeway began prattling off exactly how Poppy was putting the other ladies to shame, something that left Poppy decidedly uncomfortable, she took a moment to study the woman who was standing far too close for comfort.

Mrs. Ridgeway's gown was an interesting choice, what with it being a deep shade of crimson and adorned with flounces and numerous bows. She wore an enormous necklace set with numerous rubies, clearly chosen because the rubies matched the crimson of her gown. Her hair was the deepest black Poppy had ever seen and appeared to be dyed, but besides the color, the style was an interesting choice for a lady of a certain age to wear, pulled to the top of her head with ringlets cascading around a tiara that sparkled in the light cast from the chandeliers, that light . . .

"But my goodness, would you listen to me going on and on and with us not having been formally introduced yet," Mrs. Ridgeway said as she batted Nigel with a gloved hand. "You must rectify that situation immediately, my darling boy."

Nigel smiled and hurried to perform the expected introductions, which left Mrs. Ridgeway returning his smile before she turned to Poppy. "I feel, what with how Nigel's spoken so glowingly about you, Miss Garrison, that you and I are meant to become fast friends. And with that said, allow me to suggest that we abandon this air of formality between us. I insist you call me Lena, and I'd be honored if you'd permit me to call you Poppy—a marvelous name if I've ever heard one."

Having no idea what etiquette rule she was supposed to follow in such an unusual situation, Poppy glanced to Reginald, who'd stepped back and was simply observing her interaction with Nigel and Lena. He shrugged and sent her a small smile. That smile, she knew full well, meant he wanted to leave the decision about the abandonment of formality completely up to her, even though she knew that whatever decision she made was certainly going to earn her another notation on the list he was keeping regarding her many transgressions.

She resisted the urge to send Reginald a scowl and returned her attention to Lena. "It would be an honor for me to use your given name, Lena, and by all means, feel free to call me Poppy."

Lena clapped her hands in delight. "Oh, you are charming, Poppy, and may I say you're the spitting image of your mother when she was younger. Elizabeth made quite the impression during her debut Season, which I'm certain you're doing as well. You must be making your grandmother very proud."

"Are you friends with my grandmother?"

Lena's smile faltered for the briefest of seconds. "I wouldn't claim a close friendship with her, dear, but I'm certain that's only because I've been somewhat removed from society for the past few . . . decades." She smiled widely again. "However, as you can see, I've recently reentered society and have my darling Nigel to thank for that."

Nigel inclined his head. "Happy to have been of assistance, Lena."

"Miss Garrison, come join us," Lord Lonsdale suddenly called from the sitting room. "We've had an usher bring the bean bag game here, and you did promise to join in a game."

Excusing herself from Lena and Nigel after assuring Lena that they'd talk more later, Poppy began striding across the loge to join Lord Lonsdale. She was forced to slow her pace a few seconds later, though, because the tightness of her corset was making air difficult to come by.

Placing a hand on her side, while taking quick, short breaths as she moved at a snail's pace toward the sitting room, she jumped just a touch when Reginald appeared beside her.

"Are you all right?"

"This corset is going to be the death of me," she whispered, earning a telling arch of a brow in return.

"You did ask," she muttered before she hitched a smile into place, moving to join Lord Lonsdale and Miss Tooker in a game of bean bags.

She was not disappointed when the lights began flickering, relieved to have a reason to discontinue the game because the exertion of tossing a bean bag had begun to make her light-headed as well as queasy.

"You're very pale," Reginald said, taking her arm and walking her slowly back to her seat.

"I wouldn't mind some lemonade," she managed to get out, picking up the program an usher had left on her seat and using it to fan herself.

"I'll be right back."

As Reginald strode away, she moved closer to the balcony, hoping the sight of all the guests below her would distract her from the discomfort she was currently experiencing.

"Ah, Miss Garrison, there you are," Miss Tooker called out, waltzing through the open curtains with four of her friends and Lena. "We were looking for you because Lord Lonsdale wants to assemble a riding party sometime this week . . ."

As Miss Tooker and her friends advanced closer, Poppy began waving the program faster than ever because peculiar black dots were beginning to form in front of her eyes, making everything appear blurry and distorted.

Turning to face the stage, she struggled for air as the black dots increased. Her knees began to buckle, and then gave out, sending her surging forward and tumbling straight over the balcony.

CHAPTER 6

Reginald pushed the glass of lemonade into Charles's hand the second he noticed how unsteady Poppy seemed to be on her feet. Rushing forward, fear coursed through him when she suddenly began to topple over the balcony. Thrusting aside a lady who'd been blocking his path, he barely managed to snag hold of Poppy's ankle before she completely disappeared.

With her gown falling up past her knees, exposing petticoats and stockinged legs, Poppy was, concerningly enough, not making a single sound as she dangled from the balcony, nor were any of the guests at the Metropolitan making any noise either, which lent the situation a rather surreal air.

"I'll help you," Nigel Flaherty said, appearing by Reginald's side.

Grateful for the assistance, Reginald kept a firm grip on Poppy's ankle as he leaned over the balcony, pulling Poppy upward as Nigel leaned over the balcony as well, grabbing hold of Poppy's other leg, and together they pulled her to safety.

Alarm was immediate as Reginald helped her find her feet and got a look at her pale face.

"I can't breathe," she uttered right before her eyes fluttered shut and her body went limp.

Reginald caught her before she hit the ground. He lifted her in his arms "She's going to need some privacy, which means everyone needs to leave. Now."

"I'm not leaving," Viola argued.

"I didn't mean you," he said, striding with Poppy to the sitting room as Charles pulled the curtains closed and ushered everyone out of the Van Rensselaer box, shutting the door behind him.

"I need to loosen her laces," he said, turning Poppy over and ignoring Viola's sputtering.

"I think not, Mr. Blackburn. I'll do it."

"This is no time to worry about her modesty," he said, tackling the daunting feat of unbuttoning what seemed to be hundreds of seed pearl buttons that marched the entire back length of Poppy's gown. When he finally got her unbuttoned, he could only stare in amazement at the intricate corset she was tied into. "Why would someone use knots on her laces?" he asked, more to himself than Viola.

"I didn't want to chance having Poppy excuse herself and loosen them. It would have ruined the lines of her gown."

"And that was preferable over allowing her to suffocate?"

Not caring for how Poppy's breathing was still incredibly shallow, Reginald reached out and grabbed a paring knife that had been left on a small table, one used to cut apples Viola had requested earlier for a snack. Applying that knife to the laces, he sliced again and again through the silk until the corset fell away from Poppy's skin, revealing dozens of red welts on her back.

"I should not have been so flippant about her remarks regarding her corset," he said, anger sweeping through him. "She must have been in torture all night with how tightly she was laced up." He glanced over his shoulder, finding Viola staring at her granddaughter's back, her hand pressed to her lips.

"I didn't know," Viola whispered.

"Well, now you do, so perhaps, in the future, you might listen to Poppy when she complains. I have a feeling she's not one to complain overly much when she's in pain, but this cannot be allowed to happen again."

"If you just convinced my grandmother that I should be allowed to abandon my corset, or at least wear a larger size, I'll take back every unkind thought I've had about you since you started my etiquette lessons."

A laugh caught him by surprise. "You've had unkind thoughts about me?"

Poppy turned her head. "Several. Were you the one who caught me?"

"I was, although how I was able to reach you in time is beyond me. I'm only thankful I did. That would have been quite the drop if I'd not been able to grab hold of your ankle. Nigel Flaherty helped as well, and I certainly appreciated his assistance. I don't know if I'd have been able to haul you up on my own."

"I'll have to make certain to thank him at some later date, but as you're here right now, thank you. And because I now believe I owe you my life, I'll try to make a concerted effort to stay fully awake the next time you delve into a lesson about wine."

He swallowed another unexpected laugh. "I *knew* you fell asleep earlier. And here you told me you'd closed your eyes so the information would sink in."

"I only told you that because I didn't want to risk a lecture about how rude it was when a lady fell straight to sleep in the presence of a gentleman."

"Perhaps I'll have to restructure how I go about explaining the intricacies of wines."

"Or you could simply abandon the topic altogether. I've never been overly fond of wine."

"That's not something you should probably let get out. Society puts great stock in embracing just the right wines."

"I'm not sure I'll have to worry about what society thinks of me anymore, Reginald. I'm undoubtedly soon to be known as the notorious dangling heiress, and with a title like that, well, my acceptance into society is all but doomed."

"I would think you'll find just the opposite," he countered. "Everyone will be most sympathetic to your plight, and I imagine that will have you garnering more invitations than you'll know what to do with. But enough about that for now. Do you feel ready to sit up?"

Instead of answering that question, she caught his eye. "Do tell me that my gown stayed in place when I was dangling over the balcony."

Not believing it would do any good to tell her it had not, Reginald shrugged out of his jacket. "You may use my jacket after you sit up to cover the back of your gown. I don't think it would be wise to try and stuff you back into that corset."

"Why is it permissible for you to mention my unmentionables but a faux pas when I do?"

"A most excellent question, and one I have no idea how to answer."

"Does this mean I can go forward speaking about unmentionables without fear of a lecture?"

"No."

"That's hardly fair, but fairness aside, how much did everyone get to see of me while I was dangling in the air?"

"You're very tenacious."

"Guilty as charged, which means you're going to have to answer my question if you don't want me pestering you about it for the rest of the night."

Reginald felt the unusual desire to roll his eyes. "Very well, to spare me a bout of pestering, which I must state is hardly becoming in a lady, the audience was not afforded much time to gape at your, ah . . . petticoats and . . . limbs."

"How reassuring," she said as Viola stepped next to the settee. "I'm going to go and have the carriage brought around."

Poppy's eyes turned stormy. "I'm not leaving with two acts still left to go. I don't know how it ends."

Viola released a sigh. "You can't very well stay and watch the end, not in your disheveled state. Why, you'll be fodder for the gossips for years if you do that."

Poppy released a sigh of her own. "Which doesn't say much

about society, but I suppose you have a valid point. However, I will expect someone to spend the ride home explaining to me the conclusion of the opera that I'm now going to miss."

Viola shook her head. "Our time would be better spent discussing suggestions Mr. Blackburn has undoubtedly made regarding how we're going to turn you into a diamond of the first water."

"I would think," Poppy began, "what with how I only recently escaped what would have certainly been a most gruesome death, that you would grant me what isn't exactly an unreasonable request."

Viola blinked. "I suppose your request *isn't* unreasonable, given the circumstances. Although, you're not exactly behaving as if you just escaped a gruesome death."

Poppy waved that aside. "I'm not one to descend into a fit of the vapors every time I land into a concerning situation since, given how often that occurs, I'd spend all of my time in that state. Nevertheless, I'm not above accepting a bit of coddling, which is why I'm certain you're now going to agree that we can spend our time traveling home discussing how the opera ends."

"Assad dies," Viola said without preamble. "And with that out of the way, I'm off to summon the carriage."

Reginald wasn't surprised in the least, what with how Viola had revealed the end of the opera, when Poppy refused to speak to her grandmother on the ride home, nor did she appear to listen to any of the suggestions he made about how they were going to turn her into a diamond of the first water—a feat he was beginning to believe was going to be next to impossible to achieve.

Three hours later, as he sat in a deep-cushioned chair beside the window in his suite of rooms at the Fifth Avenue Hotel, Reginald took a sip of tea, staring out into the dark night, unable to settle his thoughts.

He'd known his time in America would be spent aiding Charles with finding a wife, and even though he'd thought he'd prepared himself for that daunting prospect, he'd not been prepared to deal with someone like Poppy.

She was everything he'd never enjoyed in a lady—outspoken, overly exuberant, and prone to the most outlandish mishaps he'd ever witnessed. But . . . there was something refreshing about being in her presence. That notion was exactly why he currently seemed to be in the midst of a bit of brooding.

Poppy was the one who'd mentioned his brooding nature—and numerous times at that, over the past few days. And while he'd brushed her comments aside, he was beginning to realize, what with how there was no other way to explain his current frame of mind, that he, Lord Reginald Blackburn, possessed the propensity to brood.

He'd always considered himself to be a very proper gentleman, stern at times, perhaps, but brooding?

Brooding, at least according to his younger sister who seemed captivated with gothic romances, lent a gentleman a romantic air, which was not an air Reginald ever wanted to embrace.

He was much too practical for romance.

Romance, in his opinion, was highly overrated and caused gentlemen to behave in very unexpected ways, penning love letters and reciting poetry from the most brooding of authors, the one to spring to mind most often being Lord Byron.

He would never recite poetry to a lady from that brooding author.

A rap on the door drew him out of his thoughts. Abandoning his chair, Reginald strode across the room, opening the door and discovering Charles on the other side.

"Ah, thank goodness I've finally found you, Reginald. I've been searching for you for what feels like hours. How's Miss Garrison?"

Stepping aside to allow Charles into the room, Reginald trudged back to his chair, taking a seat as Charles shrugged out of his overcoat, loosened his tie, then helped himself to a cup of tea.

"Poppy's fine, or at least that's what she's claiming," Reginald said as Charles sat down in a chair beside him. "But when you say you've been searching for me for hours, where have you been searching?"

Charles took a sip of tea. "Well, in all honesty, I mostly contained my search efforts to the ball I attended after I left the opera. However, after roaming through every room of the house and after I enjoyed a few dances with some lovely ladies, I finally concluded you and Miss Garrison weren't going to show up. That's when I made my excuses and took to the streets."

"You were roaming the streets of New York on foot?"

Charles waved that aside. "Of course not. I hired a cab. But when the driver asked for directions, I realized I had no idea where Miss Garrison lives, so I directed the driver to drive up and down Fifth Avenue, until I realized that there was little chance I'd simply happen upon her house or find you or Miss Garrison lingering outside, what with how the weather is taking a turn for the worse." He shuddered. "Some of the ladies at the ball told me snow may soon be coming to the city, which will certainly hinder any notion of asking young ladies to go driving with me in the park."

"Unless you offer to take them for a sleigh ride, which you've always enjoyed."

Charles immediately brightened. "An excellent suggestion, Reginald. But returning to Miss Garrison, I didn't neglect to notice you've taken to using her given name. May I assume that means you're becoming somewhat familiar with her and have made headway with determining whether she would make me an admirable countess or not?"

"The only reason I'm addressing her as Poppy is because she insisted on abandoning formality between us. I'm convinced she's done so just to annoy me."

Reginald wasn't certain, but it almost seemed as if Charles had taken to hiding a grin behind the rim of his teacup.

"It's not amusing."

"Of course it's not," Charles said pleasantly, lowing his cup. "When's your next lesson scheduled with her?"

"Tomorrow afternoon. Her grandmother is hosting a tea in a

week or so and wants to make certain Poppy's prepared." Reginald frowned. "I'm afraid I might not be up for the challenge I accepted from Mrs. Van Rensselaer because I don't think it's possible to turn Poppy into a diamond of the first water, especially since she doesn't seem willing to cooperate."

Charles frowned. "Diamond of the first water or not, I find Miss Garrison to be very beautiful, and rumor has it she's one of the wealthiest heiresses in New York at the moment. Because of all that, I do hope you won't abandon your efforts. I'd hate to have to strike her off the list of potential heiresses I wrote down a few days ago."

"You've started a list?"

"I got the idea from you after you told me about that exchange you had with Miss Garrison about committing her deviations from expected decorum to memory." Charles tapped his forehead. "You know I don't have the gift for remembering things, so I decided it would be for the best if I began writing down the names of the ladies I'm interested in."

For a man who rarely wrote anything down—or read anything, for that matter—the idea that Charles had started a list of his own left Reginald smiling. "May I ask who is at the top of your list?"

"Oh, I haven't put the names in any order. That would be taking the matter too far. But Miss Garrison is clearly on the list, as is Miss Tooker, and a few other young ladies I can't recall at the moment." Charles leaned forward. "Now, returning to Miss Garrison. What is it about her that you find objectionable?"

Reginald found that question somewhat difficult to answer.

In all honesty, the only objection he had about Poppy was that she didn't abide by the expected rules of the day. However, she was undoubtedly a lady, which was a mark in her favor, but gaining entrance into the world of the aristocracy was not an easy feat. Someone like Poppy would be eaten alive by the ladies with whom he and Charles associated, and she would probably find herself ostracized even if she held the title of countess.

"She's very exuberant," he finally settled on saying.

74

"That's it? She's exuberant?" Charles repeated.

"She also keeps pointing out that I'm a brooding sort, which means she can be slightly annoying at times."

"You *are* a brooding sort."

"No, I'm not."

"Of course you are. Everyone knows that." Charles shook his head. "The ladies in London remark upon your brooding nature all the time. They seem to believe that underneath your brooding attitude beats the heart of a romantic. Truth be told, I've spent time gazing into the mirror, trying to mimic your brooding looks, although without much success."

"I can't imagine why you'd want to adopt such an unpleasant attitude."

"What gentleman doesn't long for the ladies to sigh over him?"

"Ladies don't sigh over me."

"They do. You just haven't noticed them." Charles sat forward. "I've always been somewhat envious of that trait of yours, which is why I was rather pleased you announced you're merely my traveling companion instead of the brooding Lord Blackburn."

Reginald frowned. "You have no reason to be jealous of me."

"So says the gentleman who has no need to marry for money." Charles rose from his chair. "And on that slightly depressing note, I'm off to bed. Can you send Giles over to my room in the next hour? I need to give him this jacket so he can get it cleaned and pressed."

"I don't expect Giles to return for hours," Reginald said, rising to his feet as well. "He managed to get himself invited to a dinner one of the butlers from a house on Fifth Avenue is hosting for other butlers and valets tonight, and I encouraged him to attend."

"But what use is a valet if he's never here to assist us with dressing and undressing?"

"You do remember that I brought Giles along so he could try and infiltrate the houses of the New York Four Hundred, don't you? I'm hopeful he'll be able to ferret out information that you and I have little hope of getting for ourselves, which will be far more helpful to you in the long run than getting your jacket pressed."

Charles's brows drew together. "That does explain why Giles has been conspicuously absent over the past week or two."

Even though Reginald was quite accustomed to Charles being frequently forgetful, it did still take him aback exactly how scattered his cousin could be at times. It also left him wondering how Charles was going to be able to manage his many estates, even if he did find an heiress to fund the improvements those estates so desperately needed.

"Why don't you leave your jacket with me and I'll see to it that Giles sends it out to be laundered tomorrow?"

Charles smiled an easy smile. "Thank you, Reginald. I can't very well impress any of the ladies if I'm seen in a wrinkled jacket."

"I think your title has already impressed most of the ladies out this Season."

Charles's smile dimmed. "I suppose it has, although wouldn't it be lovely if I could find a lady in New York who didn't care about that title and simply enjoyed spending time with me?" With his shoulders drooping just a touch, Charles walked to the door and opened it, turning once again to nod at Reginald. "Good luck tomorrow with your lesson with Miss Garrison. I've been invited to ride through Central Park with Miss Tooker and some of her friends, so do feel free to join us after you're done."

With that, Charles quit the room, closing the door quietly behind him and leaving Reginald with the distinct impression that Charles was not nearly as keen about securing himself an heiress as Reginald had originally thought, especially since it almost seemed as if his cousin might have, at one time, hoped to marry for love.

CHAPTER 7

Deliberately missing her scheduled appointment with Reginald that afternoon was certainly not one of her finer moments. Even so, it had been necessary because she needed to put some distance between herself and Reginald in order to sort through some uncomfortable conclusions she'd come to about the man.

Reginald was the most proper gentleman she'd ever met, stern at times and seemingly lacking when it came to emotions, but she'd gotten a glimpse of the person behind the proper air he adopted, and that gentleman, to her very great concern, appealed to her.

He was kind, grudgingly so at times, but he'd sat beside her during the second act of the opera and explained scenes she didn't understand, taking the time to answer her whispered questions, of which there'd been many.

He'd also saved her from certain death and risked her grandmother's ire when he'd cut her from laces that had seemed intent on killing her. He'd then treated her with care as he'd escorted them home, even with her being in what could only be described as a surly frame of mind.

There was something downright intriguing about a gentleman capable of rescuing a damsel in distress, although she'd never imagined she'd find herself intrigued by the likes of Mr. Reginald—

"I was delighted to find you outside Mrs. Roderick Cameron's residence earlier," Murray Middleton was saying, pulling Poppy directly from her thoughts. "But I must admit I was somewhat surprised at how unexpectedly you exited your grandmother's carriage and joined me."

"I'm sure you did find me all but leaping out of my grandmother's carriage unexpected, but in my defense, encountering you was an opportunity I simply couldn't ignore." Poppy grinned. "It provided me with the perfect excuse to abandon another hour of tedious afternoon calls."

Murray shot a nervous glance Poppy's way before he returned his attention to the path they were on in Central Park. His hands tightened on the reins as his horse, a dapper mare that seemed rather spirited, veered to the left and straight into the path of an oncoming carriage. After tugging on the reins in what Poppy believed was a far too enthusiastic manner, and after his horse returned to her side of the path, he looked back to Poppy. "While you certainly managed to bring your calls to a speedy conclusion, I think you may have incurred your grandmother's displeasure in the process." He cleared his throat. "She was looking downright apoplectic after you jumped up on the seat beside me, and that look only intensified after you addressed me as Murray." He cleared his throat again. "I should point out that using my given name suggests that you and I share a more than familiar relationship with each other."

"How could we not share a more than familiar relationship with each other after what happened during the Gypsy Quadrille?" Poppy returned. "That experience set us on a path to friendship, and friends do not address each other formally when they're enjoying a lovely afternoon drive."

"You merely want to pursue a *friendship* with me?"

Poppy drew in a bit of chilly early December air and blew it out in a puff of mist. "Forgive me, Murray. I hope I haven't lent you the impression I'm anxious to pursue anything *but* friendship with you."

Murray, curiously enough, smiled. "Thank goodness for that. Friendship sounds lovely, but anything more would not be advisable between us."

"Why not?"

"Because my mother has warned me to maintain my distance from you."

"Why would she do that?"

Murray slumped down on the seat. "While I would love to say she did so because of the attention your mishap garnered last night at the Metropolitan, I'm afraid it might be because she sees you as a threat."

"A threat?"

"Indeed. She heard all about what transpired at the ball a few nights ago even though she was not in attendance, since she's currently suffering a cold. But after she learned that you did not throw me under the proverbial carriage wheels after our little fiasco, she's apparently decided you're no shrinking wallflower. That right there is why she feels threatened by you." Murray caught Poppy's eye. "She does not care for me to become involved with ladies she cannot manage to her satisfaction."

"I *have* been told often of late that I'm difficult to manage," Poppy admitted before she frowned. "Forgive me for pointing this out, though, but you aren't maintaining your distance from me, since we're sitting together in your two-seated buggy, tooling through Central Park."

"If you'll recall, Miss Garrison—or Poppy, rather," he quickly amended after she arched a brow. "I wasn't given much of an opportunity to discourage this outing, not after you jumped on the seat next to me, demanded I set my horse into motion, then helped yourself to the reins when I wasn't fast enough for your liking."

"I did give the reins back to you." Poppy nodded to two gentlemen who were riding past them on their horses, both of whom were tipping their hats to her. "And I'm sure you would have leapt out of a carriage as well if you'd been experiencing the trying afternoon I have. My grandmother insisted we make the rounds in the hope of heading off unfounded rumors that were brought to her attention over morning tea. Those rumors, I'm afraid, center around the unpleasant speculation that I, in a fit of pique, threw myself from the balcony because, according to the gossip that reached my grandmother's ear, I experienced some type of dramatic encounter during the opera, such as a direct slight."

"You don't really seem the type to suffer a fit of pique."

"Of course I'm not, but because I've only recently begun traveling in society, that's not common knowledge." She smiled. "However, even if I *was* suffering a fit of pique, I certainly wouldn't throw myself off a balcony. I'm much more likely to confront the person who slighted me, even though I've been told numerous times by Reginald that a lady is never to take anyone to task, no matter the provocation."

"Why would Reginald Blackburn take it upon himself to remark on something like that?"

"Have I mentioned that my grandmother has somehow procured Reginald's cooperation in schooling me in all matters of proper decorum?"

"You have not."

"Well, now I've told you, but I'm not happy about the situation in the least."

Murray gave a bit of a shudder. "I wouldn't be happy either, not with Reginald being such an intimidating sort."

Poppy waved that aside. "I'm hardly intimidated by the man. But because I don't want to earn the reputation of being a bore, and I've clearly spent more than enough of our time talking about me, let's talk about you."

"There's not much to tell."

"I'm sure that's not true, but since you seem reluctant to be the topic of conversation, tell me this—why aren't you driving those two bays you mentioned the other evening?"

Murray's cheeks turned pink. "Mother decided they're too strong-willed for me to handle. She sent the bays off to stay with Ethan, one of my older brothers, so I won't be tempted to take them out when she's unavailable to go driving with me." He nodded to the mare pulling the buggy. "Mother purchased this mare for me only a few days ago, but I'm hesitant to tell her that Clara, the name I recently chose for my new horse, seems to be far more strong-willed than the bays."

"Your mother seems to take an unusual interest in your life."

"She does, although that's because I was a very sickly sort as a child." He shook his head. "There's also my size. I've always been small—far smaller than my brothers—which lends me a fragile air. Because of that, and my ill health when I was younger, Mother tends to coddle me."

"Which would be adorable if you were three."

"True, but most of the time it's simply easier to go along with Mother. She's a difficult woman, and the few times I have defied her over the years, well, it was never a pleasant experience. That's why I don't put up a fuss over her coddling."

Turning to watch a carriage that was trundling past them, Poppy settled her gaze on the two young ladies pressing their noses against the glass windows of that carriage, their attention fixed not on her, but on Murray, who seemed completely oblivious as he steered his horse somewhat haphazardly down the trail.

Poppy fought the urge to take control of the reins again. "You said your mother doesn't care for ladies she can't manage."

"I did."

"Should I assume she wants you to settle your affections on a lady possessed of a timid and retiring nature?"

"I don't believe my mother wants me to turn my attention to any particular lady. She enjoys having me available to attend to her whims." Murray smiled. "She even enjoys having me tag along when she pays her afternoon calls, which is why I can sympathize with you about the tediousness of that particular obligation." His smile widened. "I must say, though, that since you've arrived in town, those calls have gotten much more interesting, what with all the adventures you seem to experience."

"How delightful to learn that I'm providing society with a respite from their tedium, although I haven't deliberately set out to become the most notorious lady of the Season."

"I wouldn't call you notorious, Poppy. I'd say . . . well, I don't have a word available to describe you, so . . . before I get myself in trouble, allow me to return to the subject of paying calls."

"Now you sound like Reginald when he's droning on with his lessons."

Murray's lips twitched. "I'll try to keep my droning in check, but you do need to understand the logic behind paying calls so that you don't unintentionally offend someone."

"I'm sure I unintentionally offend society members on a daily basis, so I'm not certain they'd be taken aback by anything I might say about the absurdity of spending my day calling on people."

"Do you know your voice takes on a remarkably peevish tone at times?" Murray asked.

She arched a brow, which left him grinning. "Ah, well, a sensitive topic to be certain, so returning to calls. What are you waiting with bated breath to know about them?"

"Nothing, but since I've just realized that probably came out somewhat peevish, let me try to make amends." She tapped a finger on her chin. "Why can't ladies merely send off their calling cards by mail or send a footman around with them instead of spending hours traveling around the city to deliver them in person?"

"Because that would be considered common and being a member of high society is all about appearances."

"Is that why ladies are expected to answer every correspondence they receive, something that takes up precious time every morning?"

"It is."

Poppy's brow furrowed. "Answer me this, then. Why do so many charitable organizations bother to send society ladies requests for funding when the majority of those requests are met with an engraved card declining to send funds?"

"Because they're hoping to find new sponsors, perhaps someone like you who has only arrived in the city and hasn't settled on a noble cause."

Poppy released a breath. "Choosing a noble cause is on the very long list of things I'm supposed to accomplish in the next few weeks, although I have no idea what cause needs my help because I've not traveled into the neediest parts of the city as of yet."

"Nor should you." Murray shook his head. "Ladies do not travel to Five Points or the like. You merely need to ask around at Grace Church on any given Sunday; you'll be provided with numerous causes that will be deemed acceptable in the eyes of the New York Four Hundred."

"That hardly seems like a noble way to go about selecting a noble cause, but since we've once again turned the conversation to me, and I'm growing bored with the subject of me, we should return to the subject of your mother."

"I don't have much more to say on that matter," Murray argued, "nor would any advice you may lend me do much good since, again, Mother is a difficult woman and I don't care to cross swords with her."

"Is that because she controls the purse strings and you'll be left without an allowance if you cross her?"

"You're very tenacious, aren't you?"

"That seems to be the general consensus of late, but I believe tenacity is one of my greatest strengths."

"I would have said it's more along the lines of annoying. But to answer your question, Mother does not have control over my finances. My great-aunt left me a tidy trust fund that I was able to access the day I turned twenty-one, which was a few months back. I was also then able to access the trust my paternal grandfather set up for me as well, a trust I'm all but convinced he set up to spite my mother."

"Your grandfather didn't care for your mother?"

"They learned how to rub along together, but he was of the firm belief that my mother stifles me. Grandfather also didn't like that my father, God rest his soul, left the running of the family business, which revolves around the railroad and steel industry, to my three older brothers, believing I'd never be strong enough to take on the responsibilities required of keeping our business interests on solid financial ground."

"Do you resent your father for excluding you from the family business?"

"I'm not really a business-minded person, Poppy. I've always been drawn to—" Murray suddenly pressed his lips together and began taking an interest in Clara as she clip-clopped her way down the street.

"To what?" Poppy pressed.

"I'd rather not say."

"You do recall that you only recently remarked on how tenacious I am, which means I'll simply keep badgering you until you tell me what you're drawn to."

Murray tipped his hat to a gentleman passing on his horse. "Ladies, in case you're unaware, are never supposed to badger a gentleman, especially when he's voiced a reluctance to divulge certain information."

"I must have skipped that part in the etiquette books my grandmother provided me with, and Reginald has yet to address that particular topic, so . . . if you were to decide to strike out on your own, what would you do?"

"I'd create an art studio and pursue my love of painting," Murray said in a rush. "But you can't tell anyone what I just divulged."

"Who would I tell?"

"Your grandmother, who would then tell my mother, who would then . . . well, it's best not to even consider her reaction to learning her youngest son fancies himself an artist."

"Are you any good?"

"Would I come across as a braggart if I admit I am?"

"I don't think it would be possible for you to come across as a braggart. Furthermore, if art is your passion, I see no reason for you to keep that hidden. There are many respected artists and—"

Poppy stopped speaking when Clara suddenly broke into a trot on her own accord, something Murray evidently hadn't been expecting since he let out a bit of a shriek and immediately began tugging on the reins.

Unfortunately, Clara didn't seem to appreciate shrieking because her trot turned into a gallop, which had Murray dropping the reins, leaving Clara free to gallop directly toward one of the small lakes that dotted Central Park.

"Whoa, Clara, whoa!" Poppy yelled, but the mare didn't slow in the least.

Shrugging out of her cloak as fast as she could because it was limiting her ability to move, Poppy leaned forward and tried to snatch up reins that were flapping wildly about, stretching as far as she could. She froze on the spot, though, when, out of the corner of her eye, she saw a beast of a stallion race into view. Squinting, she discovered Reginald sitting on top of that beast, his form nothing less than perfect as he turned his horse directly toward Clara.

To Poppy's dismay, it soon became clear that Clara didn't care for stallions either because she released a loud whinny and reared up on her hind legs before plunging forward again.

"Stay back!" Poppy yelled, her yell muffled as her hat fell over her face, making it all but impossible to see. Tearing the hat from her head, she threw it aside and returned her attention to a horse that was now completely out of control.

As Clara pounded down the gravel path, Poppy swallowed the fear that was rising in her throat and stretched forward again, finally snagging a piece of the reins. She began pulling it toward her, but then, the buggy flew over a bump, and she suddenly found herself launched through the air at a most troubling rate of speed.

CHAPTER 8

Fear swept through Reginald as he watched Poppy sail through the air. That fear was immediately replaced with disbelief, though, when she somehow managed to land right on the horse's back and proceeded to grab hold of the horse's mane before the horse lurched into a small lake, traveled all of a few feet, then came to an abrupt stop.

His disbelief turned to temper when the thought occurred to him that Poppy, being a lady, had no business trying to stop a runaway horse on her own, especially when he, a gentleman, had been attempting to race to her rescue.

She could have very well broken her lovely, yet far too impulsive, neck.

Kneeing his horse forward, he reined it in when he reached the water's edge, incredulity joining the temper he was experiencing when he noticed that Mr. Murray Middleton was covering his face with what appeared to be a lady's hat, frozen still as a statue, his knees drawn up to his chest on the seat of a buggy that was now sitting in at least a foot of water. Forcing his attention from that curious sight, he settled his gaze on Poppy.

"Have you quite lost your mind?" he called out, which had her lifting her head and pinning him with eyes that were flashing with what seemed to be animosity.

"I was about to say almost those very same words to you," she shot back. "Although I was planning on stating that you *had* lost your mind, and I wasn't even considering using the word *quite*." Her eyes flashed hotter than ever. "And while I'm certain you feel that peppering your vocabulary with words like *quite*, *zounds*, or *prithee* lends your speech a cultivated air, do know that in this particular instance, *quite* sounds rather ridiculous since it's your fault I'm currently sitting on the back of a horse. In December. And in a lake, for goodness' sakes."

"I have never in my life used the word *prithee*, but am I to understand you believe it's my fault for what just transpired?"

"*Quite*."

He swung from the saddle and took a step toward the water, stopping when she held up her hand. "Do not even think about coming in here. Clara has only just stopped moving, but she seems to be a most temperamental mare and one that you scared half to death when you came charging our way."

"As a gentleman, it stands to reason that the next order of business for me is to get you off that horse and out of the water without you getting a drenching in the process."

"I've been riding horses since before I could walk. I assure you, there's little likelihood that I'll suddenly lose my seat and tumble into the water. Your only order of business, as far as I'm concerned, is to unhitch the buggy, which will then allow me to get Clara out of the lake."

"You're very demanding."

"So I've been told."

Reginald took a step forward. "You're also incredibly headstrong, an attitude I'm going to assume must be responsible for you neglecting to keep our scheduled appointment today. That's why I was forced to run you down here in Central Park, after your grandmother told me you'd chosen to ride with Mr. Middleton instead of returning home with her. If you'd not missed that appointment, *you* wouldn't be sitting in the lake, and *I* wouldn't have been forced to try and save you once again. Although, because you do seem convinced it's my fault you're in the lake, I apologize about that."

"Not that I'm an expert on expected behavior, Reginald, but I don't believe it's appropriate for you to be wasting precious time yelling at me right now, nor do I believe an apology should be rendered in such a thunderous tone of voice," Poppy all but yelled back at him.

The very idea that he *had* been yelling left him speechless. But before he could find his voice and beg Poppy's pardon again, Mr. Middleton lowered the hat that had been covering his face.

"I'm certain Poppy must have simply lost track of the time, Mr. Blackburn, because Mrs. Van Rensselaer did call out to us about a scheduled appointment Poppy was not to miss as we were driving away. However, since I did remind her of that appointment, and I did see her pull out a watch from her reticule not that long—" He stopped talking when Poppy let out a noise that sounded somewhat like an angry cat.

"Thank you for that bit of unsolicited commentary, Murray. Very helpful." She turned back to Reginald. "Did you ever consider that I might have missed our appointment so as to spare you from wasting further time on me, since your endeavor to turn me into a diamond of the first water is certain to fail?"

Reginald's brows drew together. "I might need you to expand a touch on what is clearly a grasping-at-straws attempt on your part."

She gave a wave of a hand. "I'm not grasping at straws, although my explanation only just came to me, and probably on the wind that seems to be rushing over the water I'm in."

"Is that a not-so-subtle hint that you're ready for me to rescue you now?" He took another step toward the water, stilling when the horse Poppy was on let out a whinny and lunged forward, taking Poppy, along with Mr. Middleton and his buggy, another foot into the lake.

"Best give her another minute," Poppy called, running a soothing hand over the horse's neck, which seemed to keep the horse from traveling farther into the lake. "Where was I? Oh yes, I was going to explain how I was sparing you the grave disappointment of not being able to turn me into a diamond of the first water."

"I don't remember you saying a thing about sparing me a grave disappointment."

Poppy smiled. "Just came to me as I was plunging deeper into the lake, a circumstance that had me realizing exactly how to explain why your efforts will certainly fail."

"I'm listening," he was forced to call out when Poppy suddenly bent over and began whispering into the horse's ear.

"You obviously don't listen to your own lessons because I distinctly remember you telling me that patience is expected of society members, but you're not being very patient with me," she said, straightening and taking a second to pull her skirt over a knee she apparently only then realized was exposed. "Now, to continue my explanation regarding why you're certain to fail, know this; even though you're more than proficient with your knowledge about etiquette and expected behavior, you can't control my propensity for landing in the most ridiculous of situations."

"I see no reason to deny you that particular argument," he said.

"Then you shouldn't deny that you're destined for failure because you have absolutely no way of teaching me how to avoid such situations."

"If you'd kept our appointment today, you wouldn't be in your current situation," he pointed out.

Poppy, to his annoyance, ignored that. "Do know that it doesn't bother me in the least that you're doomed for failure with turning me into a diamond of the first water. If you ask me, that goal seems unusually frivolous. I'd much rather spend my time pursuing worthier endeavors, and perhaps I should also consider encouraging other society ladies to do the same."

"Oh . . . I'm not sure I like the sound of that," Reginald said slowly.

"Society ladies," Poppy continued as if he'd not spoken, "what with the resources we command, should be trying to make a difference in the world, not merely pursuing one amusement after another. Why, it's downright disturbing that so many ladies are praised for supporting their chosen noble cause when it seems to me that support only requires sending out a bit of money, instead of getting into the trenches."

"Ladies aren't expected to get into trenches."

She threw up her hands. "Would you please stop lecturing me? It's incredibly maddening."

"But he's right," Mr. Middleton chimed in. "Ladies are expected to keep themselves well removed from unpleasantness. My mother has always said so."

Poppy immediately turned flashing eyes Mr. Middleton's way. "You are not helping me to stifle the distinct urge I'm currently feeling to box your ears, which might, hopefully, knock some sense into you."

"You want to box my ears because I disclosed that ladies are expected to remain untouched by unpleasantness?" Mr. Middleton asked.

"Yes, but more importantly, I want to box your ears because you had no business taking out a horse you have little ability to control. You are a danger not only to yourself but to every poor soul who made the horrible decision to take a turn around Central Park today. You're lucky Clara didn't plow anyone over."

Mr. Middleton's brows drew together. "I've never suffered a mishap with the horse I usually drive about town."

"Then why, pray tell, did you not bring that horse out today?"

"Because Esmerelda is eighteen years old, and she prefers spending her time eating oats in her stall. She flatly refused to budge out of her stall three weeks ago, which is exactly why my mother acquired Clara for me after she decided the bays were too much for me to handle."

"*Clara* is too much for you to handle. She's clearly not been trained properly to pull a buggy through crowds. Frankly, I have no notion as to why anyone would purchase a horse that doesn't even respond to her name."

Mr. Middleton shifted on the seat as two bright patches of red stained his cheeks. "Clara might not respond to her name because I only renamed her this morning, something I do believe I mentioned earlier when I said I'd only recently named her."

Poppy's brows drew together. "I must have missed the significance of that, but do you know anything at all about horses?"

"Am I setting myself up for a blistering lecture if I admit my education as pertains to horses may be somewhat lacking?"

Poppy's shoulders drooped just a touch. "I suppose, given what you disclosed to me about your upbringing, that it shouldn't come as a surprise that your education regarding horses has been deficient. Nevertheless, your mother has not done you any favors by allowing you to be so blatantly ignorant of an animal that's essential for transportation. I suppose, since you and I are friends, there's nothing left to do but to offer to teach you the basics about horses."

Reginald cleared his throat. "While that's very generous of you to offer, now doesn't seem like the best time to give Mr. Middleton a lesson. You are, in case you've forgotten, sitting on a horse in a lake in December, and the wind seems to be picking up again."

"Since neither you or Murray have bothered to unhitch the carriage as of yet, it seems to be the perfect time."

His lips twitched. "You do know you're exhausting, don't you?"

"When you pair that with being headstrong and tenacious, one must wonder why you seem keen to continue instructing me."

Reginald found he had no easy reply to that. She *was* headstrong, tenacious, and exhausting. However, because Charles had mentioned that Poppy was on his list of potential heiresses, there was a chance Charles *would* decide she was the heiress for him, which meant he really had no choice *but* to continue on with her and try his hardest to turn her into a proper lady.

That he felt the oddest urge to discourage Charles from keeping Poppy on his list, but not because she was ill equipped to be a countess, was disconcerting to say the least, especially since Reginald knew the real reason for wanting to discourage Charles was this—

He, Reginald Blackburn, second son of a duke, found Miss Poppy Garrison somewhat fascinating.

"Not that I want to interrupt what is undoubtedly one of the most riveting conversations I've heard in years," Murray suddenly said, leaning forward on the buggy seat, "nor do I want to delay your getting out of the lake, Poppy, but I feel the need to explain why I believed that Clara would be easily handled. That explanation might allow you to conclude I'm not a completely inadequate sort."

Trepidation was swift, but before Reginald could warn Murray to have a care, Poppy was arching a brow.

"I'm listening."

"She's a she" was the only explanation Murray gave, which immediately had Reginald bracing himself as Poppy drew herself up.

"She's a *she*?" she repeated.

"Indeed." Murray gave a bob of his head. "As such, she should possess a gentle temperament, much like ladies possess, and—"

"Not only do you know next to nothing about horses, you apparently know even less about women," Poppy shot back.

"I know plenty about women," Murray argued.

"You do not," Poppy argued right back. "Simply because Clara is a mare does not mean she's possessed of a meek demeanor. She's a temperamental creature at best, and you should have shown more care with renaming her. At the very least, you should have given her more time to become adjusted to her new name before you took her out on the streets of New York."

Murray shook his head. "I couldn't very well have done that, not when the man who delivered her told me her original name was Hazel—my *mother's* name." He shuddered. "Mother would have been gravely insulted to discover her youngest son was tooling around town with a horse named Hazel. Why, she might have taken to her bed for the rest of the winter."

"And while I can't help but point out that your mother should have learned the name of the horse you told me she purchased for you before she made that purchase, if she *would* take to her bed now, you would have time to assert your independence from her."

Murray frowned. "I don't recall mentioning that I wanted to assert my independence."

"You didn't," Poppy returned. "But I imagine after your mother learns about today's events, you might begin considering the matter."

"I wasn't planning on telling her about this latest adventure."

Poppy gestured around. "If you've neglected to notice, we're beginning to draw a crowd. The likelihood that someone won't mention this to your mother is slim to none."

As Murray turned on the seat, Reginald glanced around, refusing a wince. Crowds were, indeed, beginning to gather, all of whom were casting their attention to the curious scene of a lady dressed in a lovely green walking dress who was sitting astride a horse, showing a rather shocking amount of ankle.

Knowing there was little chance Poppy would react well if he plowed through the water and snatched her off the horse so she'd no longer be the object of such scrutiny, Reginald returned his attention to Murray. "What say we get the buggy unhitched so we can then cajole Poppy and your temperamental horse out of the lake before every member of the New York Four Hundred shows up?"

Murray blinked. "You want me to get into the lake?"

"Unless you have a better suggestion of how to go about unhitching the buggy, yes, you'll need to get into the lake."

"I'm not really proficient with such matters and will probably only slow down the process of getting the buggy unhitched."

Reginald stepped closer to Murray's buggy and lowered his voice. "While I understand your reluctance to wade into water that is certainly going to be frigid, you are a gentleman. We gentlemen are occasionally required to insert ourselves into situations that are not to our liking, but you see, that's what makes us gentlemen. Surely your father has mentioned the rules of gentlemen to you a time or two over the years, hasn't he?"

"My father died over five years ago, but before he died, he didn't really have much time for me, preferring to spend his time with my older and far more masculine brothers."

Reginald suddenly found himself without a reply to what had apparently been an unexpected admission on Murray's part, given the flaming color now staining his cheeks.

Even though his father, Richard Blackburn, Duke of Sutherland, had far too many demands on his time, he had never used his lofty status as an excuse to ignore his two sons.

Richard had always been of the firm belief that gentlemen were made, not born into that role. He also believed it was his responsibility to ensure that Reginald, along with his older brother, Liam, who was the heir to the title and possessed his own title of Marquis of Stratford, were given the tools to become true gentlemen. He'd never once shown Liam favoritism, even with Liam being the firstborn and heir.

It was little wonder Murray lacked the confidence one expected in a gentleman, but that lack of confidence was not going to be cured if the man was continually excused from stepping into that role.

"I have no idea why I just disclosed that to you, since we barely know each other."

Shaking himself back to the unlikely situation at hand, Reginald frowned. "I imagine you did so because it's something that's been weighing on your mind. But I should beg your pardon for broaching such a personal question, although since the topic has been broached, I now feel the need to lend you some unsolicited advice."

"What is it with everyone wanting to advise and improve me today?"

Reginald bit back a smile and nodded toward the crowd that was growing ever larger on the banks of the small lake. "As Poppy pointed out, we are garnering quite the audience, many of whom are members of the feminine set."

Murray twisted around on the seat. "On my word but there do seem to be many ladies looking our way." He raised a hand and gave a feeble wave to two young ladies who were waving back at them. He turned back to Reginald. "I believe you've attracted the notice of Miss Maisie Leggett and her sister, Miss Helene Leggett."

"I'm relatively certain I'm not the one who has attracted their notice," Reginald said.

"Surely you're mistaken," Murray breathed, turning ever so discreetly around again and then stiffening before he gave another feeble wave. "Why do you imagine they're waving at me?"

"You truly don't understand women, do you?"

Murray blew out a breath. "Not really." He glanced to Poppy, who was leaning over Clara, whispering again into the horse's ear. "But don't tell Poppy. I don't want her to turn smug."

"Your secret is safe with me, and as for the waving ladies, I have to believe they're waving because one of the Leggett sisters fancies you. That's why I'm now going to impart some advice about embracing the role of a true gentleman."

"Will that advice explain why one of the Leggett sisters might fancy me?"

"We don't have that much time."

Murray blew out a breath. "Since we're less than acquainted with each other, Mr. Blackburn, it seems somewhat peculiar that you've decided to impart advice to me in the first place."

"True, and it's Reginald, if you don't mind, because you must know Poppy is certain to begin harping at both of us if we don't begin addressing each other by our given names."

A ghost of a smile flickered over Murray's face. "She does seem prone to harping, so please, call me Murray."

"Are the two of you talking about me?" Poppy suddenly yelled. "And if so, allow me to point out that the wind *is* picking up and, if you've forgotten, I'm still sitting in the lake."

"In short," Reginald hurried to say, surprised to feel his lips twitch at Poppy's look of exasperation, "gentlemen are often required to attend to matters that are less than pleasant in order to assist a damsel in distress."

"Poppy doesn't really fit the role of a true damsel in distress."

"Agreed, but she has asked us to unhitch the buggy, and because I'm sure the Leggett sisters will be suitably impressed if you lend your assistance to a lady they probably *assume* is in distress, I'm going to encourage you to hop in the water with me and get down to business."

"I can take off my shoes and socks, though, can't I?"

"A sensible action to be certain," Reginald agreed, shrugging out of his jacket before he kicked off his shoes, stripped off his socks, then tossed everything onto the bank and turned back to Murray.

Murray, he couldn't help but notice, seemed to be trying to hide the boots he'd just removed, and given the size of the heel on those boots, Reginald wasn't exactly surprised the young man had tried to cover them with his jacket.

"My mother believes heeled boots help me strike an attitude of authority," Murray said when he realized Reginald had noticed his attempt at concealment.

"Height has nothing to do with assuming an air of authority. Confidence does, which means you need to throw back your shoulders, keep your head up, and jump right off that seat with a sense of purpose."

Even though Murray released what could only be described as a shriek once his feet hit the cold water, he did throw back his shoulders as he sloshed through the water. Coming to a stop directly beside his horse, he released another small shriek when the horse shied away from him, but Poppy brought the mare back under control a mere second later. Once Reginald was certain the horse was not going to bolt again, and after he explained to Murray the basics of how to unbuckle and unharness the buggy, the two men set to work, joined a short time later by three other men who'd abandoned their socks and shoes and offered to assist them in wrestling the buggy out of the water after they'd gotten it unhitched.

Turning back to the lake after the buggy was returned to dry land, Reginald discovered Poppy smiling at all the men who'd helped them, her smile apparently responsible for those men smiling back at her and immediately calling out offers of help to get her and the horse out of the water.

"While I do thank you," she said with an even wider smile, which left one of the men wobbling around, as if he'd lost his sense of balance, "I'm fine. If all of you will simply allow me some room, I'll—"

"Miss Garrison! Do hold steady, my dear lady, and don't fret. I'll have you out of that cold water in a thrice."

Before Reginald could do more than turn to the man who'd shouted that nonsense, Nigel Flaherty was racing his stallion for the lake, even though Poppy was waving for him to stop.

The second Nigel's horse hit the water, Clara lunged forward. With flailing arms and billowing fabric, Poppy hung on for a good few seconds, until Clara reached a spot where she was out of her depth and disappeared beneath the water, taking Poppy with her.

CHAPTER 9

As she sputtered to the surface, finding that task difficult because her walking gown was trying its best to drag her under the water again, relief was immediate when Poppy spotted Clara swimming toward the opposite side of the lake, moving quickly, probably because the water was what could only be described as frigid.

Knowing there was little chance she'd have the strength to follow the horse across the lake, she struck out for the closest shore, her arms turning concerningly numb after only a few strokes. Just as she felt herself slip beneath the surface again, Reginald appeared directly beside her and hauled her up against a chest with which she was becoming all too familiar.

"I've got you, Poppy" was all he said before he wrapped an arm around her and began towing her toward shore.

She didn't resist him—couldn't really, not with the way her strength had been sapped right out of her.

They reached shallow water in what felt like a blink of an eye, but instead of helping her stand, Reginald lifted her into his arms and continued forward, holding her tightly against him as he stumbled his way toward shore.

They were met five feet from shore by Murray, who was looking anxious, even as he reached out to steady Reginald when he slipped.

"Is she all right?" Murray asked.

"Hard to tell. We need to get her warm and dry as soon as possible."

Reginald tightened his hold on her as he quit the water and began striding toward the large crowd gathered a few feet away from the water's edge. He came to an abrupt stop, though, when someone stepped in front of him, blocking his path.

"I'll take her from here."

Poppy lifted her head and found Nigel Flaherty standing there, his arms outstretched.

That he was almost perfectly dry except for some water splattered on his trousers lent testimony to the notion he'd not even bothered to try and save her, leaving that bit of unpleasantness to Reginald, though Nigel was directly responsible for why she'd suffered a dunk in the lake in the first place.

"I suggest you get out of my way," Reginald returned in a very proper tone that was at direct odds with the way his jaw was now clenching.

"I said I'll take her."

"I've already got her, and if you've neglected to realize, she's soaking wet. You're hardly aiding the situation by arguing with me, so . . . move."

A curious fluttery feeling swept through her, one that was obviously a result of Reginald's refusal to hand her over, that refusal accompanied by what had almost sounded like a growl, which was . . .

The sound of yapping dogs distracted her from thoughts of fluttering as a carriage painted a bright shade of red pulled to a stop before them and Lena Ridgeway poked her head out the window.

"Goodness, Poppy, what were you thinking, taking a dip in the lake? It's December, dear, hardly an appropriate month to indulge in a refreshing swim." A dog joined her at the window, licking her face. "Not now, Muffin," Lena said before she returned her gaze to Poppy. "You mustn't linger out in the cold, what with how wet you appear to be. Come, join me. I'll see you safely home." She nodded to Nigel. "You're welcome to join us as well, Nigel, after you tether your horse behind my carriage, of course."

The last thing Poppy wanted was to get into Lena's carriage, not that there appeared to be much room in that carriage, since it seemed to be filled with dogs. She also didn't want to spend the time with Nigel, a gentleman who had yet to apologize for scaring the horse, even if he had done so because of a misguided desire to rescue her. Before she could summon up any type of refusal, a young lady stepped into view.

"Forgive me, Mrs. Ridgeway, but you've no room for anyone in your carriage with all those dogs you've got with you. I've more than enough room in my carriage, which is parked only a short way from us. I also have blankets and warm bricks."

Reginald sent a nod to the young woman before he followed her to her carriage, ignoring the scowl Nigel cast his way and the disappointed look Lena sent him. Lifting Poppy up on the seat, he accepted a blanket someone handed him. Bundling it around her, he edged backward, as if to exit the carriage again.

"You need to get warm as well, sir," the young lady said from directly outside the door.

"And I will, after I see to Mr. Middleton's horse, as well as my own," Reginald said.

"No need to go after my horse," Murray said, looking over Reginald's shoulder. "Miss Beatrix Waterbury arrived on the scene a second after Poppy resurfaced. The last I saw of her, she was racing after Clara, and if anyone can catch my high-strung horse, it's Miss Waterbury. I'll send one of my mother's grooms to fetch my buggy later."

"As for *your* horse, sir," another young lady began, looking over Murray's shoulder and nodding to Reginald, "our footman will see that he's taken to . . . ?"

"The Van Rensselaer house on Fifth Avenue," Reginald said.

After calling out that direction to the footman, then calling it out again to the driver, the lady gestured to the carriage seat. "Shall we get on our way?"

"Indeed we should, Miss . . . ?"

"I'm Miss Maisie Leggett, and the lady beside me is my sister, Miss Helene Leggett, but do feel free to call us Maisie and Helene, since it's less confusing that way when we're together, but enough of the pleasantries. I'll thank both you and Mr. Middleton to get settled in the carriage without further delay so we can get all of you somewhere warmer and certainly dryer."

Even though Poppy's teeth were chattering, she couldn't resist a smile when Reginald and Murray all but jumped into the carriage, both looking rather taken aback to be ordered about by a petite lady who seemed completely at ease barking out orders. Reginald took a seat beside her, while Murray sat down on the opposite bench.

"The dogs have gotten loose!" Lena suddenly yelled.

Peering around Reginald, Poppy discovered Lena running about, trying to collect dogs that had gotten free. A poodle jumped up into Murray's buggy beside the water and dashed out a second later, one of Murray's boots in its mouth. Lena began yelling for Nigel to give her a hand, which sent Nigel hurrying after the poodle, his attempt to catch it failing the moment the poodle dropped the boot and sunk its teeth into the hem of Nigel's trousers. Before Poppy could suggest someone go to his aid, the Leggett sisters jumped into the carriage, Maisie Leggett shaking off a small dog that appeared to have attached itself to her skirts. Slamming the door shut, she banged a hand on the carriage ceiling, and as the carriage jolted into motion, she squeezed herself onto the seat next to Murray, her sister having already taken her place on Murray's other side.

"Mrs. Ridgeway might want to consider leaving her hounds behind the next time she goes for a drive," Maisie said, gazing out the window and shaking her head. "I don't imagine Mr. Nigel Flaherty appreciates having the whole pack chasing after him now."

Helene craned her neck to look past her sister. "He's on his horse now, so he's fine. I don't think those dogs can keep up with the splendid beast he's riding."

"Oh, so he is," Maisie said before she returned her attention to Murray. "Do you know that your lips are a troubling shade of blue?"

"I'm not surprised," Murray said as Maisie bent over and fished additional blankets out from beneath the seat. She handed another one to Murray and one to Reginald, then bent over again, picking up what seemed to be a brick wrapped in a cloth. She got up from her seat, placed the brick by Poppy's feet, then lifted her head.

"We need to get you out of your shoes because this brick will be more effective if it's placed directly underneath uncovered feet."

Before Poppy could do more than nod, Maisie set to work, grunting as she went about the difficult task of unbuttoning shoes that were soaking wet and obviously slippery. A second later, Reginald took over the task, something that took her aback since it was hardly proper for a gentleman to help remove a lady's shoe, especially a gentleman who seemed determined to always abide by the proprieties.

A shiver stole through her when Reginald whipped her stockings straight off her legs, but then a sigh of pure bliss escaped her lips when he placed her now-bare feet on top of the brick Maisie handed him, then wrapped another blanket around her feet and legs before he settled back on the seat, tugging his own blanket around him.

"Better?" he asked.

Poppy managed to get a "Yes" through teeth that were still chattering, a circumstance that was evidently responsible for Reginald pulling her right up against him. The heat from his body immediately began to seep into her, that warmth increasing when Maisie pulled out another blanket, which Reginald tucked firmly around the both of them. He lifted his head and sent Maisie a smile. "Thank you."

She returned the smile. "You're welcome, Mr . . . ?"

"Reginald Blackburn," Reginald supplied. "But please, call me

Reginald since you've asked me to address you as Maisie. In fact, may I suggest that all of us abandon the formalities? Seems like the thing to do, given the circumstances."

His suggestion took Poppy by such surprise that she gaped at him for a full second, until Murray shifted on the seat.

"I'm in perfect agreement with Reginald," Murray began, turning to Maisie. "And I know I speak for all of us when I tell you how much we appreciate your kind offer of a warm ride home."

Maisie's cheeks turned pink. "I'm thankful my sister and I decided to ride through the park today."

"We waved at you, Murray, before your horse took off into the lake, but you apparently didn't see us," Helene added. "Which was why we circled back, and—"

"Just happened to run across you again," Maisie hurried to say, sending her sister a pointed look, which had Helene trying to hide a grin as she turned to look out the carriage window.

Understanding was swift, and Poppy pressed her lips together to keep from grinning as well.

Miss Maisie Leggett, a most helpful and charming lady, apparently found Murray to be very intriguing indeed, so much so that she might have—or rather she *had*—taken to riding around the park in the hopes of encountering him again.

That Murray seemed to find Maisie intriguing as well, what with how he was now watching her, was an encouraging sign. Although, because Murray truly didn't seem to understand ladies, he was certainly going to need Poppy's assistance in the matter, if only to make certain he didn't make a disaster of it.

Snuggling the edge of her blanket up to her chin, Poppy turned to Maisie as the perfect opportunity to become better known to the Leggett sisters sprang to mind. "My grandmother is hosting a tea next week, and I'd like to invite you and your sister to that tea, if you'd have an interest in joining us."

Maisie wrinkled her nose. "I'm not certain your grandmother would approve of us attending your tea."

"Why not?"

Helene pulled her attention from the window. "Because we're not fashionable and are only invited to a few select events because our family has scads and scads of money." She smiled at Murray. "We were only introduced to Murray because we were present at a charity event that he attended as well."

Maisie nodded. "And after that event, even though my father made a very large donation, we were still not welcomed into high society because Mrs. Astor considers us firmly of the nouveau riche set." She blew out a breath. "Our family only made its fortune within the last twenty years, but Mrs. Astor has made it known that to be included within the New York Four Hundred, a fortune must have been held for at least three generations."

"Unless you find someone within the Four Hundred to sponsor you," Murray said before he winced. "I'd volunteer my mother for that, but . . ."

Maisie shook her head. "We would never expect you to prevail upon your mother, Murray. When I met her at that charity event, I knew she was not impressed with me."

"*Not impressed* is putting it mildly," Helene added, with a nod to Murray. "Your mother told my sister to maintain her distance from you."

Murray's mouth dropped open. "She did not."

"I'm afraid she did," Maisie said. "But you mustn't be put out with your mother. I'm convinced she only warned me away from you after I proved myself to be a complete provincial when I tried to pour myself a cup of tea and ended up losing control of the pot, splattering your mother in the process."

Helene gave a sad shake of her head. "It also didn't help your mother's impression of Maisie and me when mere minutes after the teapot incident, I ended up getting my bustle stuck to the chair I'd been sitting in." She grinned. "I'm sure most members of society aren't used to witnessing a lady hobbling to the retiring room with a chair stuck to her behind. But it was either that or rip the bustle from the chair in front of everyone, exposing my unmentionables in the process."

Poppy returned Helene's grin. "And that right there is why you and I, along with your sister, are certain to become fast friends, and why I really must insist the two of you attend the tea I'm hosting with my grandmother."

"I apparently have issues when it comes to tea," Maisie countered. "That means I don't believe attending your tea would be a good idea. Helene and I will most certainly find ourselves banished from all society events if I suffer another tea mishap or if Helene gets her bustle stuck again."

Unwilling to admit defeat so easily, Poppy took a second to strip a soggy glove from her hand, turning to Reginald when the perfect solution came to mind. "You'll have to take them on as students."

Panic flickered through Reginald's eyes as he glanced to the Leggett sisters, then back to Poppy. "I'm not a magician, Poppy. There's no way to teach a young lady how to refrain from getting her bustle stuck to a chair."

"True, but you could teach them how to maneuver around a teapot. And besides," she hurried to continue when he looked ready to argue that point, "you told me at our very first meeting that you don't own a grand ancestral estate."

Reginald leaned closer to her, peering into her eyes. "Do you imagine your time under water affected your mind? Because my not owning an ancestral estate has nothing to do with taking on additional students."

Poppy shook her head ever so slightly because her mind *had* gone curiously numb—not because she'd been under water but because he was watching her so intently. Shaking her head again, she finally remembered what she'd been speaking about and smiled. "I assure you, there's nothing wrong with my mind. To prove that, allow me to finish the point I was trying to make."

Reginald inclined his head. "By all means, continue."

She inclined her head as well. "Thank you, and consider this: If you'd agree to start accepting money from the lessons you've been giving me, and then accept a wage from the numerous society families I know would be keen to bring you on, you might amass enough funds to at least *consider* procuring an estate."

"I don't imagine I'd make enough to purchase an ancestral estate from any salary I might earn teaching young ladies proper decorum."

"True, but you might be able to, at the very least, buy yourself one of those crumbling cottages I've heard aristocrats are eager to part ways with."

"An enticing notion, to be sure."

Before Poppy could respond to that, or even puzzle out why there seemed to be a hint of amusement in Reginald's tone, Maisie leaned forward. "Reginald's teaching you decorum?"

She nodded. "He's an expert on everything proper, although he does tend to pontificate on certain subjects, like wine, which can send you into a trance, but other than that, I've found his instructions to be quite illuminating. A word of warning, though, he's rather strict about ladies mentioning their unmentionables in public."

"Or ever," Reginald muttered.

Helene's brows drew together. "But you're already traveling in high society, Poppy. Why would you need decorum lessons?"

"My grandmother has decided I need to become a diamond of the first water."

"Why would anyone want to become that?"

"I have no idea, but apparently that's a status many young ladies aspire to, so Reginald's taken on the difficult feat of turning me into one of those."

Maisie exchanged a look with her sister before she turned her sights on Reginald. "Could you do that? Turn me and Helene into diamonds?"

Reginald blew out a breath. "Perhaps, but I have to state that I have limited time these days, what with how difficult Poppy has been with keeping to our schedule. I'm also Lord Lonsdale's traveling companion, although I haven't been much of a companion to him lately."

Poppy smiled. "I don't believe Lord Lonsdale is missing your company much, Reginald. He's in high demand at all the society events, which, even though the Season hasn't started in earnest, must keep him busy almost every hour of the day. Besides, he's apparently entrusted you with aiding him in his search for a proper countess, and I see no reason why Maisie and Helene shouldn't be brought forth for consideration."

Maisie began looking rather horrified. "I don't want to become a countess." She shot a glance to Murray, who completely missed the glance because he, for some reason, had pulled his blanket completely over his head. "I prefer to keep my sights set on American gentlemen."

"Understandable." Poppy turned to Helene. "What about you? Any interest in becoming a countess?"

"None at all," Helene said without hesitation. "Although I wouldn't be opposed to learning how to comport myself better, which might go far in convincing a certain society mother that it wouldn't be the end of the world if her son . . ." Helene's eyes widened right before she turned to the window and began taking an absorbed interest in the scenery.

Realizing that Helene had almost divulged something she was evidently not comfortable divulging, Poppy turned to Reginald. "So, that's that, isn't it? You'll take on instructing them?"

"Should I assume you'll continue badgering me until I agree?"

"Most certainly."

Reginald's lips curved just the slightest touch. "Then I suppose I have no choice, although"—he nodded to Murray—"Murray's going to have to help me."

Murray poked his head out of the blanket. "What was that?"

"I'd like you to help me teach Maisie and Helene, along with Poppy, of course, some of the basics of how to go about in society. At the very least, agree to accompany us as I take them out in public to assess their abilities."

If Poppy wasn't convinced Reginald was a no-nonsense sort, she would have sworn the man was up to a bit of matchmaking.

107

"I suppose I could help," Murray said, looking rather pleased when Maisie beamed a smile at him before she nodded to Reginald.

"My mother will be more than happy to pay you whatever wage you feel is warranted. She longs to fit into society and has descended into a rather melancholy state over us not being immediately welcomed into the New York Four Hundred."

"We certainly can't allow that melancholy state to continue, can we, Reginald?" Poppy asked, which had Reginald's lips curving again.

"Of course we can't, which means the matter is apparently settled." He smiled. "However, Poppy, I really must insist that you be the one to tell your grandmother you've volunteered me to spend time away from instructing you."

"I'm not overly concerned she'll take issue with that, although she might be a bit surprised when I tell her she needs to sponsor Maisie and Helene this season."

As horror once again settled on Maisie's face and Helene turned rather green, Reginald's eyes began to gleam. "Do promise me you'll tell her that when I'm in the same room."

Poppy waved that aside. "She'll be fine with the idea because I have to imagine that after she's presented with the challenge of introducing two additional young ladies into society, she'll throw herself into that challenge with relish."

"That's one way to imagine what her reaction is going to be," Reginald said.

Pretending she hadn't heard him, Poppy looked out the window as the carriage pulled up in front of her grandmother's Fifth Avenue residence.

It was an impressive brownstone, although not as impressive as the new mansions that were springing up on the other side of Fifth Avenue, closer to Central Park. Four stories tall and created in an Italianate design, it sported elaborate carved ornamentations hanging from the gables and a tall stoop with cast-iron railings flanking the steps. The front door, complete with golden knocker, was flanked by two stained-glass windows, and many a guest had been impressed with the way light filtered through the stained glass after they'd been ushered into a majestic entranceway, the receiving room directly to the right of that.

As a footman opened the carriage door, Poppy drew in a breath and braced herself for what she knew was going to be a somewhat questionable encounter with her grandmother. Viola was hardly going to enjoy learning Poppy had experienced another bout of mayhem, something that couldn't be withheld given Poppy's sorry state. And even though she'd just proclaimed Viola would be delighted to take on the responsibility of sponsoring an additional two young ladies into society, Poppy was fairly certain that was *not* going to be the case.

Chapter 10

There was one conclusion about Miss Poppy Garrison that Reginald could no longer deny.

She was the most exhausting lady he'd ever encountered.

She was also a magnet for mayhem, and yet, she was a lady who accepted the consequences for that mayhem without hesitation, even when what she experienced was not all of her making.

Frankly, he was more to blame for the lake fiasco than Poppy, but she'd flatly refused to accept his offer of explaining their latest adventure to Viola. In fact, after the Leggett carriage had drawn to a stop in front of Viola's Fifth Avenue brownstone, Poppy had scrambled over him and jumped to the sidewalk, nodding pleasantly to Viola, who'd been standing on the front stoop, looking outraged as she'd gotten a look at Poppy's bedraggled state. Reginald had tried to intervene on Poppy's behalf, but his intervention had come to a speedy end when Poppy slammed the door on him and encouraged the driver to make haste from her grandmother's house.

The last Reginald had seen of Poppy, she'd been marching her way toward the front stoop, apparently determined to face Viola's wrath on her own.

He didn't know many ladies who would have willingly taken on such a daunting task or who would have dismissed an offer of assistance so easily.

Leaning his head back against the rim of the tub as the hot water finally began to banish the chill he'd been experiencing ever since he'd gone after Poppy in the lake, he willed his thoughts to settle, admitting defeat when thoughts of Poppy immediately sprang back to mind.

She was an enigma to him, but more concerning than that, he seemed powerless to refuse her.

Her enormous request of instructing Maisie and Helene Leggett in the finer points of etiquette was a feat that was going to be daunting in the extreme. He was not a gentleman prone to accepting challenges that might end in failure, but attempting to turn not one, but three ladies into diamonds of the first water, was a challenge he had little hope of successfully accomplishing, even with Murray agreeing to help him.

The thought of Murray left Reginald smiling as he reached for the cup of tea on a small table beside the tub.

Murray Middleton was certainly a young gentleman who seemed to be floundering quite spectacularly when it came to matters of the feminine sort. Miss Maisie Leggett had been more than obvious regarding her interest in the man, but Murray, other than seeming oblivious to that interest at first, now seemed at a loss as to what was expected of him next. For some reason, Reginald felt compelled to provide Murray with at least a few basics when it came to ladies, although why he felt such a compulsion was rather confusing, and—

A knock on the bathing chamber door interrupted Reginald's thoughts, and before he could even inquire as to who was knocking, the door suddenly burst open and Charles bounded into the room.

"Ah, Reginald, I cannot tell you how delighted I am to find you still amongst the living" was how Charles greeted him before his cousin threw himself into a dainty chair a few feet away from the tub. "I was about to travel to the local hospitals to see if you'd been admitted there, but Miss Edith Iselin, one of the ladies I was driving around town with today, suggested I start here at the hotel first." He smiled. "I'll need to send her a note, telling her I found you in the bath."

"I think you can leave the bath part out. That's not really information a proper young lady expects to find in a note."

"Too right you are." Charles's smile widened as he looked Reginald over. "I *am* delighted to find you alive and seemingly well given the circumstances you experienced today. You had me worried there for a while."

"I take it you heard what happened in Central Park?"

Charles bobbed his head. "I ran across Nigel Flaherty, and he divulged all, telling me that I wasn't to worry because he believed everyone was fine. However, given that he kept looking over his shoulder and muttering something about dogs, I wasn't certain I should put much stock in his assessment of the situation."

"He was set upon by Lena Ridgeway's dogs after I got Poppy from the lake."

"How peculiar. We actually ran across Mrs. Ridgeway after we spoke to Nigel. She was searching for Nigel, saying something about him not showing himself to advantage, but she didn't expand on that, probably because one of the dogs in her carriage began trying to eat the flowers on her hat. I was forced to bid her a hasty good day because Miss Tooker and Miss Roche descended into hysterics, a state that Mrs. Ridgeway, given the look on her face, didn't seem to appreciate."

"I'm not sure what to say to all that."

"Not much to say, really, except that New York is an unusual place, isn't it?"

"Can't argue with you there. But how did you come to the conclusion I might be dead?"

Charles gave a wave of his hand. "Gossip has you all but buried, or so said the occupants of numerous carriages we encountered as I was escorting Miss Iselin, Miss Tooker, and Miss Roche home." He shook his head. "I should know better than to put much stock in gossip, but you know I've always been a man drawn to the intrigues of the day, and how could I not be drawn into a story that had my very dearest friend and cousin dead?"

"You're a complicated man, Charles—a bit mental at times, but

I'm thankful you would have mourned my death if I'd actually been killed in the lake."

"Of course I would mourn you," Charles said firmly before he settled his attention on a stack of papers Reginald had left on the corner of the sink. "What are those?"

"Notes from Giles about some of the heiresses you've been squiring about town."

Charles picked up the notes and riffled through them. "Seems like he's been remarkably busy, given the extent of his notes."

Reginald raked a hand through his wet hair. "Indeed, and he'd just stopped by to drop off his notes when I arrived back here. Giles took one look at me and ordered me out of my soggy clothing and into the bath, determined to get my clothing to the laundry as soon as possible in the hopes it could still be salvaged."

"That might be overly optimistic on his part."

"That's what I told him, but since he was heading out again anyway, mentioning something about a meeting with a lady's maid, he said it was worth a try."

Charles tilted his head. "What lady's maid is Giles off to meet?"

"Not sure. He was rather sketchy with the details, although he did say he hoped to get additional information about a lady he's *almost* convinced will not be an appropriate choice for you, given her questionable character."

"Sounds like Giles is putting a great deal of effort into researching the backgrounds of all the heiresses out this Season."

"I would expect nothing less of Giles." Reginald smiled. "He's been a tremendous help to me over the years, and not just because of his abilities as a valet. He's got a wonderful aptitude for uncovering facts many people want to keep hidden, and he's saved me numerous times from investing in deals that turned out to be anything but ethical. He's putting that same tactic to work over here."

Charles blew out a breath. "It seems somewhat troubling to have to resort to such measures as well as a bit disrespectful to all the ladies in question. It's as if we don't trust any of them."

"We *shouldn't* trust any of them at this point, Charles."

Reginald nodded to the papers in Charles's hand. "Perhaps you should read Giles's notes so we can begin narrowing down your search for a countess."

"You're right, of course, but I have to go run down my spectacles first." Charles set the papers aside. "Can't see a word on the page without them."

It took a good twenty minutes for Charles to find his spectacles, during which Reginald finished his bath, bundled himself into his warmest dressing robe, and settled himself into his suite's small sitting room.

"Found them," Charles said, striding into the sitting room and brandishing the spectacles. "No idea why I stuffed them into one of my socks, but at least they're not overly bent." He sat down in a nearby chair, shoved the spectacles on, then looked around. "Where do you suppose I left those notes?"

"You left them in the bathing chamber, but I brought them out here. They're right beside you on the table."

"Oh, quite right." He picked up the notes, took an inordinately long time to read through them, then frowned as he looked up and caught Reginald's eye. "Why am I reading these again instead of you?"

"I was in the bath when we first started discussing them, but I didn't think you'd appreciate me taking over since you did have to go on a bit of a journey to find your spectacles."

"Ah, excellent reasoning there, and I thank you for being so considerate."

When Charles didn't say anything else and seemed to get distracted by something out the window, Reginald gave a bit of a cough, which had Charles turning his way.

"You're not taking ill, are you, Reginald?"

"Not at all. Just a tickle. But returning to Giles's notes, anything of interest you want to share with me?"

Charles shuffled through the pages he'd been reading. "He's listed at least twenty names, then added tidbits about how much each lady's dowry is rumored to be as well as how much their fathers are worth. He's added a few personal observations, such as he finds Cynthia Roche to be a bit of a spendthrift, believes a lady by the name of Miss Mary Kip, whom I must admit I can't recall meeting, is prone to suffering from frequent fits of the vapors, and noticed that Miss Adele Tooker is less than pleasant to members of her staff." He raised his head, peering at Reginald over the rim of his spectacles. "Why would he write that down about Miss Tooker? I find her to be a most pleasant lady."

"Many people believe that a true test of a person's character can be seen by how they treat those beneath them. If Miss Tooker is unkind to her staff, it shows a weakness of character and should give you pause about pursuing her."

Charles removed his spectacles and rubbed a hand over his face. "Concerningly enough, I haven't had to put much effort into pursuing *any* lady since they seem only too keen to pursue *me*." He caught Reginald's eye. "I never thought I'd say this, but I'm not sure I enjoy all this feminine attention. I've even witnessed ladies shoving other ladies out of the way in order to get closer to me."

"Perhaps I should begin accompanying you to events, Charles. You've often mentioned that I'm an intimidating sort, which might dissuade some of these ladies from pursuing you so earnestly."

Charles suddenly began looking a tad guilty. "You're not going to have time to accompany me, Reginald, not when word has gotten out about those decorum lessons you're giving Miss Garrison. Quite a few other ladies are now determined to take lessons from you as well."

Reginald blinked. "How did that information get out?"

"I . . . ah . . . might have been . . . perhaps a bit . . . responsible for that."

"You were either completely responsible for it or not. Which is it?"

Charles winced. "Completely."

"And . . . ?"

"You know, I neglected to inquire on how Miss Garrison is faring after her dip in the lake."

"She's fine, or at least she was when I returned her to her grand-mother's house, but getting back to—"

"Not many young ladies would be fine after suffering such an un-usual adventure in a lake, in December at that. Should I take that to mean she's a lady possessed of unusual fortitude and survival skills?"

"Perhaps, although I would say she's more along the lines of a lady possessed of an unusual ability to become entrenched in unlikely situations, but getting back to what we were discussing before—"

"Mind if I help myself to some tea?"

"Will it help bolster your courage?"

Charles grinned. "Wouldn't hurt."

Returning the grin, Reginald watched as Charles moved to the teapot, poured himself a cup, then returned to his chair, taking three sips before he set the cup aside. "Where was I?"

"You were about to explain how it became known I'm giving etiquette lessons to Poppy."

"Ah, so I was." He reached for his tea again. "I believe that came about after I, along with Miss Tooker and Miss Roche, ran across Mr. Nigel Flaherty in the park. After he explained what happened, Miss Tooker and Miss Roche began wondering why Miss Gar-rison has been spending so much time in your company. I got the distinct impression they were implying you had set a romantic eye her way, and knowing that was not the case, I'm afraid I blurted out the bit about you giving her lessons as a way to disabuse them of that rather laughable notion."

The fact that it wasn't exactly a laughable notion at all left Reginald reeling ever so slightly.

"But then, Miss Tooker and Miss Roche began to, well, al-most mock Miss Garrison for needing decorum lessons in the first place," Charles continued, "something I was surprised to hear from ladies who'd been nothing but sweet when in my presence. I realized I'd done Miss Garrison a disservice and wanted to make amends. I then told Miss Tooker and Miss Roche that you were actually assisting Miss Garrison in learning more about what is expected of a proper countess, and . . . that's why I know you're soon to be in high demand with the ladies." He caught Reginald's eye. "Are you completely disgusted with me?"

"You know I'm not, since you were trying to come to Poppy's defense, although allow me to suggest that you distance yourself from Miss Tooker and Miss Roche. There are many eligible American heiresses out this Season, some of whom I have to imagine aren't nearly as unpleasant as those two ladies seem to be."

Charles buried his head in his hands. "I'm rubbish at deciphering who is pleasant and who is not." He looked up and frowned. "This choosing an heiress business is downright daunting and I'm tempted to wash my hands of it and simply return to London—a temptation I know I don't have the luxury to embrace, what with my finances being in such woeful shape."

Reginald leaned forward. "If you truly don't want to continue this search for an heiress, we *can* return to London. I did offer to help you with some investments, which would see a stream of revenue flowing back into your accounts, although it will take time to build up any substantial amount of funds."

"I'm even more rubbish at investments than I am at choosing an heiress, and I know full well I'll never have the patience needed to become successful at investing, even with your assistance," Charles returned. "And don't forget that my mother is notorious for overextending her allowance, which means any profit I might see won't last long." He shook his head. "No, an heiress is my best chance at this point, although I do think, what with my mother's proclivity for spending money in such a willy-nilly fashion, I might need to consider choosing a no-nonsense type of heiress, one who would be capable of keeping my mother in check."

"A prudent decision."

Charles smiled. "And an unusual decision coming from me, but . . ." He raked a hand through his hair. "Do you believe Miss Garrison is a no-nonsense sort?"

For some reason, Reginald felt it difficult to nod in agreement, but when Charles sent him an expectant look, he forced a nod as well as a smile. "She is."

"She is remarkably beautiful, and rumor has it her dowry is quite extensive."

"True," he agreed even as his stomach began to churn most unpleasantly.

Charles abandoned his seat. "Then I'll keep her in the running. Although . . ." He took a step closer to Reginald. "You *haven't* turned a romantic eye her way, *have* you?"

"Why would you ask me that?"

"You jumped into a lake to save her. That's a romantic act if I've ever heard one."

"Or I jumped into the lake because it's really not in my nature to stand back and watch a lady drown."

"There is that, but do know if you had turned a romantic eye Miss Garrison's way, I wouldn't be troubled in the least to stand aside. In fact, I think it might be rather amusing to watch you try your hand at romance, what with how you've always been such a sensible sort and definitely a bit disdainful when it comes to matters of love."

"I'm not in the market for romance."

Charles sent him a rather sad smile. "Apparently nor am I. More's the pity since I've never been a sensible sort and do believe I'd enjoy falling in love." He turned and headed for the door. "And on that happy note, I'll bid you adieu for now. I'm off to take a short nap before I head out to enjoy yet another night of being pursued."

As Charles closed the door quietly behind him, Reginald shook his head and reached for the notes Charles had abandoned.

While there was no debating that Charles was a most impractical sort, he was a good man at heart and could make the right lady a more-than-acceptable husband.

The problem with that, though, was the sheer number of ladies who were interested in being considered for the position of Charles's countess.

Looking through the names written on the pages, Reginald suddenly stilled when he realized that Poppy had not proclaimed any interest at all in Charles, an idea that left him feeling, curiously enough, rather relieved.

CHAPTER 11

"It was absolutely brilliant on your part, Reginald, to get us well away from my grandmother's house. And, because of that brilliance, I've decided to apply myself most diligently to our lesson today."

Reginald turned on the seat of the hansom cab and arched a brow Poppy's way. "Even if I decide to drone on and on about how to fold a proper napkin?"

Poppy wrinkled her nose. "Why in the world would anyone feel the need to drone on about napkin folding?"

"To see how diligent you're really prepared to be."

"Maybe I should have given this more thought," Poppy muttered as the cab pulled to a stop in front of Rutherford & Company, one of the leading stores of the day and the place Reginald had decided would be perfect for a lesson.

Sending her what almost seemed to be a grin, Reginald opened the door and stepped to the sidewalk. Turning, he helped her down, paid the driver the fare, then took hold of her arm, scowling when she pressed a few coins into his gloved hand.

"What are these for?"

"To reimburse you for the fare."

"Why would you think it necessary to reimburse me for the fare?"

"Because you're on duty as my instructor, so it's only fair that I, or rather my grandmother, pick up any expenses we incur. Besides, you'll never be able to purchase yourself a grand ancestral estate if you spend your coins so frivolously."

"Saving my coins will never be a viable plan, especially when ancestral estates are entailed, rendering them impossible to purchase."

Poppy frowned. "You can't purchase a grand estate over in England?"

"Not if they're owned by the aristocracy and are entailed—which is how aristocrats have managed to hold on to their land over the years instead of being able to parcel it off to pay debts and keep up appearances."

Something began niggling at the back of Poppy's mind, but before it could fully develop, she was distracted by the Rutherford & Company doorman who was holding the door open for them. Hurrying as a blustery wind swept around her, Poppy stopped directly inside the door and looked around. "How lovely. I wonder where ladies' fashions are located?"

"Those are on the third floor, miss," the doorman said, nodding to the elevator that was a few feet away from them and to the elevator operator standing by the open grate. "James will be more than happy to take you there."

"An elevator," Poppy breathed. "I love riding in those."

"We're not going to ladies' fashions. We're here to visit the tearoom," Reginald reminded her.

"That would be on the fourth floor, sir," the man said.

"Then fourth floor it is," Poppy said, taking Reginald's arm as they walked to the elevator. She immediately returned the smile that James sent her. "We'd like to go to the tearoom, please," she said, stepping into the elevator, Reginald joining her a second later.

James inclined his head, shut the grate, and moved to stand beside a gilded lever.

Poppy edged closer to him, peering over his shoulder. "How fast can this elevator go?"

"Don't even think about it, Poppy," Reginald muttered.

"I'm merely asking a question," she returned, watching as James slid the lever to the right and the elevator glided upward. "How quickly can it stop?"

"Almost immediately, if one has the right touch," James said.

"Which you won't have, Poppy, so put that idea right out of your head."

Poppy ignored him, but before she could figure out a way to convince James to let her have a try at the lever, he was bringing the elevator to a stop. Opening the grate, he gestured her forward with a smile. "Enjoy your tea."

Blowing out a disappointed breath, she returned the smile. "Will you be manning the elevator all afternoon?"

Reginald had hold of her arm a second later as he all but towed Poppy out of the elevator. "It doesn't matter if he's manning it or not, Poppy. We'll be taking the stairs."

Annoyance was swift as Reginald exchanged a far-too-knowing look with James before that man closed the grate and the elevator whizzed away.

"I wasn't going to badger him into letting me have a go at the elevator."

"Weren't you?" Reginald countered, steering her into a tearoom that was tastefully decorated and afforded a lovely view of Broadway. After being greeted by a young woman who quickly showed them to a round table draped in fine linen, Reginald helped Poppy into an upholstered chair before he sat down opposite her and took the menu the young woman handed him. Telling them she'd send a server right over to take their order, she walked away.

"This is much nicer than remaining at home with Viola to receive callers," Poppy said, glancing around. "I must admit I'm confused about why so many people seemed keen to pay my grandmother a call today. It seemed to me, given the number of carriages lining the street, that every lady from high society was descending on Viola, even though my grandmother let it be known through a few well-placed whispers that I was fine after my swim in the lake."

Something that looked like resignation flashed through Reginald's eyes. "I'm sorry to say that I think those ladies, besides being curious about your many adventures, were at your grandmother's house because of me."

"Why would you think that?"

"I might need to get some tea first. It's a tricky matter to explain and tea always helps settle my thoughts."

"You don't seem unsettled to me. Out with it."

"Have I mentioned that bossiness is not a trait a young lady should embrace?"

"Only about a hundred times, but since that lesson doesn't seem to be sticking, you might as well get on with it."

He released a sigh. "Your grandmother has so many callers because Lord Lonsdale told Miss Tooker and Miss Roche that I was giving you decorum lessons."

She frowned. "Why would he have done that?"

Reginald took a moment to explain, ending with "but in Charles's defense, he did originally think that Miss Tooker and Miss Roche were under the impression that I was, ah, courting you."

Poppy's lips curved. "Oh dear."

"Yes, oh dear is right, and it's not amusing. I'm afraid I'm soon going to find myself under siege from ladies intent on learning what's expected of a proper countess—or better yet, intent on learning how to *become* that proper countess." Reginald raked a hand through his hair, leaving it standing on end, a look that was at complete odds with his usual tidy appearance. "After I saw all those carriages at your grandmother's, I decided you and I needed to get well away and with undue haste."

Poppy allowed herself a moment to take that in before her amusement at the situation bubbled out in the form of a laugh, one that was quickly followed by another.

"I don't find anything about this situation amusing," Reginald muttered.

She snatched up her napkin, dabbed at eyes that were beginning to water, then gave a wave of her hand. "If you could see your face, well, disgruntled doesn't do your expression justice." She gave one last hiccup of amusement. "On the practical side, though, just think of all the funds you can earn by instructing so many additional ladies."

"I'm not really keen to take on all of the young ladies who are now determined to get to Charles through me. You take up a great deal of my time, and now I have to carve out additional time to assist Maisie and Helene Leggett."

"Two ladies I was hoping you'd invite to join us in tea today, which would have allowed us to share whatever lesson you're about to embark on, saving you some of your precious time."

Reginald looked more disgruntled that ever. "I *did* invite them, but their mother decided she needed to interview me first to see if I'm qualified for the task of instructing her daughters." He raked a hand through his hair again. "I'm meeting Mrs. Leggett later this afternoon, where I'll be expected to give her an accounting of my teaching abilities, which will then have her deciding whether or not I'm qualified to teach her daughters."

She swallowed another bubble of amusement. "I imagine that got your stiff upper lip twitching."

"Who would have ever thought I'd be expected to suffer through an interview with a lady about my abilities when it wasn't even my idea to offer instruction in the first place?"

"I could go with you, explain to Mrs. Leggett that you're more than qualified."

"Of course I'm more than qualified, especially given that I'm—" He suddenly stopped talking, picked up his menu again, and disappeared behind it.

"You're what?" she pressed.

He peered at her over the menu. "Friends with many aristocrats."

Poppy tilted her head. "How many aristocrats do you know? And could you possibly know any dukes, or better yet, princes?"

He retreated behind the menu again. "I just admitted that I'm soon to be under siege. Do you honestly think that condition will improve if I admit I might be acquainted with a few dukes and a prince or two?"

"A fair point, and even though you might have to stretch yourself a bit thin, it'll be good for your bank account, as I mentioned before." She smiled. "Society mothers can be very generous if they think a specific service will improve their daughters' chances on the marriage mart."

"This notion you seem to have about me being in desperate need of money is very disconcerting."

"Aren't you?"

He looked at her over his menu again. "That's beside the point, and I should mention, as your instructor, that it's not remotely acceptable to speak about money to a gentleman at any time, and you certainly shouldn't imply a gentleman is impoverished."

"I never said you were impoverished."

"I believe you did, just a moment ago, or at least suggested it."

"Then I owe you an apology."

"Yes, you do, one that I'll now magnanimously accept, which means we'll put this discussion behind us and get down to the important business of ordering tea." He glanced at his menu again. "I'm going to order the house tea. What would you have me order for you?"

"Why are you going to order it for me?"

"Because proper etiquette demands it."

"Oh."

"Yes, oh, and after I order our tea, we'll then proceed with our daily lesson, one that centers on proper conversation to enjoy while having tea. And before you argue with that, allow me to remind you that you said you were going to be cooperative today since I did get you away from your grandmother's house."

"I'm not certain I should be held to that promise since I've now learned it was self-serving on your part."

"But you already promised, so . . . what tea are you going to impress me with by ordering?"

Poppy glanced over her menu. "They do offer an impressive assortment of teas, but . . ." She looked up. "Will you find me quite beyond the pale if I admit I don't actually care for tea, preferring coffee instead?"

"You don't care for *tea*?"

"Shocking, I know."

"Scandalous more like."

"That's because you're British, although I'll understand completely if my admission means you'll never be able to turn me into a diamond of the first water because a fondness for tea is a requirement to become one of those. And, I'll even take it upon myself to explain to my grandmother why you now have to back out of her challenge."

The corners of Reginald's lips twitched. "Nice try, but I'm more than up for the challenge, although your tea admission does suggest it may be more difficult than I imagined. I can only hope the Leggett sisters don't disclose they have no liking for tea either. That might send me over the edge, swimming back to London where tea lovers will certainly be waiting for me on the shores with open arms." His lips twitched again. "And while I know this may be setting myself up for horror, dare I hope that you'd care for a few scones with clotted cream?"

"Your sense of horror may immediately commence because I've never had clotted cream."

"Remind me to tell your grandmother that I'm going to need an increase in that wage I finally agreed to let her pay me."

"Perfectly understandable. But I wouldn't be opposed to trying clotted cream."

Reginald tilted his head. "I have to say that I find it fairly bewildering, what with how your grandmother told me you adore everything English, that you don't care for tea, nor have you ever tried clotted cream, a British staple if there ever was one."

"I've never claimed to adore everything English, only British accents, although I'm no longer quite as susceptible to those as I once was, not after listening to all your reprimands."

His eyes crinkled at the corners. "I have to wonder how susceptible you truly were to British accents since you did take me to task for using the word *quite*, and you find words like *prithee* and *zounds* to be ridiculous."

"Prithee *is* a ridiculous word, but I'm not completely opposed to zounds. It's rather charming, if used in the proper context." She smiled. "Frankly, I only made such a to-do with you because I was furious that you'd frightened Murray's horse."

"As your instructor, allow me to state that ladies are expected to weigh every word before they speak, even when they are infuriated. That will then alleviate the chance of insulting a gentleman who merely believed he was rushing to save a damsel in distress."

"You would have been more insulted if I'd jumped off the horse and punched you instead of taking you to task, a temptation that I did contemplate after Murray's horse charged into the water."

"A temptation I'm pleased you resisted since ladies are never to resort to physical violence, no matter how provoked."

"Duly noted," she said cheerfully as a young woman stepped forward to take their order.

"We'll have a pot of coffee," Reginald began, "as well as an order of scones with clotted cream and a small plate of cakes and finger sandwiches."

Poppy's heart did a bit of a lurch as the young woman inclined her head and hurried away. "You ordered coffee."

Reginald arched a brow. "You said you don't care for tea."

"But you could have ordered tea for yourself."

He leaned forward. "Since you've agreed to try clotted cream, I don't believe it will kill me to drink a cup of coffee, although in fairness, I must admit that I like coffee." He smiled and lowered his voice. "Don't let that get around, though. I do have a proper British reputation to uphold."

Settling back into her seat, she returned the smile. "Your secret is safe with me, and now that our refreshments have been ordered, what's next?"

"Proper conversations to engage in while sitting down to tea with your guests."

"That hardly sounds amusing."

"Missteps pertaining to conversation can get you expelled from society's inner circle, so amusing or not, that's what we're going to cover this afternoon." He settled his full attention on her, which left her feeling the distinct urge to fidget. "Pretend we've just sat down at your grandmother's house. There are two other ladies sitting with us and it's up to you to get the conversation going. How do you start?"

She folded her hands in her lap and considered his question before she smiled. "It's such a pleasant afternoon, what with the way the sun is shining so brightly. I felt a touch of moisture in the air this morning, though, which might suggest we're in for snow later."

Reginald inclined his head. "Nicely done, and I suspect your guests will reply with their own observations regarding the weather, and then . . ."

"We'll have exhausted that topic and I'll need to move the conversation forward."

"Weather can be used as the focus of conversation for at least fifteen minutes if you allow everyone an opportunity to state their opinion."

Poppy smiled. "True, but it's a less-than-riveting subject, and I don't particularly care to see my guests nodding off from sheer boredom. That'll hardly earn me a spot as a charming hostess or encourage any of my guests to long to be invited to a future tea I'm sure my grandmother will insist I hold."

"An excellent point, and because you're obviously keen to host a memorable tea, tell me how you'll direct the conversation to achieve that goal."

"I've always found discussions about books to be rather fascinating."

"What type of books?"

She tapped a finger against the table. "I suppose that depends on whether or not my grandmother will allow me to switch up what was originally planned as a ladies' tea and invite gentlemen as well."

"Gentlemen don't enjoy attending teas."

"How many teas have you been invited to over the years?"

"Well, none, which goes to show it's not really something gentlemen enjoy."

Poppy leaned forward. "But you see, I don't believe ladies actually enjoy these teas either. And given the ladies my grandmother took it upon herself to invite, I have to admit I've not been looking forward to the tea at all."

"You seem to like Maisie and Helene."

She nodded. "I do, and because they're now attending, I thought it would make the experience more enjoyable for them if gentlemen were included, which also might have Miss Tooker and her friends behaving themselves. And then, well, there's Murray."

Reginald considered her for a moment. "So this is to be a matchmaking tea, is it?"

"You have to admit it's a brilliant strategy, not to mention discreet. Murray won't have an inkling as to what I'm about."

"I don't think Murray would have an inkling you've turned your sights on matchmaking even if you sent him an invitation that titled your tea the matchmaking event of the Season."

"You could be right. Although do know that I'm going to expect you to prevail upon my grandmother to invite gentlemen—"

"Why would she listen to me?" he surprised her by interrupting.

"Because you're going to tell her you'll bring Lord Lonsdale, of course, which will make the tea one of the most anticipated events of the year."

"I suppose I could convince Charles to attend."

Poppy smiled. "All you have to do is tell him there will be a variety of heiresses gathered there, and that, no doubt, will have him agreeing without hesitation."

"Aren't you concerned that providing him with a variety of heiresses to chat with might diminish your chance of winning his affection?"

She waved that aside. "I've barely spent any time with Lord Lonsdale, which, if you think about it, is somewhat telling."

"How so?"

"If he were determined to win my affection, I would think he'd go out of his way to spend time in my company, not rely on you to feed him little tidbits on whether or not I'd make an acceptable countess."

"You think I'm feeding him tidbits?"

"Of course you are, although I do hope you're not trying to encourage him to pursue me, since we both know without a doubt that I'd make an abysmal countess, even with the instructions you've been giving me."

Reginald's gaze sharpened. "Aren't you interested in becoming a countess?"

"Not in the least, but don't tell my grandmother. She's enjoying the idea of my procuring a title for the family, and there's no harm in allowing her to hope."

"Until you shatter that hope by not ending the Season with a title."

"I doubt Lord Lonsdale would choose me in the end, even if we do get to know one another better. That will leave my grandmother feeling sorry for me, which will take the place of any disappointment she'd feel."

Reginald frowned. "Forgive me for asking, but if you're not interested in procuring Charles's attention, why have you agreed to continue with our decorum lessons?"

"Because my grandmother, even though she annoys me at times, wants me to become a diamond of the first water. And even though I think that's a feat I'll never achieve, I don't deliberately set out to disappoint her." Poppy grinned. "I also haven't neglected to notice how competent you are about getting me out of social obligations my grandmother wants me to attend."

"So it's to your benefit to continue on with our lessons?"

"Indeed." Poppy smiled. "And now, with that settled, I'm going to artfully redirect the conversation. Since I'm now convinced there *will* be gentlemen in attendance at the tea, I need to stick with books that would appeal to both genders, such as *Frankenstein* or *Wuthering Heights*."

"You enjoyed *Frankenstein*?"

"I found it to be a thrilling read. *Wuthering Heights*, on the other hand, was somewhat depressing, but it's one of those reads that people seem to enjoy discussing in earnest."

"Unless you get a guest who delves into a touch of pontification about the literary merits of that work, which will hardly lend the conversation that enthralling air you seem determined to provide."

"I didn't consider that. So . . . *Frankenstein* it is."

Reginald shook his head. "Some ladies find *Frankenstein* too disturbing."

"But that could lead to a rousing debate, which would be entertaining."

"Unless some of the ladies take offense and depart your tea early because their tender sensibilities have been offended."

"That would definitely offend my grandmother."

"Indeed, so . . . ?"

She wrinkled her nose. "This may be a trickier topic than I first assumed, but since it's getting close to Christmas, what about Charles Dickens's *A Christmas Carol*?"

Reginald nodded, albeit rather slowly. "While I've never particularly cared for that story, it is a popular tale this time of year and would be a safe book to bring up for discussion."

"How can you not care for *A Christmas Carol*?"

"My older brother staged an in-home reenactment of the tale when I was young and impressionable, which left me unable to sleep for a solid month because I kept expecting spirits to show up at the end of my bed and whisk me away."

Poppy fought a grin. "Since we certainly don't have time to stage a reenactment of the tale as Christmas is rapidly approaching, we won't need to worry about you suffering nightmares again, so that will be the book I broach during the tea." She shook her head. "It's a shame, though, that we won't have time to do a reenactment. You would make a wonderful Scrooge."

"And here's where I remind you that a lady is expected not to toss what might very well be construed as an insult at her guests."

"I couldn't resist."

"Try."

She fought another grin. "Now that we've discussed the weather and books, should I move the conversation to the latest fashions?"

"Riveting subject matter, to be sure. But since it's just the two of us, and because you do seem perfectly capable of holding your own in a polite conversation, why don't we abandon our lesson for just a bit. You can tell me something about yourself instead."

Unexpected heat settled on her face, evidently brought about because Reginald was suddenly watching her far too closely. "What do you want to know?"

She couldn't be certain, but it almost sounded like he muttered "Everything" before he cleared his throat and leaned back in his chair. "Tell me how it came to be that you're having your first Season at the age of twenty-two."

"I'm almost twenty-three, but don't tell my grandmother I told you that," Poppy said, her disclosure having Reginald blink somewhat owlishly back at her. She pretended not to notice as she launched into the whole story of how she'd come to the city, ending with "And then after my parents secured a large loan from our local bank, they purchased land in Kentucky, where the horse industry is settling. Unfortunately, before they could get the new facility up and running, the bank ran into some unexpected financial difficulties, which forced them to call in my parents' loan two years before it was due."

Reginald frowned. "Were your parents delinquent with their payments?"

"Not at all. Garrison Farms has always turned a nice profit, and we were still selling horses from our location in Pennsylvania. The only reason my father couldn't immediately pay off the full amount of the loan was because of all the expenses he'd incurred with our new operation."

Poppy traced a finger over the lace-embroidered tablecloth.

"The owner of the bank offered to hold off foreclosing on the loan if Father wanted to take steps to sell our farm in Pennsylvania. My parents were hesitant to sell, though, because they'd always planned on dividing up the farm between my two brothers and me. Their hesitancy to sell is apparently why the bank began foreclosure proceedings."

"And that's when your grandmother entered the picture?"

"It was. I reached out to her, let her know about the dire situation, and she was perfectly willing to step in and save Garrison Farms if I would agree to allow her to bring me out for a New York Season."

"Sounds like blackmail on your grandmother's part."

"Oh it was, but I wasn't completely opposed to coming to New York." She smiled. "I'm not widely traveled and thought the city would be quite an adventure." Her smile dimmed. "Little did I know, though, that I would be expected to change so much about myself in the process."

"I think you'll eventually discover that you're delightful just the way God made you, my dear."

Turning, Poppy found an older lady standing behind her, holding a silver pot of coffee, which she immediately set down on the table.

"I do beg your pardon for interrupting your conversation," the lady began, "as well as eavesdropping, although it wasn't exactly eavesdropping since I was coming to deliver your coffee." She smiled. "I'm Miss Mabel Huxley, but you must call me Miss Mabel, and you're Miss Poppy Garrison."

"You know who I am?"

"But of course." Miss Mabel turned her smile on Reginald, who'd already risen from his chair. "And you're Mr. Blackburn."

"You've heard about me as well?" Reginald asked, taking the hand Miss Mabel offered him and placing a kiss on her knuckles.

Miss Mabel laughed. "Do you honestly believe that rumors wouldn't swirl around the city regarding the tall, dark, and brooding traveling companion of Lord Lonsdale?"

"Why does everyone seem to have come to the conclusion I'm a brooding sort?" Reginald asked to no one in particular as Miss Mabel actually reached out and patted his cheek.

"If you don't care to be considered brooding, my dear man, perhaps you should try harder not to brood" was all Miss Mabel said before she waved Reginald back into his seat and returned her attention to Poppy. "I hear your first Season has been rather interesting."

"How did you hear that?" Poppy asked weakly.

"Rumors run through this tearoom faster than the tea is poured, but do know that you're not the first young lady to have an adventure at a society event. Why, I know of one lady who was responsible for almost burning Delmonico's to the ground, another who caused mayhem by misunderstanding the rules to the Go-As-You-Please Quadrille, and yet another young lady who got herself firmly attached to a fainting couch because of an unusually crafted bustle."

Poppy's spirits immediately lifted. "How reassuring to learn that other ladies seem to have difficulties with bustles."

"Bustles are horrid contraptions made by men who'll never have to wear them." Miss Mabel released a sniff. "I've elected to not embrace the new rage of wearing such large atrocities on my behind, but only because with age comes certain privileges, although . . ." She caught Poppy's eye. "You seem to be an original, my dear, so perhaps you won't feel the need to wait so long before you abandon what's expected of you, embracing who you truly are and who God meant you to be, instead of trying to embrace a sense of who others want you to be."

Before Poppy could come up with a response to that, Miss Mabel was suddenly squinting across the room. "Speaking of originals," she began, "Mr. Murray Middleton is heading this way, and . . . he looks like he could use a cup of coffee. I'll fetch an extra cup." Excusing herself, Miss Mabel hurried away right before Murray appeared beside the table and all but flung himself into an empty chair.

"I've done it now," Murray said by way of greeting.

"That doesn't sound encouraging," Poppy said as Reginald picked up the silver pot and poured coffee into the cup that had been meant for him, then placed that cup directly in front of Murray, who nodded his thanks and picked it up.

Murray took a sip, winced because the coffee was apparently still hot, then set aside the cup and shuddered. "I've had an enormous row with Mother. She was most distraught about my adventure in Central Park yesterday and was convinced I'd most certainly caught any number of illnesses from being in that cold water. Her distress quickly changed to outrage, though, when I refused to take her suggestion of retiring to my bedchamber for an entire week to build up my strength." He shuddered again. "Our conversation only went downhill from there, ending with me threatening to move out."

Poppy blinked. "You told your mother you're considering moving out of her house?"

"There's no considering left about the matter," Murray said, his voice quivering. "Mother was furious with me for even broaching the topic, which is exactly why she took it upon herself to throw me out of her house, rendering me, I'm sorry to say, homeless."

Chapter 12

While Poppy set about trying to console Murray, Reginald rose from his seat as Miss Mabel hurried back to their table, handing him the cup she'd gone to fetch. After noticing Murray's distress, she didn't bother to wait for Reginald to pull out a chair for her, but took a seat directly next to Murray, giving his arm a good pat as Reginald resumed his seat.

"My dear Murray," she began, "do not tell me you've had another row with that mother of yours."

"I'm afraid I have, Miss Mabel," Murray said, taking a gulp of his coffee, his eyes immediately watering since the coffee was still not cool enough to drink. "She's probably even now tossing all of my worldly belongings into the street to prove how put out she is with me."

Miss Mabel's eyes twinkled. "You've always been so wonderfully dramatic, but I doubt if Hazel will go through the bother of tossing your belongings into the street. She's never been one to enjoy overexerting herself."

Murray immediately brightened. "She *doesn't* enjoy exerting herself."

Miss Mabel inclined her head right as the young woman who'd originally taken their orders returned, bearing a tray filled with cakes, scones, jams, and the clotted cream. As the woman went about setting the plates on the table, Miss Mabel beamed a smile all around.

"I took the liberty of adding a few extra helpings of everything after I noticed Murray's arrival, and good thing I did. There's nothing quite like a plate of cakes to cheer a person up." She turned to Murray. "If that's not enough to improve your spirits, do remember that you're in possession of two substantial trusts, left to you from relatives who obviously wanted to make certain you'd have plenty of funds available if the day ever arrived where you'd want to strike out on your own. Thankfully, that day does appear to have arrived."

"I completely forgot I'm not a pauper," Murray said before he accepted a plate from their server and immediately dove into one of the cakes, shoveling forkfuls into his mouth so quickly Reginald couldn't help but wonder if the man had also forgotten to eat that day.

"You've apparently forgotten you're a gentleman as well since a gentleman usually waits until everyone has been served before tucking in," Miss Mabel said, which had Murray immediately choking on the bite of cake he'd just taken.

After giving Murray a sound pounding on his back, Reginald turned his attention to his own plate, setting aside his knife when he noticed Poppy slathering clotted cream on a scone that she then topped with jam.

"The cream always goes on top," he pointed out, earning a scowl in return.

"Why would that matter?"

"It's just how it's done."

"It's cream, somewhat like butter I have to imagine, and I never put butter over my jam, always under it."

"Clotted cream is not like butter," Murray said, pausing with another forkful of cake halfway to his mouth.

Poppy's mouth made an O of surprise. "What does it taste like then?"

Murray frowned. "Since you didn't like the comparison I made between snail and chicken, I'm not certain you should be seeking my counsel on the matter."

"It's not as horrid as snail though, is it?" Poppy asked as she, much to Reginald's surprise, set aside the scone she'd improperly fixed, spread jam over a new scone, then added a hefty dollop of clotted cream before she looked to him. "Is it?" she repeated.

"I like snail," he reminded her. "But no, clotted cream is not horrid at all, although it is heavier than the cream you're probably used to."

"Fine, I'll try it, although I still don't understand why the cream has to be on top." Without waiting for him to reply to that bit of nonsense, she took a bite, her nose wrinkled, and then, after giving a linen napkin a longing look, Poppy began chewing at a furious rate. A moment later, she swallowed, shuddered, then turned a rather concerning shade of green.

"Oh dear. I think you might need a refreshing glass of lemonade to wash that down. I'll be right back," Miss Mabel said, jumping from her chair to all but sprint across the tearoom and through a door that evidently led to the kitchen.

"Whatever is the matter with you now, Miss Garrison?" a lady asked from behind Reginald, before Miss Adele Tooker stepped into view. She smiled brightly at Poppy, who was looking less than pleased at the appearance of a lady who seemed to show up at the most inconvenient times.

"There's nothing the matter with me," Poppy returned coolly, summoning up a smile that must have taken a great deal of effort since she was still green. "I was merely savoring the taste of clotted cream for the first time."

Miss Tooker, along with Miss Edith Iselin, whom Reginald only then noticed as he rose to his feet while Murray did the same, stepped closer to the table.

"Lord Lonsdale adores clotted cream," Miss Tooker said, raising a hand to her chest. "I'm afraid he was somewhat taken aback to learn I've never tried it before, but I assured him I would rectify that at my earliest convenience."

"But the two of you must join us now," Poppy said, waving the two ladies forward. "Be a dear, Murray, and fetch two additional chairs. I say there's no time like the present to introduce Miss Tooker and Miss Iselin to the pleasure of clotted cream."

Even though Poppy's invitation to Miss Tooker and Miss Iselin was what was expected of a society lady, Reginald had the distinct feeling that allowing those two ladies to join them was a certain recipe for disaster. Even so, since there was no way to politely rescind the invitation, Reginald assisted the ladies into the chairs Murray had pulled from an empty table, taking his own seat right as Miss Mabel rejoined them.

"Ah, more guests. How delightful," Miss Mabel exclaimed, setting a tall glass of lemonade in front of Poppy before she nodded to Miss Tooker and Miss Iselin. "Shall I fetch you some tea, or would you two ladies prefer a pot of coffee?"

Miss Tooker turned eyes filled with clear longing to the coffeepot. "Everyone is drinking coffee?"

"Poppy apparently prefers it over tea," Murray said, his cheeks turning red when Miss Tooker turned her attention his way.

"What would your mother say, Mr. Middleton, if she were to hear you address Miss Garrison so informally?"

"Since Mr. Middleton is not a boy, Miss Tooker," Poppy said before Murray could get a word out of his mouth, "I'm sure she wouldn't have much to say about it at all. However, because I'm of the belief that sharing clotted cream and coffee is far more pleasant when it's done in an informal atmosphere, I suggest *all* of us abandon formality. You may address me as Poppy, Mr. Blackburn as Reginald, Mr. Middleton as Murray, and . . ." She raised an expectant brow.

"This is most improper," Miss Tooker said, exchanging a look with Miss Iselin. "But in the spirit of informality, you may call me Adele."

"I'm Edith," Miss Iselin added before Adele could introduce her.

"How lovely," Poppy exclaimed, setting aside her now-empty glass of lemonade. "Now, with that settled, what shall it be . . . tea or coffee for the two of you?"

Adele glanced to Reginald. "Do you believe Lord Lonsdale would find it distressing to learn Edith and I enjoy having an occasional coffee?"

"I don't believe that would distress him overly much," Reginald said, earning a smile from Adele, who then nodded to Miss Mabel. "Coffee sounds splendid, Miss Mabel."

As Miss Mabel promised to return directly with additional cups and a fresh pot of coffee, Poppy sat forward. "I'm surprised to discover the two of you here. It's not yet two o'clock, and both of you are known to maintain a diligent calling schedule."

Adele nodded as she accepted a plate from Murray. "Edith and I *were* making our calls with our mothers earlier. However, after calling upon your grandmother and learning you weren't at home because you'd agreed to accompany Mr. Blackburn, or rather, Reginald, to the tearoom, we decided we simply had to stop by Rutherford & Company to check on your welfare. Edith and I have been most concerned about you after your unfortunate swim yesterday."

"How thoughtful," Poppy murmured, picking up a plate of scones and holding it out to Adele and Edith. "Scone?"

After Adele and Edith each took one, they began spreading on clotted cream, and then placing jam on top of that cream, something that left Reginald wincing. However, since they weren't students of his, he refrained from correcting them, even though that earned him a scowl from Poppy. Thankfully, Murray distracted her when he cleared his throat and looked to Edith.

"Did you enjoy your visit with Mrs. Van Rensselaer today, Edith?"

Edith smiled. "It was enjoyable, but then, I always find Mrs. Van Rensselaer to be a more-than-amiable hostess. She's very charming and tells the most captivating stories."

Poppy's brows drew together. "Are you certain we're talking about the same Mrs. Van Rensselaer? As in my grandmother, Viola?"

"But of course." Edith set her knife on the very top of her small plate. "I'm often disappointed that calls are restricted to thirty minutes because that doesn't seem like enough time to truly enjoy her company."

"She's a very gracious lady, Poppy," Adele added. "You're fortunate to have a leading society matron as your grandmother, although why you waited so long to have her bring you out into society is a mystery." She smiled sweetly, even though something less than sweet flickered through her eyes. "I will admit, though, that today's call at your grandmother's house turned somewhat unusual after Miss Beatrix Waterbury arrived."

"Beatrix paid a call to my grandmother?"

Adele shook her head. "I believe she was looking for you, Poppy, as well as you, Murray."

Murray's face turned pink. "Why was Beatrix looking for me?"

"She apparently still has possession of your horse."

"I forgot all about my horse."

"Which would explain why Beatrix was trying to run you down," Adele said. "She apparently stopped by your house first, Murray, and from what little I overheard Beatrix say to Mrs. Van Rensselaer, your mother and Beatrix had words."

The color began leaking from Murray's face. "Why would my mother have words with Beatrix?"

"It had something to do with you naming your horse Hazel, which, in my humble opinion, was not well done of you, since your mother's name is Hazel."

"I didn't name my horse Hazel. She was already named that when my mother purchased her, although, clearly, Mother wasn't aware of that at the time of the purchase." Murray frowned. "I wonder how Beatrix knew my horse was originally named Hazel."

Edith sat forward. "From what I overheard, Beatrix had intended on purchasing Hazel for herself, but your mother evidently beat her to the sale." She turned to Poppy. "I then overheard Beatrix say that Murray's mother demanded she take the horse out of her sight, which is why I believe Beatrix was looking for you, hoping you'd know where to find Murray."

Poppy's brows drew together. "If she was looking for me, why didn't she accompany the two of you here?"

Adele began smoothing a linen napkin over her lap. "Because then Mr. Nigel Flaherty stopped by your grandmother's house." She lifted her head. "He apparently wanted to check on your welfare, and he brought you flowers."

Something peculiar took that moment to unfurl in Reginald's stomach, something that rumbled around and felt very much like . . .

"He brought me flowers?" Poppy repeated.

"A lovely bouquet of hothouse roses. He apparently wanted to take you for a ride through Central Park, and when you pair that with the flowers, well, I must say it does appear that the gentleman is smitten with you." Adele leaned toward Poppy. "Rumor has it Mr. Flaherty is well on his way to becoming one of the wealthiest gentlemen in the country, a circumstance that certainly makes him appealing to more than one young lady."

Poppy shrugged. "Mr. Flaherty and I are merely friends, that friendship formed because we share a love of fine horses."

"He helped rescue you when you were dangling from a balcony."

"True, but that's hardly a reason to set my cap for him."

"Rescuing a lady from certain death most assuredly can be considered a romantic gesture," Adele said firmly.

Poppy waved that aside. "I beg to differ." She nodded to Reginald. "Reginald saved me as well, but I don't believe he felt compelled to do so because he was thinking of romance as I tumbled over the railing." She arched an expectant brow at him.

"Ah . . . quite right" was all he could think to respond.

She smiled and returned her attention to Adele. "See? Not a romantic gesture in the least. And before you come up with another reason why you believe Nigel and I would suit, you should remember that the man is at least twice my age."

"Most ladies find older gentlemen very compelling."

Poppy inclined her head. "Perhaps they do, but I'm not most ladies."

"No truer words have ever been said," Adele said sweetly. "And with that settled, shall we turn the conversation to something less contentious, such as . . . Lord Lonsdale?"

Poppy frowned. "But you didn't finish explaining why Beatrix didn't accompany the two of you here."

Adele lifted her chin. "Allow me to simply say this—Beatrix Waterbury and I aren't close. And, with that said, I now feel compelled to offer you some sage advice: It will not benefit you to further your acquaintance with Miss Waterbury because she's garnered a reputation of being eccentric."

Reginald found it less than encouraging when temper flashed through Poppy's eyes.

"I find Beatrix's eccentricity to be refreshing," Poppy said. "She's a charming lady, and I have no intention of distancing myself from her, no matter that *some* in society believe differently."

Adele's eyes flashed with temper as well before she directed a smile Reginald's way. "Forgive me. Here Poppy and I are going on and on about a trifling matter and neglecting you most assiduously. I believe we were, at one time, discussing scones and clotted cream."

"A less volatile topic of conversation for certain," Reginald said.

"Unless you decide you don't care for clotted cream," Poppy muttered, "and are concerned that it may leave you at distinct odds with British gentlemen who were raised on the—"

"This looks simply delicious," Adele interrupted, picking up her scone, but pausing when Poppy shook her head.

"I'm going to suggest you wait for Miss Mabel to return with your coffee cup, Adele. You might need something at the ready if you decide clotted cream is not to your taste."

Adele frowned. "You said you were savoring clotted cream when I first arrived."

"Savoring, detesting," Poppy said with a wave of her hand. "It's all somewhat debatable, but I will say this—clotted cream, no matter how delectable it may sound, might very well be an acquired taste, so I'd advise you to proceed with caution." She shot a look to the scone on her plate and grimaced. "Frankly, I found it to be incredibly heavy, and instead of tasting like butter, or the cream I enjoy with cake, it had a slightly nutty taste, and I'm not partial to nutty."

A hint of defiance flickered over Adele's face right before she took a large bite of her scone. Something curious settled in her eyes as she chewed, but then she swallowed, squared her shoulders, and smiled. "Delicious, although I can see where a person with less sophisticated tastes might not find it so."

That was all it took for Poppy to snatch up her scone and begin eating with relish, Adele doing the same with her scone a second later.

It was a riveting battle if Reginald had ever seen one, although one where clotted cream, jam, and scones were the weapons, instead of the usual pistols, swords, or knives.

As Poppy and Adele polished off their first scones and reached for seconds, Miss Mabel returned with additional cups and a fresh pot of coffee. After depositing those on the table, she glanced to Poppy, then Adele, then turned straight on her heel and beat a hasty retreat, saying something about pressing business in the kitchen.

"Wish I had some pressing business in the kitchen," Murray muttered before he turned to Edith, who'd taken a small bite of her scone before setting it aside, perfectly content, or so it seemed, to abandon the scone for the small cake she was nibbling in a most ladylike fashion—unlike Adele and Poppy, who were devouring their scones as if they'd not eaten in months.

"What news have you heard about the snow that some believe is soon to be coming to the city?" Edith asked as she and Murray began discussing the weather in earnest.

Sitting back in his chair, Reginald took a sip of his coffee and watched as Poppy and Adele reached for their third scones.

Edith sat forward and nodded to Reginald, drawing his attention away from the madness at hand. "And how do you find the weather here in New York, Reginald? Is it much different than what you're used to over in England?"

Reginald smiled, realizing that he'd not paid much attention to Edith, while also realizing that she was a charming young lady, what with her quiet demeanor, impeccable manners, and an understated beauty that had been eclipsed by Adele's classically beautiful face and Poppy's, well, everything.

"I find that the weather has been most marvelous in New York." He set aside his cup. "Have you lived in the city long, Edith, and do you reside here the entire year or only spend the Season here?"

Before Edith could answer, Adele pushed away the plate in front of her that only had crumbs remaining upon it, and blotted her lips. She sent what seemed to be a look of warning to Edith before she turned her full attention on Reginald. "Edith's family has numerous homes scattered around the country, quite like my family." She blotted her lips again. "But enough about Edith. I'm much more interested in hearing about Lord Lonsdale's homes, as I'm certain Edith is too." She half-heartedly tossed a smile Edith's way but apparently missed the frown Edith sent her in return.

Before Reginald could say a single word about Charles's many properties, Murray sat forward, his eyes narrowed on Adele before he smiled pleasantly and nodded to the empty clotted cream bowl. "Shall I take the liberty of ordering more clotted cream?"

A look of absolute horror crossed Adele's face, whereas Poppy, on the other hand, returned Murray's smile, a distinct twinkle in her eyes.

"How thoughtful of you to notice, Murray. And yes, I would love nothing more than to share another tub of it with my dear friend Adele."

The moment the word *tub* slipped out of Poppy's mouth, Adele blanched, but she rallied quickly, taking a second to fiddle with the small watch attached to her sleeve.

"My goodness, would you look at the time." She lifted her head. "I'm afraid the afternoon has gotten away from me, so I'll need to excuse myself." She looked expectantly at Reginald, who immediately rose to his feet and helped her out of her chair. She turned to Edith. "Coming, dear?"

Even though Edith looked less than thrilled to have what could only be considered a most riveting afternoon outing come to such a rapid end, she smiled pleasantly at Murray, who was already on his feet, and allowed him to help her from her chair.

After telling Poppy they were looking forward to the upcoming tea at her grandmother's house, the two ladies quit the tearoom, Adele all but running away, as if she was convinced if she lingered even a second longer she'd be obligated to have more clotted cream.

"May I still claim a victory, even though I'm fully aware I completely failed in regard to proper decorum?" Poppy asked, looking less than contrite about her failure as Reginald and Murray resumed their seats. She turned to Murray and grinned. "What a brilliant strategist you are, Murray. It was sheer genius on your part to offer to fetch more clotted cream, although I must admit I was worried there for a moment that Adele might actually accept your offer, which would have seen the both of us sick for certain."

"You could have graciously declined Murray's offer," Reginald pointed out.

"Which would have been no fun at all and would have left us to suffer Adele's company longer." Poppy picked up her coffee cup and took a dainty sip. "I do believe I like Edith, though." She caught Reginald's eye. "You should tell Lord Lonsdale that she might make him a worthy countess."

"You'd make a worthy countess," Murray said, taking a sip of his coffee.

"And while that's kind of you, I don't believe I would." Poppy settled back in her chair. "I'm never going to have clotted cream again if I can help it. It's far too rich for me, and that right there is reason enough for Reginald to take me off Lord Lonsdale's list of potential heiresses."

"Edith didn't appear to like clotted cream either," Reginald pointed out.

"True, but she didn't make a fuss about it, which is exactly how I would expect a real countess to behave."

"Good point." Reginald considered her over the rim of his coffee cup. "Should I assume you don't believe Adele would make a credible countess?"

Poppy shrugged. "She's probably more than up for that challenge. However, I don't believe Lord Lonsdale would find her easy to live with, so unless you secretly don't care for him, I'd take her off the list as well."

Because he couldn't argue with that, since he'd already come to the conclusion that Adele wasn't a likeable sort, he settled for finishing his coffee as Murray and Poppy discussed where Murray might begin searching for a new residence. They were joined a moment later by Miss Mabel, after Reginald had seen her making certain Adele and Edith had taken their leave.

"Not that everyone is in agreement that French flats are appropriate for a bachelor gentleman to let, but may I suggest considering the Osborne flats on Fifty-Seventh Street?" Miss Mabel said. "Those flats offer very luxurious spaces, complete with steam heat, four Otis elevators, and secret passageways for the help." She smiled at Murray. "The basement level hosts a florist, but more importantly, a physician and pharmacy."

Murray returned the smile. "That might prove handy, since I do seem to suffer from a variety of ailments." His smile dimmed. "Even so, I'm certain my mother would hardly approve of me letting space in a flat. She finds them most disagreeable."

Miss Mabel's lips thinned. "Hazel would find any residence you set your sights on disagreeable, dear. But since you're the one who will live in that residence, you're the one to make the final decision. Did I mention most flats at the Osborne come complete with fourteen-foot ceilings, windows designed by Tiffany, and modern plumbing? And the Osborne is situated not far from Central Park, which would make it convenient for you to walk over and do a bit of that sketching I know you're so fond of doing."

"It's very disconcerting how you know so much about everyone," Murray muttered.

"I'm sure it is." Miss Mabel nodded at Poppy. "Just as I'm sure that if anyone can convince him to give the Osborne a look, it's you."

Poppy smiled. "And because I have nothing else on my schedule this afternoon, there's no need for us to delay. Thank you for being so attentive to us today, Miss Mabel. I thoroughly enjoyed myself and will certainly return soon to this lovely tearoom."

"See that you do," Miss Mabel said. "I'll go fetch your bill."

"You can simply put it on my grandmother's account," Poppy said before Reginald could tell Miss Mabel he was settling the bill.

Inclining her head, Miss Mabel strode away, stopping to chat with guests seated at another table.

Reginald narrowed his eyes on Poppy. "That was not well done of you."

"Probably not, but since I'm the one who ate most of the food, as well as consumed most of the beverages, it's only fair." She rose from the chair. "And with that settled, shall we go look at that French flat?"

Without waiting for Reginald or Murray to offer her their arm, Poppy took off like a shot through the tearoom, the reason for her haste becoming crystal clear the second she stopped in front of the elevator.

"I think not" was all Reginald said as he took a firm grip of her arm, and with Murray falling into step behind him, they moved to the stairs, ignoring Poppy's complaints about having to travel down four flights when there was a perfectly good elevator at hand.

"You just consumed a large quantity of clotted cream," he reminded her when they reached the second floor. "You should appreciate the opportunity for some exercise."

"Why didn't we make use of the elevator?" Murray huffed, taking a swipe at his perspiring brow.

"Because I suspect that Poppy had intentions of cajoling the elevator operator into letting her try her hand at bringing us down to the first floor."

Murray's eyes widened. "No need to say anything else."

Poppy muttered something that sounded like "traitor" under

her breath right as they reached the first floor, and soon they were standing outside, heads bent against a brisk wind that was howling up and down Broadway.

"May I offer the two of you a ride?" Murray asked right as the wind tore his hat from his head, which Poppy immediately darted after, even though the hat was already in the street.

"Watch out for the—"

The rest of Reginald's warning got lost as Poppy dodged around a closed carriage that had almost run her over and raced after the hat, making it to the other side of Broadway without incident.

Thankful that she'd not been flattened before their eyes, Reginald, with Murray by his side, strode after her, their progress delayed when a large delivery wagon trundled in front of them, blocking their path. Craning his neck, he frowned when he realized Poppy was now almost an entire block away from them, rushing after Murray's hat in what could only be considered a run.

"She's unusually fast for a lady who just ate that much clotted cream," Murray said as they hurried around the delivery wagon.

"Indeed, but . . ." Reginald stopped talking as he noticed three large men darting out from an alley Poppy had just raced past. Trepidation slid through him when he noticed that their attention, or so it seemed, was directed at the reticule dangling from her wrist.

Breaking into a run, Reginald could only pray he was mistaken about the three men's intentions. But since this did involve Poppy, and she seemed to get herself entangled in the most unlikely of situations, he was afraid he wasn't mistaken at all.

CHAPTER 13

By the time Poppy caught up with Murray's runaway hat, she was distinctly regretting all the scones and clotted cream she'd consumed, what with how her stomach was currently roiling in protest. Brushing dirt from the brim of the hat, she lifted her head, then narrowed her eyes on a troubling sight occurring directly across from her on Broadway.

A deliveryman was wielding a whip on a horse in an aggressive manner, yelling obscenities at the poor beast. The man was evidently trying to get the horse to move, but it was quite clear that the load was too heavy for one horse and could have possibly needed four to pull it easily.

Charging through the traffic that clogged the street, Poppy thought she heard someone yelling behind her, but because the deliveryman now seemed to be whipping the horse even more aggressively than before, she plowed forward, stopping directly beside the driver's seat and craning her neck to meet the deliveryman's gaze.

"I insist you stop such horrid treatment of your horse at once, sir," she demanded.

The deliveryman, a big, burly sort who probably caused small children to flee from him in terror at the sight of his frightening face, stopped lashing his horse and glared down at her.

"Ain't none of your business how I be treatin' this nag. I ain't gonna be able to make this delivery on time if I can't get him to move."

"Your load is too heavy. Beating the poor creature isn't going to change that. You'll only end up causing irreparable damage."

"That's my choice to make, and now you best be steppin' out of the way." The man turned his attention back to his horse, lifting the whip over his head, an action that had Poppy's temper going from simmering to boiling.

Tossing Murray's hat aside, Poppy leapt up on the wagon and wrenched the whip straight out of the now very surprised-looking deliveryman's hand. Fury soon replaced the surprise on the man's face, and a second later, Poppy found herself in the middle of a dangerous game of tug-of-war as the man tried to wrestle the whip away from her.

Stumbling backward, she tumbled out of the wagon, hitting the hard surface of the street a second later. Ignoring the pain that was radiating from her left elbow, Poppy felt satisfaction rush through her when she realized she'd somehow managed to maintain her hold of the whip. Jumping to her feet, she opened her mouth to unleash a blistering tirade about treating horses and humans so shabbily but swallowed that tirade when she realized the deliveryman wasn't paying her the least little mind. Instead, his attention was settled on something behind her. Turning, she drew in a sharp breath as she took note of three derelict-looking men who were standing a few feet away from her.

For the briefest of seconds, she thought they might be standing there because they were considering coming to her aid, but then the biggest of the bunch suddenly lurched forward and grabbed hold of the reticule attached to her wrist, breaking the delicate chain and pulling the reticule into his beefy hand.

Poppy did the only thing she could think of—she brought the

whip down on the man's head, earning a howl of rage from him in return.

"Run!" Reginald yelled as he barreled into view, looking absolutely furious as he drew back his arm, and then fists began to fly.

Finding herself rooted to the spot, Poppy saw Murray enter the fray, jumping on the back of one of the men and looping his arm around the man's neck as that man set about trying to shake Murray off him.

A second later, and to Poppy's astonishment, Beatrix Waterbury rode into view on the back of Murray's horse, and before Poppy could do more than gape at her friend, Beatrix leapt to the ground, rushed toward Murray, and began brandishing her riding crop in a most impressive fashion.

Realizing she wasn't doing any good by gawking at the bedlam unfolding around her, Poppy surged into motion, setting her sights on the man who'd grabbed her reticule and who was only now picking himself up from the ground, his eyes narrowed on Reginald, who was exchanging blow after blow with the other assailant.

"Oh no you don't," she yelled, raising the whip and aiming for the man's head. Unfortunately, her aim was less than accurate and before she could do more than blink, the man grabbed the whip right out of her hand. He smiled in a way that had her blood turning to ice as he broke the whip in two and took a step toward her.

Poppy's mind went curiously blank until Reginald appeared right beside the man, and with a "Get out of here, Poppy!" he spun the man around, planting a fist in his face. That earned another howl of rage from the man in return, and then fists were flying in every direction, only ending when the man Reginald was fighting fell to the ground and stayed there.

"Impressive," Poppy breathed as Reginald turned back to the original man he'd been fighting, tossing a "I mean it, Poppy. Get out of here!" over his shoulder before he threw himself at the other man, who'd just lumbered to his feet.

Knowing there was little she could do to assist Reginald, Poppy dashed toward Beatrix and Murray. Before she could reach them, though, police whistles rent the air. At the sound of those whistles, the man Beatrix was hitting with her riding crop, and who had his arms over his head trying to avoid the blows, turned and fled into the crowd Poppy only then realized was gathering around them.

Temper flashed anew at the sight of people watching the brawl instead of helping, that temper turning hotter when the man who'd taken her reticule suddenly bolted past her, her reticule swinging from one hand while he brandished a pistol he'd apparently pulled from his jacket in the other. With a twitch of her skirts, Poppy began plowing through the crowd, pulled to a stop a moment later by a strong hand that wouldn't let go of her arm, no matter how hard she tried to tug free.

"And where do you think you're going?" Reginald rasped from behind her.

"After my reticule."

"I think not."

"How do you plan on stopping me?"

The next thing she knew, she was hanging upside down over his shoulder. Opening her mouth to utter a protest, she managed to get out a "Put me down" before the ground began whizzing by her as Reginald strode back the way they'd just come.

"It's becoming obvious that you do not need an instructor so much as you need a keeper."

"I don't need a keeper," she argued. "But before you launch into a hundred reasons why you believe differently, I must encourage you to set me down. If you've forgotten, I did ingest a rather large quantity of clotted cream and dangling upside down isn't doing a thing to settle my stomach."

"You should have thought about that before you went off on your madcap rush down Broadway and before you confronted some random deliveryman."

"I don't confront random deliverymen."

"So you recognized that man and, what, decided to jump up on his wagon for a bit of a chat?"

A small belch took that moment to escape through her lips,

a belch Reginald apparently heard since he stopped dead in his tracks. A second later, she found herself back on her feet, blinking as she got a good look at Reginald's face.

His right eye was already puffy and showed signs of soon sporting an impressive bruise. His nose was bleeding, and his lip was swollen. He was also missing his hat, his hair was sticking up every which way, the sleeve of his jacket was torn, and dirt covered his trousers. She winced when she lifted her gaze and found him watching her with aggravation in his eyes.

"What were you thinking?" he demanded.

"I was thinking I have quite a bit of pin money in my reticule, and I don't believe members of the criminal set should get to enjoy it."

"Not about that—about jumping up on that wagon. But do know that it's never permissible for a lady to take it upon herself to chase down members of the criminal persuasion."

"That's completely ridiculous." She shoved aside a strand of hair that had unsurprisingly escaped its pins. "Who decided that ladies can't react accordingly when someone has the audacity to relieve them of their personal possessions?"

"Ladies are not physically equipped to defend themselves in dangerous situations. You're fortunate you weren't grievously injured when you so foolishly tried to intervene in what turned into nothing less than a brawl."

"Perhaps instead of trying to instruct me on how to speak properly about mundane topics like the weather, you should teach me how to handle myself in a brawl. That would better prepare me in the future if I find myself involved in another similar situation."

"One would hope you'll never find yourself in a brawl again, and no, I'm not teaching you how to fight."

Poppy's lips thinned. "If you ask me, gentlemen always seem unwilling to lend ladies practical knowledge, which then leaves us reliant on their assistance, although I didn't notice any of the men in the crowd who were watching the brawl try to stop the man who snatched my reticule." She lifted her chin. "And returning to the matter of the deliveryman, I would not have jumped onto the man's wagon if any of the many men roaming around Broadway had intervened, since surely a few of them had to have witnessed that man abusing his horse."

Reginald's one good eye narrowed. "What do you mean the man was abusing his horse?"

"You didn't notice that?"

"How could I have been expected to notice that since I was trying to keep an eye on the three rough-looking men who'd taken to following you."

"Should I assume you didn't notice the deliveryman shove me off his wagon?"

"He shoved you off his wagon?"

Before Beatrix could do more than nod, Reginald took a firm hold of her arm and began pulling her through the crowd, not stopping until they were a few feet away from the delivery wagon. The deliveryman was still sitting on the driver's seat, gesturing wildly as he spoke to a policeman who was standing near the wagon and taking notes.

"There she is," the deliveryman yelled, pointing a dirty finger Poppy's way. "That's the woman who accosted me and you need to get her locked up. The streets ain't safe with nutters like her running amok."

The policeman turned his attention Poppy's way, looked her up and down, then turned back to the delivery driver. "She doesn't look like a nutter to me. She looks like quality, and no, I won't be locking her away. The Four Hundred don't take kindly to having their members arrested." The policeman tucked his notepad away before he strode off toward where another policeman was leading away the one and only criminal captured.

"Wot's the matter with everyone today?" the deliveryman yelled. "Ain't no one gonna help me get some justice for sufferin' through an attack from that madwoman?"

"I didn't attack you," Poppy said before she slipped out of Reginald's hold and moved to stand beside the horse, needing to put a bit of distance between herself and the deliveryman who certainly didn't seem to hold so much as a smidgen of remorse for what had happened. Giving the horse's nose a rub, she looked into its eyes, her heart breaking at the resignation she saw there.

She'd spent her life around horses, loved them more than people at times, and that there were so many horses frequently abused because their owners didn't value their worth was something she'd never understand.

"You're a beauty," she whispered, dashing a hand over eyes now swimming with tears. "I'm sorry your owner doesn't realize that."

The horse gave her a nuzzle, and after she gave him a nuzzle in return, she lifted her head, finding Reginald watching her closely. He sent her the barest hint of a smile, glanced at the horse, shook his head, then turned back to the deliveryman.

"While I feel the distinct desire to pummel you," Reginald began in a curiously cheerful tone, "we have seen a lot of violence today, so I'm going to ignore that particular desire."

"Kind of you," the deliveryman growled, his beady eyes traveling over the breadth of Reginald's shoulders. "And since I do need to get on with my day, I'll not press to have that woman hauled off to jail for assaulting me."

"Kind of *you*," Reginald returned. "However, I do believe there needs to be some type of retribution for your unacceptable behavior, so what say you agree to turn your horse over to me and we'll call it a day?"

"I ain't givin' you my horse."

"I'm not asking you to give it to me." Reginald reached into his pocket, pulled out his billfold, and a second later, thrust some bills into the deliveryman's hand. "I think you'll find that more than enough compensation."

Right there, in the middle of Broadway, surrounded by carriages, strangers, and belligerent deliverymen, and having only recently been relieved of her reticule, Poppy lost a bit of her heart.

She'd not voiced a single word about getting the poor horse away from its abusive owner, but Reginald had taken it upon himself to do just that—prompted, or so it seemed to her, after he'd witnessed her distress.

"I'll pay you back," she whispered.

Reginald's brows drew together. "Don't be ridiculous. It's a gift, although I'm not certain it's a gift anyone else would want."

"He's beautiful. The most beautiful horse I've ever seen."

Reginald looked at her for a long second, then shook his head. "Should I be concerned that you suffered an injury to your head in the melee?"

"My head is in fine form, thank you very much."

"A scary thought." He turned back to the man. "You'll need to unhitch the horse."

"You bought it, you unhitch it."

Poppy didn't hear Reginald's response, but whatever he said had the man off the wagon and unhitching the horse in the blink of an eye.

She gave the horse a last pat and moved to stand beside Reginald. "You seem to have a most impressive ability to get people to do your bidding, even when they're reluctant to do so. Was that a trait you were born with, or have you developed it over time?"

A trace of a smile flickered over Reginald's face. "I imagine I acquired it after associating with so many aristocrats through the years. They're demanding sorts and are very good at getting people to see after their demands."

"How . . . disconcerting."

He arched a brow. "Is it?"

"Of course," Poppy said right as Beatrix strode up to join them.

"I've given the police an account of what I believe happened," Beatrix began. "They recognized the one man detained as being a habitual criminal and are hopeful he'll disclose the names and whereabouts of his two friends, although I doubt those hopes will amount to anything." She brushed dirt from the sleeve of her jacket as she looked Poppy over. "Are you all right?"

Poppy nodded but frowned as she got a closer look at her friend. "I'm fine, but you seem to have blood on your face."

"It's not mine. It's Murray's." She nodded to where Murray was sitting on the sidewalk across from them. "He took an elbow to the nose, and I'm afraid he'll be sporting two black eyes before long."

Taking Beatrix's arm, Poppy hurried through the street, relieved to discover that the crowd of gawkers had dispersed while she'd been dealing with the deliveryman.

"Don't start hovering" were the first words out of Murray's mouth. "I'm fine."

Murray looked anything but fine.

Blood was seeping from his nose, something he didn't seem to realize, and both of his eyes were swollen. For some odd reason, he was missing a shoe, but because he was sporting a rather dazed look, Poppy didn't think it would improve matters if she pointed that out. Before she could summon up a single thing to say, though, a horse stopped directly beside them, and then Mr. Nigel Flaherty was swinging down from the saddle, striding her way as he held out her reticule.

"May I dare hope that this belongs to you?" he asked, looking remarkably pleased with himself.

"It does, but how did you get it back for me?" Poppy asked.

Nigel gave a wave of a gloved hand. "Bit of luck. I just happened to be traveling down Broadway, wondering what all the ruckus was about." He shook his head. "You cannot imagine my dismay when I finally edged my way closer and discovered you'd been accosted by men of the most derelict sort." He shook his head. "By the time I was able to squeeze through the crowd, the altercation had ended, but I saw one of the criminals racing away, so I followed him." He touched his face, drawing attention to a red mark that seemed to be in the shape of a hand. "The man was, as you can imagine, reluctant to hand over the spoils, but even though he put up a fight, I overpowered him in the end and managed to retrieve your reticule."

Beatrix frowned. "If you overpowered him, should we assume he's now been taken into custody?"

"I'm sorry to say that after I secured the reticule, the man hit me again and slipped away, but at least he left empty-handed."

Nigel returned his attention to Poppy and dipped his head. "I'm only thankful I'm able to be of such small service to you, and . . ."

Whatever else Nigel had been about to say got lost when a bright red carriage came trundling up the street, Lena Ridgeway all but leaping out of that carriage the moment it stopped, not bothering to wait for the groom riding on the back of the carriage to get the door for her. Five dogs leapt after her, yipping and scrambling around her skirts as she advanced toward them.

"Nigel, there you are, my dear. I just missed you at Mrs. Van Rensselaer's house."

Nigel blinked. "Were you following me?"

Lena released a titter. "Goodness no. I merely decided after you mentioned you were going to call on the Van Rensselaers that I should pay Viola a call today as well."

"But why were you driving down Broadway?" Nigel pressed.

Lena leaned over and picked up a small black dog that had been trying to burrow underneath her skirt. "Simply wanted to take the dogs for a ride, since they do enjoy traveling in the carriage. I must say I wasn't expecting to see you, Nigel, chasing down a member of the criminal persuasion." She smiled. "You made such a dashing figure, although you did frighten me half to death when you leapt from your horse and engaged in an honest-to-goodness fistfight with that ruffian, muscling the reticule away from him and winning the day in the end."

Nigel smiled somewhat weakly, but before he could respond, Lena returned her attention to Poppy. "You're looking somewhat bedraggled, dear, but still charming all the same."

"Ah, well, thank you" was all Poppy could think to say right as two of Lena's dogs, both poodles, began circling Nigel, baring their sharp teeth.

"Pebbles, Cookie, be nice to darling Nigel," Lena cooed before she returned her attention to Poppy. "What say all of us repair to the tearoom at Rutherford & Company? It's turning downright frigid out here, and I, for one, wouldn't mind a nice hot cup of tea."

Poppy was spared a response when Nigel suddenly stopped trying to shoo Cookie and Pebbles away from him and frowned.

"What's Mr. Blackburn doing leading that decrepit-looking horse our way?" Nigel asked.

Looking past him, she smiled as Reginald drew closer, holding out the reins to her once he was about a foot away.

"Here you go, Poppy. Your new horse." Reginald shook his head. "And before you ask, he does not have a name, so no need to worry that it'll be a Murray situation where you've come into possession of a horse named Viola."

She moved to take the reins, stroking the nose of the horse. "Perhaps I should name him Reginald since you saved him from a horrible fate."

"Well, quite like Mrs. Middleton, I find I'm not keen to share my name with a horse."

"And you mustn't name him Nigel either, even if Nigel did save your reticule from that criminal," Lena said, taking a firm grip on Pebbles's collar when the poodle let out a growl, its sights settled on Poppy's new horse. "Nigel would probably take offense at that, although I have been considering getting another dog and naming it Nigel. Perhaps an Irish Wolfhound would be able to bear the name admirably."

Nigel began looking rather pained, which left Poppy smiling, although Lena seemed to miss the expression on his face since Pebbles took that moment to begin barking at a gentleman walking past them.

"We can discuss the matter further over tea," Lena said, pitching her voice louder to be heard over the barking. "And with that said, I should return the dogs to the carriage, although I do hate to deprive my darling Wags of what seems to be his new friend."

Glancing to where Lena was now looking, Poppy's gaze settled on Murray, who was still sitting on the curb, one of Lena's dogs sitting right beside him, licking a face that was, unfortunately, smeared with blood.

"I'm afraid we're going to have to enjoy tea another day, Lena," Poppy said. "I need to see Murray home."

"Would appreciate that," Murray called out. "If someone could call to have my carriage brought around, I'd appreciate that as well. I left it and my driver at Rutherford & Company."

Lena's eyes widened. "Goodness, Mr. Middleton, you're bleeding, and rather profusely at that."

"I'm not bleeding," Murray argued as Reginald strode over to Murray, handing him a handkerchief as he bent down and examined Murray's face.

"I beg to differ, Murray. Looks to me as if you might have broken your nose, but no need to fret. We'll summon a physician as soon as we get you off the streets. I'm certain he'll be able to set your nose back to rights with one good twist."

Murray stopped dabbing at his face with the handkerchief, his eyes widening at the sight of the blood now marking the fabric, and then, without a word, he keeled forward, Reginald grabbing hold of him before he hit the ground.

Chapter 14

By the time Beatrix returned with Murray's carriage, Murray was stirring somewhat feebly, muttering something about how he was certain to come down with some deadly illness after Lena's dog had been licking his bleeding face.

Reginald turned to Lena. "It might be for the best if you were to take your leave before Murray becomes fully conscious. If you've neglected to notice, your dogs are now earnestly sniffing him, and I don't think it will help the situation if they decide he's a prime piece of beef because, well, that might ruin the poor man's nerves forever."

Thankfully, Lena was only too happy to oblige. With a nod to Nigel, who released a rather resigned breath before he returned Lena's nod, she sailed off toward her red carriage, her pack of dogs trailing after her, although rather reluctantly. After sending Poppy a smile, Nigel swung himself up on his horse and followed Lena's carriage down Broadway.

"She's rather odd, isn't she?" Beatrix remarked, nodding at Lena's departing carriage.

"A bit, and her dogs are a menace—not that I think she realizes that," Poppy said, wincing when she noticed a large lump on Murray's head. "This doesn't look good."

Reginald squatted down next to Murray, who was finally open-ing his eyes. "Do you think you'll be able to get to your feet?" he asked him.

"I can try," Murray said weakly.

The second he stood, it became clear he was not going to be able to make it into the carriage on his own, not when his eyes suddenly rolled back in his head and he fainted dead away.

Catching him again before he hit the ground, Reginald hauled him over his shoulder, striding to the carriage Beatrix had found and got him inside as gently as he could.

"Watch his head," Poppy urged, wincing when Murray's head conked against the seat.

"If you think you'll do a better job, then by all means, have at it," Reginald shot back. "But he's a dead weight and even though he's slender, it's tricky to maneuver him about."

"No need to turn grouchy."

"I thought you considered me more along the lines of brooding."

"Brooding, grouchy, highly irritable, they're really all the same, aren't they?"

Having nothing of worth to say to that, Reginald got Murray on the seat, turned, and helped Poppy into the carriage, then nod-ded to Beatrix who told him she'd follow them back to the Van Rensselaer residence on Hazel.

"You don't want to ride in the carriage?" Reginald asked, look-ing up at the large snowflakes now falling.

Beatrix shuddered. "There's every chance if Murray comes to that he'll toss up his accounts, so no. I'll ride Hazel back, thank you very much."

"I thought Murray decided he needed to figure out how to get Hazel to answer to Clara, which means you're probably not help-ing the situation by referring to his horse by her original name."

Beatrix grinned. "Since the human Hazel, as in Mrs. Middleton, decided she never wanted to see this horse again, I purchased it from her and can now use the name my new horse is accustomed to, that being Hazel."

"That'll make you one of Mrs. Middleton's favorite ladies of the Season."

"Won't it, though?" After Reginald gave her a hand up into a side saddle that Beatrix sat on with ease, Beatrix kneed Hazel into motion, stopped beside the horse he'd purchased for Poppy, snagged the reins, then began riding down the street, moving at a snail's pace because Poppy's new horse seemed to lack the energy to move faster.

Climbing into the carriage, Reginald settled himself on the seat beside Poppy, then turned his attention to Murray as the carriage jolted into motion.

"How are we going to explain this to your grandmother?" he asked.

"We'll tell her the truth, of course, although she might not believe us because it's a rather outlandish tale."

"You do realize she might terminate the lessons she asked me to give you?"

"Which I'm going to believe you'll see as a relief, since it does seem as if you are going to be in demand by quite a few society ladies soon, all of whom are most assuredly going to beg you to take them on."

A sliver of disgruntlement pricked at him. That Poppy didn't seem overly distressed by the idea their lessons might soon come to an end spoke volumes, and in all honesty, it rankled, while also leaving him feeling slightly morose because, even with the outlandish adventures they'd shared of late, he enjoyed being in her company.

Life was never dull whenever he was with Poppy.

"Viola won't fire you, though, not if I tell her I long to continue our lessons and that I believe I'm certain to achieve diamond of the first water status if you continue instructing me."

"You don't want to become a diamond of the first water," he pointed out.

"True, but Viola wants me to." She smiled. "Then there's the idea that you and I have become friends, even with you annoying me when you point out all of my inadequacies, and I'd miss spending time with you."

His spirits immediately began to lift, which was telling in and of itself, but before he could consider the matter further, Murray began to stir. Then, to Reginald's dismay, the man began to moan. Realizing the moaning was certain to lead to something else, Reginald called for the driver to stop the carriage, and a few seconds later, Murray was outside on the street, tossing up his accounts.

By the time they finally reached the Van Rensselaer residence, they'd been forced to stop the carriage an additional three times, and Murray was an alarming shade of white beneath the blood and bruises all over his face.

As Reginald all but carried Murray into the house, stumbling past Viola, who'd greeted them at the door looking completely horrified, he sent a smile of thanks to the Van Rensselaer butler, Mr. Parsons, who immediately came to his assistance. Together, the two men managed to get Murray up one flight of stairs and into a guest bedchamber.

"I've sent for a physician," Poppy said, stopping just inside the door. "What else can I do to help?"

"I think we should get Murray out of these clothes because they're covered in blood," Reginald said. "Since you clearly can't help with that, if you could find something for him to wear, I'm sure he'd appreciate it."

"I *would* appreciate it," Murray muttered.

With the help of Mr. Parsons, Reginald soon had Murray stripped of his clothing, sponged off, then dressed in a nightshirt Poppy had left outside the door. The physician arrived soon after that, but when he went about setting Murray's nose to rights with one good twist, Murray fainted dead away again, and stayed that way for a good thirty minutes.

Leaving Mr. Parsons to watch over Murray after the physician took his leave, Reginald made his way down to the first floor. The sounds of a heated argument led him straight to the library.

Stepping into the room, he found Poppy glaring at Viola, Viola glaring back at her granddaughter, and Beatrix calmly sipping a cup of tea.

"Should I return later?" he asked.

"Don't be a coward, Mr. Blackburn. Of course you shouldn't return later. I have much to say to you, so do stop lingering by the door and join us," Viola barked.

Striding across the room, he took a seat in a chair next to Poppy, turned his attention to Viola, then refused the most unusual urge to fidget as she considered him for a very long, very silent, moment.

"I'm waiting," she finally said.

Reginald blinked. "Should I take that to mean you're waiting for me to explain what happened today?"

"Don't toy with me, Mr. Blackburn. I'm not in an accommodating frame of mind."

"Understandable, since I'm certain you were alarmed when we arrived in such a deplorable state, but I must say that the situation we experienced today was completely unexpected and—"

"You were only supposed to be taking Poppy out for tea," Viola interrupted. "And because you know she has the unfortunate propensity for landing herself into mischief, how is it possible you let her out of your sight long enough to become engaged in an altercation with a deliveryman, and then get accosted by members of the criminal persuasion?"

"Well, as to that, you see—"

"I thought you were a gentleman who'd be up for the task of managing her mischief, but clearly, I was mistaken about that. You may consider yourself dismissed from your position as Poppy's decorum instructor."

"Honestly, Grandmother, that's enough," Poppy said, rising from her chair, her color high and her blue eyes blazing. "Reginald is not to blame for what happened today, nor has he ever agreed to manage any mischief I might get into, at least not to my knowledge." She shot him a smile, which faded when she returned her attention to her grandmother. "In all fairness to Reginald, he's been a most diligent instructor, even with me *not* being as diligent with learning the lessons he's been attempting to give me." She drew in a breath and released it. "However, what with how he's been so gallant coming to my rescue time after time, I feel I owe it to him to now put my heart into his lessons, and in the process, I'm confident I will become that diamond of the first water of which you seem so keen for me to become. But I'll only attempt that feat if you apologize to him."

Viola drew herself up, considered Poppy for a long moment, and then turned to Reginald. "My apologies, Mr. Blackburn."

Reginald managed a nod, even though he was so taken aback by Viola's unexpected apology that he was tempted to allow his mouth to gape open. "Apology accepted."

Viola inclined her head and looked to Poppy. "And with that settled, I'd now like your word that not only will you strive to become proficient with all matters of proper behavior, you'll also strive to refrain from becoming embroiled in additional ridiculous situations."

Poppy's brows drew together. "You have my word that I'll do my best to become proficient with proper behavior. However, before I agree about the ridiculous situation business, not that I'm convinced there's really anything I can do to prevent that, I need you to agree to allow me to invite gentlemen to the tea we're hosting a week from now."

"Gentlemen are never invited to tea, and I'm not certain you're in a position to negotiate terms with me in the first place."

Poppy waved that aside. "Of course I am, since I'm apparently the one responsible for landing in ridiculous situations and am the only one capable of trying to avoid them. As for the tea business, I believe it's an original idea, and one that could very well launch me into becoming a rousing societal success."

"How so?"

"Reginald has agreed to get Lord Lonsdale to attend, which will certainly have our tea becoming one of *the* events of the Season."

"Lord Lonsdale's presence would most assuredly guarantee that."

Turning toward the door, Reginald frowned as Murray wobbled his way into the room, looking rather pathetic since the physician had stuffed wads of cotton up his nose to staunch the bleeding. His eyes were alarming shades of purple and black, as well as being swollen, and what little unmarked skin that could be seen on his face was palest white.

Striding across the room to take Murray's arm, Reginald helped him into the nearest chair, his frown turning into a small smile when he realized Murray was wearing a pink dressing gown, one that had frills around the neckline.

"Are you wearing my dressing gown?" Viola asked, her hand raised to her throat as she moved closer to Murray and looked him up and down.

"I'm afraid I might be, Mrs. Van Rensselaer," Murray said. "Mr. Parsons fetched me one of his dressing gowns, but since it was far too long, he then returned with this. I didn't know it was yours, though, but do know that I'll have it properly laundered before I return it to you."

"Perhaps you should have considered staying in bed, which would have rendered your need of a dressing gown unnecessary."

"I considered that, but it would have hardly been right for me to stay in bed when I knew you were probably putting Poppy, Beatrix, and Reginald through the wringer."

Viola blinked, then blinked again. "That was very, well, noble of you, Murray." Her lips curved the slightest bit. "Pink suits you, dear. You may consider the dressing gown yours."

With that, Viola glided across the room, sank into a lovely chair of palest blue that matched the afternoon gown she was wearing, and folded her hands demurely in her lap, apparently having nothing else to say.

Silence descended over the library until Beatrix spoke. "I left your new horse out in the carriage house, Poppy. I also took the liberty of instructing the stable hands to feed, water, and brush him."

Viola sat forward. "You have a new horse?"

"Reginald bought the horse that was being abused for me."

"I thought you told me that horse was ancient and on its last legs. Why would you want it?"

"Because it deserves a better life than what it has evidently had thus far."

"And I had a good look at its teeth," Beatrix added. "If you ask me, that horse isn't more than four or five years old, and might, with some proper care, make someone a lovely companion."

She exchanged a look with Poppy before they both turned toward Murray, who immediately seemed to shrink against the chair he was sitting in.

"If memory serves me correctly," Murray began, "and I cannot be certain about that after taking what I was told were a few blows to my head, I was under the impression that horse was somewhat intimidating and stood at least sixteen hands tall."

"He's not intimidating in the least, even with him being sixteen hands tall, because he's possessed of a very gentle nature," Beatrix argued.

"But I already have a horse."

Beatrix shook her head. "I'm afraid you don't because I bought Hazel from your mother this morning after she and I had a bit of a row."

"So you really *did* have a row with my mother?"

Beatrix winced. "I'm afraid so, and it culminated with her stating she never wanted to see your horse, an unwelcome namesake in her opinion, again." Beatrix smiled. "Seeing that as a prime opportunity to procure a horse I wanted for myself, although I realize that does not speak overly well of me, I offered to buy her, and your mother didn't hesitate to sell. That means you *do* need a horse, and I'm convinced the horse now in the carriage house will be perfect for you, once we have an opportunity to train him up some."

Murray frowned. "He's not trained?"

Beatrix shrugged. "Hard to say at this point. But once you're feeling better, you can come with Poppy and me to Jerome Park.

That's where I usually take my horses when I need to put them through their paces."

"But you bought that horse for Poppy," Murray said, sending Reginald a look of panic mixed with a bit of hope.

"That I did," Reginald began, "but since that horse is now Poppy's, it's not up to me to tell her what to do with it."

"Aren't you going to be disappointed if she gives me her horse?"

Reginald turned to Poppy. "Are you going to regret parting ways with this horse?"

"I have numerous horses I call my own back in Pennsylvania," she said. "And while I wouldn't be opposed to keeping him if Murray doesn't want him, I think this particular horse might be perfect for Murray."

"And if you're feeling guilty about the matter, Murray," Beatrix added, "you could always pay Reginald the amount he paid for the horse, which would alleviate all of that guilt and plump up Reginald's billfold again."

Even though Reginald could easily afford the cost of the horse and wasn't bothered in the least that Poppy wanted to give it to Murray, he forced himself to nod at Murray after he proclaimed he'd happily pay the cost of the horse if he decided they'd be well suited.

"Wonderful," Poppy said, smiling all around. "And with that settled, perhaps we should—"

Viola cleared her throat, interrupting whatever Poppy had been saying, as she turned a stern eye Reginald's way. "You must know that buying a lady a horse is an action that will have the gossips coming out in droves if it becomes known. Those gossips will certainly turn your gesture into something I need you to reassure me it wasn't."

Reginald frowned. "I'm not sure what you're getting at, Mrs. Van Rensselaer."

"The purchase of a horse for a lady is a sure sign a gentleman is intent on a courtship with that lady."

Silence was swift as everyone turned their undivided attention Reginald's way.

The collar on his shirt suddenly felt remarkably snug. He would have liked to believe that unusual occurrence was a direct result of being the object of such scrutiny, but he'd never been a gentleman uncomfortable with attention before.

That left him with the disturbing conclusion that his feeling of strangulation was a direct result of the thought that was even now whirling around his mind.

While the notion of courtship had not prompted him to buy the horse for Poppy, something of a more troubling nature most certainly had.

He'd been moved by the sight of Poppy's distress when she'd been standing next to the abused horse, and he'd been powerless against the tears in her eyes. His only goal at that time had been to soothe her anguish, and he'd known without a doubt that buying the horse for her would do exactly that.

He was not a gentleman, though, who was given to impulsive acts, and that the lady who'd brought about such an unusual occurrence was Poppy Garrison, well, it was a bit of an alarming revelation.

She was the most irritating lady he'd ever known, as well as being completely unpredictable. She was also woefully negligent in maintaining a sense of proper decorum. However, even with all her deficiencies, she'd somehow wormed her way under his very proper British skin, and . . . she'd begun to matter to him.

Drawing in a much-needed breath of air, while reminding himself yet again that the last lady he should ever allow to matter to him was an American, and one who didn't seem overly impressed with anything having to do with British aristocracy, Reginald struggled to come up with some reasonable reply to Viola's demand, stunned when not a single thing came to mind.

Thankfully, the Van Rensselaer cook took that moment to bustle into the room, bearing a tray of raw meat. Stopping directly in front of him, and without even a by-your-leave, she picked up a slab of meat, slapped it over his eye, and as blessed coolness immediately seeped through an eye that was almost swollen shut, she marched her way over to Murray. After slapping two pieces of meat over Murray's eyes, rendering that man blind, she marched out of the room again.

"Should I be worried that I'm soon to come down with an infection from having uncooked meat on my face?" Murray asked to no one in particular.

"What in the world are they trying to do to you?" someone suddenly demanded from the doorway right as Mr. Parsons rushed into the room, pulling down a waistcoat that had begun to lift because of the rushing.

"Mrs. John Middleton has come to call," Mr. Parsons announced, sending Viola a look of apology before he spun smartly around and quit the room as Mrs. Middleton advanced across the Aubusson carpet, not stopping until she reached her son.

Murray, who'd been holding the beef over his eyes with both hands, stripped off one filet, blinking owlishly at his mother who was bristling with indignation.

"Mother, what are you doing here?"

Mrs. Middleton's indignation increased. "What am I doing here?" she all but shrieked. "Rumors are swirling around town about the unfortunate trouble you've recently experienced, rumors I was quite certain were nothing more than fabricated bits of mischief, but apparently, they were nothing less than the truth." She leaned over and peered at Murray's face, straightening as all the color leached from her cheeks. "What happened to your face, and why do you have cotton shoved up your nose?"

"It was bleeding after the physician reset it." The corners of Murray's lips twitched. "I broke it, you see, after I, along with Reginald and Beatrix, rushed to save Poppy from a band of criminals intent on stealing her reticule."

Mrs. Middleton raised a hand to her chest. "You intentionally threw yourself into a band of criminals?"

Murray slapped the filet over his eye again. "'Course I did. As a gentleman, could you expect me to do anything less?"

For a second, Mrs. Middleton didn't say a thing, but then she rounded on Viola, who seemed completely unfazed about having an irate woman in her drawing room, given the cool nod she sent to Murray's mother.

"I'm holding you and your granddaughter responsible for my son's condition, Viola, as well as responsible for whatever he's wearing, which appears to be a lady's dressing gown."

Viola drew herself up. "While I will accept responsibility for the dressing gown, since it is mine, even if I didn't know he was going to be wearing it, I cannot accept responsibility for Murray's condition. I was not present when he was injured, but I do believe you're missing the greater point here. Murray, I'm pleased to say, rose to my granddaughter's defense in what I can only imagine was a magnificent fashion, and at great peril to his person. That, my dear, suggests you raised him right. So instead of berating him, or anyone else for that matter, you should be thankful you can claim a chivalrous gentleman as your son."

Color began returning to Mrs. Middleton's face. She opened her mouth, closed it a second later, then sent Viola the barest hint of a nod before she turned back to Murray.

"It *was* well done of you, darling, to save Miss Garrison, but to spare you from suffering additional mayhem in the future, I'm now going to have to insist you discontinue your association with her. I also must insist you take that meat off your face because I need to get you home and seen by our physician straight away."

Murray peered at his mother after he lifted one of the filets. "Poppy is my friend, and I have no intention of discontinuing my association with her. Furthermore," he continued as Mrs. Middleton seemed to swell on the spot, "I'm not going home. If you've forgotten, you tossed me out on my ear."

"That was done in the heat of the moment, brought about because you were being obstinate, a new trait of yours that I'm going to demand you immediately discontinue. You must know I was never serious about tossing you out of the house. And now, with that settled, come along. It's time you and I went home."

Murray shook his head. "I think not, Mother. It's past time I lived on my own, and just so you won't be worried I've nowhere to go, I've decided to take up residence at the recently completed Osborne flats. I'll send my direction around to you after I get settled."

That declaration was all it took for Mrs. Middleton to completely lose her composure. As she began railing at Murray, who merely returned the filet to his eye and seemed to go deaf as well as blind, Reginald found himself at a complete loss of what to do next.

He'd never been privy to such a spectacular display of dramatics before. Turning his attention to Poppy to see how she was reacting, he found her, along with Beatrix, calmly sitting on the settee, both ladies swiveling their attention to Murray, then his mother, then back to Murray again, quite as if they were watching a tennis match and not an ever-escalating argument.

"I must say this isn't exactly the homecoming I was expecting," a voice suddenly boomed over the din.

Reginald turned to the door and found a gentleman standing there—a gentleman who looked vaguely familiar.

As he tried to place the man, Poppy jumped up from the settee and bolted across the room, sidestepping Mrs. Middleton, who'd stopped railing at Murray and was gaping at the man in the doorway.

"Grandfather!" Poppy exclaimed before being scooped up into an enthusiastic hug by a man who was apparently Mr. George Van Rensselaer—Poppy's grandfather, Viola's husband, and a man Reginald now distinctly remembered seeing at a business meeting he'd attended with his father.

Unfortunately, Mr. Van Rensselaer was a man who, if he recognized Reginald, would know he was no mere traveling companion, but rather the second son of one of the most influential dukes in Britain.

CHAPTER 15

"I see you've inherited your mother's flower-arranging abilities."

Wincing when a thorn pierced her finger, Poppy looked up from the disaster she was creating and smiled as her grandfather moseyed into what her grandmother referred to as the sunroom.

It was an appropriate name for the room, what with the floor-to-ceiling windows that encompassed two complete walls. And even though the day outside was gloomy and marked with fitful spurts of snow, the sunroom was cozy, the fire in the fireplace crackling merrily away, and any chill that seeped through the windows kept at bay because of the forced heat her grandparents' house enjoyed.

"I remember watching Elizabeth in this very room, although she was usually not smiling when she attempted to create her floral arrangements." George's lips curved. "She deliberately paired the most unlikely of flowers together, often annoying your grandmother by choosing colors that did not complement each other."

"If Mother deliberately went out of her way to annoy Grandmother with her flower arrangements, I'm surprised Grandmother didn't discontinue asking my mother to arrange flowers in the first place."

"One would have thought that to be a logical solution, but your grandmother is a stubborn woman and wasn't one to pick her battles, preferring to fight daily with Elizabeth over the most absurd topics."

"Which does explain why they've been mostly estranged for so many years." Poppy picked up another rose and began stripping the thorns from the stem, regretting that she hadn't chosen a less hostile flower to use for all the arrangements Viola wanted her to assemble for the next day's tea.

Sticking the rose in the vase and grimacing when she realized she'd cut it at least five inches too short, Poppy reached for another flower, stilling when her grandfather stepped beside her.

"How about you go take a seat by the fire and let me do this," he surprised her by saying.

"You know how to arrange flowers?"

"When your grandmother and I were first courting, we used to spend hours scouring the flower vendors in the city, looking for the perfect blooms. We'd then repair to her parents' house, and under the watchful eye of Viola's chaperone, we'd spend the afternoon arranging each flower exactly so."

Poppy moved to a chair next to the fireplace and sat down. "It's difficult to imagine you and Grandmother courting or picking out flowers because—"

"We don't strike you as romantic types?" George finished for her as he expertly stripped the rose he was holding of its thorns, eyed the stem, then snipped the stem two inches before he placed it into a crystal vase.

Poppy's lips curved. "I can't say 'romantic' is what first springs to mind when I think of you or Grandmother, but were you truly possessed of a romantic nature back in the day?"

"I'm not ancient, Poppy. I'm certain I could still be a romantic type if I set my mind to it."

"And how do you think Grandmother would respond if you set your mind to romance?"

George snipped the stem off another rose. "She could very well conclude I've taken leave of my senses. But speaking of your grandmother, where is she? Has she vacated the premises to avoid the numerous callers who've stopped by today, anxious to see if you've experienced any new adventures?"

Since Poppy had resolved to comport herself as a diamond in the making, she'd not had a single adventure over the five days that had passed since the incident on Broadway. It was a dreary way to spend her time, but since she had made a promise to her grandmother, she'd been trying to embrace the role of true lady, even though she found the activities she was limited to relatively dull.

Afternoon calls had been a must and then there'd been a few dinners and small balls where she'd found herself participating in conversations about the weather and the latest fashions. She'd been tempted to enter into a conversation about suffragists that Beatrix had started at a dinner held by Mrs. Stuyvesant Fish but refused to give in after the society matron she'd been standing beside had proclaimed the discussion inappropriate.

The only enjoyment she'd had of late was the time devoted to her lessons with Reginald. He'd suggested she share her lessons with the Leggett sisters since he did seem to be in much demand. And because Maisie and Helene's mother was still a little leery about Reginald's abilities, they'd decided to hold the lessons at the Leggett residence, something Reginald seemed relieved about, although she had no idea why that was.

He'd also made himself scarce before and after those lessons. And even though she understood he had limited time these days, what with how many young ladies were clamoring for his services, she found herself somewhat put out over his lack of attention, and . . . she missed his company.

Her grandfather suddenly cleared his throat, recalling Poppy back to the question he'd asked her.

"Forgive me, Grandfather. I seem to have gotten lost in thought. As for Grandmother, she has not gone out. She's in the attic with Murray."

"Ah, Murray, now there's an interesting gentleman. But what could Viola and Murray possibly be doing in the attic?"

"Grandmother converted the attic into an art studio some years ago and spends almost all of her spare time up there painting."

"Viola created an art studio?"

"You *do* know that she enjoys painting, don't you?"

George nodded as he stripped off a few more thorns. "She's done that since I've known her, but I suppose I never considered that she might enjoy it. I merely thought she pursued painting because it's what ladies do." He placed the thorn-free rose into a vase and picked up another one. "She and your mother were always at odds over that. Elizabeth, as I'm sure you're aware, is horrid with a paintbrush, although your grandmother was of the belief that Elizabeth was deliberately trying to sabotage any artistic endeavor as a way to annoy her."

"Mother doesn't need to deliberately sabotage her art. She simply possesses no talent for it." Poppy smiled. "I seem to have inherited that lack of talent from my mother as well, which is why I was banished from the attic and sent to arrange flowers. Grandmother was becoming frustrated with my efforts with oil and canvas, but she certainly is enjoying her time with Murray as they paint."

"Murray's a talented painter?"

"Indeed. When I left them, he was showing Grandmother how to capture a ray of sun just so. I must say she seems to have changed her opinion about him." Poppy lowered her voice. "She warned me a while ago to keep my distance from him because he's not considered fashionable in the inner circles of society. Now, however, she's invited him to stay here until he secures himself new premises and seems to be enjoying his company."

George abandoned the flowers, settling himself into a chair across from Poppy a moment later. "I imagine you've been wondering why Viola offered Murray such unexpected hospitality."

Poppy smiled. "I can't deny that, although I'm almost convinced she did so to annoy Mrs. Middleton."

George returned the smile. "While Viola is certainly capable of deliberately annoying a person, I'm relatively certain, in this case, that she offered Murray a place to stay to alleviate the anxiety Hazel was most assuredly experiencing after Murray refused to return home with her. You have to admit that Murray was looking beyond pathetic a few days ago, which certainly must have been of grave concern to his mother."

George's eyes began to twinkle. "I know you've probably not seen much in the way of compassion from your grandmother, dear, but deep down—*very* deep down—Viola is a good woman. She's merely a victim of her own strict and unemotional upbringing, but before I continue on with that tale, allow me to take the liberty of ringing for coffee and a few treats." George got up from his chair and moved to where an annunciator was attached to the wall. Pushing a knob that would alert the kitchen that service was required in the sunroom, George was just settling back to his seat when Mr. Parsons walked into the room.

"Ah, Mr. Parsons, my granddaughter and I would like a pot of coffee, along with some small cakes, if Mrs. Hardie has any of those available."

Mr. Parsons inclined his head. "Very well, Mr. Van Rensselaer." He turned to Poppy. "Would you like me to include a few of those pastries you baked this morning?" His lips curved. "I must say I enjoyed them immensely, although I do believe I may have insulted Mrs. Hardie by stating that I thought the pastries you made surpassed hers."

Poppy fought a grin. "That was not well done of you, Mr. Parsons. Mrs. Hardie is a most excellent cook, but you must know that she's a sensitive sort. I fear you may find yourself regretting making such a statement when you sit down to your dinner this evening."

"You might be correct about that." Mr. Parsons suddenly smiled. "Or Mrs. Hardie might find herself unable to resist rising to the challenge of besting your recipes, which could very well see the kitchen producing an abundance of sumptuous treats." With that, Mr. Parsons executed a perfect bow, turned on his heel, and walked out of the room, leaving Poppy alone with George, who was regarding her closely.

"You bake?"

Poppy nodded. "I do, and unlike my less-than-stellar painting and flower-arranging abilities, I'm rather proficient in the kitchen."

"Does Viola know you bake?"

"She does, but she doesn't really approve, which is exactly why I was in the kitchen this morning at the unheard of hour of five." She smiled. "Grandmother does not step foot out of her bedchamber until nine, so if I find myself with a hankering to stick my hands in some dough, I have to get up well before that."

George frowned. "Does Elizabeth bake?"

"Indeed, but don't start taking yourself to task for not knowing that. Mother didn't discover a love for the kitchen until after she married my father."

"It is regrettable, though, that I know so little about my own daughter."

"It's difficult to know a person when you only see them for a few days every year, and from what I remember, there were many times when you weren't in New York when Mother came for her yearly visit."

"Another regret of mine." George looked up as Mr. Parsons walked through the door again, bearing a tray with a silver coffeepot and a plate stacked high with treats.

After Mr. Parsons poured the coffee and handed Poppy and her grandfather a small plate of pastries, he inclined his head and quit the room.

As her grandfather took his first bite of pastry, Poppy watched him closely, grinning when he released a groan and proclaimed it the best pastry he'd ever tasted.

"Which is exactly what I'd expect a grandfather to say to his granddaughter," she returned before she picked up her cup.

"I'm afraid I've not been much of a grandfather to you, dear," George said, picking up his own cup. "Your grandmother and I have failed your entire family by allowing hurts from the past to keep us apart for so long."

"I'm beginning to think some of that may have been a direct result of that upbringing you mentioned Grandmother had."

George nodded. "Viola's mother, Martha Rhinelander, God rest her soul, was a staunch knickerbocker, believing it was a lady's place to be a picture of decorum. She raised Viola in a household that put great emphasis on abiding by all the rules." George took another sip of his coffee. "After Viola made her debut, her mother soon set her sights on me. I was an acceptable gentleman because my family was also of the knickerbocker set, although Viola's mother was concerned that I showed an interest in industry."

"Were members of the knickerbocker set not expected to work back in those days?"

"Most of the oldest knickerbocker families earned their fortunes through real estate, so no, it was somewhat scandalous that I wanted to become involved with railroads, shipping, and investments." He smiled. "My family encouraged me to court Viola because they too were somewhat scandalized by my interest in industry. They knew that a proper lady like Viola would make it possible for me to pursue my interests while also maintaining a presence within society."

"That sounds more like a business arrangement than a romantic courtship."

George nodded. "To a certain extent it was, but there was something about Viola that I found fascinating. Even though she was always dressed to perfection, abided by all the social rules, and never had so much as a hair out of place, she had this glimmer in her eyes that suggested she wanted to break free of the societal bonds that kept her from seizing life with zest. I'm afraid, though, after we married, that glimmer disappeared, and I must take some of the blame for that."

"What happened?"

"I was consumed with matters of business and increasing my fortune. That had me leaving Viola far too frequently, and while I was gone, she turned into a version of her mother, minding our home and attending society events. After Elizabeth came along, Viola threw herself into the task of making certain Elizabeth would grow up to become a . . . what is that term everyone uses for the crème of society?"

"A diamond of the first water?"

"That's it, although between the two of us, I've always found that term to be rather confusing."

Poppy grinned. "I feel the same way, but because Grandmother seems to have her heart set on me becoming one of those diamonds, I've decided to at least attempt to achieve that status."

George frowned. "You should only attempt that if it's something you really want."

"It won't kill me to try, Grandfather, and my abiding by the rules this week certainly seems to have lifted Grandmother's spirits."

"But if it begins to feel like that attempt is killing you, you'll need to abandon it." George blew out a breath. "Viola has always clung to unrealistic expectations, especially since she was raised to believe that it was her job as a mother to produce a daughter who'd be nothing less than sheer perfection. When Elizabeth balked, and then ran away with your father, Viola felt she'd failed in what she apparently believed was her life's ambition, and has now, I'm afraid, decided that her redemption lies with you."

Poppy took a sip of her coffee. "Did my mother spend all her time balking at the rules?"

George's eyes crinkled at the corners. "Elizabeth was a terror before she could even walk. And then, after she learned to walk, she decided running was far better, no matter that Viola tried her very best to convince Elizabeth that a lady never moves faster than a glide." He suddenly sobered. "They used to argue all the time when Elizabeth didn't adhere to the rules, and I, being a typical father, found it much easier to make myself scarce than step between them." He gave a shake of his head. "Failure at its finest. Elizabeth needed someone to speak up on her behalf, but I couldn't be bothered."

"There are many fathers who have no idea what to do with daughters."

"True, but because Viola and I were never blessed with any additional children, I should have made a greater attempt to have an impact in my only child's life." He caught her eye over the rim of the cup. "I've decided to remedy that."

"How?"

"No idea, but I figured a good first step was to return to New York. I'm going to make certain your grandmother doesn't decide to try and coerce you into one of those nonsensical aristocratic marriages that seem to be all the fashion these days."

"You know that's what she has in mind for me?"

"She sent me a letter after you agreed to a Season, and from that letter, I concluded she had some lofty goals for you." He tapped a finger against the arm of the chair. "I'm not keen to sell you off for a title, unless, of course, you've decided you're keen on that Lord Lonsdale, a gentleman your grandmother keeps talking about."

"Grandmother may have her sights on Lord Lonsdale, but considering that the gentleman has not bothered to seek me out nor do more than exchange the expected pleasantries with me when I encounter him at numerous society events, I'm afraid she's doomed for disappointment."

George frowned. "Unless spending limited time with you is his peculiar version of courtship."

"It's not impressing me if that's the case."

"Why would Reginald Blackburn continue on with your lessons if Lord Lonsdale doesn't have an interest in you?"

"I would imagine he's doing so because he sees it as a challenge laid down by Grandmother." Poppy smiled. "Not that I know him all that well, but Reginald doesn't seem to be the type of gentleman who is accustomed to failing, and he seems most determined to win this challenge by turning me from a diamond in the rough into a diamond of the first water."

"I've heard Reginald has come to your rescue more than a few times. That speaks highly of the man, and I must admit that I'm somewhat disappointed he's not come around since that first time I met him. Wouldn't mind getting to know him better since every grandfather appreciates a man who doesn't balk at rescuing a granddaughter from one disaster after another."

"I don't experience that many disasters."

"So far this season you've gotten your grandmother's tiara stuck on poor Murray's sleeve, tumbled over a balcony, ended up in a lake

. . . and, well, I could go on. With that said, do you find Reginald to be an intriguing gentleman?"

Uncomfortable with the direction the conversation seemed to be heading, Poppy got up from her chair and moved back to the flowers, picking up a rose and immediately pricking her finger on a thorn. Setting it aside, she frowned. "You're not trying your hand at matchmaking at the moment, are you?"

"Of course I am. You're my granddaughter, and you're obviously in need of some help in the romance department." He ignored the arch of a brow she sent him. "I have to admit I've been wondering if you're somewhat fond of Reginald, given how much you've mentioned him in conversation over the past few days."

She picked up another rose, needing a distraction because the truth of the matter was . . . she *was* rather fond of Reginald.

There was something undeniably appealing about a gentleman who always seemed to be available whenever she found herself in a spot of trouble.

"Even if that were true," she finally settled on saying, "Grandmother would never speak to me again if I set my sights on a man who doesn't seem to have much of an established place in the world. If you'll recall, she cut Mother off without a dime after Mother ran off with my father, and Father was in the process of creating a very well-respected and lucrative horse business."

George frowned. "Did Reginald tell you he doesn't have an established place in the world?"

"Not in so many words, but he came to New York as Lord Lonsdale's traveling companion, which does seem to suggest he's not a man of business. And I know he's not a man of property because he told me he doesn't own his own estate."

"Hmm . . ." was all George said to that.

"What does that mean?"

He shrugged. "Nothing at all, my dear. But returning to the matter of your mother and her estrangement from me and your grandmother, do know that Elizabeth was never cut off from her funds. Rather, she refused to accept the trust I created for her. That right there is why I was stunned to discover she and Harold took out a loan to expand Garrison Farms when there was absolutely no need for her to do so."

"Mother wouldn't have wanted to feel indebted to either you or Grandmother."

"Which is unfortunate because she'll end up with most of my money eventually. I didn't spend so many years working to build up my fortune only to turn all of it over to charities."

"Charities are noble causes."

"True, and I will leave some of my fortune to charities, but the rest will go to Elizabeth as well as you and your brothers." George smiled. "Have I mentioned that, along with my return to New York, I've decided to cut back on the amount of time I spend on business matters?"

Poppy blinked. "I thought you got a great deal of enjoyment out of matters of business."

"Oh, I do—or rather, I thought I did. But I've recently realized pursuing one business deal after another has not provided me anything of true worth over the years."

George looked out the window where snow was falling in earnest, drew in a deep breath, then returned his attention to Poppy. "I had a bit of a revelation about four months back when I was out west, checking on a new railroad venture." George shifted in the chair. "You see, the terms of the deal I'd thought I'd arranged to my satisfaction suddenly changed, and I allowed my temper to get the best of me. While in that temper, I suffered what the doctors called an apoplectic fit. Everyone, even the doctors, felt I didn't have much longer to live, so a traveling pastor named Reverend Wilbur Goodall was summoned, rarely leaving my side as I lingered on."

"You almost died?"

"I did, but to everyone's surprise, I began to recover, but I didn't have the strength to get out of bed, which is how it came to be that I was able to have long, in-depth conversations with Reverend Goodall." George shook his head. "Now I've never been what one would call a religious man, although I have always attended church when the opportunity presented itself. Truth be told, I've never faced any trials that had me turning to God as so many seem to do when they're experiencing difficulties. I was content to believe that God was pleased with the way I was living my life since I've been able to do so well financially. I've now come to believe, after speaking so much with Reverend Goodall, that what I thought was a fulfilling life was really nothing of the sort.

"Reverend Goodall, you see, was a man with no materialistic wealth, but he was completely content with the life he believed God carved out for him, and that right there was a bit of an eye-opener for me." George's gaze locked with Poppy's. "When you're facing death, my dear, you really do contemplate how you've lived your life, and I'm afraid to say that my life has been consumed with matters that are unimportant. How much money I've amassed or how many deals I've struck will not matter in the end. Family matters. Friends matter. Embracing a relationship with God matters. And it's past time I rectify that."

"What do you mean . . . when you were facing death?"

In the blink of an eye, Viola was standing directly in front of George, looking furious while Murray lurked in the doorway.

"Well?" Viola demanded when George simply gazed back at her, as if he had no idea where to begin to explain the whole facing death situation, something he clearly had yet to discuss with his wife.

Poppy rose to her feet. "I think this is where I excuse myself and take Murray for a bit of fresh air. I've been meaning to see how he handles Wilbur, his new horse."

Ignoring the look of panic now on Murray's face, she walked to Viola's side and gave her grandmother a quick kiss on the cheek. Stepping back as Viola began looking flustered, Poppy smiled. "While I would be furious as well for being left in the dark, Grandmother, I don't believe it'll do Grandfather any good to become engaged in a loud argument with you, given his recent ill health." She turned and headed for the door, only realizing after she and Murray quit the room that Viola had, surprisingly, not corrected her when she'd been addressed as Grandmother.

CHAPTER 16

"Did I mention that I've been given the extreme honor of participating in the Dresden China Quadrille that's to be held at the first Patriarch Ball of the year?"

Reginald pulled his attention from the snow-covered path down which he'd been steering a rented sleigh, trying to ignore the ache in his head that had started from almost the moment Miss Adele Tooker had taken a seat beside him.

"I don't believe you have mentioned that yet," he said, which had Adele launching into a description of the ball in question, barely taking a breath as she discussed the location, which was Delmonico's again, the people invited, and why she believed Mr. Ward McAllister had chosen her to participate in what was apparently a most desirable quadrille.

While she chattered on and on, his attention began to drift until another sleigh drew up beside him. Giles, his valet, sat behind the reins, his expression somewhat pained, clearly because he'd been given the challenging task of driving Miss Cynthia Roche around Central Park. Cynthia was chattering away quite like Adele was doing, apparently trying to impress Giles, who Charles had let it become known was a man he often sought counsel from—although why he'd done that was a mystery. Giles was now finding himself besieged by young ladies whenever he stepped foot out of the Fifth Avenue Hotel, which had brought a rapid end to his undercover investigation work.

Thankfully, Giles had completed background notes on almost every young heiress out this Season, and it was because of those notes that Charles had suggested the day's outing to Central Park.

Charles had always been reluctant to believe the worst of anyone. And even though Giles had turned up some less-than-appealing qualities in quite a few of the heiresses, Charles, being Charles, was convinced that ladies like Adele and Cynthia were not the spiteful shrews Giles had heard them to be, so he'd tasked Reginald and Giles with getting to know the ladies better.

"The snow's beginning to accumulate," Giles called out. "Think we should call it a day?"

"Don't be silly," Adele called back before Reginald could speak. "It's delightfully refreshing out here."

Giles pulled down the black cap that was covering his brown hair and pulled up his scarf to where it almost touched his nose. With a significant look to Reginald, one that said the information regarding Adele's spoiled nature was spot-on, he flicked the reins and set his horse into a canter, the sound of Miss Roche explaining why she was always in high demand drifting after them.

"Where was I?" Adele asked.

"Something about a quadrille?"

And with that, Adele launched into more details regarding the quadrille in question. She didn't seem to expect Reginald to participate in the conversation, something he was experiencing often of late, what with how he was now gainfully employed as an instructor for over twenty society ladies.

That rather peculiar state of affairs meant that while Charles was off enjoying one frivolity after another, Reginald was traveling from one young lady's house to the next. Some of those young ladies had even cheerfully abandoned their evenings out once they'd learned his morning and afternoon schedule was full. And while he could certainly appreciate their competitive spirit, their determination to secure a chance at becoming Lady Lonsdale was downright terrifying.

"Ah, there's Lord Lonsdale and Edith," Adele exclaimed, waving frantically as Charles drove past them in his sleigh, Miss Edith Iselin sitting beside him.

Of all the society ladies Charles had been spending time with, Edith was the only one who didn't seem to be trying to impress him. She, unlike Cynthia and Adele, had not clamored to spend the afternoon in the company of Reginald or Giles. She'd not uttered a single protest when Adele had encouraged her to partner up with Charles, and from what Reginald could tell, she'd been spending her time with Charles simply enjoying his company as they'd been sliding over the frozen grounds of Central Park.

Now that Reginald considered the matter, it was somewhat interesting exactly how often Edith was found next to Charles, and it was interesting how Charles never brought her into the conversation whenever he and Reginald met in the Fifth Avenue Hotel to discuss his situation. It was also interesting how Charles rarely asked him about Poppy, even though Reginald was still continuing on with her lessons, but had begun giving her those lessons at the same time he met with Maisie and Helene Leggett.

Self-preservation had been behind his suggestion to combine their lessons, in the hope of keeping his identity from George Van Rensselaer for as long as possible, or at least until he explained to Poppy that he possessed a rather impressive pedigree.

His reluctance to disclose all, though, rested squarely with how he thought society, as well as Poppy, was going to react to the fact he'd not been exactly truthful about who he really was. Society members would certainly feel slighted that he'd withheld his relationship to a duke from them, and they could very well take to slighting not only him but Charles as well, which could see their time spent in New York all for naught.

As for Poppy, she was going to be furious, of that he had no doubt. Frankly, her reaction to his deception was more concerning than society's reaction. That was exactly why he was putting off revealing what had turned into a very large secret, and why he was currently growing a beard to disguise his appearance, and . . .

"Dear Edith, she looks to be practically frozen, but she's such a good friend, willing to suffer the elements because I asked her to join us today."

Shaking all thoughts of Poppy and his beard aside, Reginald turned to Adele, finding her watching Charles's sleigh with a small smile on her face. That smile dimmed as she glanced Reginald's way. "I hope Edith won't be distressed to learn she's not going to be a participant in the China Quadrille."

Reginald frowned. "Why not?"

Adele gave an airy wave of her hand. "Because Mr. McAllister left it up to me to decide who was going to have a spot in the quadrille, and I decided to limit the ladies to those in whom I know Lord Lonsdale has shown a specific interest."

"But he's with Edith right now."

Adele released a titter. "Only because Lord Lonsdale wanted you and Giles to spend additional time with me and Cynthia, which does suggest he's beginning to narrow down his search for an heiress."

"And you don't believe Edith is under consideration?"

"I'm afraid not. Edith, although one of my *dearest* friends, is possessed, unfortunately, of merely passable looks. Since I'm quite convinced a countess is expected to be as lovely as her title, Lord Lonsdale is hardly likely to set his sights on her." She batted her lashes. "I didn't include her because I don't want to set her up for certain disappointment."

Reginald fought a grimace. "How very . . . magnanimous of you."

"Wasn't it though?" she chirped. "I *did* request that Poppy Garrison be chosen to dance the quadrille, though, because she's certainly drawn Lord Lonsdale's interest." She shook her head. "Granted, she's not drawn as much interest from Lord Lonsdale as some of the other ladies, since he doesn't actually seem to spend much time with her, although I have noticed him making a point to greet her whenever they encounter each other at a society event."

Trepidation was immediate.

Wishing he'd been paying more attention when Adele had been discussing the quadrille, Reginald summoned up a smile. "Tell me more about this quadrille."

Adele was only too happy to oblige. "Oh, it's a most spectacular dance, and ever since Alva Vanderbilt had it performed at her grand mansion on Fifth Avenue a few years back, everyone has been hoping it would be included again at one of the balls. I'm pleased to report that, after I convinced Mr. McAllister that the Dresden was a quadrille that demanded to be performed this season, he then convinced Mrs. Astor to choose that quadrille to open the first Patriarch Ball, held the first week of January."

Reginald frowned. "That doesn't leave much time to prepare, unless, of course, some of the young ladies you have in mind participated in the Dresden China Quadrille at Alva Vanderbilt's ball."

Adele shook her head. "I'm afraid none of the ladies I suggested to Mr. McAllister were even out in society at that time. I certainly wasn't, although my older sister, Marie, was a participant." She got a faraway look in her eyes. "I well remember watching her practice the intricate steps, and after I saw the elaborate costume she was required to wear, I then began to dream of the day I'd get an opportunity to dance the Dresden. That day, I'm delighted to say, is almost here."

Ignoring the snow that was now falling in earnest, Reginald considered Adele for a long moment. "I imagine that after you watched your sister learn this particular quadrille you then went about learning the steps as well."

"I suppose I did at that."

"And you don't think that you'll have an advantage over all the other ladies since you're already familiar with the steps?"

"I'm certain a few of the ladies I suggested, those being Miss Emily Thorne, Miss Cynthia Roche, and Miss Julia Newberry, are somewhat acquainted with the steps, but it's not the dance that draws the eye—it's the costumes we'll be expected to wear. Made of the snowiest white with flounces cascading down the back, each lady will also be wearing a towering white wig and have her face powdered. That right there is why I felt compelled to give Mr. McAllister the names of every lady who has drawn Lord Lonsdale's interest, proving that I am, indeed, a lady who believes in embracing a sense of fairness."

Deciding right then and there that he really didn't need to spend additional time in Adele's company since Giles was spot on with believing the lady unworthy of Charles's attention, Reginald gave another flick of the reins, hoping to catch up with Giles so he could suggest a change of partners.

"Oh, look, Lord Lonsdale seems to be driving his sleigh out of Central Park, and . . ."

Whatever else Adele had been about to say was lost when the sound of a gunshot split the air. Pulling the sleigh to a stop at the entrance to Central Park right as five young lads came running toward him through thick flakes of snow, Reginald watched as the lads split apart and ran separate ways right as a sleigh came racing after them, a lady at the reins.

He could not claim to be overly surprised when that lady turned out to be none other than Poppy.

"Get back here," he heard her yell as she raced past him, Murray beside her and, curiously enough, laughing heartily as he held on to the side of the sleigh for dear life.

Realizing he couldn't very well go after them with Adele sitting beside him because he couldn't put her welfare in jeopardy, he turned to her and nodded.

"Would it be too much to ask you to get out of the sleigh?"

Her mouth dropped open. "You want me to get *out* of the sleigh?"

"I do, and quickly if you please."

"Why I never . . ." was all she said to that, but before he could ask her again, Charles suddenly pulled up alongside them.

"Was that Poppy driving that sleigh?" Charles asked.

Reginald nodded. "I'm afraid it was. I need to go after her, so—"

"Adele should get into our sleigh," Edith said without hesitation, waving Adele over.

Thankfully, Adele didn't need additional convincing, and thirty seconds later, Reginald was off.

Another gunshot rang out, and because that shot sounded from the direction Poppy had been heading, Reginald turned the sleigh that way, finding it difficult to see the road, what with how the snow was doing its best to blind him.

Peering through the flakes, he pulled on the reins when he caught sight of a sleigh that was tilted at a precarious angle in a ditch, pulling on the reins harder when he saw two bodies lying motionless in the snow.

Fear raced through him as he jumped from his sleigh before it came to a complete stop, that fear turning to temper when Murray sat up and grinned at Poppy, who was now sitting up and grinning back at him.

"Have you lost your mind?" Reginald demanded, sliding his way over to her.

"You seem to ask me that rather frequently," she replied, wiping snow from her face. "But no, my senses are in fine working order, thank you very much."

"You're trying my patience."

"I don't know why. You asked me a question and I answered it. It's not like I ignored you, which, if I had, would be a reason to try your patience."

Reginald drew in a breath, stepped forward, held out his hand, then hauled Poppy to her feet. "Explain to me, if you please, why you were chasing those lads, and do not tell me you're the one responsible for those gunshots I heard, because that would be beyond the pale, even for you."

This time, instead of answering him, Poppy held out a hand to Murray, and while he was struggling to get to his feet, she began looking around. "I'm afraid I might have lost my pistol when the sleigh went careening off the road. Murray, be a dear and help me find it. I don't believe it would be very responsible if I were to leave it lying out here somewhere. Someone could very well stumble upon it, and, well, the outcome might be distressing."

"So you *did* fire that pistol, not Murray?" Reginald asked, earning a surprising roll of a blackened eye from Murray in the process.

"Really, Reginald," Murray began, "my mother is the type to expect me to take to my bed for an entire week after I've suffered a chill. Do you honestly believe she would have ascertained I learn how to handle a pistol?"

Reginald frowned. "You've never fired a pistol before?"

"I've never even held one," Murray admitted before he took a few steps forward, bent over, then plucked the missing gun out of the snow, holding it gingerly as he straightened. "They're much heavier than I expected."

"Good heavens, Murray, don't point that at Reginald. You're likely to shoot him, and then he'll be annoyed with both of us," Poppy said, marching her way to Murray and taking the gun from his now-trembling hand. "I believe, what with you already getting rather proficient with handling your new horse, the next lesson I'll have to teach you is how to use a pistol." She glanced to Murray's horse. "How reassuring to learn that Wilbur doesn't seem to be skittish around loud noises."

"Is that why you took control of the reins?" Murray asked.

"Of course, but since he's not skittish, that proves he's the perfect horse for you, and he's not nearly as plodding as you feared he was going to be. We were moving at a remarkably fast clip before we slid into the ditch."

"Which was surprisingly exhilarating," Murray said, his eyes trained on the pistol Poppy was now wiping free of snow. "But I don't believe I'd find you teaching me how to shoot as exhilarating."

"Why not?" Poppy asked as she tucked the pistol inside the reticule that was hanging from her wrist.

"You're a girl."

Poppy lifted her head and frowned. "Observant of you to notice, but what does me being a girl have to do with teaching you how to use a pistol? I assure you, I'm more than capable with them."

"You didn't take out even one of the criminals we were chasing."

Poppy's nose wrinkled. "I wasn't trying to take out one of those boys, Murray. I shot my pistol in the air the first time to frighten them away from that vendor they were robbing. I then shot it in the air again in the hopes it would frighten them enough to stop their flight so we could then recover whatever goods they'd been able to pilfer."

"Oh" was Murray's only response to that before he suddenly squared his shoulders. "Well, even so, you're not teaching me how to shoot. It won't help what little reputation I have around town if word gets out a girl is teaching me how to use a firearm."

"And here I thought we were friends," Poppy muttered before she threw up her hands and began stomping her way toward the sleigh.

"What's wrong with her?" Murray asked.

"I imagine she's annoyed with you for pointing out she's a girl."

"She is a girl."

"Clearly, and with that settled, what say you go and apologize to her for refusing her offer of assistance?"

When Murray refused to budge, Reginald gave him a bit of a push, earning a scowl from Murray in return. Thankfully, though, Murray didn't continue arguing with him, instead marching his way over to Poppy, who refused to look at him.

"I didn't mean to insult you by refusing your offer," Murray began. "But you must admit that normal ladies don't carry around pistols in their reticules, nor do I believe they're—"

"You should have stopped while you were ahead," Reginald muttered as Poppy's eyes narrowed.

"Are you suggesting I'm not normal?"

"Was that in question?" Murray asked weakly, relief settling over his face when another sleigh took that moment to stop beside them.

"Good heavens, Poppy, have you experienced *another* mishap?" Adele called out as Charles and Edith jumped from the sleigh and slid their way over to join them.

Poppy ignored Adele's question as Charles took hold of her hand and gave it a quick kiss. "I trust you've not been harmed?" he asked.

"I'm fine," she said with a surprising smile, her ability to go from annoyed to perfectly affable leaving Reginald shaking his head. "Murray's fine as well, although his tumble has apparently left his wits slightly scattered."

Charles shot a glance to Murray, who shrugged and then wisely chose to direct his attention to trying to tug the sleigh free from the ditch.

Poppy's smile dimmed as she considered Murray for a moment before she nodded to Charles. "As you can plainly see, my sleigh is stuck, so I'd appreciate your help getting it unstuck."

Charles blinked. "You want me to help get the sleigh out of the ditch?"

"Of course she does," Edith answered for him before she grabbed his arm and began tugging him toward the sleigh. "I'll help as well."

"*I'm* not helping," Adele called.

"Nor would anyone expect you to," Edith called back, and if Reginald wasn't mistaken, she rolled her eyes right as Giles rode up in his sleigh to join them, Miss Cynthia Roche still chattering away by his side.

It took a great deal of effort not to grin when Giles gave a roll of *his* eyes before he pulled the sleigh to a smart start and all but leapt out of it, clearly intent on getting away from Miss Roche, if only for a brief moment.

After Poppy introduced herself to Giles, everyone except Adele and Miss Roche turned to getting the sleigh from the ditch, a feat that took barely a minute to accomplish, what with how many hands were now available to help.

Charles dusted snow from his jacket and smiled. "Well, that's that. Since it's snowing harder than ever, may I suggest we get everyone back to their respective homes?"

Reginald refused a sigh when Poppy immediately shook her head.

"I'm afraid Murray and I can't repair home just yet," she said.

"We can't?" Murray asked, stumbling a step backward when Poppy sent him a scowl.

"Surely you must want to check on the welfare of that poor peddler we saw being robbed, don't you?"

Reginald braced himself when Murray began shaking his head, but when the scowl she was still sending him turned slightly terrifying, his shaking turning into a nod a mere second later.

"Wonderful," Poppy exclaimed. "And with that settled, if all of you will excuse us, Murray and I need to be on our way."

CHAPTER 17

"Can't thank you enough, Reginald, for insisting on accompanying Poppy and me as we search for that peddler," Murray said from the far side of the sleigh, staunchly ignoring the frown Poppy, who was squished in between Reginald and Murray, was sending him.

"You say that as if you're worried our search for that peddler is going to turn into another bout of mayhem," Poppy returned.

"I'm not worried . . . more along the lines of resigned," Murray muttered before he leaned forward and nodded to Reginald, who'd not only insisted on accompanying them but had also insisted on taking the reins.

In all honesty, Poppy was rather relieved Reginald was with them as well because there *was* a possibility, however slight, that looking for the peddler could result in another instance of mayhem. Reginald was a gentleman who'd proven himself capable of rescuing her time and time again. And even though she still found him annoying, somewhat arrogant, and . . .

"We're simply fortunate Edith stepped in and offered to drive the sleigh I'd been using today," Reginald said, drawing Poppy's attention. "Although I'm afraid Adele wasn't pleased with Edith's offer."

Murray grinned. "Adele apparently wasn't finished telling you about some quadrille, but I have to say that I don't believe Giles was pleased when Miss Cynthia Roche refused to give up her seat beside him and ride with Charles, although . . . now that I think about that, it was a peculiar tactic on Cynthia's part if she's trying to win Lord Lonsdale's affections."

Reginald grinned. "She must realize Giles has a lot of sway with Charles, although I do think Adele's tender sensibilities regarding me abandoning her have probably been soothed since Charles is very good at peacemaking when he puts his mind to it. I imagine she's even now telling him all about that quadrille she'd been prattling on about, but . . ." His grin faded as he caught Poppy's eye. "Speaking of quadrilles, you don't happen to be familiar with the Dresden China Quadrille, do you?"

"Have I given you any reason to believe I'm familiar with any quadrilles?"

Reginald rubbed a hand over his face. "You did manage to get through the Gypsy Quadrille."

"Only because Murray practically dragged me through the steps, but . . ." She frowned. "Since when have you taken to growing a beard?"

"He's been growing it for a few days now," Murray answered before Reginald could. "How did you not notice that, what with how he's got hair all over his face?" Murray leaned forward. "I must say I'm impressed with how quickly you're able to grow a beard, Reginald. Frankly, I've been wondering if I should follow suit and do the same. Maisie might . . . ah, like it."

Poppy grinned. "Maisie seems to like your face just as it is."

"You really think so?"

"Would I have told you that if I didn't?"

Looking remarkably pleased, Murray nodded toward Reginald. "What do you think of Reginald's beard?"

"I think if I remark on it, I'll suffer a lecture from Reginald regarding how inappropriate it is to make such personal observations when in mixed company, so it's probably for the best if I keep my opinions about his beard to myself."

"Nicely done," Reginald said with a grin before he suddenly sobered. "But beards aside, I did raise the question of the quadrille for a reason."

"Am I going to like what you're about to say next?"

"Probably not." With that, Reginald explained everything Adele had told him, giving Poppy's hand a pat every now and again. "But if it makes you feel any better," he finished, "Adele did say that the Dresden is more about the costumes than it is the steps."

"And you'll look exquisite dressed all in white," Murray added.

"How, ah, reassuring," Poppy managed to get out. "May I dare hope, though, that the steps aren't that difficult and that I should be able to learn them in a day or two?"

Murray winced. "Afraid not. The steps are intricate and need to be exactly coordinated with all the other dancers."

Her shoulders slumped. "Then I suppose I'm doomed for failure."

"Of course you're not," Murray argued. "I know the steps, and I'll teach you until you know them by heart, even if we have to work night and day to achieve that."

"And I'll lend a hand in whatever way is needed as well," Reginald promised.

Even though the thought of being asked to perform in another quadrille left her distinctly queasy, Poppy also felt a wonderful warmth begin to swirl through her. That the two gentlemen sitting on either side of her were willing to go above and beyond to make certain she was prepared for what was really only a silly dance was lovely in the extreme. And that Reginald would be assisting Murray in what sounded like hours and hours of work, well, it was . . .

"There's someone in the street up ahead," Reginald said. "Do you think that's your peddler?"

Poppy leaned forward, peering down a street that was almost completely devoid of other carriages and sleighs, spotting a hunched figure limping down the very center of the road.

"Hard to say if that's her, but if it is, it looks like she's been injured."

"I'll get us closer," Reginald said, urging the horse forward and drawing up beside the person a moment later.

Leaning around Reginald as he brought the horse to a stop, Poppy was shocked to discover that the person beside the sleigh, while certainly being the peddler who'd been robbed, was not a woman at all, but a young girl of no more than ten. She was bundled up in a threadbare coat and had a scarf wrapped around her head, although it was not large enough to cover her face. Lashes covered in snow blinked up at them, but before Poppy could get a single inquiry past her lips, the girl let out a shriek, spun around, and dashed straightaway.

"Poppy really is incredibly fast for a lady," Murray said after Poppy flung herself from the sleigh and took off after the fleeing girl. "She's remarkably agile as well and didn't even stumble when she hit the ground, and that was after she scrambled over you."

Rubbing a hand over a stomach that had suffered an elbow from Poppy as she'd done her scrambling, Reginald scooped up the reins he'd dropped and handed them to Murray. "I'll be right back. Don't go anywhere."

"Where would I go?" Murray asked as Reginald hopped from the sleigh and took off after Poppy, who was now only a blurry figure in the distance.

Increasing his pace, which only succeeded in having him slip to the ground, Reginald pushed himself out of the snow, wondering for what felt like the millionth time how his life had turned so interesting of late.

Brushing snow from his jacket, he started forward again, stopping when he saw Poppy marching his way, holding the arm of the peddler who seemed to be trying her hardest to shake free.

"Stop fighting me," he heard Poppy say.

"I'm a good girl, I am, and I don't want you to take me to that flesh peddler over there."

Poppy stopped in her tracks. "Good heavens, child. I'm not taking you to a flesh peddler."

The girl pointed a finger Reginald's way. "He looks like a flesh peddler to me, and lookie at that poor lad behind him. He's taken a beatin' for sure, probably since he don't want to go with the flesh peddler either."

"Those two gentlemen are only looking in such a sorry state because they helped me with a band of thieves I ran into a few days ago, something I was trying to help you with earlier."

"That was you?"

Poppy nodded. "It was, but I'm afraid to say that—"

"You didn't hurt the boys, did you?" the girl interrupted.

Poppy frowned. "Were those boys not robbing you?"

"'Course they was tryin' to rob me, but that's just because they didn't recognize me at first." The girl shook her head. "They're boys from my neighborhood, and my mama will be boxin' their ears once she hears what happened." She pushed aside hair that was blowing into her eyes, revealing a wind-chapped face and delicate features. "They didn't mean me no harm. They was just desperate cuz there ain't no swells ambling around the park or in the streets today, what with all the snow."

Poppy's brows drew together. "They're pickpockets?"

"Sure, but they usually only steal from the rich, so it's not like they're hurtin' anyone. They gotta eat, don't they?"

"I imagine they do," Poppy said as her gaze sharpened on the girl. "Do you pick pockets as well?"

"Mama would take a belt to me for sure if I took to pickin' pockets," the girl said. "'Sides, Reverend Lewis—he runs the House of Industry that helped Mama find work—believes God don't like us to steal. He's always sayin' that we need to stay on the right path, no matter how tough life gets, and I decided to do just that." Her slim shoulders sagged. "Me, Mama, and one of my sisters take in piecemeal work, makin' fancy lady things. I save up the scraps and turn them into flowers. I thought I'd be able to sell some of those today, what with the flower vendors stayin' inside, but I didn't sell a single one."

"We'll buy all your flowers," Poppy said firmly. "But first we need to get you home. You must be freezing."

The girl shook her head. "I live down on the Lower East Side. That's too far for you to take me."

"We're giving you a ride whether you want one or not," Poppy countered.

"I can catch a ride on the back of a delivery wagon. It's how I got here."

"Do you see any delivery wagons still on the street?"

The girl looked around. "No."

"Then it's settled. We'll take you home, and I'll hear no more arguing from you."

Poppy marched the young girl to the sleigh and helped her into the back seat. After getting her settled, she pulled a blanket from underneath the seat and nodded to Reginald as he climbed up beside Murray. "Do you know how to get to the Lower East Side?"

"I'm from England, so no." He nodded to Murray. "You?"

"I have an overly protective mother. Do you honestly believe she'd ever take me to that part of the city?"

Reginald turned his attention to the girl, now huddled under the blanket. "Do you know how to get back to your home?"

"'Course I do. Go down Sixth Avenue, get on Broadway, then turn down a side street that will lead us to Mulberry Street. Mulberry Bend is not far from there."

He turned back to Murray and arched a brow.

Murray shrugged. "I can get us to Broadway, but I have no idea where to find Mulberry Street."

"I'll tell you when we get close," the girl said.

"I suppose that'll have to do," Reginald said, flicking the reins and setting Wilbur into motion.

As they traveled down a nearly deserted Sixth Avenue, Poppy chatted easily with the girl, discovering her name was Maria Romano. She lived with her father, mother, three sisters, and a baby brother, in tenant housing. Her papa had only recently returned to work, doing something with plumbing after he'd recovered from breaking a leg at another job some months before.

"That's why we don't have much money right now, and why we had to move from Fulton Street to Mulberry Bend."

"Did you like Fulton Street better?" Poppy asked.

"It was much nicer. We had three rooms, a balcony, and only had to share the privy with two other families. Now we only have the one room and share the privy with ten families."

"I never knew people had to share a privy with other families," Murray said quietly, exchanging a look with Reginald as Maria continued talking with Poppy. "And how do you imagine seven people, if I'm counting correctly, manage to live in one room?"

Reginald, unfortunately, didn't have an answer to that. His family owned numerous residences, including three grand country estates and a house in London that was equipped with every luxury. He'd always had his own room in all those homes and had never had to worry about waiting his turn to use a retiring room.

That Maria spoke so matter-of-factly about her life suggested she was accustomed to living in dire conditions and had accepted that there wasn't anything she could do about them.

"How long have you lived in the city?" Poppy asked her.

"About seven years. We came on a boat from Sicily—me, Mama, Papa, and Isabella. My other three siblings was born here. That boat took us right to Castle Garden, where they took down our names, but they misspelled my mama's name because she's Catalida, not Catherine, which makes Mama so mad. Papa thought there'd be more opportunities here than in Sicily, but we have yet to see them."

"And is this Castle Garden near where you live?"

"It is. That's why so many immigrants live near Five Points. You don't have to travel far and rooms are cheap. Plus, they got places that teach English, but Mama don't speak much English. I've been helpin' her since I stopped goin' to school."

"You don't go to school?"

"Can't very well make the money we need if I'm spendin' hours at school. I'll go back there someday, hopefully soon since Papa is back to work."

Something that felt very much like guilt settled in the pit of Reginald's stomach.

He'd been given the best of everything money could buy, including an education. That education had allowed him to pursue his love of investments, which had, in turn, allowed him to amass an impressive fortune. Not once, though, had he ever considered using that fortune to help better the lives of those less fortunate. How he was going to alleviate the guilt he now felt as a result was completely beyond him, but listening to the young girl sitting behind him was one of those moments he knew was going to impact his life forever.

It had been so easy to distance himself from the hardships of strangers, but now that he'd been made aware of those hardships, it would not be easy to enjoy all the frivolities life offered while children were forced to help support their families, even in the middle of what was turning into a storm for the ages.

"I think we should be getting close," Murray said, leaning forward and peering through snow that was coming down in earnest. "We're definitely moving into a less prosperous area."

Looking around, Reginald found that to be nothing less than the truth. Gone were the fine stores and houses, replaced with ramshackle buildings that seemed to go on and on, some of those buildings sporting snow-covered balconies every ten feet or so, while many of the windows seemed to be covered with paper.

There were also more people moving about the sidewalks, some of them standing around fires that had been lit in large barrels. Young boys were darting in and out of the street, dodging snowballs other boys were throwing, their squeals of laughter at distinct odds with the squalor that surrounded them.

"My street is coming up," Maria said, appearing directly by his shoulder. "But you can leave me off here. I'll get in trouble if my mama sees me getting out of this fine sleigh."

"Won't she simply be thankful you were able to find a ride home from Central Park?" Murray asked.

"Not since I didn't bother to tell her I was goin' up that far to try and sell my flowers."

Poppy appeared right next to Maria. "That reminds me, I told you I'd buy all your flowers from you. How many do you have?"

"About twenty, but you don't need to buy them from me, Miss Poppy. You was kind enough to give me a ride. I'll just go back out tomorrow." Maria smiled. "I'm tryin' to earn some extra money so we can have a proper Christmas. We've not had money to buy presents this year, and it's not a proper Christmas if you don't got a few presents, or at least a nice meal."

Reginald pulled the sleigh to a stop and reached for his billfold, right as Murray did the same. Pulling out all the bills he had on him, which were quite a few since society mothers kept handing him what they called "bonus money"—although that money was more likely bribes, given in the hopes he'd convince Charles their daughters were worthy of being a countess—he pressed them into Maria's cold hands, shaking his head when she tried to give the money back to him.

"You keep that. Buy some presents and perhaps a ham for your Christmas dinner."

"This is a lot of money," Maria whispered.

Ignoring Poppy, who was watching him with something warm lingering in her eyes, he forced a smile. "I want you to have it, and I won't take it back from you, so put it inside a pocket, then give it to your mama once you get inside. It's my Christmas present to you, and before you argue with that, remember this—Christmas is supposed to be more about giving than receiving, something I might not have really understood until just now."

Murray handed Maria some money as well. "Too right you are, Reginald, and I want you, Maria, to give this to your papa. Tell him it's to help all of you get into a place where you don't have to share a privy with ten other families."

"It's too much," Maria protested.

Murray waved that aside. "I have plenty of money, Maria, but you've just had me realizing that I've never appreciated that before, nor have I ever done anything worthwhile with the money I have. You'll be allowing me to feel useful for once if you simply accept my gift. Your Christmas present to me."

Maria looked to Reginald. "And do you have plenty of money as well?"

"I have enough to get by," he settled on saying, which seemed to satisfy her since she tucked all the money into a pocket and nodded. "Thank you." She handed the bag she'd been clutching out to Poppy. "Here's the flowers."

Reginald wasn't surprised when Poppy shook her head. "Why don't you keep those, sell them tomorrow if the weather turns nicer." She unbuttoned her jacket, and then, to his surprise, she unbuttoned the high neckline of her gown, reached underneath the fabric, pulled out bills from her bodice, handed them to Maria, then calmly buttoned back up again, as if it was a usual occurrence for a lady to pull bills from the neckline of her gown in the first place.

"Wasn't taking any chances after my reticule got snatched the other day" was all she said when he arched a brow at her before she turned back to Maria. "And now, how about we get you home? I'll walk with you to make certain you're not set upon again by those neighbor lads."

Maria shook her head. "I'll be fine. I walk these streets all the time by myself. You're dressed too nicely for this neighborhood and will draw attention."

"I'm not allowing you to walk home by yourself," Poppy said before she sent Reginald a telling look.

"I'd be delighted to walk you home," he said to Maria, who looked horrified at the offer.

"No offense, but you look like you've seen more than your fair share of fights, and if you go roamin' into this neighborhood lookin' like that . . ." She shuddered. "You'll be set upon before we make it a block."

206

"Then I'll walk her home," Murray surprised him by saying.

Giving him a good once-over, Maria finally nodded. "I don't think anyone will take issue with you."

"How reassuring" was all Murray said before he climbed from the sleigh and held out his hand to Maria, which had her grinning as she took it. He then shook his head at Poppy, who was trying to hand her reticule to him—or more specifically, her pistol.

"Really, Poppy? I'll be in more danger if I'm armed and besides"—he grinned—"you'll hear me if I run into trouble. I'm very proficient with shrieking." With that, Murray began walking with Maria through the snow, bending his head to hear whatever she'd begun saying to him.

"Do you think we should follow them?" Poppy asked.

"Murray would find that insulting, and since he's just now beginning to come into his own, I say we let him do this with no help from us."

"I suppose you're right, but his mother will hunt both of us down if anything else happens to him," Poppy muttered before she climbed onto the seat beside him and gestured around. "I never knew people lived like this."

"I can't say I did either."

"She lives with six other people in one room."

"Troubling indeed."

"She told me some of those boys who tried to rob her don't have parents." Poppy began blinking rapidly, trying to stop the tears that were now swimming in her eyes from falling. "Surely there must be something that can be done about the situation down here."

A sense of apprehension slid down his spine. "What are you thinking?"

"I'm thinking it's appalling that I have so much when many others have so little. And I'm thinking I've just found that noble cause my grandmother suggested I find."

While Reginald certainly found it commendable that Poppy wanted to throw herself into helping those less fortunate, he was fairly certain Viola was going to be less than thrilled. Poppy, he'd discovered, was not the type to stay on the sidelines, and he knew, without a doubt, she wouldn't settle for donating money but would want to get into the thick of the matter . . . which would undoubtedly lead to mayhem.

Chapter 18

"I'm afraid the conditions may prevent anyone from coming to our tea today."

Joining Viola by the window, Poppy peered through glass that was speckled with snow, a small measure of relief washing over her at the notion the tea might not take place.

"I think you're fretting for no reason, Viola," Murray said, striding into the drawing room and banishing Poppy's feeling of relief in a blink of an eye. "Everyone invited was most excited to get what are being considered coveted invitations. You mark my words, every guest will show up promptly at two, which"—he pulled out his pocket watch—"is less than ten minutes from now." He repocketed the watch and lifted his head. "How do I look? Is my face going to put anyone off their tea, coffee, or treats?"

Taking a second to look Murray over, Poppy bit back a grin. In all honesty, Murray was still looking grim, now that his eyes were ringed with an unusual shade of green. His nose, though, seemed almost back to normal, and thankfully, he'd gotten rid of the cotton he'd stuffed up his nostrils the night before after his nose had begun bleeding for no apparent reason.

Even with his face still looking a little worse for wear, his jacket and trousers were expertly tailored, fitting him to perfection, instead of the baggy fit he'd been wearing before he'd paid a visit to a tailor Viola recommended. That tailor had seen fit to convince Murray that extra fabric did nothing to enhance his slight stature, which had led Murray to decide to have all his garments altered. He'd also taken to holding himself differently, keeping his head up and his shoulders thrown back, lending him a far more dignified air, and he'd abandoned his heeled boots and lifts, which suggested he was finally becoming comfortable in his own skin.

"I *am* going to disgust the guests, aren't I?" Murray said, pulling Poppy directly out of her thoughts.

"Forgive me, Murray. I was admiring the cut of your new suit and got distracted by what a dashing figure you make today. But to answer your question, no, you're not going to disgust anyone today. Your face may still be somewhat battered, but it lends you a dangerous air, one I'm going to assume Maisie will find most intriguing."

Murray grinned. "Dashing and intriguing. Two words I never thought I'd hear spoken about me."

Viola turned from the window. "Have I missed something? It almost sounds as if you've taken a special interest in Miss Maisie Leggett."

Two bright patches of pink stained Murray's cheeks. "I don't know if I'd go so far to say I've taken a *special* interest in Maisie, although I do find her to be a most engaging young lady."

Viola sent Murray what almost seemed to be an approving sort of smile. "I must admit that Maisie and her sister have surprised me with their engaging natures, especially after both of them penned me charming notes, thanking me for allowing them to share Poppy's time with Reginald for decorum lessons." She nodded. "That charm is exactly why I've decided to honor Poppy's request of sponsoring the Leggett sisters this Season. I've already reached out to Mrs. Leggett, presenting her my offer. Unsurprisingly, she accepted without hesitation, and also penned me a very gracious note of appreciation."

Poppy blinked. "You didn't tell me you'd decided to sponsor Maisie and Helene."

Giving a wave of a hand, which sent the gold bracelets she was wearing jangling, Viola shrugged. "I didn't see a need to make a fuss."

"On the contrary, there's every need for a fuss," Poppy argued. "Sponsoring the Leggett sisters will require a great deal of effort on your part since Mrs. Astor has spread it around that Maisie and Helene are not worthy of admittance into highest society."

Viola's lips thinned. "Caroline Astor should have a care with whom she deems unworthy these days. Society is rapidly changing, and if she's not careful, she'll find her position as the queen of society taken away from her."

Poppy wrinkled her nose. "Who are you and what have you done with my grandmother?"

Viola ignored that as she sent Murray another smile. "Do know that I'm more than happy to assist you, dear, if you decide to take that special interest in Maisie." Her eyes began to sparkle. "Why, I could offer you lessons in how to attract and hold a lady's attention, quite like the lessons Poppy is taking to turn herself into a diamond of the first water."

A hefty dose of terror settled on Murray's face, replaced with relief when her grandfather suddenly strolled into the room, dressed in a suit and tie, his hair combed and a smile on his face.

"I'm not interrupting, am I?" George asked, stepping next to Poppy and giving her a kiss on the cheek before he shook Murray's hand, then moved to join Viola, giving her a kiss on the cheek as well, which had her turning somewhat flustered.

"I was just offering to assist Murray with a young lady he might have set his eye on," Viola said, smoothing a hand over hair that was perfectly in place. "Getting ready to go out to one of your clubs, dear?"

"I'm here to present myself for the tea."

Viola blinked. "You're attending the tea?"

"Of course I am, since gentlemen have now been included on the guest list." He nodded to Murray. "And good thing, what with the conversation I heard as I was walking into the room." He smiled.

"You'll be delighted to hear that I'm more than willing to offer *my* assistance as well in regard to your lady issues because there's nothing quite like getting a male perspective on the workings of the feminine mind."

Murray edged closer to Poppy as Viola let out what almost sounded like a snort. "Since when have you understood the workings of the feminine mind?"

"Since I began reading all those novels Elizabeth left behind." George's eyes twinkled. "I overheard some gentlemen speaking at the Union Club the other night, reminiscing about how two gentlemen a year or so back decided to read romance novels in an attempt to understand women. Sheer brilliance, if you ask me, which is why I then hurried home and dug out some of Elizabeth's old novels."

"I thought I got rid of all of her books," Viola said slowly.

George nodded. "You did—or at least got them out of the house. I had all of her belongings sent up to the loft in the carriage house after she ran off with Harold."

"Why would you have done that?"

"Because she's our daughter and I thought you were being overly hasty." George turned from a now-scowling Viola and settled his gaze on Murray. "Returning to what I'm now considering excellent research fodder, I've been spending time reading Jane Austen, and I have to tell you, Murray, Jane's books are quite riveting and have lent me some wonderful insight."

Viola crossed her arms over her chest. "I hardly believe you've gained any credible insight into ladies through reading Jane Austen."

"The only way for you to discern whether or not that's true, dear, is for you to begin reading those books with me," George returned pleasantly, ignoring that Viola was now sputtering. "Why, we could make an event of reading romance novels, and perhaps even include Poppy and Murray, taking turns reading out loud to one another."

Viola stopped sputtering and looked to Poppy. "And here is

where you should ask who this gentleman is and what he's done with your grandfather."

George chuckled before Poppy could compose a suitable reply. "Should I take that as a yes, that you'll join me in a spot of romantic reading?"

Viola drew herself up. "You must recall that I blame those types of books for filling Elizabeth's head with nonsense and swore after she ran away that I'd never read fiction again."

"That sounds like a definite yes to me, so we'll start our reading this evening." George smiled. "I'm just about ready to crack the cover on *Pride and Prejudice*, but I'm flexible on that, as long as we settle on an Austen book to begin tonight." He rubbed his hands together. "I'm hoping that we'll make it through at least two of Jane's books before Elizabeth joins us for Christmas. It'll give us something to discuss over Christmas dinner."

Poppy frowned. "I don't believe Mother is planning on coming to New York for her yearly visit, Grandfather. She's beyond annoyed with Grandmother over what she considers blackmail. And because Mother's never pleasant to be around when she's annoyed, I suggested she stay home this year, which will allow everyone to enjoy a Christmas devoid of drama."

Viola released a sniff. "I didn't blackmail you. I merely used my impressive proficiency for persuasion to get you to agree to a Season."

"Persuasion that seemed rather like blackmail to Mother."

The edges of Viola's lips curved. "Perhaps it was somewhat like blackmail, but admit it. You've been enjoying yourself."

"I'm sure Poppy has been enjoying herself more now that you, in an unexpected move, summoned a seamstress to let out all of her gowns," George said, which had Viola's face turning a delicate shade of pink.

Poppy's eyes went wide. "I *thought* breathing was becoming easier. Although, frankly, I attributed that to restricting how much I eat at society events, since I've been told annoyingly often that ladies aren't supposed to be seen eating much in public."

"I couldn't very well continue having you fainting all over town, could I?" Viola said, her cheeks still pink as she narrowed her eyes on George. "And thank you for bringing that to Poppy's attention, dear. Are you quite certain you don't have any business matters you need to attend to this afternoon? Perhaps a new railroad stock you need to acquire, or better yet, acquaintances at one of your clubs with whom you need to catch up?"

George gestured around the room. "And miss all this? Not on your life." He winked at Poppy. "I'm particularly looking forward to the cake you made bright and early this morning—assisted, or so I was told, by Murray."

"Murray did help, and wait until you see how he decorated that cake. It's absolutely stunning and shows off his considerable artistic talents."

Viola sent a fond smile Murray's way. "I'm sure it is a sight to behold, but I would prefer that talk doesn't settle on the fact Poppy baked the cake. It's curious enough that we're hosting a tea for ladies *and* gentlemen."

"And speaking of those ladies and gentlemen," George said, moving to the window and peering out, his face wreathed with a smile. "A carriage has drawn up, and . . ." He blinked. "Good heavens. Lena Ridgeway just practically jumped out of that carriage, and she's now walking rather quickly for the front door, on the arm of a man I've seen before, but don't personally know."

Viola peered out the window as well. "Ah, that's Mr. Nigel Flaherty."

Poppy frowned. "I didn't invite Nigel Flaherty or Lena Ridgeway."

Viola turned. "I did, dear, after Lena payed a call on me yesterday and broached the matter of the tea. I couldn't very well not invite her after that, as well as include Mr. Flaherty, after she made a point of telling me he's been kind enough to squire her about town this Season. Frankly, I'm delighted to find Lena enjoying herself. She spent years as a recluse, even when her husband was alive, only appearing infrequently at the occasional society event.

After he died, she all but disappeared from sight, which is why I'm happy Nigel Flaherty has somehow managed to convince her to get out and about." Viola blinked a far-too-innocent eye at Poppy. "That's why I didn't hesitate to include him today, although I also didn't feel it would hurt to have another eligible man present at the tea."

"You believe Nigel Flaherty, a gentleman who is twice my age, is someone I should consider as a potential suitor?"

"Not at all, since he *is* twice your age. But it never hurts to have numerous gentlemen show an interest in a lady. Gets that competitive spirit going and all." Viola looked back at the window. "And would you look at that. More carriages are arriving."

"Which means we should move to the entranceway to greet the guests who were willing to brave the fierce elements to attend today's tea," George said, extending his arm to Viola.

Viola ran another hand over hair that was still perfectly in place, smoothed down the skirt of her lovely green-and-blue day dress, then took George's arm, turning a bit pink in the face again when he gave her arm a pat. Clearing her throat, she looked to Poppy and inclined her head. "George and I will welcome the guests, but I think it might be for the best if you and Murray stay here to see to the guests' comfort after we've greeted them."

"I'm certain we'll be able to manage that with little problem," Poppy said.

Viola seemed to give a bit of a shudder. "That's an encouraging thought, although I would have felt much relieved if Reginald would have been able to arrive before any of the other guests began descending on the house."

"Why would you be relieved about that?" Poppy asked.

"Because you seem to turn an ordinary event into something extraordinary, and Reginald has proven himself useful when events turn concerning."

"I highly doubt anything unusual will occur during the tea," George said. "It's a somewhat simple occasion that one really shouldn't be able to disrupt."

"Unless you happen to be named Poppy," Murray mumbled before he hitched a smile into place and ignored the scowl Poppy tossed his way.

"You might have a point," George conceded before he gave Viola's arm another pat and walked with her toward the entranceway.

"Nothing unusual is going to happen today," Poppy said firmly as they waited for the guests, earning a grin from Murray right as Beatrix Waterbury strolled into the room. She was holding the arm of a gentleman Poppy assumed was Mr. Thomas Hamersley, since Beatrix had suggested Poppy extend that gentleman an invitation, telling her Thomas was her *special* friend, the one with whom Beatrix shared a certain *understanding*.

Moments after Beatrix introduced her to Mr. Hamersley, Poppy knew without a doubt the two were not remotely romantically interested in each other, especially not after Beatrix poked Mr. Hamersley's arm in a less-than-loving way after he'd contradicted her about the weather.

"We will certainly see at least ten inches of snow before this storm is finished," Beatrix said, giving Mr. Hamersley another poke.

"Eight inches at the most," Mr. Hamersley countered, rubbing his arm. "And stop poking me. You're probably leaving a bruise."

"You do realize you're sounding a bit whiny, don't you?" Beatrix asked. "You're hardly likely to impress Miss . . ." She abruptly stopped talking, shook herself ever so slightly, then sent Poppy a rather weak smile. "But would you listen to me and Thomas go on and on. It's hardly well done of us, and we really shouldn't monopolize your attention."

Before Poppy could argue with that, or even ask Beatrix why she and Mr. Hamersley were lending society the impression they were romantically involved with each other, when clearly, they weren't, additional guests began swarming into the room. Those guests were dressed in the first state of fashion, although most of them were shivering as they moved close to the fireplace, evidence that the weather was less than inviting for a person to be out and about.

"Ah, and there's Lord Lonsdale," Beatrix said, glancing over Poppy's shoulder as Poppy turned around.

Her gaze, however, did not settle on the man at whom everyone else was gawking but went immediately to Reginald, a thrill of something unexpected running over her when she got her first look at him.

His hair, which was normally combed with every strand in place, was what could only be described as tousled, and his beard was certainly thicker than it had been the previous day. It gave Reginald a most dangerous air, one that, oddly enough, left her distinctly wobbly at the knees and somewhat breathless.

Calling herself every sort of ridiculous because Reginald had not lent her the impression he found her anything other than a friend, nor had he ever seemed to have an issue with his knees going wobbly or becoming breathless when he looked at her, Poppy squared her shoulders. She then shoved aside all thoughts of dangerous men, and forced her knees to steady.

CHAPTER 19

"I'm not sure what to make of your appearance," Charles muttered, keeping a smile firmly on his face as he and Reginald paused in the entranceway of the drawing room.

"There's nothing to make of it," Reginald muttered back, realizing that it might have been prudent to explain to Charles exactly why he was trying to alter his looks before he'd met up with him at the Van Rensselaers', instead of springing his new look on his cousin as they'd walked up the steps to the front door.

"You look like you work on the docks."

"I doubt a dock worker would be wearing a custom-made suit."

"True, but that beard you're sporting would fit in nicely on the docks, and do not even get me started on your hair." Charles glanced at his head. "How *did* you get it to look like that?"

"Rubbed it with a towel after I put a touch of Macassar oil in it."

"But . . . why?"

"Because George Van Rensselaer was at a meeting I attended in London. I don't want him to recognize me. That's why I started growing a beard in the first place, and why I've rearranged my hair."

"Perhaps it might be easier just to come clean and tell everyone the truth about your illustrious father." Charles blew out a breath.

"Frankly, I've been having a touch of difficulty remembering you're merely supposed to be my traveling companion. I'm not sure you noticed this, but I've slipped up several times and told people Giles is your valet, not mine, although I do believe I've recovered nicely, telling everyone I've magnanimously offered you the use of my valet."

Reginald grinned. "Kind of you to be so magnanimous, which is a word I don't believe I've ever heard you utter."

"Miss Edith Iselin, curiously enough, enjoys discovering new words every day from a dictionary she recently purchased at a book shop. She's been sharing some of those words with me, magnanimous being one of them, although she already knew the definition." Charles's brows drew together. "I must say, I've been finding the dictionary to be far more interesting than I ever gave it credit for."

"And I must say that I find it interesting you'd enjoy spending your time reading from a dictionary with a lady."

"Yes, well, it's been an interesting time here in New York. But weren't we speaking about you and how you might want to consider telling society the full truth about yourself since withholding that information seems to be turning into a lot of work?"

Finding it interesting as well that Charles wasn't keen to continue on with talk of Edith or dictionaries, Reginald inclined his head, taking a minute to consider Charles's suggestion of revealing his truth to society.

He couldn't dispute that keeping his true identity a secret was becoming more and more difficult, especially since George Van Rensselaer could, at some point, recognize him even with his attempt at disguising himself, but . . . he simply wasn't ready to disclose the truth just yet.

The reason behind his reluctance centered squarely around Poppy. She was hardly likely to take his duplicity well and would see that duplicity as a direct insult, and then, well, she might very well decide to discontinue their association.

"So . . . are you going to take my suggestion?" Charles prodded, drawing Reginald out of his thoughts.

"Not just yet."

"Why not?"

Unwilling to admit the real reason, since that would undoubtedly lead to questions Reginald wasn't prepared to answer, he smiled when the perfect response sprang to mind. "I don't believe it'll serve our agenda of finding you a countess if the truth gets out about me right now."

Charles's eyes widened. "Ah, brilliant thinking on your part. I didn't even consider that, but you've evidently concluded, as I evidently did not, that society may very well become annoyed with both of us. Why, we might find ourselves ostracized from society events, and where would that leave us?"

Reginald blinked. "Did you just use the word *ostracized*?"

"Edith, or rather, Miss Iselin, brought the word to my attention yesterday." Charles grinned. "Never thought I'd find an appropriate time to use it, but I believe it worked well just now." He leaned closer to Reginald. "But returning to what we were discussing, perhaps it would be for the best if we simply carry on as we've been doing. And even though you're not looking like the very proper and well-groomed Reginald I've always known, you still hold yourself the same, and it's a distinctive stance. That means you might want to limit the time you spend with George Van Rensselaer, although because that man seemed delighted to welcome you into his home a few minutes ago, you might not be able to avoid him as much as you ought."

"He didn't seem overly delighted to greet me."

Charles grimaced. "Well, he was, which was odd, unless he's decided to cozy up to you in an attempt to get cozier with me."

"George doesn't really seem to be the type of man to cozy up to anyone."

"Grandfathers are known to act in peculiar ways when it comes to seeing their granddaughters well settled." Charles raised a hand and waved at someone. "And speaking of Poppy, she's right over there, and"—Charles shot him a rather curious look—"she seems to be watching you."

Reginald looked across the room, finding Poppy standing on the other side of it, and . . . she *was* watching him. She was also looking enchanting, dressed in an afternoon gown of palest blue that hugged her figure and was cut in the first state of fashion. Her hair was drawn up in a knot on the top of her head, little wisps of curls descending out of that knot to tease cheeks that were a lovely shade of—

"Did I mention that Miss Cynthia Roche is incredibly put out with Giles?"

Reginald blinked. "What?"

Charles peered back at him. "I say, you're suddenly looking rather odd, Reginald. Are you feeling all right?"

It was a question that was difficult to answer.

He'd somehow, and he didn't quite know how, become slightly fascinated with Poppy Garrison, the most unusual lady he'd ever met, and one who certainly was not the type of lady with whom he'd ever thought to become fascinated.

"Shall I fetch you something cool to drink?" Charles asked, pulling Reginald abruptly from his thoughts again.

"Forgive me, Charles. I'm fine. What were you saying about Giles?"

Frowning, Charles considered Reginald for a brief moment, then shrugged. "You don't look fine, and if I didn't know you better, I'd say you were flustered. But returning to Giles—he apparently insulted Miss Roche yesterday, something to do with him not responding to one of her comments to her satisfaction." Charles blew out a breath. "Mrs. Roche then sent a note around to me, complaining about Giles's inattention to her daughter, although why she did that is beyond me."

"She was probably hoping you'll give her daughter more attention to make up for Giles's inattention."

Charles's brows drew together. "This searching for an heiress business is growing rather tedious, Reginald, although I have been meaning to thank you for agreeing to take on those additional decorum lessons. I know those ladies aren't interested in learning about etiquette, and I also know that your time with the ladies must be trying your patience. However, with that said, you've taken a great deal of pressure off me and afforded me precious time from being pursued, time I used for . . . well . . ."

"Used for what?" Reginald pressed when Charles simply stopped talking.

"This and that."

"Hardly helpful."

"And annoying as well, I imagine," Charles returned. "And on that note, we should go say hello to Poppy."

As Charles began walking across the drawing room, Reginald fell into step beside him. "I've just noticed that you've begun calling Poppy by her given name."

"Finding that annoying too, are you?" Charles asked cheerfully, and before Reginald could question what he could possibly mean by that, Charles stopped directly in front of Poppy, took her hand, kissed it, then smiled. "And aren't you looking simply delightful today, Poppy?"

Poppy dipped into a curtsy and then straightened. "Thank you, Lord Lonsdale, or should I address you as Charles, since you seem to have abandoned a sense of formality between us?" She leaned toward him and lowered her voice. "Reginald and I have yet to delve into the intricacies of the aristocracy, so if I've just stepped over the line, do take it up with him."

Releasing a booming laugh, one that drew everyone's attention, Charles released his hold on Poppy's hand. "Besides looking delightful, you're charming as well." With that, Charles stepped back and all but shoved Reginald forward. "Isn't she just one of the most charming ladies you've ever met?"

Deciding the stress of choosing an heiress had finally caught up with his cousin because Charles had apparently misplaced his wits, Reginald took Poppy's hand and raised it to his lips. "You are, of course, charming, Poppy, although I must point out that I have covered the intricacies of the aristocracy with you—in depth at that—only two days ago." He smiled. "If you'll recall, Maisie and Helene were present during that lesson as well, and—"

"Was that the lesson where Helene almost fell out of her seat after she'd drifted off to sleep?" Poppy interrupted, her eyes twinkling.

Reginald fought to stifle a grin. "Quite right."

Poppy didn't bother to hide her grin. "Well, there you have it." She stepped back. "And now, to prove that I do occasionally listen to your lessons, allow me to remark upon your appearance, since you were so kind to compliment me on mine."

When she simply took to looking him up and down and didn't bother to say anything else, he winced. "Well?"

"I'm trying to decide whether I should say that you're looking rather—"

"Dashing?" he finished for her.

"I was going to say *derelict*, but I was then going to follow that by saying that it seems to suit you, oddly enough."

"Charles believes I look as if I belong on the docks."

She nodded. "I can't argue with that, although I believe you look more like a pirate than a dock worker."

Reginald's lips curved. He'd never been compared to a pirate before, as most people found him to be rather stuffy, and he had to admit he enjoyed the comparison.

"I've been considering growing a beard as well," Charles said, running a hand over his clean-shaven face. "Do you think it would give me the look of a pirate?"

"I imagine you'd make a delightful pirate, Lord Lonsdale," Edith Iselin said as she moved to join them. "Although I'm not certain you'd be able to adopt the attitude needed for a pirate, since you seem to be a most proper English gentleman all the time."

"Miss Iselin!" Charles exclaimed, taking the lady's hand and bringing it to his lips, although he didn't let go of her fingers after he'd kissed them. "How splendid that the snow didn't keep you from attending today."

Edith smiled. "I'm fairly certain my mother would have hired sled dogs to get me here if she thought that necessary, but thankfully, my driver had no difficulty making it down Fifth Avenue."

She turned to Poppy. "Thank you again for the invitation, Poppy. May I dare hope you suffered no ill effects from being out in the storm yesterday as you went to search for that peddler? And may I also dare hope that you found her?"

Poppy smiled. "I'm healthy as a horse, Edith, thank you for asking. And as for the peddler, we did find her." Her smile dimmed. "After providing her a ride home, though, I was dismayed by the mean surroundings she lives in, which is why I've decided something needs to be done about the conditions in Five Points. I've begun to develop an idea for how I could help down there, and I'm hoping a few guests here today will want to assist me with the project I'm going to broach later, after we've had tea and coffee."

"What type of an idea?" Reginald forced himself to ask.

"You'll find out after we've had some refreshments."

Before Reginald could press her further, Poppy excused herself, saying she needed to greet the other guests.

"There's Cynthia Roche and her mother," Edith suddenly said, nodding to the doorway.

Charles squinted at the doorway and winced before he thrust out his arm to Edith. "I've heard there is a most wonderful painting in the parlor. Care to join me?"

Edith took Charles's arm, nodded, and a second later they dashed away, leaving Reginald standing all alone.

"Was that Lord Lonsdale with Miss Iselin?"

Turning, Reginald found Miss Cynthia Roche already standing behind him, her gaze narrowed as she watched Charles disappear into the parlor that was located next to the drawing room.

"It was," he admitted.

"Where's he going?"

"I believe he wanted Miss Iselin to see a painting in the parlor."

"It's probably the Jean-Louis Ernest Meissonier I recall Viola has hanging in there," Mrs. Roche said, stepping up to join her daughter. "*The Chess Players*, if memory serves me correctly. But how nice to see you again, Mr. Blackburn. I trust your decorum lessons with my Cynthia are going well?"

After assuring Mrs. Roche that her daughter was more than competent when it came to all matters of decorum, Reginald soon found himself held hostage by the two ladies, both of whom seemed determined to impress him with their knowledge of paintings. He spent the next five minutes listening to them tell him all about their favorite artists, and then, after they apparently ran out of things to say about that topic, Cynthia switched the conversation to quadrilles, or more specifically, the Dresden China Quadrille.

". . . it's a most exacting dance, but Mother's convinced I'll not have a bit of trouble with it, not since I've spent so many years taking dance instruction from one of the leading dance masters in New York."

Dread began seeping through Reginald's veins. "And is that dance master helping you with this particular quadrille?"

"But of course," she returned with a smile.

Reginald was not disappointed when Beatrix suddenly appeared, begging the Roches' pardon, then took hold of his arm and hurried away, tugging him across the room to introduce him to some of her friends.

"You were looking a bit glassy in the eyes," Beatrix said as she drew to a stop. "I'm sure you'll enjoy this group much better, and with that, allow me to introduce you to my Mr. Hamersley."

It took all of three minutes to conclude that Mr. Thomas Hamersley was not Beatrix's beau, although both Thomas and Beatrix, for some unknown reason, seemed to be going out of their way to convince everyone otherwise. Thomas, if Reginald wasn't mistaken—and he was certain he wasn't—was smitten with Miss Helene Leggett, given the manner in which he was watching that young lady, who'd only just arrived with her sister, Maisie.

"Why do you look as if you're trying to puzzle something out?" Beatrix asked, stepping closer to Reginald as Mr. Hamersley casually wandered away, stopping beside Miss Helene Leggett a moment later.

"Why are you perpetuating a clear deceit on society?" Reginald countered.

Beatrix batted her lashes. "I'm sure I have no idea what you're talking about."

Reginald nodded to Mr. Hamersley, who was lifting Helene's hand to his lips, clear adoration on his face as he did so. "I think that speaks for itself."

Beatrix squinted at Mr. Hamersley, before she rolled her eyes. "Honestly, I told him to have a care with showing any unusual amount of affection for Helene when he's in public, but apparently he's somewhat confused about what constitutes an unusual amount of affection."

"So you *are* perpetuating a deceit on society, aren't you?"

Beatrix blew out a huff. "Fine. Thomas and I *are* being less than forthcoming to society about our true relationship, but we're not doing so to harm anyone. It merely suits both of us to allow society to believe we have an understanding."

"Why?"

"Because Thomas's mother has always wanted their family to form an alliance with mine via marriage with me. She can be a most unpleasant woman, not above resorting to plots and schemes to get her way. Our supposed relationship has provided Thomas with a way to avoid his mother's drama."

"Until she becomes aware that he's fonder of Helene Leggett than you."

"Thomas is fond of me, just in a different way."

Reginald inclined his head. "I'm sure he is, but tell me this. I now understand his motivation for keeping up the pretense, but what of yours?"

Beatrix shrugged. "My motivation is relatively simple. I have no desire to be pursued for my fortune, nor do I really see a need to marry."

"You don't want to marry?"

"Not particularly."

"But what if you fall in love?"

"Then I'll need to revisit my decision, although I have no intention of falling in love until I'm at least forty and have experienced more of what life has to offer."

Reginald frowned. "And you expect to continue with the charade you and Thomas are perpetuating until you're forty?"

She glanced to where Thomas was still standing beside Helene, his head bent close to her as Helene whispered something to him. "I give it, at the most, a year, although I'm not sure how Thomas is going to go about breaking the news to his mother. She was recently seen inquiring about china patterns at Rutherford & Company."

"Perhaps both of you should divulge your duplicity before Mrs. Hamersley buys that china or begins ordering monogrammed linens."

Beatrix shook her head. "I have no intention of spending this Season dodging potential suitors, nor has Thomas gotten up enough nerve to disclose his affection for Helene to his mother just yet. He certainly doesn't want to provide his mother with a reason to try and disrupt Helene's entrance into high society."

"Wouldn't Helene's entrance into society actually help Thomas's case with his mother?"

"Not when Helene's family is nouveau riche. Mrs. Hamersley finds that state to be unacceptable."

"A complicated situation to be sure."

"Indeed," Beatrix agreed, frowning. "But speaking of a complicated situation, Poppy seems to have been cornered by Nigel and Lena. If you'll excuse me, I believe I should go see about rescuing her."

As Beatrix hurried away, Murray moseyed over to join Reginald, shaking his head as he nodded to where Poppy was now beaming a bright smile at Beatrix, clearly relieved to see her friend.

"We might have to intervene with *that* at some point," Murray said.

"That?"

Murray frowned. "And here I agreed to accept your advice and expertise about women and romance, when you're not nearly as savvy as you think you are."

"I have no idea what you're saying."

"Poppy has no interest in Nigel Flaherty. But, he, if you haven't realized, has an interest in her. And, if I'm not mistaken, Lena Ridgeway has that matchmaking gleam in her eye that so many older women seem to get when they're around eligible ladies and gentlemen. I believe she's interested in seeing her dear Nigel matched up with Poppy."

Reginald's jaw clenched. "You don't say."

"I do say. Nigel's been having flowers delivered here daily, and he brought chocolates with him today, but not for Poppy—for Viola. That was a rather shrewd move on his part because Viola readily admits her greatest weakness is chocolate, something I heard Lena say she remembered. That means Lena is probably the one who encouraged Nigel to bring Viola the chocolates, and it was Lena who managed to secure them an invitation to the tea." Murray shook his head. "Nigel doesn't seem to me to be the type of gentleman to accept defeat—or rejection for that matter—so you, being Poppy's most intimidating friend, at least in my humble opinion, will probably need to have a chat with him at some point."

"I can't simply stroll up to the man and tell him to leave Poppy alone."

"Sure you can, although I'm not going to encourage you to do that right now. Poppy seems to be fine, and I doubt Viola would appreciate the argument that's certain to erupt between you and Nigel." Murray smiled. "Did I mention that Viola's invited me to live in this house for as long as I want?"

Finding it beyond peculiar that Murray would switch the conversation so abruptly, Reginald frowned. "No, you didn't, but since when have you taken to calling Viola by her given name?"

"Since she and I became friends."

"Are you considering taking her up on her offer?"

Murray shook his head. "Probably not. Poppy's been relatively vocal about me getting out on my own. Doesn't think I should exchange living in one domineering woman's house for another. Believes it'll ruin my chances of discovering the man I'm meant to be, or something like that." Murray smiled again. "That's why Poppy and I are going out tomorrow or the next day to take a look at those Osborne Flats. Poppy doesn't want to leave me with too much time to consider Viola's offer."

"I thought you found Viola to be a frightening sort?"

"Oh I do, but we share a common love of art, and even though I'm going to strike out on my own, Viola has offered me the use of the attic here to use as a studio. Since the lighting is wonderful, I'm going to take her up on that offer."

"And I'm going to take Murray up on his offer of helping me become more proficient with watercolors," Viola said, causing Reginald to jump as she suddenly appeared beside him.

Apprehension slid through him when she smiled and then reached out and actually patted his arm, nodding to where Poppy had somehow managed to escape from Nigel and Lena and was now chatting with some other guests. "I believe I have you to thank for the wonderful way Poppy is comporting herself today. Why, she's taken it upon herself to greet every person here and has even gone so far as to spend extra time with the few friends of mine we invited." Her smile widened. "Some of my friends, I'm sure you can imagine, are somewhat—how did you just describe me?—oh yes, frightening sorts, but Poppy doesn't seem bothered by that at all."

"You weren't supposed to hear that bit," Reginald said.

"And I also probably shouldn't have admitted I heard you, but . . ." Viola's eyes twinkled. "I do think Poppy might be having an influence on me." She nodded to Murray. "We'll be taking our seats in the dining room soon. You'll be pleased to discover that Poppy and I put your name card directly beside Miss Maisie Leggett's." Leaving Murray looking completely delighted, Viola strolled away, joining Poppy on the other side of the room right as the butler, Mr. Parsons, announced that tea and coffee were ready to be served and encouraged everyone to follow him to the dining room.

After walking down the painting-lined hallway that led to the dining room, Reginald moved through the doorway, taking a second to appreciate the sight of the long table, expertly set for thirty with bone china and crystal. Numerous flower arrangements ran down the center of the table, while gilt-engraved place cards were waiting on gilded charger plates to direct guests to their proper seats.

Even though he'd known he wouldn't be sitting beside Poppy because Charles had been given the seat of honor, he was a bit surprised to find Adele sitting next to him. She was looking rather smug, and given the look Poppy sent her when she noticed where Adele was sitting, Reginald got the distinct impression Adele had taken a few liberties with the place cards. Resignation settled in as Adele immediately began to launch into another discussion of her accomplishments, but it came to an abrupt end when Beatrix, who was sitting on the other side of Reginald, changed the subject to how everyone was intending on spending Christmas.

As everyone in their near vicinity began telling their plans while they sipped cups of steaming tea or strong coffee that was served by liveried members of the Van Rensselaer staff, Reginald found his gaze going back time and again to Poppy, who was sitting at the opposite end of the table, chatting away with Charles, as well as with Miss Edith Iselin, who was sitting on Charles's other side.

Poppy suddenly looked up, caught his eye, sent him the barest hint of a wink, then returned her attention to Edith and Charles.

"Isn't it curious?" Beatrix asked quietly, nodding toward Edith, but then going still when Adele leaned forward and rolled her eyes.

"There's nothing curious about Edith sitting next to Lord Lonsdale," Adele said shortly. "Edith is one of those ladies who gentlemen find nonthreatening. I'm sure Poppy decided to seat Edith beside Charles as a way to avoid unwelcomed animosity being raised between any of the ladies he's set his eye on."

Beatrix's brows drew together. "How do you know he hasn't set his eye on Edith?"

Adele waved that aside with a flick of a wrist. "Because Edith hasn't spent any time with Reginald, or for that matter, with Giles. Everyone knows Lord Lonsdale is counting on Reginald and Giles to help him choose the perfect countess in the end." She smiled and batted her lashes Reginald's way.

"More tea?" Beatrix asked, and not waiting for one of the servers to refresh Reginald's cup, she took it upon herself to do it for him, earning his undying appreciation for saving him from additional attempts on Adele's part to impress him.

Beatrix then started a discussion about horses, a subject on which she was clearly passionate. And Adele, after trying unsuccessfully to broach the subject of her many accomplishments once again, finally joined in with her opinion about horses, proving that she could actually speak, and quite nicely at that, on subjects other than herself.

When all the tea and coffee was gone, along with the small sandwiches, fruit, and cheeses, Poppy rose to her feet, clinked a knife against a crystal glass, then waited until the guests grew silent before smiling all around.

"On behalf of the Van Rensselaer family," she began, "I'd like to take a moment to thank all of you for joining us today. I know the ride to get here was treacherous, and I'm hoping all of you found the effort worthwhile."

Polite applause sounded about the two rooms, although Beatrix and Murray were clapping enthusiastically, and Murray might have released a bit of a whistle.

Poppy inclined her head. "We'll be serving a delightful cake in a few minutes, one that was, well . . ." She shot a glance to her grandmother and grinned. "I'll simply leave it at delightful, but before we get to the cake, I'd like to broach the topic of Five Points. I've only recently discovered that part of the city, and I must say I was disheartened to view the horrible conditions there. Because we are quickly getting into the Christmas season, a time when goodwill should be shared by all, I'm looking for some volunteers to go with me to Five Points and assess the situation down there."

Adele raised her hand, quite as if she were in the classroom. "Forgive me, but that's madness," she said after Poppy nodded her way. "Everyone knows there are nasty criminals roaming freely down there."

"A most excellent point, but I'm hoping some of the gentlemen in attendance will volunteer to help as well, which will lend us some much-needed protection."

"Wouldn't it be easier if you just asked for donations for this cause of yours?" Adele pressed.

Poppy narrowed her eyes. "Well, yes, but then we would never know for sure if our money was reaching the right people. If we go there, we'll be better equipped to understand what needs to be done."

Adele frowned. "It almost sounds as if you'd like us to dirty our hands, so to speak, in Five Points."

"That's exactly what I'd like to do."

"That's not how we do things in society," Adele returned. "We give money; we don't get in the trenches."

Poppy's smile dimmed, but just as Reginald was getting to his feet, Charles rose from his chair and smiled.

"I, for one, believe this to be a most exciting idea, Poppy," he began. "And while I've never been to Five Points, I'd like to be the first to volunteer to come with you."

Edith was suddenly standing as well. "I'd like to volunteer as well."

Poppy smiled. "How lovely. Thank you, Lord Lonsdale, Miss Iselin."

George rose to his feet. "And you know I'll be there, as well as your grandmother, and we'll make a sizable monetary donation to the cause." He nodded to the guests. "Feel free to do the same."

"I'll donate," Murray said as Beatrix stood as well and added, "As will I."

"Anyone else?" Charles asked, and before Reginald knew it, Adele was rising from her chair, although she did so rather reluctantly, and was soon joined by every other guest in the room.

"I believe Charles has just cemented Poppy's standing in society, along with coercing society members to actually volunteer to do some real good in the world," Beatrix muttered.

"I believe you're right," Reginald returned as Poppy beamed all around.

"Your willingness to help is quite overwhelming," Poppy said. "And to celebrate, I'll now have the staff bring out that cake I mentioned."

Feeling an odd sense of pride as Poppy nodded to one of the servers, Reginald allowed his gaze to linger on her, wondering how it had happened that he'd become so involved in her life and accomplishments.

In all honesty, he'd not been responsible for many of her successes, even with him instructing her on proper behavior. Those successes had come about when Poppy was simply being Poppy, an original as Miss Mabel had deemed her, and . . .

"If you'll excuse me, Cynthia seems to be trying to get my attention," Adele said, rising from her chair as Reginald did the same, retaking his seat after she walked over to where Cynthia was sitting a few feet away. She leaned closer to Cynthia, and a second later, the two ladies were whispering furiously.

"And here it is," Poppy exclaimed, stepping away from the table as she moved toward the two servers who were bringing in the cake.

"Poppy baked it and Murray decorated it," Beatrix whispered. "But don't let that get out. Viola wants to keep it quiet about Poppy's love for the kitchen and baking."

Reginald nodded and glanced to the cake, one that was three tiers tall and iced in white, with exquisitely painted flowers splashed over the icing.

"If you'll put the cake right over here"—Poppy nodded to a side table against the wall as she moved to direct the servers—"we'll allow everyone to appreciate it for a second before we . . ."

The next moment seemed to happen in slow motion.

One minute Poppy was gliding along, passing where Adele and Cynthia were still whispering, and the next, she seemed to be rolling across the floor, her arms flailing about, right before she careened into the two servers who were carrying the cake.

A second after that, the cake was flying through the air.

And a second after *that*, shrieks rang out as it landed on the table, splattering cake and icing on numerous guests in the process.

Chapter 20

"Tell me again why we have to go riding before the sun comes up?" Murray called through the door of the carriage house.

Poppy tugged up the trousers she was pulling on, cinched the belt she'd borrowed from one of the grooms, then strode over to the carriage house door. She opened it a crack and frowned. "Shh, keep your voice down. We don't want to wake my grandmother."

"Why not?" Murray shot back, his voice ringing out in the crisp December air.

"We're going to have to teach him a thing or two about stealth," Beatrix said, looking up as she went about the tricky business of getting all her curls stuffed underneath a hat. "Since you're now dressed, though, Poppy, perhaps you should bring him inside to join us before he wakes up the entire neighborhood."

With a nod, Poppy opened the door a few more inches, grabbed hold of Murray's arm and yanked him inside, rolling her eyes when he let out a touch of a shriek. "If you don't stop making so much noise, Beatrix and I are going to leave you behind."

Murray's gaze slid over Poppy. "What are you wearing?"

"They're called trousers, something you're wearing as well."

"But . . . why are you wearing trousers, and . . ." He turned to

Beatrix. "Why are you stuffing your hair underneath that ratty old hat?"

"Poppy and I can't very well dress as ladies today. We'll draw too much notice down in Five Points, nor can we ride astride if we're wearing skirts."

Murray immediately turned indignant. "No one said anything about us riding down to Five Points. I was under the impression we were simply going to take Wilbur over to Central Park to see how he reacts to me using a saddle on him."

Beatrix waved a hand toward Wilbur, where he stood fully saddled in his stall. "I already took him around the block. He's fine carrying a rider and has a lovely gait, which means you'll enjoy a pleasant ride to Five Points."

Panic flickered through Murray's eyes. "But why would I *want* to ride to Five Points? That's hardly a suitable destination for what I thought was supposed to be a relaxing morning ride."

Poppy crossed her arms over her chest. "Did you or did you not agree to help me come up with a plan to improve the lives of the people living in tenant housing?"

"You know I did, but I thought that meant I'd act as your secretary, penning out all of your ideas since I have such fine penmanship." He lifted his chin. "I'm not sure I would have agreed to assist you if I'd known you were planning to travel to Five Points, dressed in disguise no less, and with only me and Beatrix to accompany you, unless . . ." He suddenly looked hopeful. "Dare I hope that Reginald is soon to arrive to accompany us?"

Poppy allowed herself the luxury of a snort. "Can you honestly believe Reginald would agree to peruse the conditions in Five Points after it was discovered that someone—and probably on purpose—let loose a handful of musket balls two days ago to trip me up at my own tea?"

Murray's face fell. "He does seem to have adopted a most protective air around you."

"He's taken to treating me with kid gloves, which is rather sweet, but I'm feeling a tad stifled." Poppy blew out a breath. "He also convinced my grandparents that additional attempts to sabotage me are a distinct possibility, since he believes someone is determined to see me become the laughingstock of society. That has turned my grandparents overprotective as well and is exactly why we're sneaking out of the house at the crack of dawn. With winter setting in, the people living in Five Points are certainly suffering, and I'm determined to help them as soon as I possibly can. I won't be able to do that, though, if I'm only allowed to travel to society events under the watchful eyes of Reginald and my grandparents."

"Couldn't you send Reginald and a few of the other gentlemen who offered to help down to Five Points to scout it out while you remain safe on Fifth Avenue?" Murray asked.

Poppy shook her head. "It's my cause, and sending others in my stead is no better than merely handing over some money and allowing someone else to do the dirty work."

"But it's dangerous in Five Points," Murray argued.

"Which is why Beatrix and I are armed as well as disguised. And it's also why Beatrix didn't bring Hazel today because—"

"Why would Beatrix want to bring my mother along?"

Beatrix grinned. "Not that Hazel, Murray—my horse, Hazel, the one with distinctive markings, which is why I can't bring her with me."

Murray winced. "Oh, right. I forgot you bought my horse, although it's really not well done of you to continue calling it Hazel. My mother is certain to be most put out when she learns you've not changed its name."

"And *I'm* certainly put out with all of you, unless there's a reasonable explanation as to why you're skulking around in the carriage house, dressed in . . . are those trousers, Poppy?"

Poppy closed her eyes for the briefest of seconds before she forced herself to turn, finding Viola standing in the doorway, wearing a flannel dressing gown with her hair wrapped in rags, looking exactly as if she'd only just rolled out of bed.

"This is certainly an unexpected surprise" was all Poppy could think to say.

"I'm certain you are surprised, just as I'm completely astonished to discover you out here and intent on no good, if I'm not much mistaken."

"Aren't you supposed to be sleeping?"

"I heard you creep downstairs thirty minutes ago. And then because I was already awake and thought you were heading for the kitchen to do some of that baking you seem to enjoy so early in the morning, I decided to join you and have a cup of coffee with you while you baked."

"You've never once joined me for a cup of coffee in the morning."

"True, but does that mean I *shouldn't* start doing so?"

"Why do you want to?"

For a second, Poppy didn't think Viola would answer, but then she blew out a breath. "Because I *did* blackmail you into accepting a Season. But because you didn't grow up with the other young ladies out this Season and because I let the extent of your dowry become publicly known, I never considered that I was placing you in such a hostile environment." She heaved a sigh. "I've been involved with society for decades and know firsthand how malevolent it can be, and yet I threw you to the wolves, even knowing as I did that you had no experience dealing with wolves."

"I do have experience dealing with foxes, though," Poppy said. "They're pesky creatures, crafty as well, and they do enjoy stirring up drama with the chickens on the farm."

"An unusual analogy, but I suppose it's an apt one." Viola caught Poppy's eye. "You've handled yourself with grace and good humor through all the trials you've faced and rarely complained, except occasionally about the lessons you take from Reginald, and you've made me finally realize that I don't know you at all." She nodded, just once. "I'd like to rectify that, even though I must admit I'm afraid that if you and I get closer, you'll have the ability to hurt me, just the way your mother hurt me when she ran away."

"I've no intention of leaving you, Viola."

"Grandmother," Viola corrected.

Poppy inclined her head. "Grandmother, then, and with that settled, I suggest you return to the house since it's chilly outside and you're not dressed for the conditions. I'm sure there's hot coffee waiting for you in the kitchen."

"Do you honestly believe that I'm going to shuffle off to the kitchen and leave the three of you to continue whatever madness you've evidently got planned for the day?"

"It was worth a try," Poppy muttered as Beatrix stepped forward.

"We're not planning any madness, Mrs. Van Rensselaer. We're merely going out for a ride."

"Dressed in trousers and at the crack of dawn?" Viola countered.

"They want to go down to Five Points to do a touch of investigating, or more specifically, to visit the House of Industry," Murray said in a rush, keeping his attention squarely on Viola, which had him missing the scowl Poppy sent him, although he most assuredly heard the "Traitor" Beatrix said under her breath because he winced.

Viola's eyes flashed. "Five Points? Young ladies never go to Five Points on their own."

"We'll have Murray with us," Poppy pointed out.

"Murray doesn't seem too keen about your plan."

"Well, clearly, or he wouldn't have spit it out to you like that," Poppy said. "However, as I told Murray earlier, I want to help the people in Five Points sooner than later. But because I've become such a peculiar attraction of late, what with people showing up to pay calls every single day in the hopes they'll witness me do something unexpected like dangle myself from a balcony or dump a cake on someone's head, if I don't slip away this morning, I won't have another opportunity to get to Five Points until after the holidays. Christmas is in two days, and then after that, well, I have to learn all the steps to the Dresden China Quadrille."

"I'm sure many of those people paying you calls, especially the gentlemen, would be more than willing to accompany you to Five Points—or better yet, go in your stead," Viola said.

"I'm sure you're right, but I've had a change of heart about having numerous society members come with me the first time or two I travel into a less desirable part of the city. I believe including those society members will make the outing seem more like a social occasion rather than a mission. I don't think the people living in Five Points are going to disclose their true needs if they conclude I'm down there on some type of lark."

Viola considered Poppy for a very long moment before giving a bob of her head. "An excellent point, my dear. But because you are your mother's daughter and because I know full well if I forbid you to go you'll end up climbing out a window or some such nonsense, risking that stubborn neck of yours in the process, I'm coming with you."

"What?" Poppy and Beatrix asked together.

"I'm coming with you," Viola repeated.

"You, well, ah, can't come with us," Poppy all but sputtered. "We're going in disguise, but our disguises as ordinary men will never work if we're seen in the company of a member of the New York Four Hundred."

Viola waved that aside. "I'll go in disguise as well."

"We're riding astride," Poppy said, wincing when she heard the trace of desperation in her voice.

"I've always wanted to ride astride."

"We don't have the time to teach you. If you've forgotten, I'm meeting Reginald after lunch to begin quadrille lessons."

Viola arched a brow. "Even though you seem to land yourself in the most unusual of circumstances, Poppy, you're inherently graceful, something I'm convinced you inherited not only from your mother but also from me. I assure you it won't take me long to learn how to ride astride, so stop arguing and let us get on with matters."

Thirty minutes later, Poppy was fighting a grin as she watched her grandmother canter down Broadway, dressed as a man and riding astride, quite as if she'd been riding that way since birth.

239

Five minutes had been all it had taken for Viola to get accustomed to the new method, and given the way her grandmother's lips kept curving, Poppy was certain Viola had discovered a new love in life, one that was going to see her donning trousers whenever she felt she could get away with it. She certainly seemed keen to be out and about without wearing a corset, something Viola had abandoned after she realized her form didn't look remotely masculine under the shirt she'd borrowed from Mr. Parsons, fetched for her by Murray, as were the trousers she was wearing.

"I wonder what George is going to say, Viola, when he learns what you've been up to today," Beatrix said, riding her horse with ease beside Viola, as Murray bounced along beside her on Wilbur, not quite having found his seat yet.

Viola blinked innocently at Beatrix. "I don't think there's any reason for me to tell George about our little adventure today. We rarely confide all the details of our day to each other, and I see no reason to change that now."

Beatrix grinned. "And you're afraid he'll decide you've taken leave of your senses."

Viola, surprisingly enough, returned the grin. "There is that." She steered her horse, a spirited mare by the name of Trotter, around a delivery wagon, waited for everyone to do the same, then nodded to Poppy. "But speaking of your grandfather, he didn't uncover any new information last night while visiting the Union Club about who might have dropped those musket balls at our tea."

Poppy frowned. "I wouldn't imagine he *would* find out anything new. There was plenty of time after my accident for someone to claim responsibility. But since no one stepped forward at the tea, I doubt anyone will suddenly feel overwhelmed with guilt and do so now."

"I think Adele is to blame," Beatrix said. "She's the most likely culprit, given how much she clearly dislikes you, Poppy."

"And I think you're wrong about that," Murray argued. "Adele ended up with more than her fair share of cake on her head and suffered a fit of the vapors directly after that happened, which did not show her to advantage to Charles."

Beatrix smiled. "She did look a fright, but I have to imagine if she is to blame, she wasn't counting on the cake going airborne when Poppy slipped on the musket balls." Her smile faded. "Does anyone else find it peculiar that someone used those to trip Poppy up?"

Viola nodded. "It was a most unusual weapon of choice, but highly effective."

"But only for a brief moment," Murray said. "Oddly enough, Poppy's accident seems to have made her one of the most sought-after ladies of the Season."

"Only because I've become a curiosity," Poppy said, slowing her horse as she looked around. "Shouldn't we be turning off onto a side street soon to return to the area where little Maria lives?"

"Are you intending to find this little Maria?" Viola asked.

"Not unless I can't find the House of Industry." Poppy nudged her horse forward. "I thought we'd start there, seek out the Reverend Lewis who Maria mentioned and see if he might be able to point us in the right direction, where our efforts to help the needy would be most useful."

It took them fifteen minutes of winding their way through side streets that were less than reputable before they stumbled upon the House of Industry—and only by accident, after a man Poppy had asked for directions sent them almost to the Battery before a woman selling hot chestnuts got them turned around. Reining her horse to a stop, Poppy glanced over the five-story building in front of her, one that took up at least half the block.

"It's an impressive size," Murray said, digging into the paper sack of chestnuts he'd purchased and popping one in his mouth. "I wonder what type of services they offer here."

"I believe they offer classes in a variety of subjects but mostly teach immigrants English and offer children standard lessons," Beatrix said, digging into her own sack of chestnuts before she looked up and caught Poppy's eye. "I'm ashamed I don't know much more than that though, having never thought to investigate this particular mission effort further."

"At least we're here now," Poppy said as four lads burst through the door of the House of Industry and came charging their way.

"We'll hold your horses for you if you're here to see Reverend Lewis," one of the larger lads said, stopping directly beside Viola.

"And how do we know the four of you are to be trusted with our horses?" Viola asked in her most intimidating voice, which, instead of leaving the boys looking properly terrified, had them descending into giggles.

Viola frowned. "What could they possibly find so amusing?"

Poppy grinned. "I imagine they weren't expecting you to sound like a lady since you're dressed like a man."

Viola rolled her eyes. "Well of course they weren't, and here I thought I was doing so well with my masquerade." She cleared her throat. "Can you be trusted?" she asked the boys in a voice she'd lowered a good octave, which had them giggling harder right as an older gentleman walked out of the House of Industry and strode over to join them.

"Are you lost?" he asked.

"You have no idea," Murray muttered as Poppy swallowed a laugh and inclined her head toward the man.

"We're here to speak with Reverend Lewis."

A trace of wariness flickered through the man's eyes. "What do you want with him? Or better yet, why are three of you dressed like men when you're obviously nothing of the sort?"

Poppy winced. "Apparently we need to perfect the art of assuming the role of men, but to answer your question, Maria Romano told me that Reverend Lewis ran the House of Industry. We're here to question him about how we could best go about improving the lives of those living in Five Points."

The man blinked before he smiled. "You're Miss Poppy, aren't you?"

"You know my name?"

The man nodded. "Maria told me all about you when she came

with her mother to visit me. I'm Reverend Lewis, dear, and I with-held my name because we often encounter questionable sorts here, mostly men looking to hire on some of the women who work here, but hire them under false pretenses, which can leave those women in dire straits."

"No wonder you were wary," Poppy said before she swung from the saddle and went to help her grandmother, who seemed rather annoyed that she was having difficulty getting down from her horse.

After Reverend Lewis instructed the young boys to take the horses to the stables located on the side of the building, he mo-tioned for everyone to follow him into the House of Industry. He led them to the third floor, where the offices were kept, pointing out along the way the sewing room, dining hall, and then classrooms where they taught students, young and old alike.

Gesturing them into chairs once they reached the office, he took a seat, then launched into the history of the House of Industry, explaining all the services available at the mission.

"We offer women a new chance at life here, as well as take in orphans from the streets," he eventually concluded with a smile. "We're always in need of supplies, and we could use a few extra hands to serve up a Christmas meal."

Viola sat forward. "I would be more than willing to donate."

"Would you also be willing to come here on Christmas and help us see after those most in need?" he asked.

To Poppy's surprise, Viola didn't hesitate to nod. "Of course. I can also have my staff prepare more hams and whatever else you may want to serve, which I'll deliver after my granddaughter and I, along with her grandfather, present ourselves for service."

"I'll help too," Beatrix said as Murray nodded and added, "As will I."

Reverend Lewis beamed a smile all around. "How marvelous." He turned to Poppy. "Maria told me you were an unusual woman, and clearly she was right. But I am thankful she mentioned the House of Industry to you because we could use your assistance.

The number of poor in the city is increasing at an unprecedented rate, and I'm afraid the resources we have don't go as far as they used to. I've been praying every morning and every evening, asking God to send us desperately needed assistance, and"—he caught Poppy's eye—"here you are."

Poppy smiled. "I wouldn't be surprised if God did direct me here, what with the strange circumstances I experienced that led me to Five Points in the first place. And now that I'm beginning to understand the need in this area, I'm going to make a concerted effort to strongly encourage other members of society to step up and help. Hopefully, we'll be—"

Before she could finish, a boy suddenly rushed into the room, skidding to a stop directly in front of Reverend Lewis. "You'd best come quick, sir. There's been another accident at that laundry up the street and someone said people died. A crowd's already gathering to protest the conditions at the laundry, and they're turning rowdy."

"You should get on your way" was all Reverend Lewis said before he strode from the room.

"I believe he's right," Viola said, rising to her feet and heading for the door, Poppy falling into step beside her with Beatrix and Murray close behind.

By the time they reached the street, they could see that the crowd was on the move, streaming down Worth Street in front of the House of Industry, their demands of better working conditions shouted in voices raw with fury.

"Too bad Reginald never caught up with us after I sent that note around to him," Murray said, his eyes wide as he took in the chaos unfolding around them.

"You sent Reginald a note?" Poppy asked, craning her neck as she tried to discover exactly where the stables were located.

"'Course I did, and no need to get up in arms, Poppy. Everyone knows mayhem follows in your wake, and here's the proof." Murray gave a somewhat feeble wave of his hand to the crowd surrounding them, one that seemed to be swelling by the second.

"I see the stables," Beatrix yelled, raising her voice to be heard over the noise.

Tugging her hat lower over her face, Poppy grabbed hold of her grandmother's hand and began hurrying through the crowd, tightening her grip as they were jostled by the horde of people. Ignoring a fight that broke out directly to her left, she plowed forward, coming to a stop when a burly man suddenly stepped directly in front of her.

"Excuse me," she muttered, but when the man didn't move, she lifted her head, disbelief flowing through her when she recognized him as being none other than the man who'd tried to steal her reticule.

By the way his eyes widened when his gaze settled on her face, she knew he'd recognized her as well. What she wasn't expecting, though, was for him to shove Viola away from her and then pick her up as if she weighed nothing at all. He slung her over his back, rather like one would sling a sack of potatoes, then began pushing his way through the crowd, completely ignoring her shrieks of outrage.

"Poppy! I'm coming, hold—"

For the briefest of seconds, Poppy thought the voice calling out to her belonged to Reginald, but before she could respond, the man holding her picked up his pace. Growling at someone to get out of his way, the man suddenly stopped dead in his tracks as police whistles rent the air.

In a blink of an eye, Poppy found herself dumped to the cobblestones as the man abandoned her and fled into the crowd.

Dodging people as she scrambled to her feet, she shoved aside a man who'd lurched into her, raising an arm to deflect the blow the man she'd just shoved seemed about ready to render.

To her relief, the man suddenly lowered his arm and raced away, but her relief was short lived when she turned around and discovered a policeman scowling back at her.

"Thank goodness you've arrived on the scene, officer," she began, "for a minute there I thought—"

Whatever else she'd been about to say got lost when the policeman took hold of her arm and began marching her through the crowd, not letting go of her until he'd all but tossed her into what, unfortunately, turned out to be a police wagon bound for jail.

CHAPTER 21

Traveling to a local jail had not been on his agenda for the day—or ever, if the truth were known.

Coming to a stop in front of the cell a policeman had directed him to, Reginald blinked as he peered through the bars and got his first glimpse of Poppy, Viola, and Murray.

To say they looked the worse for wear was an understatement.

Murray's nose was once again dripping blood. He'd lost his hat and his hair was standing on end as he slouched on the wooden bench he was sharing with Poppy.

Viola was sitting stiff as a poker on the other side of Poppy. Her face, what could be seen of it since she'd pulled a woven cap down almost over her eyes, was smudged with dirt. Her jacket was torn and filthy, and the trousers she was wearing, which were something he'd never imagined a grand society lady wearing, were covered in mud and sported a large tear in one of the knees.

Poppy, quite like her grandmother, was filthy from head to toe, her cap pulled down as well, but not far enough to where the curiosity in her eyes was hidden as she leaned closer to Viola, whispering something that had Viola nodding.

Relief flowed freely as Reginald realized Poppy was unharmed, although that relief was mixed with a hefty dose of exasperation, since she'd once again managed to become involved in another bout of mayhem, this one of epic proportions.

When he'd received Murray's hastily scribbled note, telling him that Poppy, Beatrix, and Viola were insisting on traveling to the House of Industry, Reginald had thrown on his clothes and summoned a hansom cab a mere five minutes later. Bouncing his way through the early morning traffic, he'd thought he'd prepared himself for whatever mischief Poppy was certain to have landed in, never imagining he'd be forced to fight his way through a mob.

He certainly hadn't imagined he'd find Poppy slung over some man's back, yelling at the top of her lungs as the man carried her through the crowd.

His heart had missed a beat as he'd plunged into that crowd after her, but before he'd been able to catch her, he'd been surrounded by furious men who'd begun swinging their fists at anything that moved.

By the time he'd fought his way free of those men, Poppy had somehow managed to become parted with the man who'd seemingly been about to abduct her and was being thrown into a wagon stuffed with protestors. Knowing he'd have little chance of seeing her removed from the wagon, not with all the chaos surrounding it, he'd had no choice but to run behind the wagon as it trundled away, keeping pace until it had passed through a gate that led directly to a jail.

A good two hours had passed before he'd finally been able to talk to someone about seeing her released. His plan to pay her bail, however, had come to a rapid end when he'd realized he'd become parted from his billfold at some point in time, probably while he'd been fighting his way through the mob. That pesky problem meant he had no available funds to secure her release, a situation he could certainly rectify, but one that annoyed him because if he'd realized his billfold had been pilfered, he would have returned to his hotel straightaway to fetch more funds instead of waiting around.

"Ah, Reginald, thank the good Lord you got my note."

Reginald blinked as Murray charged his way, gripping the bars that separated them with white knuckles, relief evident in his eyes. "Please tell me you've been able to secure our release."

Wincing, Reginald shook his head. "I'm afraid not, Murray. I've apparently been a victim of a pickpocket, so all of you will need to sit tight a bit longer until I can fetch more funds. I'm simply here to tell you not to worry because I will get all of you released at some point today, but . . . where's Beatrix?"

"Last I saw her, she was leading some young girls out of the crowd," Murray said, "which has me hoping she managed to avoid the dastardly business of being carted off to jail."

"And has me hoping that when she finds us here, she'll know exactly how to get us released," Poppy said, moving up to join Murray.

"Unless she was a victim of pickpockets as well," Reginald said, trying to ignore that Poppy, even in her bedraggled state, was looking rather adorable, what with the dirt smudged across her nose and bits of hair straggling out from underneath the cap on her head. He felt the oddest urge to reach through the bars and pull her toward him, needing to feel her in the flesh to truly ascertain she'd not been harmed.

"On my word, I forgot. I have money with me," Poppy said right before she unbuttoned her jacket. A second later she began rummaging around underneath her shirt, stilling when Murray drew in a sharp breath and gave a bob of his head toward two men on the other side of the cell, who were now watching Poppy far too closely.

"Do you want to start another riot?" Murray whispered furiously.

"Since I've just realized my money must have fallen out when I was upside down over that man's back, there's nothing to riot about," she whispered back as she withdrew her hand and buttoned herself back up. She caught Reginald's eye. "I guess it'll be up to you to track down our bail money now, and may I suggest you get on your way so that we don't have to linger long in this cell?"

Reginald's jaw clenched, as did his hands as he realized the two men were now watching her more intently than ever. "I'm not leaving you now, not when those men have apparently realized you're no man and are looking at you like they've just found their next meal."

She lifted her chin. "How was I to know I'd draw such attention?"

Reginald ran a hand over his beard. "You wouldn't be drawing attention at all if you'd had the good sense to remain in your home today, trimming the house for Christmas instead of dashing off to Five Points on a madcap adventure."

Poppy's chin rose another inch. "We weren't on a madcap adventure, and we couldn't have known we'd find ourselves dragged into a riot."

"But you should have known, what with your peculiar proclivity for attracting trouble, that something unforeseen would transpire. At the very least, you should have waited for me, or even your grandfather, to accompany you."

"My grandmother accompanied us," Poppy shot back.

"Which is rather bewildering in and of itself, although given that she's languishing with you in the jail cell, I'm not certain I understand your point."

"A valid observation." Poppy nodded to Murray. "We brought Murray with us."

"Who is also behind bars."

Murray sent him a weak smile before turning to Poppy. "I don't believe you're going to win this particular argument." He gave a sad shake of his head. "I imagine Maisie will not think as highly of me once she learns I was unable to keep us all out of jail."

Poppy rubbed a soothing hand down Murray's arm. "Nonsense. I imagine Maisie will be nothing less than impressed with the dashing way you ran afoul of an enraged mob and lived to tell the tale." She caught Reginald's eye and gave a slight nod, quite as if she was encouraging him to agree with her.

Reginald, no matter that Poppy *was* looking adorable, was not in an accommodating frame of mind. "There's nothing remotely dashing about being arrested, and Murray will be fortunate if Mrs. Leggett, whom I've discovered is a rather overprotective mother, ever allows him to see Maisie again."

"That's hardly helpful," Poppy said, crossing her arms over her chest.

"I'm not feeling the urge to be helpful at the moment." He turned to Murray. "You should have tried harder to dissuade Poppy and Beatrix from today's madness."

Murray's brows drew together. "I did send you a note, begging for help. Besides, it's not as if *you've* seen much success in dissuading Poppy from anything she's set her mind on lately."

Reginald frowned. "True, but I bet Viola could have been persuaded to see reason."

"Where do you think Poppy gets her stubborn nature?" Murray countered before he shot a glance to Viola, who was inching her way from the man on the bench with her, her inching coming to an abrupt end when she ran out of room. Murray returned his gaze to Reginald and shuddered. "Viola was adamant about joining us after she discovered us making plans in the carriage house. She even made me fetch her men's clothing, not particularly concerned that I was going to have to do some fancy talking to explain to Mr. Parsons why I needed to borrow clothing in the first place, since I was already dressed for the day."

"She actually *wanted* to come with us," Poppy added, leveling a stern gaze on Reginald. "Which means you can swallow that lecture I'm sure you're dying to give me about dragging my poor, elderly grandmother to the slums, where she then, quite accidently, got arrested."

"I'm not elderly, dear," Viola suddenly called. "And it's my own fault I got arrested, what with how a policeman saw me slap a man after he almost bowled me over." She waved a hand covered in a tattered glove toward a man sitting on the opposite side of the cell. "He's right over there if you'd like to corroborate my story."

The man waved back at Viola and smiled, revealing a few missing teeth. "I sure am sorry about shovin' you, ma'am. Knew I'd made a mistake after you slapped me instead of punched me, which had me realizin' you were no man."

Even though Viola looked a bit taken aback that the man was speaking to her, she did incline her head. "Apology accepted, and you did try to intervene with the policeman who unjustly hauled me to a police wagon . . . which is exactly what landed *you* in jail, which I am sorry about." She smiled. "It was a gallant gesture on your part, so do know that I'll make sure you're released today as well, just as soon as that young man over there gets on with matters and goes off to fetch bail money." She caught Reginald's eye. "But don't go seeking the funds from George. I don't think there's any reason for him to learn about this little jaunt of mine. Wouldn't want to give him fodder for whenever he becomes cross with me over the next twenty years or so."

"You should have thought about that before," Reginald said, which earned him a narrowing of the eyes from Viola before she deliberately turned away from him.

"You've annoyed her now," Poppy muttered, a statement Reginald didn't believe there was any need to address.

"Why did that man try to make off with you?" he asked instead.

"Probably because he was the same man who stole my reticule and recognized me."

"Are you certain about that?"

"Of course I am, although what are the odds that I'd just happen to encounter a member of the criminal persuasion more than once, and in different parts of the city?"

"I would think those odds would be slim to none, which could mean this man's been following you."

Poppy released a bit of a snort. "I highly doubt that. Why would anyone of the criminal persuasion bother to stalk me? It's more likely this was only a chance encounter that lent the man an opportunity to extract a measure of retribution for thwarting him the first time."

Murray swiped a hand over a nose that was still dribbling

blood, ignoring that blood as he settled his full attention on Poppy. "Maybe the person who seems intent on disrupting your first New York Season has decided to up the stakes and get you to leave New York once and for all, and has hired members of the criminal persuasion to persuade you to do just that."

Poppy wrinkled her nose. "While I can certainly see Adele or a few of the other ladies out this Season scattering some musket balls to disrupt my tea, I can't imagine, given the sheltered life those ladies lead, that any of them would know how to go about hiring someone from the criminal class."

"True," Murray said with a nod right before he froze on the spot and emitted what sounded like a squeak.

"What?" Poppy asked, craning her neck to look at something behind Reginald before her eyes widened. "Grandfather . . . what are you doing here?"

Before Reginald could turn, George was standing directly beside him.

"What do you think I'm doing here? I've come to bail you out," George said, peering through the bars, his gaze settled on Viola, who had taken an absorbed interest in the ceiling, completely neglecting to acknowledge her husband, almost as if by not acknowledging him, he wasn't really standing directly outside her cell.

George's lips began to twitch. "Imagine my *astonishment*," he began cheerfully, "when Beatrix came to fetch me after being forced to leave all of you behind in Five Points because you'd been arrested and thrown into jail."

Viola abandoned her perusal of the ceiling and looked at her husband. "We were fairly astonished to find ourselves behind bars too."

George nodded as he looked his wife up and down. "You're a mess, Viola, and I've never seen you wear trousers before. Do you know there's a tear in one of your knees?"

Viola glanced down. "Ah, so there is. Must have happened when I was shoved aside."

"And then she slapped me, which had me knowin' she was no

253

man," the man missing a few teeth said as he sent a smile Viola's way. "I'd not mistake you for a man again because you're the most beautiful critter I ever seen."

"I believe you mean *creature*, dear," Viola corrected, which had the man smiling wider than ever as he nodded.

"Creature, that's the word. Don't know what I was thinkin' callin' you a critter."

"And I'm certain I don't know what to think about any of this," a lady drawled from behind Reginald, which had him turning as Poppy suddenly reached through the bars and took the hand the lady immediately held out to her.

"Mother!" Poppy exclaimed. "What in the world are you doing here?"

The lady, who was apparently Elizabeth Garrison, a lady Poppy distinctly resembled, let out a throaty laugh. "Why, I've come to New York for Christmas, my darling." Her gaze shifted from Poppy to Viola. "Good thing I have because I must say, there's something about seeing you behind bars, Mother, that lends the impression that Christmas has certainly come early this year."

CHAPTER 22

"Perhaps we should suggest another task for your mother and grandmother, Poppy," Murray said quietly, nodding to where Elizabeth and Viola were currently slicing up ham to serve to the people who'd come to the House of Industry for a warm Christmas meal. "Those knives they're wielding are making me nervous, what with how furious those two seem to be with each other at the moment."

Poppy stopped mashing potatoes and looked up, frowning when she saw Viola toss aside her knife, snatch up a platter of ham, and stalk out of the kitchen, muttering something under her breath.

What she was muttering was anyone's guess, but since Elizabeth looked Poppy's way, grinned, and sent her a bit of a wink before picking up another platter of ham and heading out of the kitchen as well, Poppy was fairly certain Elizabeth had been doing her best to annoy her mother again.

Poppy glanced back to Murray. "Since they've abandoned their knives, I don't believe we need to worry about any stabbings, but they're obviously not ready to put their mutual resentments behind them just yet."

Murray's brows drew together. "Don't you find their renewed animosity toward each other somewhat curious? They were getting along quite well last night at the Christmas Eve service and were even sharing a hymnal at one point. They were also being perfectly pleasant with each other this morning before I left to enjoy a Christmas breakfast with my mother."

"True," Poppy said. "But that pleasantness changed into palatable anger a mere second after my parents presented me with my Christmas present."

"Viola doesn't strike me as the type who'd begrudge her only granddaughter a nice present from her parents."

Poppy winced. "It was more than simply a nice present, Murray. My parents deeded me Garrison Farms in Pennsylvania."

"They gave you an entire horse farm?"

"They did, and while it was a more than generous gift, it was the one present that was certain to infuriate my grandmother."

"And the reason behind that fury would be . . . ?"

"Garrison Farms, while a much smaller operation than the new horse facility my parents are building in Kentucky, is still a viable business. The horse farm comes with acres and acres of land, along with a reputation of raising some of the best horses in the country."

"But your parents are moving to Kentucky. I would think they'd move all the horses there."

Poppy shook her head. "There was never any intention to abandon the operation in Pennsylvania; rather, they want to expand the family business into Kentucky, where the bulk of the horse industry is moving. The pastures we own in Pennsylvania allow our horses prime grazing land, while the farmhouse I grew up in is a lovely home, and none of us wanted to part with it because of its sentimental value." She smiled. "My paternal grandfather was born in that house, which is one of the reasons why my parents were willing to go through with having the bank foreclose on their land in Kentucky in order to save Garrison Farms, even though the foreclosure would have left us with very little money."

"But Viola stepped in before the foreclosure could happen, didn't she?"

"She did, which is why she's now so furious with my mother."

Murray tilted his head. "Because your mother wanted to make certain you have a reason to leave society after this Season?"

"Exactly, and I'm relatively certain Mother also wanted to make certain that I knew there was no reason to accept the dowry Grandmother has settled on me because Garrison Farms will provide me with a suitable dowry—not that I believe I need a dowry in the first place."

"It's very complicated, isn't it?"

"I can't argue with that," Poppy said, returning her attention to the potatoes. "And while I understand my mother's reasoning, and understand that she's apparently under the belief I want nothing more than to spend my life raising horses, I'm going to have to have a long chat with both of my parents in the not-too-distant future to clear up a few misunderstandings."

Murray nodded. "You need to tell them that you're not meant to live on a horse farm."

She stopped her mashing. "How do you know that?"

"Please," Murray said as he returned to his potatoes. "Even though you've proclaimed time and time again that you're not suited to society life, you enjoy the hustle and bustle of New York." He nodded to the room at large. "You've also just found your noble purpose, and I don't believe you'll want to abandon it to return to a peaceful life in the country." He leaned closer to her. "I am curious as to what you'll do with the farm, though. Hire someone to manage it for you?"

"No. I'll simply ask my parents to divide it up equally between my two brothers and me, something I was under the impression they'd been intending to do anyway." She smiled. "I'm certain my younger brother, Robert, would be more than willing to take over the operation there, seeing as how he's completely mad about horses. He's actually been running the farm for the past few months on his own while my parents have been spending their time on their new venture in Kentucky."

"What about your other brother?"

"Nathan's intent on pursuing a career in law."

Murray frowned. "Seems like you have it all figured out, but, and don't get annoyed with me for saying this, but what if you happen to find a gentleman you adore who'd want to help you manage a horse farm? He might be disappointed to learn you refused your parents' generosity."

Poppy returned the frown. "I'd hope that any gentleman I might end up adoring would want to spend his life with me simply because of me, not because marrying me would give him access to a profitable horse farm—or a large dowry, for that matter."

"And *is* there a certain gentleman on whom you've turned an adoring eye as of late?" a lady asked from behind her.

Poppy jumped ever so slightly before she turned around, discovering Lena Ridgeway standing a foot away from her, a touch of flour on her nose and a warm smile on her face.

To say Poppy had been surprised when Lena, along with Nigel Flaherty, had shown up at the House of Industry to assist with serving the Christmas meal, was an understatement. But because they'd thrown themselves into the spirit of volunteering, Lena helping with the rolls and Nigel helping Reginald and George set up tables and chairs, Poppy was grateful for their help. She was also wondering if she might have misjudged them, having been of the belief they weren't the type to want to help others.

"How long have you been standing there?" Murray asked, abandoning his potatoes as he nodded to Lena.

She waved aside his question with a hand sprinkled with flour. "Not long, but I couldn't help but overhear the part about gentlemen, although"—she caught Poppy's eye—"I do hope you're not too disappointed to have lost Lord Lonsdale's interest." She gestured around. "He's not here this afternoon, which does lead me to believe that your unfortunate mishap at your tea might have been responsible for taking you out of the running to become a countess."

Having been required to spend hours and hours attempting to learn the intricacies of how to comport herself within high society, Poppy couldn't help but wonder why it was that established ladies didn't seem very keen to abide by those very same rules of comportment—especially the one pertaining to pointing out unpleasant truths.

Nevertheless, since she knew it would hardly be adhering to etiquette rules if she pointed *that* out to Lena, Poppy summoned up a smile.

"While it's very sweet of you to be concerned that I am disappointed about Lord Lonsdale's lack of interest in me," Poppy began, "allow me to put your mind to rest. Contrary to what I'm going to assume is popular opinion, I never considered myself in the running to become a countess, nor do I have any desire to spend my life living amongst the aristocracy."

Lena, oddly enough, immediately reached out and gave Poppy's arm an unexpected pat. "Good for you for attempting to rise above your disappointment with such a declaration, although there's no need to pretend with me."

Poppy frowned. "I'm not pretending. I'm not bothered in the least that Lord Lonsdale isn't considering me as one of his potential countesses, nor am I disappointed he's not here today."

"But why isn't he here?" Lena pressed. "Mr. Blackburn is here, and given that Mr. Blackburn is Lord Lonsdale's traveling companion, well, I would expect those two gentlemen to want to enjoy Christmas together."

"Lord Lonsdale accepted an invitation to spend Christmas dinner with Miss Adele Tooker."

"Did she not extend an invitation to Mr. Blackburn as well?"

"Reginald had already committed to joining us here at the House of Industry."

Lena considered Poppy for a long moment before she suddenly shifted her attention across the room, settling it on Reginald, who'd just walked through the kitchen door from the dining hall where the Christmas dinner was being served. He was holding an empty bowl in one hand, while holding Maria Romano's hand in the other, and something about the way he was giving the child his undivided attention as she brightly chattered away stole the very breath from Poppy's lungs.

Reginald was a man who certainly had the propensity to brood as well as adopt a rather surly nature upon occasion, but he was also undeniably kind, and . . . she was finding it more and more difficult to ignore that the affection she felt for him was growing at an extraordinary rate.

That affection, if she was honest with herself, was sheer lunacy because Reginald had not given her the slightest reason to believe he viewed her as anything other than a friend, and—

". . . struck me as unpleasant and brooding, but there is something about him that I suppose some ladies find appealing, such as his blatant masculinity."

All thoughts of affection disappeared as Poppy returned her attention to Lena, who was now watching her with speculation in her eyes.

"Forgive me, but my thoughts were wandering," Poppy said. "Are we still discussing Reginald?"

"I was pointing out that I believe he has a certain appeal, even with him deciding, for some unknown reason, to take on the look of a barbarian, what with that thick beard and disheveled hair. He's also very attentive to you, and young ladies can be predisposed to read too much into that. However, he's not an aristocrat, nor do I get the impression he's a man of business because I've never heard him broach the topic of business with anyone. That right there suggests he's a man with limited wealth, and given that you're an American heiress, I feel an obligation to warn you against a man who may be looking to secure himself a fortune."

"Reginald has never so much as hinted he's after my fortune."

"But of course he hasn't, my dear," Lena argued. "That would harm his chances of getting closer to you."

"Reginald and I are friends," Poppy said coolly. "And I must tell you that I take offense at your implication he's a fortune hunter, and I urge you to proceed with caution because I won't be held responsible for what might come out of my mouth next if you insult him again, because, as I mentioned, he's a friend of mine."

Lena's eyes narrowed ever so slightly, but then, she blinked, smiled, and inclined her head. "Allow me to beg your pardon if I've offended you, Poppy. That was not my intent. I simply thought to caution you against a man we really don't know that much about, other than he's Lord Lonsdale's traveling companion." She inclined her head again. "I'm allowing my imagination to get the better of me, especially since you've adamantly stated that you and Mr. Blackburn are merely friends. And with that settled, allow me to broach a different matter that I've been longing to talk through with you for days."

Instead of saying anything else, though, Lena suddenly nodded to Murray. "Your potatoes seem to be well mashed, Mr. Middleton. I imagine they're waiting for them out in the dining hall."

Murray stopped mashing potatoes that, indeed, almost seemed overly mashed, handed the bowl to little Maria who just happened to be walking past them, then pulled the bowl of potatoes Poppy had abandoned toward him, sending Lena an innocent smile. "No need for me to go to the dining hall now" was all he said as he began mashing the potatoes with enthusiasm.

Poppy pressed her lips together to keep from smiling, forcing herself to look back at Lena, who'd clearly wanted to speak to her alone, but had been thwarted from that by Murray—a gentleman who was certainly coming into his own.

"Yes, well, as I was saying," Lena said, taking Poppy's arm and pulling her less than discreetly away from Murray, who simply scooted his bowl down the table as Lena began whispering furiously in her ear.

". . . not aware . . . Nigel . . . very fond of you . . . caught his eye" was all Poppy managed to hear, although it was enough to understand the gist of Lena's whispers.

Lifting her head, she directed her gaze to the far side of the enormous kitchen where Nigel was currently up to his elbows in water at the sink, scrubbing pots, while George stood right beside him, drying them.

"And he seems to get along wonderfully well with your grandfather, what with how they're smiling at each other and talking as they go about the mundane business of dishes," Lena continued, abandoning her whispering as she nodded toward Nigel.

Nigel took that moment to glance over his shoulder at them, as if he could feel them watching him. He arched a brow Lena's way, but a second later, he was directing a smile at Poppy, sending her a nod before he returned to dishes still waiting to be scrubbed.

"Isn't he simply the most lovely gentleman?" Lena chirped.

"I imagine he is, although it's not as if I'm overly familiar with him" was all Poppy could think to say to that.

"Forgive me if this comes across as being too forward, but I know for a fact that Nigel is hoping that'll change."

Poppy shot a glance at Murray, who sent her a grimace in return, as if he had no idea how she could possibly respond politely to that bit of nonsense.

Poppy forced a smile. "Nigel and I are merely friends as well, Lena, and not close friends at that. We simply share an appreciation for horses."

"He fancies you."

"How . . . ah . . . well . . . ah . . ."

"He has no need of your fortune, and . . . he's in much demand," Lena continued, quite as if she didn't notice Poppy's sputtering. "I wanted to make certain you were aware of his interest before some other society lady snaps him up." She released a titter. "Men are known to be somewhat fickle creatures when it comes to matters of the heart, and I would so hate it if you allowed Nigel to slip away because you weren't aware of the great affection he holds you in."

"Ah, Mrs. Ridgeway," Beatrix Waterbury suddenly exclaimed, bustling up to join them, holding a tray filled with pastries Poppy had made. "Could you be a dear and take this into the dining hall? I'm afraid that the young lads who've been helping me unload the wagon filled with the desserts have begun eyeing those desserts far too longingly, which means I need to get back outside without delay."

Not waiting for Lena to agree, Beatrix thrust the tray into the startled-looking lady's hand, and after Beatrix gave a less-than-discreet nod to the door, Lena walked away, saying something about progressive ladies being the death of society as she walked.

"Looked like you needed rescuing," Beatrix said, shaking her head as she watched Lena disappear through the door. "Do you find it as odd as I do that Lena Ridgeway seems to be around so much these days? I've been out for quite a few years now, and I rarely encountered that lady before this Season."

Murray frowned. "An excellent point, Beatrix, and yes, I have thought her attendance at so many societal events is odd." Murray laid aside his potato masher and moved closer to Beatrix and Poppy. "Given that I've spent so much time in my mother's company over the years, which has allowed me to spend additional time in the company of her friends, I do have an unusual amount of knowledge at my disposal. That is why I know that Lena Ridgeway has always been considered a willful and peculiar sort. She was apparently coddled by overindulgent parents in her youth, then married a man chosen by her parents who was quite a bit older than she was. From what I recall, they often retreated from society, preferring to spend their time together. After he died, she all but disappeared from society, until this year, of course, when she began traveling to events with Nigel." He frowned. "I've never heard that Lena's put any of the fortune her husband left her to charitable causes, which is why I was surprised to see her here earlier, willing to give up her Christmas day in order to serve the needy."

"Perhaps she's decided it's time for her to put some effort into philanthropy now," Beatrix said, earning a shake of a head from Murray in return.

"From what I overheard as I was blatantly eavesdropping on Lena and Poppy, Lena's decided to put some effort into match-making—more specifically matchmaking as pertains to Poppy and Nigel."

"What was that?"

Poppy swallowed the yelp that almost escaped her lips as Reginald appeared directly by her side, something dark and dangerous lurking in his eyes.

Beatrix looked around, then moved closer to Reginald. "Lena's apparently trying her hand at matchmaking, and she has Poppy and Nigel in her sights."

Reginald glanced to where Nigel was still scrubbing pots, waving a soapy rag in the air as he evidently made some enthusiastic point to George.

"Lena told Poppy that Nigel fancies her," Murray added, which had Reginald stiffening as the look in his eyes turned more dangerous than ever.

"Does he now?"

"I'm sure Lena's mistaken," Poppy said, trying to ignore the fluttery feeling that had settled in her stomach because, clearly, she was reading far too much into the look in his eyes. "So many older society women turn their thoughts to matchmaking, and because Nigel does appear to be her close companion, it's only natural that she would set her sights on seeing him well settled."

"You seem to enjoy his company," Reginald pointed out.

"Not enough to where I long to become more permanently attached to him."

Reginald considered her for a long moment before his lips curved ever so slightly. "Ah, well, good. Glad that's settled." He picked up the bowl of potatoes Murray had been mashing, sent nods all around, then turned and strode out of the kitchen without another word.

"Now that was an interesting development," Beatrix said.

"Interesting how?" Poppy asked.

Beatrix glanced across the room and frowned. "Oh dear, there's my Thomas and he's looking rather harried." She nodded to Murray. "You'll have to explain to her what I meant."

"So . . . explain away," Poppy said as Beatrix hurried away and joined Mr. Thomas Hamersley, her gentleman friend, with the emphasis being on *friend*.

Murray's lips curved. "For a lady who is usually an intuitive sort, you've turned concerningly obtuse when it comes to Reginald."

"What do you mean?"

"Just as you apparently didn't realize Nigel fancies you, I've come to believe Reginald fancies you as well, but he seems almost reluctant to accept that, because—"

"He doesn't *want* to fancy me?"

"That's not what I was going to say."

"It was. You're just too polite to actually tell me what I'm sure you believe I'll take as an insult."

"It *would* be an insult if he didn't want to fancy you."

"He doesn't fancy me," Poppy argued.

"'Course he does, and all we need to do now—" He held up his hand when she opened her mouth. "Don't even bother trying to convince me you don't fancy Reginald, because—"

"I have never said I fancy Reginald."

Murray arched a brow. "You haven't balked at all about him spending all of his time with you ever since you got arrested, which, in my humble opinion, is telling."

"I haven't balked because Reginald and my grandfather believe there's a possibility that someone who wants to frighten me out of New York—or more specifically, out of society—has hired on ruffians to do their dirty work. They've been stubbornly reluctant to change their minds about that, even though I've stated numerous times that it's ridiculous, since I've yet to achieve that diamond of the first water status, nor have I received so much as a single proposal of marriage."

"Is that a hint of dejection I hear in your tone, brought about because Reginald seems reluctant to . . . well . . . approach you about a courtship?"

"I have no idea how to respond to that."

Murray nodded. "Don't blame you a bit. You've not puzzled out your feelings for Reginald yet, or his feelings for you, but don't fret. Now that I'm getting a better inkling about the situation, I'll set right to work coming up with a plan."

Trepidation was immediate. "What kind of plan?"

Murray gave an airy wave of a hand that Poppy only then noticed had mashed potatoes stuck to it. "I haven't the foggiest idea. But rest assured that whatever plan I devise will leave Lena Ridgeway realizing there's no reason to continue any further matchmaking attempts because you'll, hopefully, find yourself firmly off the shelf."

CHAPTER 23

"I might have to have a bit of a chat with Nigel Flaherty, make certain he realizes that Poppy has no interest in pursuing more than a friendship with him," Reginald said, leaning back against the seat of his rented carriage, as Murray turned from the window, smiling a somewhat curious smile.

"And *why* would you want to do that?"

Reginald frowned. "Do you not think I should have a chat with Nigel?"

"Of course you're going to have to have a chat with him, but that's not what I asked—I asked *why* you would want to have a chat with him."

"To spare Poppy the awkwardness of discouraging a man she's claimed not to have a romantic interest in."

"And?" Murray pressed.

"And what? There's nothing more to add."

"Isn't there?"

Reginald rubbed a hand over a beard that was growing in nicely—perhaps too nicely, since it completely covered a great deal of his face. "I'm afraid I have no idea where you expect me to go with the conversation from here."

"This is going to be much more difficult than I imagined."

"And no idea what to make of that statement either."

Murray sat forward and rubbed a hand over his perfectly shaven face, something Reginald actually envied since he was quickly coming to the conclusion that beards were incredibly itchy. "What are your feelings for Poppy?"

"What?"

"Your feelings."

Reginald blinked. "I'm not really a gentleman who is comfortable discussing feelings. If you've forgotten, I'm British. We don't discuss our feelings."

"Ah, so you haven't really considered how you feel about Poppy, have you?"

Reginald blinked again. Frankly, he had been thinking about Poppy far too often of late, but he hadn't actually delved into how he felt about her, because, well, there was little point in doing that, not when Poppy was so clearly unsuited to an aristocratic lifestyle. There was also the pesky notion that, when she did discover the truth about him, she'd be furious with him for withholding that truth so long, that fury possibly leaving her unwilling to ever speak to him again.

"I hate to have to bring this riveting discussion to an end," Murray suddenly said, drawing Reginald from his thoughts. "But we're pulling up to the Van Rensselaer house, and I told Maisie I'd ride over to her house to enjoy a nice piece of Christmas pie with her family after I was done at the House of Industry. I'm running late and don't want her to conclude that I've forgotten about her." Murray reached for the door the second the carriage came to a stop and caught Reginald's eye. "We'll continue our talk tomorrow, shall we? You still intending on helping me teach Poppy the Dresden?"

"I am, but as I said, I'm not comfortable talking about my feelings, although there's not much to discuss since Poppy and I are strictly friends."

"Which is exactly why we will continue our talk because you, my friend, are in need of some advice—and romantic advice, if that was in question."

Before Reginald could do more than gape at Murray, he was out the door, bending his head against a fierce wind, heading not for the front door but for the carriage house, clearly anxious to get a horse saddled and be off to visit Maisie Leggett.

Stretching for the door that Murray, in his haste, had neglected to shut, Reginald stilled when George suddenly poked his head into the carriage and then, after nodding to Reginald, climbed inside, closing the door firmly behind him.

"It's a wicked wind out there," George began, settling himself on the seat Murray had just vacated. "I wanted to see if you'd like to join me and Harold in a game of billiards." He blew out a breath. "It's been slightly uncomfortable between Harold and me, what with Viola and Elizabeth being so annoyed with one another. I would appreciate having you act as a buffer—if you'd care to join us, that is."

"I thought you told Lena Ridgeway and Nigel Flaherty that you wanted to spend the rest of Christmas with your family."

"Of course I did. I've never been overly fond of Lena Ridgeway. And after spending all afternoon with Mr. Flaherty talking my ear off about matters of business—or, more specifically, opportunities he was certain I'd like to invest in—the last thing I wanted was to invite them back to the house." George smiled. "You, on the other hand, I like, and I wouldn't be opposed to talking matters of business with you . . . Lord Blackburn."

Reginald refused to allow himself the luxury of wincing. "How long have you known?"

"That you're the second son of the Duke of Sutherland?"

Reginald forced a nod.

"I had my suspicions the moment I met you, but given the state of your face at that meeting, what with it being so battered, I couldn't immediately place you. However, when I visited the Knickerbocker Club the very next morning, I ran across Lord Kenyon, who attended a most insightful business meeting with me in London, one that you and your father, the duke, attended as well. That's when I remembered exactly who you are and that you're no mere Mr. Blackburn."

"Why are you only now confronting me about what you must see as a bit of subterfuge on my part?"

A distinct twinkle settled in George's eye. "After you began growing a beard, I was curious how far you'd take it to disguise yourself from me, while also wanting to try and discern on my own why you decided to withhold the truth about your title in the first place."

"Should I assume you've been unsuccessful with figuring that out?"

George nodded. "I have many theories, mind you, but none that make much sense, which is why I decided that now is an appropriate time to request an explanation."

Knowing there was nothing to do except disclose all, Reginald took a moment to gather his thoughts. "It's not a sordid tale why I withheld my title from everyone. I thought that if I allowed it to become known that my father is a duke, I'd attract notice from young ladies interested in obtaining titles, and that would, unfortunately, take attention from Charles, who is my cousin by the way, and who . . . ah . . ."

"Needs to marry an heiress?" George finished for him.

"Indeed."

George settled back against the seat. "Understandable, but you must know that my Poppy has shown no interest in your cousin, nor does Lord Lonsdale seem to have an interest in Poppy. That begs the question of why you've kept your true identity from her."

Reginald blew out a breath. "Not that this shows me in a good light, sir, but when I first arrived in New York, I was somewhat, shall we say, prejudiced against American young ladies, and . . . I'm afraid I assumed Poppy was one of those young ladies intent on securing herself an aristocrat. Frankly, when she asked me if I owned any grand ancestral estates, I might have left her with the impression that I'm all but impoverished as a way to discourage any interest she might have had in me at that time."

George released what sounded exactly like a snort. "No wonder you've yet to tell her the truth. It's bad enough that you've allowed her to believe you're a mister; you've also apparently convinced her you're a pauper."

"She's certain to be furious with me."

"Furious is putting it mildly, but your reluctance to have Poppy furious with you, oddly enough, explains much."

"What could that possibly explain?"

"You've changed your mind about American ladies—or more specifically, about my Poppy."

Reginald fought the distinct urge to jump right out of the carriage and run his way back to the Fifth Avenue Hotel. "You're not about to begin questioning me endlessly about my feelings, are you? Murray just tried to do that and found little success."

"Ah, so Murray figured this out before I did." George smiled. "He's a very intuitive young man and is showing great promise these days."

Grateful for a change of topic, Reginald nodded. "He is showing promise, although—"

"So, how *do* you feel about Poppy?"

"I thought we put that to rest."

"Barely scratched the surface of the matter, if you ask me."

Turning to look out the window, Reginald struggled for a response that might satisfy George, a man who was quickly showing himself to be a rather persistent sort.

There was no arguing the point that he did care for Poppy—cared more than he should, if the truth were known—but she truly was *not* a lady suited for living an aristocratic life, and unfortunately, he *was* an aristocrat.

Poppy approached life with an exuberance that intrigued him, but that exuberance wasn't something that would be accepted in his world. Societal ladies in London were far more proper than those in America, and they wouldn't be keen to accept Poppy into their midst, nor would they be kind.

George suddenly chuckled, drawing Reginald's attention.

"Since it is still Christmas, in the spirit of the day, I'll stop badgering you—for now. What say we go have that game of billiards?"

"You're not going to press me about when I'm going to reveal myself to Poppy or society?"

"That's up to you, although I am going to encourage you to tell Poppy sooner rather than later. Secrets have a way of coming out, and she'll not be forgiving if someone beats you to it." George reached for the door, then waited for Reginald to join him on the snow-covered pavement.

After greeting Viola and Elizabeth, who met them right inside the door, and after learning that Poppy had repaired to her room to change into a dress that didn't have potatoes smeared on it, Reginald followed George down a hallway.

"Viola didn't seem very pleased when you didn't expand on what you and I were discussing in the carriage," Reginald said.

"I'm sure she and Elizabeth are even now lamenting how frustrating it is when I don't disclose every snippet of information they desire." George grinned. "But that might have them turning the animosity they've been holding fast to all day on me, instead of on each other. However, while I'm perfectly willing to set myself up as their common enemy, I have no desire to linger and deal with that animosity in person. Ladies, if you're unaware, can turn scary when they feel they've been thwarted." He turned down another hallway, then into a room that had a billiard table placed directly in the center of the room, surrounded by heavy pieces of masculine furniture in shades of brown and black.

Harold Garrison, Poppy's father, a large man with hair a shade darker than Poppy's, was standing beside the billiard table. "I was wondering if you got lost." He nodded to Reginald. "Decided to join us, did you?"

"Wasn't really given a choice," Reginald replied, earning a grin from Harold as he handed him a billiard cue.

"I wasn't either, but I've discovered that George becomes sufficiently deaf when one tries to oppose him, so here I am."

"You've been opposing me ever since you ran off with my

daughter," George said, picking up a cue of his own and moving to the table.

Harold inclined his head. "I suppose that is true, but in my defense, I fell in love with Elizabeth the first time I saw her. I really had no choice *but* to oppose you after Viola made it clear that my pursuit of her daughter was not going to be tolerated."

"Perfectly understandable," George surprised Reginald by saying. "And with that out of the way, shall we play?"

Reginald soon discovered both George and Harold were competitive sorts, which had him throwing himself wholeheartedly into the game, pleased when he held his own against such worthy opponents.

The conversation never lagged as they played, although it never returned to anything of a personal nature, revolving instead around matters of industry.

"I've heard that talk at the Union Club has been centered around John Rockefeller of late," Reginald said, taking a step away from the table after he missed a tricky shot. "He's apparently been colluding with the railroads to maintain his control over the oil industry."

George nodded. "Rockefeller's been known to embrace some questionable tactics. I've managed to best him a few times over the years, although he undercut my bid for a new railroading venture a few months back, which infuriated me and brought on that apoplectic fit I suffered." He nodded to Harold. "I've been told I need to cut back on stress-inducing business matters, which is why I'm considering investing in the horse industry. I like horses, and from what I know of your business, it's a lucrative one."

Harold leaned over the table, took his shot, then straightened. "You're not thinking about investing in horses as a way to pour money into my new venture down in Kentucky, are you?"

"You're very suspicious, aren't you?" George countered.

Harold smiled. "You'd be suspicious as well if you'd lived with a wife who was at distinct odds with both of her parents for the past twenty or so years—a wife, I might add, who did tell me a story or two about the crafty nature of her parents."

"I'm sure Elizabeth did have quite a few stories to tell you about us. And since you've brought the topic of you and Elizabeth into the conversation again, I'm going to ask Reginald to forgive me, but I feel I need to address some family matters."

Reginald set aside his cue. "I'll leave the two of you alone."

"I wasn't asking you to leave," George said before nodding to Harold. "I need to tell you how much I regret not reaching out to you and Elizabeth over the years. More specifically, I regret not reaching out to you and attempting to get to know you better." George took a step closer to Harold, who was watching him warily. "You've clearly made my Elizabeth happy, as well as given me three fine grandchildren. Because of that, I owe you my most sincerest apology, and know I'll be forever in your debt for providing my only child with a life in which she delights."

Harold cleared his throat before he nodded. "Thank you for that, George. You've taken me completely aback, but I appreciate what you've said, and I'm only too willing to accept your apology. I suggest we now put the past behind us and concentrate on the future."

George's brows drew together. "Viola and I rejected you as our son-in-law for years. I find it difficult to believe you can forgive me so easily."

Harold laid aside his billiard cue and stepped closer to George. "Forgiveness is not as difficult as you seem to believe. When I was younger, I *was* hurt by your rejection. However, Reverend Thomas Cameron, a minister who serves our small church in Pennsylvania, has preached more than a few sermons on the topic of forgiveness over the years, or more specifically, how God forgives us time after time for our sins. I then realized that if God can forgive us our sins, I could certainly find it in me to forgive the slights I felt I'd received from you and Viola. From the moment I made a concerted effort to stop holding fast to the animosity I'd felt for you and Viola for far too long, I felt a sense of peace, along with a sense of hope that someday we'd be able to put the past behind us—and that someday seems to be here, on Christmas, of all days." He placed a hand on George's shoulder. "I'm also hoping that you'll someday be able to forgive me. I realize I caused you and Viola a great deal of anguish when I stole Elizabeth away. And while I don't regret making her mine because we've always loved each other, I could have gone about the matter differently."

George took a swipe at eyes that were suspiciously bright. "Thank you, Harold, but there's really no need to ask for my forgiveness. You and Elizabeth were young and in love, and, well, there's really no need to say more."

"Then we'll consider it settled," Harold said before he smiled. "With that out of the way, what *were* we discussing before the conversation took such an emotional turn?"

Reginald returned the smile. "I believe you were asking George if his newfound interest in the horse industry was a sneaky way to invest in your new venture."

"Yes, thank you for that, Reginald," George said dryly.

Harold grinned before he shook his head. "Do know that even if that is your intention, George, I'm not taking your money."

"Don't know why not. You and Elizabeth, along with the children, will be getting all of it eventually anyway," George said, looking somewhat grumpy before he brightened. "Besides, you, as an astute man of business, must realize that with my funding behind your new venture you'll be able to become the largest horse farm in the country, and—" He suddenly stopped talking as Elizabeth sauntered into the room with Poppy by her side, Viola following a few steps behind.

That Viola and Elizabeth were both scowling was not an encouraging sign.

"Come to join us in a game of billiards, have you?" George asked cheerfully, as if his wife and daughter weren't still put out with each other.

Elizabeth tossed her scowl Viola's way before she returned her attention to her father. "I was actually attempting to get away from Mother's incessant harping regarding my supposed audacity in deeding Garrison Farms over to Poppy, but . . . why not? I'd love a game of billiards." She turned back to Viola. "Care to join me, Mother?"

Reginald was not reassured when Viola suddenly smiled, moved to take the billiard cue away from George, then nodded pleasantly at the table. "You go first, dear."

It turned into a battle of epic proportions.

It quickly became clear that both ladies were more than adept at playing billiards, which was rather surprising, at least when it came to Viola.

"Who would have thought she'd be good at this?" Poppy whispered as Viola straightened and smiled after she'd made a surprisingly difficult shot.

"Who indeed?" George whispered back, earning an arch of a brow from Poppy.

"You didn't know she played?"

"Afraid not."

"I don't spend all my time at society events and painting," Viola said with a bit of frost in her tone, evidently listening far more closely than George or Poppy had realized.

"Of course you don't, dear," George muttered weakly.

She lifted her chin. "I'm capable of embracing a good sense of fun, and I'm not opposed to seeking out a few adventures now and again either."

Elizabeth gave a twirl of her billiard cue. "Was that what you were doing when you dressed in disguise and managed to get yourself arrested?"

Viola leaned over the table, took a shot, missed, and straightened. "I didn't set out to get arrested, Elizabeth, and I'll thank you to discontinue bringing that up every other minute. I was mortified about the arrest, as well as mortified that an article ended up in the newspapers about my misadventure."

Elizabeth frowned. "I don't bring your arrest up every other minute, Mother. Perhaps every other hour, but not minute. And since the reporter of that article made a point out of writing about the grave injustice you suffered after being mistakenly arrested, you've garnered society's sympathy instead of censure."

"You're still so very exhausting," Viola murmured.

"Thank you, but you wouldn't currently have to experience that exhaustion if you hadn't blackmailed my daughter into accepting a Season. If you'd refrained from doing that, I would have simply come for my usual two-day visit, exchanging a few presents and a few strained hours of conversation before I returned home. But since you did blackmail my daughter, you've now been forced to spend additional, and apparently exhausting, time in my company. You have no one but yourself to blame for that." Elizabeth took her shot, made it, then began walking around the table, eyeing the remaining balls.

"You're right about the blackmail, of course, but did you have to get back at me by giving Poppy the farm in Pennsylvania? Couldn't you have simply allowed me to enjoy her for one short Season, holding fast to the unrealistic hope that she might choose to stay in New York instead of leaving me like you did all those years ago?"

Silence settled over the room as Elizabeth's cue dropped to the ground, not that she seemed to notice since her gaze was firmly settled on her mother.

"Did you just admit that you blackmailed Poppy?"

A jerk of her head was Viola's only response.

Elizabeth took a single step toward her mother. "Why didn't you merely ask Poppy if she wanted a Season instead of going to such extremes?"

"Because that would have allowed her the opportunity to refuse me, and I just wanted to . . ."

"Wanted to what?" Elizabeth pressed when Viola faltered.

"I wanted to make amends with you, and I thought, foolishly so, that if I was able to get Poppy accepted into society, allow her to experience the delight of a Season, that you would finally understand that I'm not the monster you've always thought me to be, but simply a concerned parent who wanted what was best for her only child."

Elizabeth took another step toward Viola. "You could have simply apologized, told me you were sorry for not giving me your blessing to marry Harold."

"I didn't know how to do that," Viola whispered.

"You could try now," Elizabeth shot back. "You could try and explain to me why you always seemed to loathe me so much and why you were always unwilling to allow me to simply be me, not some preconceived notion of who you thought and expected me to be."

For a second, Reginald didn't think Viola was going to say anything else, especially not when she gave the door a rather longing look. But then, she straightened her spine, drew in a breath, and inclined her head toward her daughter.

"I never loathed you, Elizabeth. I was jealous of you."

Elizabeth drew in a sharp breath. "Jealous?"

"But of course. You always stayed true to who you wanted to be, never abiding by any of the rules I tried to force upon you or letting your strict upbringing stifle your spirit." Viola dashed a hand over eyes that were bright with unshed tears. "How I envied that, longing to join you when I'd see you fleeing down the road in the early morning hours, dressed in trousers and riding your horse at full gallop, the wind tangling your hair as you rode."

"You could have joined me, Mother."

Viola shook her head. "No, I couldn't, nor would I have known how to ask." She smiled rather sadly. "I never had the courage to balk against the many rules my mother expected me to follow, nor did I have any idea what to do with a daughter who was rebellious from the moment she learned how to walk. And even though I tried to rein you in, there was a part of me that envied your rebellious nature. That right there is why I never fought to repair our relationship after you married Harold. I was relieved you were no longer around so I could quit comparing my life with the more fulfilling one I knew you were making for yourself."

For a long moment, Elizabeth didn't say a word, but then she moved to stand in front of her mother, swiping away tears that were trickling down her cheeks. "I never imagined you were jealous of me."

"I was."

Elizabeth drew in a shaky breath. "That certainly explains much, and . . . because it's still Christmas, a time for new beginnings, I say you and I agree to begin again, put the past firmly behind us this time and see if we can't find a way to enjoy the future together."

Viola's lips began trembling right before she pulled her daughter into her arms and held on as if she never wanted to let go.

"And that," Poppy began, accepting the handkerchief Reginald fished out of his pocket and dabbing her eyes, "has got to be one of the best Christmas presents my mother and grandmother have ever received."

Reginald certainly couldn't disagree with that. And when Poppy unexpectedly slipped her hand into his, leaving him decidedly unbalanced, he couldn't deny that he *did* have feelings for Poppy—feelings that were unquestionably not of the strictly friendly sort.

What he was going to do about those feelings, though, now that he'd admitted to himself he had them, was quite beyond him at the moment.

CHAPTER 24

"Are you certain you're not too disappointed that your mother and father returned to Kentucky before they got to see you perform in the Dresden China Quadrille?" Murray asked as he stepped to the right, waited for Poppy to step around him, then offered her his arm. Together, they moved around the other dancers assembled in the Tooker ballroom at the last quadrille practice before the first Patriarch Ball of the Season.

"I'm not disappointed at all. My parents are still in the process of completing the new horse facility in Kentucky, and I knew they needed to get back. They were also anxious to reunite with my younger brothers." She smiled. "I believe they were feeling guilty about abandoning them for Christmas, but I think their sense of guilt was misplaced. They did celebrate Christmas early with Nathan and Robert, and Mother told me Nathan couldn't have come to New York even if he'd wanted to because he's only recently entered law school and had to study over the Christmas break. As for Robert, well, he apparently wanted to prove he's capable of looking after the horses without anyone's supervision." Her smile turned into a grin. "Besides, there's every chance I'll do something unexpected during the quadrille, so it's best all around if my parents aren't here to witness that. If you've neglected to notice, my mother has a rather questionable temperament, and I'd hate to see her have to take Mr. McAllister to task in front of society if he decides to lecture me again over my lack of . . . er . . . grace."

Murray returned the grin. "I doubt you'll get your tiara stuck to my sleeve again."

"Only because my costume won't include a tiara."

"And thank goodness for that, but there's really no need for you to worry you're going to suffer a mishap," Murray said as they wove their way through the ballroom. "You have practiced endlessly with me and Reginald for a solid week, so I doubt anything will go wrong—at least during the quadrille." His grin widened. "Even Reginald has been finding it difficult the past few days to come up with any suggestions to improve your proficiency with the steps."

"Something he seems surprised about."

Murray shot a look to where Reginald was leaning against a wall, watching their progress as they moved across the floor. "He seems incredibly proud of you, as if you've become his star student."

Turning to the right and taking three steps forward, Poppy paused as Murray completed his expected steps and wrinkled her nose. "You don't think Reginald only sees me as his student, do you?"

"I believe we've already covered this, what with how I told you I thought he fancied you. But why do you care?"

Biting her lip as she completed a complicated turn that had her ducking underneath Murray's arm, Poppy took a second to consider the question, even though the answer was fairly obvious.

She might, perhaps, fancy Reginald a bit as well.

He was an exasperating man, far too proper for his own good while also being far too opinionated in how a proper lady was meant to behave. Nevertheless, he'd come to her rescue time and time again, helped her master the steps of the Dresden China Quadrille even though he'd had to recuse himself from giving any of the ladies who'd hired him additional lessons, annoying all of them in the process, and . . . he was the only man who'd ever made her weak at the knees.

"I didn't realize I'd posed such a difficult question, but I must say your silence is telling," Murray said, pulling her from her thoughts as he sent her a wink before he twirled her around, steadying her when she stumbled.

"And here I was considering telling you how thankful I am that you somehow convinced Mr. McAllister to partner you with me in this quadrille, but I don't think I'll do that now, not with how annoying you've suddenly turned."

"You've already thanked me about a hundred times," Murray said. "And even though what I'm about to disclose does not show me to be a man of great character, I asked Mr. McAllister to pair me with you out of a sense of self-preservation. You must remember how most ladies in society balk at having me partner with them, so you're actually doing *me* a service since you're sparing me from being the object of some other lady's scorn."

Poppy rolled her eyes before she nodded discreetly toward a gathering of five young ladies who were standing on the edge of the ballroom, having come at Adele's request to watch the practice. All five of those ladies, even with them being disappointed they'd not been asked to participate in the dance, had apparently been unable to refuse Adele's invitation. And even though Poppy thought it rather spiteful on Adele's part to extend such an invitation in the first place, the ladies seemed to be enjoying themselves, and they especially seemed to be enjoying watching Murray as he danced her across the floor.

"I don't think any of those ladies currently watching you so intently would be opposed to being your partner," she said, which had Murray looking up so quickly he stepped on her foot.

Recovering nicely, while mumbling an apology, he grinned. "Curious what participating in a bit of scandal can do for a person's reputation—not that I have any intention of landing in jail again, nor participating in a brawl that might leave me with another two black eyes." Murray steered Poppy in a circle before they began making their final turn around the floor. "Did I tell you that Viola took it upon herself to pay a visit to my mother to make certain she wasn't overwrought after that article appeared in the paper about our arrest? From what Mother told me, Viola spun a marvelous tale about me, telling her that I single-handedly protected you and Viola from the ruffians who were sharing our jail cell."

"Grandmother's gotten somewhat peculiar of late."

"I caught her only this morning coming in from the carriage house. She was wearing trousers and looking rather windblown."

Poppy smiled. "It seems she's trying to make up for abiding by all the rules for so many years." She sank into a curtsy as the notes of the piano faded away, then straightened and sent a discreet nod to the group still watching Murray. "Shall we mosey over there so you'll have an opportunity to speak with those ladies?"

"Can't," Murray said, shaking his head. "I'm meeting Maisie and her mother for tea at Rutherford & Company in about thirty minutes, but I need to swing by my mother's house and pick her up before that."

"Should I assume you've mended fences with your mother?"

"All thanks to Maisie. She's been rather bossy about me making time for Mother, and I must say, Mother, once she learned about that, just adores Maisie these days." He leaned closer to her. "And speaking of adoration, remind me to thank Viola again for paying a call on Mrs. Leggett after word got out about the jail incident. I don't know what she said to her, but Mrs. Leggett absolutely seems to adore me now as well. She even went so far as to pull me aside after I called on them yesterday to tell me she and Mr. Leggett would welcome any attention I might want to give Maisie." He frowned. "I think that means they'd give me their blessing if I wanted to ask Maisie to marry me."

"That's exactly what that means, Murray, but *are* you considering asking Maisie to marry you?"

"Can't deny I haven't considered the matter, which might be why I've yet to move out of your grandparents' house and find a place of my own."

"Because you're uncertain how large a residence you might need in the not-too-distant future?"

He grinned. "Perhaps. Or perhaps I enjoy being around your family and don't want to give that up just yet."

"My family does seem to have taken to you."

"That's because I'm a likeable sort, not prone to drama or theatrics."

"You passed out cold in my grandmother's parlor after we returned from jail and your nose started bleeding again."

"True, but I didn't pass out while we were *in* jail and my nose started bleeding, although that might have been because I was terrified one of those criminals sharing our cell would take that as a sign of weakness and I needed to stay strong to defend you or Viola if anyone tried anything."

"You're a complicated man, Murray."

"And dashing as well, or so I've been told."

Exchanging grins, Poppy walked with Murray to the edge of the ballroom floor, her knees turning a tad weak when Reginald pushed himself away from the wall and strode her way.

"You stumbled once" were his first words to her, although because his eyes were crinkling at the corners, she didn't take it to heart.

"That's because Murray stepped on my foot."

"No, he stepped on your foot after you stumbled."

"How closely *were* you watching us?"

Reginald shrugged and sent her a smile that made her feel unusually tingly all over. "Close enough."

Before she could summon up a remotely coherent retort, Lena Ridgeway, who'd volunteered to play the piano for their quadrille practices that week, began waving for Poppy to join her by the piano. Telling Reginald she'd be back directly, Poppy walked over to Lena, returning the smile the woman was sending her.

"How graceful you looked on the floor today, Poppy," Lena said, reaching out to give Poppy's arm a squeeze. "Why, I daresay you'll be the belle of the ball tomorrow night, which is exactly why I wanted to speak to you." She leaned closer. "Nigel will be here soon to escort me home, and I know this is rather untoward of me, but I'd like to ask you on his behalf to allow him to escort you to the ball tomorrow."

Poppy frowned. "I'm not certain Nigel would appreciate you speaking for him, Lena. He's never struck me as a gentleman unable to speak for himself."

Lena nodded. "And while that is true, my dear, Nigel's been occupied with some troubling business matters of late, which is why he's not found an opportunity to ask you personally."

Having no idea what she should say next, Poppy almost jumped out of her skin when Reginald suddenly appeared directly beside her, took hold of her arm, then smiled at Lena, although the smile didn't reach his eyes.

"Forgive me for interrupting, but I'm afraid Poppy and I need to get back to the Van Rensselaers'."

Lena narrowed her eyes. "I'm sure you can wait a few minutes, Mr. Blackburn. Poppy and I have yet to finish our conversation, nor have we agreed on a time when Nigel Flaherty and I can pick her up before the ball tomorrow."

"Then allow me to be of assistance, Mrs. Ridgeway," Reginald said pleasantly. "There's no need for you or Nigel Flaherty to fetch Poppy tomorrow because she's already agreed to go to the ball with me." He inclined his head. "And now, with that settled, we really must be going."

Leaving Lena gaping after them, Reginald pulled Poppy into motion, moving so quickly across the floor that she almost had to break into a trot to keep up with him.

"That was a bit of a surprise, finding out you're escorting me to the ball," she said, which had him slowing his pace.

"Forgive me, Poppy. That was not well done of me, and quite rude. But because I know you never consented to attend the ball with Nigel and because I didn't like that Lena seemed to be badgering you into something you didn't want to do, I felt obligated to act—and rashly, so it appears."

A distinct sense of disappointment settled over her. "You certainly don't have to escort me to the ball if you don't want to."

Reginald stopped walking. "Who said I don't want to escort you to the ball?"

"You did. Just now."

"I said nothing of the sort."

Poppy lifted her chin. "I don't care to feel as if I'm an obligation, Reginald."

"I never said you were an obligation. I said I felt obligated to act."

Frowning, Poppy nodded. "True. However, you've yet to ask me if I *want* to go to the ball with you."

"Oh."

"Indeed."

He frowned. "Do you want to go to the ball with me?"

She returned the frown. "One would think, what with you being so proficient in matters concerning all the proprieties and expected behavior of ladies and gentlemen, that you'd know you're supposed to approach such questions with a bit of delicacy, and perhaps even using a more . . . poetic turn of phrase rather than being so direct."

"So you *don't* want to go to the ball with me?"

"Of course she'll go to the ball with you," Murray said, rolling his eyes as he strode up to join them. "She's just being difficult, and you're just being, well, you. And, with that settled, I have some news."

"What kind of news?" Poppy asked.

"Lord Lonsdale has apparently let it be known that he's intending on making a big announcement tomorrow night."

Reginald's brows drew together. "Who told you that?"

"Adele."

"I need to speak with Charles," Reginald said, steering Poppy for the door as Murray fell into step beside him.

Unfortunately, before they could make their escape, Adele stepped in front of them, blocking their exit. "You can't leave just yet. I still have to impart a few details about the ball tomorrow." She spun around and clapped her hands, drawing everyone's attention.

"Before anyone leaves, I must tell you that your costumes are being delivered to your respected houses as I speak. I apologize again for having them delivered so late, but since I gave the seamstresses everyone's measurements, the ones provided to me by each of you, I have no doubt they'll fit to perfection and will not need additional alteration."

"And why were they delivered so late again?" a young lady called from the far end of the room.

Adele's lips thinned for the briefest of seconds. "Because they weren't as elaborate as I'd requested, a circumstance that had to be rectified. I'm sure all of you will be more than delighted with the results."

"When you say weren't as elaborate," Poppy said slowly, "what do you mean by that, and what steps were taken to rectify the situation?"

"Oh, it was nothing too dramatic. I simply wanted a bit, well, *more* added to the costumes." Adele turned from Poppy and settled her attention on Reginald, batting her lashes. "I was hoping you might have a few additional tidbits to share about what Lord Lonsdale is intending on disclosing tomorrow night at the ball. All he said to me was that he was going to be making a grand announcement, but the darling gentleman wouldn't expand on that, no matter how I pleaded with him."

Reginald shook his head. "I'm afraid I don't have anything else to add, although if he told you it was going to be a *grand* announcement, I would think that might mean he's—"

"Going to announce who he's chosen to become his countess?" Adele finished for him, excitement sparkling in her eyes.

It seemed as if every lady surrounding Poppy suddenly sucked in sharp breaths of air, before releasing those breaths in one loud whoosh as whispers began flying about the room.

"I suppose that could be a possibility," Reginald said slowly. "But I wouldn't get your hopes up since Lord Lonsdale has been known to—"

Adele waved that aside as she turned to the crowd of ladies who were edging closer to them, not wanting to miss a single word of the seemingly riveting conversation taking place between Adele and Reginald.

"Ladies, I assume you've now become privy to the information about Lord Lonsdale's grand announcement, and with that said, allow me to wish all of you the best of luck." She smiled and clasped her hands in front of her. "Additionally, I think we should make a pact right here and now, one where we promise not to hold a grudge against the lady who will soon find herself a countess." She arched a brow, which had almost every lady nodding back at her. "Lovely." She turned to Reginald again. "Do give Lord Lonsdale my warmest regards when you see him next. I was expecting him to show up this afternoon, but I imagine he must have been delayed at the Union Club." Sending Reginald a waggle of her fingers, Adele turned and moved away, quickly surrounded by ladies who immediately began peppering her with questions about Charles's intentions.

"Charles isn't at the Union Club this afternoon," Reginald said as he steered Poppy for the door.

"Where is he?"

"He said something about shopping, but he didn't say much more than that."

After fetching Poppy's cloak from a maid, Reginald helped her into it. Then, holding on to her arm, they stepped out into an afternoon that was so cold it was difficult to draw breath, bidding Murray a hasty good-bye as they hurried for the carriage. After seeing her tucked into a fur-lined carriage blanket, Reginald took a seat beside her.

"It's too cold for us to sit apart" was all he said as the carriage jolted into motion, traveling down Fifth Avenue at a fast clip. "Now that it's just the two of us, with no Murray to interrupt, are you going to the ball with me tomorrow?"

"I suppose so, since I'm certainly not going to go with Nigel, and I don't want to show up without an escort."

"You might want to review some of your etiquette books about the proper way to accept an invitation from a gentleman."

"And I'll do just that after you've refreshed yourself on how a gentleman is supposed to extend an invitation to a lady," she shot back, not quite able to hide a grin when he immediately took to looking somewhat brooding.

He didn't have long to brood, though, what with how the Tooker residence was only minutes away from her grandmother's house. As the carriage rolled to a stop, Poppy waited for the driver to get the door, took Reginald's hand as he helped her from the carriage, then walked with him to the front door, smiling at Mr. Parsons, who was already holding the door open for her.

Her smile faded straightaway, though, when Viola stepped around Mr. Parsons, her face unusually pale, nose red, and dark circles under eyes that were watery.

"Goodness, Grandmother. What's wrong?"

Viola gave a wave of the hand that was clutching a handkerchief. "I'm feeling a touch under the weather, as is your grandfather, who has already taken to his bed for the day."

"Where you should be."

Viola inclined her head. "And I'll repair to my room soon, but I can't very well do that until after I tell you about the situation that's currently waiting for you in the parlor."

"There's a situation in the parlor?"

"Indeed, and it revolves around the costume that was just delivered for you."

"My costume can be considered a situation?"

"I'm afraid so," Viola said, dabbing at her nose. "But perhaps instead of trying to explain it, we should repair to the parlor so you can see for yourself." Viola dabbed at her nose again and shook her head. "I'm afraid, given my somewhat foggy state of mind at the moment, that I won't have sufficient words to describe the horror that's waiting for you."

"It is horrific," Poppy said five minutes later as she walked around the costume that Mr. Parsons had set up on a dress form.

Yards and yards of velvet made up the gown, but what was truly astonishing was the bustle underneath the fabric, one that looked quite as if it might have been made from a barrel. It was difficult to say exactly what it resembled except that it was enormous—or perhaps gargantuan was more accurate.

Whatever the word, though, it was going to leave her decidedly back heavy and would make it more than difficult to glide gracefully across the floor.

"It would seem Adele is of the belief that revenge is a dish best served unexpected," Poppy finally said, shuddering when her attention settled on the shoes that were sitting beside the gown, the heels looking quite as if they were at least six inches high.

"I'm not certain you're going to be able to even walk in those, let alone dance," Viola said, nodding to the shoes Poppy was inspecting.

Poppy turned to her grandmother and squared her shoulders. "There's no need for you to worry about this, Grandmother. You need to be in bed."

"But . . ."

"Bed, and now." Poppy took hold of her grandmother's hand. "I'll handle this. You go rest, and I don't want to see you out of your room before morning. I'll be up to check on you and help you get settled soon."

"My lady's maid can get me settled."

"True, but I'm your granddaughter, and it seems like a granddaughter thing to do, so stop arguing with me and go to your room."

A hint of a smile crossed Viola's pale, drawn face. "You're very bossy."

"And you're very obstinate. You need to be in bed. As I mentioned, I'll handle this."

"How in the world do you believe you'll handle this?"

Poppy blew out a breath. "Since you're not going to repair to your room until you feel this is settled, know that I have no intention of meekly going along with what is apparently Adele's dastardly plot. She's probably been practicing in this absurd costume for weeks and hopes to make herself stand out as the most graceful lady on the floor tomorrow night, while making the rest of us look clumsy and ridiculous."

Viola blinked. "What are you going to do?"

"I'm going to summon all the other young ladies who are participating in the quadrille, except for Adele, of course, although . . ." She frowned. "I might have to have someone find Murray because I'm not well acquainted with all the ladies, and I don't know if I'll remember all of them."

Reginald cleared his throat, drawing Poppy's attention. "There's no need for Murray. My—or rather, Lord Lonsdale's—valet, Giles, has a list of all the ladies participating in the Dresden."

"Of course he does," Poppy said before she frowned again. "But speaking of Giles, where's he been the last few days? The last time I saw him was when he was with Miss Cynthia Roche in the sleigh."

"He's been keeping a low profile because he apparently annoyed Cynthia that day and Giles has concluded that society ladies are now terrifying. He's currently hiding out at the Fifth Avenue Hotel, but I'll be happy to fetch him." With that, Reginald inclined his head, told Viola to go to bed, then strode from the room.

Turning to Viola, Poppy arched a brow, earning a shake of Viola's head in return.

"I'm not going anywhere until you tell me why you're going to summon all of those ladies."

Poppy considered Viola for a moment before she nodded to Mr. Parsons. "Since my grandmother is not going to cooperate until I explain my plan to her, may I count on you to see if you can find some seamstresses who would be willing to come here as soon as possible—as in this evening?" She glanced to the towering heels Adele had chosen. "We might need a shoemaker or two as well."

Viola raised a hand to her throat. "What in the world are you planning?"

Taking hold of Viola's arm, Poppy began steering her out of the room. "I'm going to stage a rebellion, of course. One that, in my humble opinion, is long overdue."

CHAPTER 25

"Sorry I'm late, Lord Blackburn," Giles said, rushing into Reginald's suite at the Fifth Avenue Hotel the next day, dashing a hand over a brow that was dotted with perspiration, even though the temperature outside had been dropping at a rapid clip all afternoon. "I had no idea that offering my assistance to the gentlemen who were trying to get ready for the quadrille would take so long after you and I took Miss Garrison, along with all the bags she'd packed her costume in, over to Delmonico's."

Reginald smiled. "I'm sure your assistance was much appreciated, but getting the gentlemen ready must have been a rather daunting feat because you seem a bit rattled, and . . . you just addressed me as Lord Blackburn."

Giles stopped directly in front of Reginald and raked a hand through hair that was standing on end. "Daunting is putting it mildly, sir, but do forgive me for the slip with your title. I'm afraid I *am* somewhat rattled, what with how demanding those gentlemen were." He shook his head. "You can't imagine how many times I was asked to re-powder a wig or repaint a face, and don't even get me started on what lengths I had to go to in order to get some of the gentlemen dressed. Since they apparently were unwilling to hand over their true measurements, they found themselves not quite able to button pieces of their costumes. You would not believe the arguments I was forced to listen to after I suggested the only solution was to bind the men with strips of linen, a suggestion that was met with vehement protests until I suggested stuffing them into corsets."

Reginald grinned. "I'm sorry I wasn't there to witness that. It sounds rather amusing."

Giles returned the grin. "It was, but I could have done without the arguing." Giles took a step back and looked Reginald up and down. "You've done a remarkably fine job of pulling yourself together without my help, but you do have some lint on your sleeve. Allow me a moment to wash up since I still seem to have powder on me."

"I might need some assistance as well, Giles," Charles said, strolling into the room, his tie askew, his hair less than perfect, and his white waistcoat improperly buttoned.

Giles's eyes widened. "I'll be right back."

Reginald smiled as his valet dashed toward the retiring room before he turned to Charles, looking him over. "Here, let me at least help you with your tie."

He moved to stand in front of Charles. "Where have you been all week? I feel as if I've not seen you at all and I have been wanting to talk to you about—"

"If I've made a decision about who I want to make my countess?"

Reginald frowned. "Since Adele told me yesterday that you're intending on making a grand announcement tonight, I assumed you'd already made your decision, although I would have thought you'd seek my counsel before announcing to the New York Four Hundred who you're planning on marrying."

Charles's brows drew together. "Adele wasn't supposed to tell anyone about my announcement tonight."

"Clearly you've yet to get Adele's full measure. Please tell me you've not settled on her as your choice, have you?"

Charles released a snort. "I'm not a complete idiot."

"So you're not intending on asking Adele to marry you?"

"Again, I'm not an idiot, unlike you who—" Charles stopped

talking as he caught sight of himself in a mirror. He grimaced, then ran his fingers through his hair, which only left it looking more rumpled than ever.

"Did you just call me an idiot?" Reginald asked, taking a seat and catching Charles's eye in the reflection of the mirror.

"What *possible* reason would I have to call you that?"

"How could I *possibly* know how to answer that, unless . . ." Reginald frowned. "Are you put out with me because I recently abandoned all the etiquette lessons I'd been giving, which might have left you to the mercy of swarms of young ladies trying to impress you?"

Charles leaned closer to his reflection, smoothing the tie Reginald had just fixed. "I'm perfectly capable of dealing with determined young ladies, Reginald. Frankly, those ladies were so put out about your abandonment that they began complaining about you, as well as Giles, who has evidently gone into hiding. Curiously enough, that allowed me to see their true characters." He turned and smiled. "Not that I didn't find their attempts at disparaging you somewhat amusing, since I've never known anyone to find you so lacking before."

"Glad I could be a source of amusement, but getting back to why you think I'm an idiot . . . ?"

Consulting his pocket watch, Charles shook his head. "I don't have enough time to do justice to that question. We're expected at the ball in less than an hour, but do know I'll be more than happy to discuss the matter with you later. But speaking of the ball, aren't you supposed to be escorting Poppy?"

"She's already there. She, along with the other quadrille participants, except for Adele, decided they'd get ready at Delmonico's. That establishment has a few rooms for just that purpose, which Poppy decided to use, as did all the rest of the quadrille participants, except, again, Adele." He smiled. "They don't want any of the guests to get a glimpse of them or their costumes before the quadrille begins."

"Why isn't Adele getting dressed there?"

"Because no one asked her to join them," Giles said as he hurried back into the room. "And before you ask me why they didn't ask her, did you bother to read the notes I made about Miss Tooker?"

Charles nodded. "I did, but I don't recall anything that mentioned anything about the ball tonight."

"I didn't make any notes specifically about the ball, Lord Lonsdale, only about her character, which is why she wasn't asked to join the other ladies this evening. She's not been behaving admirably."

Charles looked to Reginald, then back to Giles, then abruptly took a seat. "I think a more thorough explanation is needed, if you please, but be quick about it because we're running out of time."

Five minutes was all it took for Reginald to sum up the situation. "And that's why Giles and I, every member of the Van Rensselaer staff, five seamstresses, and two shoemakers spent most of the night modifying costumes that Adele had embellished, evidently in the hope of causing the other ladies participating in the quadrille to be at a disadvantage. I'm convinced Adele spent hours practicing in the ridiculous heels she chose without anyone's knowledge, and I would bet she didn't have her gown sewn to where it was inches too small in the waist, something many of the ladies who arrived at Poppy's last night discovered about their gowns."

"There was so much work to be done," Giles added, expertly setting Charles's waistcoat and hair to rights as he spoke. "Even I was given a needle and thread and set to work hemming until four in the morning." He smiled. "I was vastly relieved when Mr. Murray Middleton returned to the house and immediately joined me. We weren't as competent as the seamstresses, but Murray was very good with reattaching glass beads to the heels of the shoes the cobblers had whittled down to a more manageable height."

Reginald nodded to Charles. "And now, with all that explained, please tell me Adele isn't in the running to become your countess, or better yet, tell me you'll put off this grand announcement until you and I have a chance to discuss everything thoroughly."

"My grand announcement doesn't actually involve Adele, but

I'm not going to put it off. Mrs. Astor, the esteemed queen of New York society, has most likely heard about my announcement. That means she will be disappointed if I don't go through with it, but no need to worry. It's not an announcement that's going to ruin my life." Charles rose from the chair. "With that said, let us get on our way. We do, after all, have a ball to attend."

Fifty-five minutes later, Reginald stepped from his rented carriage, bending his head against the wind that all but pushed him toward Delmonico's. Hurrying up the steps, he joined Charles, who'd ridden in a separate carriage, in the receiving line, along with Miss Edith Iselin, who'd ridden to the ball with Charles that evening.

"You're looking very well, Edith," he said.

Edith smiled. "Thank you, Reginald. You're looking well yourself. You've shaved off your beard."

"You did shave off your beard," Charles said, leaning closer before he straightened and arched a brow. "Do you think that's wise?"

Reginald realized with a start that he'd never gotten around to explaining to his cousin that George had already recognized him. He'd also not told Charles that he was almost ready to divulge the truth to Poppy, although how he . . .

"Ah, Lord Lonsdale, there you are," Mrs. Astor exclaimed, gesturing for Charles to join her even though there were a good number of guests ahead of him.

"We'll talk later?" Charles asked.

"We will, and it seems as if we're going to have much to discuss," Reginald said, unable to help but notice that Charles had slid his hand for the briefest of moments against Edith's back, before he'd offered her his arm, which she took without hesitation.

"Too right we do," Charles said with a wink before he walked with Edith past the guests waiting to greet Mrs. Astor.

After he finally made his way through the receiving line, Reginald moved down a hallway, stopping when Murray suddenly stuck his head around a door that looked as if it led to a flight of stairs. Striding over to join him, he soon found himself tugged through the door, Murray closing it firmly shut behind him.

"You're looking very . . . powdered" was all Reginald could think to say as he took in his friend's appearance.

Murray was looking exactly as if he'd stepped out of time, wearing a powdered wig, white knee breeches, and a dazzling white waistcoat sporting hundreds of glass beads, which sparkled even in the dimly lit hallway they were standing in.

"Giles got a tad carried away when he was powdering me," Murray said, waving a billowy sleeve and causing powder to float aimlessly in the air. "But look at you. You shaved."

"I didn't want to attend the ball looking like a mountain man."

"You wanted to look nice for Poppy."

Reginald frowned. "Or I was merely tired of the beard."

"You're clearly still in denial about your feelings for her, but now's not the time to discuss the matter. Adele just arrived, and I thought you and I should sneak upstairs and hover outside the room where all the other ladies participating in the quadrille are gathered."

"I'm not really the type of gentleman to hover."

"That's too bad because we're going to, and if it begins sounding like it's turning nasty, you may then feel free to burst in and save Poppy yet again, this time from the wrath of a spiteful lady."

"I'm not certain Poppy would appreciate that."

"Of course she would," Murray said, turning and heading up the steps, the heels of the buckle shoes he was wearing ringing out against the wooden floors.

Knowing there was no choice but to follow, since Murray was determined to get as close as he could to what might turn into an unpleasant situation, and that there was every chance that Murray would attempt to drag Reginald up the stairs if he balked, he began climbing the steps after his friend. He made it almost to the top before shrieking met his ears, undoubtedly coming from an enraged lady, one he was going to assume was Adele.

CHAPTER 26

"What is the meaning of this?"

Looking over her shoulder as she set aside the handkerchief she'd been using to blot some of the paint from her lips, Poppy settled her attention on Adele, who looked absolutely furious as she marched past ladies who were not wearing the expected outlandish costumes.

Adele, on the other hand, was wearing that outlandish costume, complete with enormous bustle, yards and yards of white velvet that barely moved as she stormed forward, and sky-high shoes that she'd obviously been practicing in since the height of those shoes didn't seem to affect her ability to storm across the room.

Coming to a stop directly in front of Poppy, Adele nodded, the action causing the towering wig on her head to shift forward ever so slightly. "I'm sure you're responsible for this, aren't you?"

Poppy rose from the stool she'd been sitting on. "I see no reason to deny it."

Adele's heavily painted lips pursed as her nostrils flared. "And I see no reason to deny to the many guests in attendance tonight that you're the one responsible for ruining the quadrille."

Poppy lifted her chin. "I haven't ruined anything except your plan to show yourself more favorably than the rest of us."

"We're expected to be wearing identical costumes."

Gesturing to the ladies who'd gathered in a semicircle, Poppy shrugged. "All of us *are* wearing identical costumes, Adele. We each have white elbow-length gloves, white gowns, white wigs, identical beauty marks on our painted faces, and"—she lifted up the hem of her skirt, revealing sparkly white shoes—"matching shoes."

Miss Cynthia Roche stepped forward. "All of us, including yourself it seems, Adele, are even wearing gowns we can actually breathe in. I am curious as to why when the rest of us tried on the monstrosities you sent to our respective homes yesterday that they were a good two sizes too small for all of us."

"Mine wasn't too small," Poppy said. "But that's only because my grandmother, being a surprisingly insightful lady, thought it would be wise to add a few inches on my behalf to the measurements you asked for, Adele."

Furious mutters erupted around the room, which Adele tried to ignore until Miss Virginia Thorne stepped forward. "Why were our gowns so snug, Adele?"

Adele inclined her head. "I imagine yours was snug, Virginia, because of that pastry I saw you consume at Rutherford & Company."

"That was three weeks ago."

Adele shrugged. "Once past the lips, a lady will certainly find it on her hips." She turned back to Poppy. "I won't forget this, and you can be certain Lord Lonsdale will hear about your duplicity."

"Since his valet was up half the night helping with alterations, I'm fairly convinced Lord Lonsdale's already heard about my . . . duplicity, was it?"

Adele's eyes narrowed, but before she had an opportunity to release what Poppy knew would certainly be a scathing tirade, Lena Ridgeway suddenly breezed into the room, announcing to everyone that it was time to take their places.

Sending Poppy one last animosity-filled look, Adele stalked away, taking up her position directly in front of the door.

"And here come the gentlemen," Cynthia Roche said, the scowl she'd been wearing disappearing in a thrice as gentlemen dressed all in white began streaming into the room.

Shoving all thoughts of Adele aside, Poppy smiled as Murray stepped up to join her.

"You look lovely, Poppy," he said, taking hold of her hand and giving it a good squeeze as he looked her up and down. "Why, I would never know that you've had relatively little sleep, although your eyes do look somewhat bloodshot. You're not getting sick, are you?"

"I'm fine," Poppy said, even though her stomach was a touch queasy, which she hoped was a direct result of knowing she was soon to perform in front of society again.

"Thank goodness. I was afraid you were coming down with whatever Viola and George have. They've got a nasty case of something, what with how much they're both tossing up their accounts."

"Before I left the house, Grandfather told me he was feeling much better," Poppy said. "Which has me hoping they won't be suffering for long." She shook her head. "I was afraid Grandmother was going to try and attend tonight even with her still under the weather, but I finally convinced her she wasn't fit to leave the house."

"She was most disappointed about not getting to see you perform."

"I'm sure there'll be other quadrilles."

Murray's gaze sharpened. "You've begun enjoying society, haven't you?"

Poppy gazed at all the other couples looking resplendent in their costumes, although all the ladies still seemed to have some lingering fury in their eyes, a sight that left Poppy smiling. "While I might have said only yesterday that *enjoying* society was definitely a stretch, I'm not sure that's still the case."

"Viola will be delighted to hear that. Now, shall we get in line?"

Taking hold of the arm Murray extended her, they found their place, Poppy drawing in a few deep breaths in the hopes of settling a stomach that had, indeed, turned queasy.

"Nervous?" Murray asked.

"A bit."

"We'll be fine," he said, giving her arm a squeeze. "I won't let you falter."

Her vision grew a little misty. "Thank you for that, Murray. You've become such a dear, dear friend."

He leaned closer to her. "And because of that, allow me to be the first to tell you that I spoke with Maisie's father this afternoon before I spoke with Maisie, and . . ." He wiggled his brows her way.

"You're getting married?" Poppy whispered.

"Indeed, and it's all thanks to you and Reginald because I would have never noticed her interest in me if the two of you hadn't pointed it out."

"I'm sure you would have eventually noticed Maisie's interest in you," Poppy said right as everyone in front of them began moving forward, Cynthia Roche having to stop for a moment when her wig, the one item of their costumes they'd not been able to alter much, listed to the left.

"This is going to be a very interesting quadrille," Murray said as three women who'd been hired to assist with the wigs rushed forward, sticking numerous pins into Cynthia's wig, which had her wincing every other minute.

Once Cynthia's wig was set to rights, the line began moving again, and before Poppy knew it, they were standing in front of the ballroom that had gone completely silent.

"We'll be fine," Murray said for what seemed like the hundredth time.

"'Course we will," Poppy returned as they glided on to the dance floor.

Taking her position, she drew in a breath, smiled when she heard Murray whispering a quick prayer, whispered one of her own, and then . . . she was dancing.

It soon became clear that all the hours she'd practiced the quadrille with Murray had been hours well spent because she missed not a single step, nor, from what she could tell, did any of the other ladies.

Adele and her billowing costume certainly stood out, something she seemed well aware of since she kept sending Poppy smug looks as she glided around the room on the arm of her partner. That smugness, though, disappeared in a blink of an eye when Adele suddenly lost her footing and stumbled about for a good moment, which had everyone freezing in place.

To everyone's surprise, Adele suddenly kicked off her shoes, which her partner then kicked straight off the dance floor, and with a charming smile sent to the assembled guests, she surged into motion again, a recovery Poppy couldn't help but appreciate.

As the music drew to a close and wild applause sounded throughout the ballroom, Murray gave her arm a squeeze.

"We did it," he said waving a gloved hand in front of his perspiring face while the guests continued applauding.

"That was more enjoyable than I was expecting."

Murray sent her a wink. "Of course it was. You were dancing with me—a dashing, intriguing, and newly engaged gentleman." He leaned closer. "Reginald couldn't take his eyes off you."

The queasiness in her stomach that had yet to disappear suddenly intensified. "I'm afraid I didn't notice. I was much too busy trying not to lose my wig and remember the steps. But, with that said, I'm certain he was watching me so closely so he could take note of any mistakes I made."

Murray let out a snort. "Don't be coy. It doesn't become you."

"I'm not being coy."

"Then you're being obtuse because he truly does fancy you."

The queasiness took a turn for the worse. "He does not."

"He does, although he may not have actually realized that."

"I'm not certain that even makes any sense."

Murray grinned. "You might be right, but I'm a man in love, and again, newly engaged, so my thoughts might not be as clear as they normally are. But know this: with me being newly in love, I've decided it's a state that everyone should embrace, and I'm going to do my very best to make certain you and Reginald . . . well, at the very least, admit you both hold each other in great affection." He looked up. "But he's heading our way, so we'll discuss the matter further after the ball."

Handing her over to Reginald a moment later, then sending

her another wink, Murray hurried away, claiming he needed to find Maisie.

"Did he tell you his news?" Reginald asked, taking Poppy's hand and bringing it to his lips.

"He did, just before the quadrille, and after Adele's rant about my apparent duplicity."

He caught her eye. "Murray and I were directly outside the door when she started shrieking, but before we could intervene, Lena Ridgeway showed up. She told us in no uncertain terms that our presence in a room filled with infuriated ladies would not help the situation."

"I imagine that you couldn't get away fast enough."

Reginald grinned. "Indeed, but only after Lena assured us she'd get the situation well in hand."

"That was kind of her. I wouldn't have expected her to make such an offer, at least to you, since you seemed to annoy her yesterday when you told her you were escorting me tonight."

"Which turned out to be less than the truth since I merely deposited you here earlier and came to the ball on my own."

"Why didn't you come with Lord Lonsdale?"

"He promised Miss Edith Iselin a ride here."

Poppy smiled. "That was thoughtful of him. I've been thinking Edith was most likely upset about Adele, her supposed friend, excluding her from the quadrille, but I would think Charles's kind gesture more than made up for that."

"Have I mentioned yet that I found you to be the most beautiful lady on the floor, or that I didn't neglect to notice that you performed the quadrille flawlessly?"

Poppy blinked as her stomach did a bit of a flip, which was worrisome since she was still feeling queasy. "I don't believe you did, but that was a rather abrupt change of topic."

"I didn't want to forget. But you are looking exceptionally beautiful this evening."

As her knees began wobbling, she started to lose her balance, but before she could do something mortifying, such as plunge to the ground, Reginald's arm was around her, steadying her.

"Are you all right?"

"In all truthfulness, I'm feeling a little queasy."

"Should I take you home?"

"No, I just need to find a quiet place to sit for a moment. Perhaps you could get me something cool to drink?"

"Of course."

After Reginald escorted her to a chair sitting against the far wall of the ballroom, he strode away, disappearing into the guests who were milling around, waiting for the orchestra to begin the first waltz of the evening.

Drawing in a breath, which did nothing to still her queasiness, Poppy rubbed a hand over a cheek that seemed unusually hot. Realizing her queasiness, aching head, and evidently increased temperature were not simply her being anxious about the quadrille, but rather a direct result of coming down with the same illness as her grandparents, Poppy pressed a hand to her forehead right as Lena Ridgeway, with Nigel Flaherty by her side, walked into view.

"Ah, Poppy, there you are, my dear," Lena said cheerfully. "I've been looking for you because I have a most interesting tale to tell you."

Wondering if the curious smile on Lena's face was simply a figment of her imagination because there really was no reason for Lena to be looking almost smug, Poppy forced a smile of her own, praying she wasn't about to toss up her accounts as Lena and Nigel stopped directly in front of her.

"I'm afraid I'm not—" Poppy began, interrupted from saying anything else when Reginald suddenly rejoined her, handing her a glass of what appeared to be water.

"Here, drink this," he said, straightening right as Lena let out a laugh.

"Ah, and here you are as well. Perfect," she all but purred.

Reginald frowned at Lena. "Why is it perfect?"

"Because I've got something incredibly interesting to tell Poppy,

Reginald, something that involves you, or should I say involves . . . Lord Blackburn, second son of the Duke of Sutherland."

Poppy swallowed the sip of water she'd taken, trying to make sense of the conversation. "What are you talking about?" she asked as Nigel sent a frown Lena's way.

"I'd like to know that as well," he said. "What *are* you talking about?"

Lena released a titter. "I'm talking about uncovering a bit of subterfuge that Lord Blackburn has been perpetuating on society, because he, for some unknown reason, has withheld his true identity from all of us, but as to why he's done that, well" —she shrugged—"I've yet to puzzle that out to satisfaction."

Nigel shot a look to Reginald, then looked back to Lena. "Where did you hear this?"

Lena smiled, looking quite like the cat who'd captured the canary. "I've had suspicions about the man for ages, especially after he grew that beard, which, in my humble opinion, did nothing for his appearance. I didn't broach my suspicions to anyone, though, until I realized that he seemed far too interested in our dear Poppy." She pinned Reginald with a malevolent eye. "My husband used to socialize with numerous Englishmen when he visited the Knickerbocker Club, so that's where I decided to go to see if I could ferret out any information about Lord Lonsdale's traveling companion."

She shook her head. "I was most annoyed to have to cool my heels outside the Knickerbocker because they wouldn't allow me, a mere lady, entrance into that hallowed club. But a member of the staff did find me a few Englishmen who agreed to talk to me outside, and imagine my surprise when I broached the topic of Mr. Blackburn to those gentlemen and was immediately taken to task because I'd not used the proper title for Lord Blackburn, second son of the Duke of Sutherland."

Nigel frowned. "But how are you so certain Reginald Blackburn is the same man as Lord Blackburn?"

"Because I made a point of mentioning Lord Lonsdale and was

told he's Lord Blackburn's cousin and is often seen in his cousin's company."

Poppy's hand began trembling, causing some of the water to spill from the glass and onto the silk of her gown. She caught Reginald's eye, not caring in the least for the wariness that was now resting there. "You're the son of a duke?"

He gave a quick jerk of his head. "I am."

Trying to ignore the roiling her stomach was now doing, she frowned. "You lied to me."

"I didn't. I simply withheld a few details about myself."

"You told me you don't own any ancestral estates and led me to believe you're a pauper."

"I don't own any ancestral estates. My family estates are entailed, which means they'll eventually go to my older brother."

"But you're not a pauper, Lord Blackburn, are you?" Lena drawled, taking a step forward. "I was told you're incredibly wealthy—information I believe might explain why you didn't let any of us know the truth about you. You're one of those British gentlemen who believes you're too good for Americans, and you were making sport of our fine young ladies over here, weren't you?"

"Don't be ridiculous," Reginald said shortly. "I was doing nothing of the sort. But now, if all of you will excuse me, I need to speak with Poppy in private."

When Reginald held out his hand to her, Poppy handed him the glass of water she knew she wouldn't be able to drink. Swallowing past the lump that had formed in her throat, she shook her head.

"I'm afraid I'm not up to having a discussion with you right now, *Lord* Blackburn. I'm feeling quite unwell, so if you'll excuse me, I'm going home—and no, I don't want you to escort me."

Before Reginald could voice the argument he clearly wanted to voice, a loud cheer from the crowd suddenly erupted as Charles's voice rang out. "If you'd all gather around, it's time for my announcement."

"You'd better go see what Charles has to say. Don't, for any reason, try to follow me home. I'm much too furious, as well as ill, to have to suffer your company," Poppy managed to say as Lena hurried to her side, took hold of her arm, and gave it a good pat.

"My carriage is right out front, my dear. I'll see you home."

Without hesitation, and praying she'd make it out of Delmonico's before she lost the small bit of lunch she'd eaten that day, Poppy stumbled through the crowd that wasn't paying her any mind at all, thankful when Lena didn't try to engage in conversation but instead got her outside and into her carriage, shooing two dogs off the seat as she helped Poppy get settled.

"Nigel, stop dallying and get in the carriage," Lena demanded, which, surprisingly, had Nigel, who'd never struck Poppy as a gentleman fond of being ordered about, climbing into the carriage. Before he had an opportunity to find his seat, though, Lena rapped on the roof of the carriage, setting it into motion.

Rubbing a shaking hand over a face that now felt on fire, Poppy managed a nod toward Lena. "Thank you for offering to take me home."

"But of course, my dear. You've suffered quite a shock. And while I know this may seem like an unusual time to broach this topic, broach it I shall so you won't worry needlessly that you're soon to be made the laughingstock of society."

Forcing herself to concentrate on what seemed to be a very unusual conversation indeed, Poppy rubbed a hand over a stomach that was turning incredibly painful. "Why would I be considered the laughingstock of society?"

"Because Reginald Blackburn deceived you. You were growing fond of him, what with how you were only too willing to agree to have him escort you here this evening, but you must realize now that he was merely amusing himself with you, which is why . . ."

Lena suddenly elbowed Nigel, who was sitting beside her on the seat opposite from Poppy. "Go on, dear."

Nigel winced and pressed a hand against ribs that were evidently smarting. "I'm not sure what you want me to go on with, Lena."

"Of course you do, and now is the perfect time for you to declare yourself, which will alleviate any concerns Poppy may have about having to face society as a . . . well . . . duped woman."

Trying to ignore the intense pounding in her temples, Poppy frowned. "I don't think you need to worry about that, Lena."

Lena gave a dismissive flutter of her hand. "We're waiting, Nigel."

Nigel shook his head. "I'm afraid you're going to have to wait a long time, Lena, if you believe I'm going to declare myself to Poppy. And while I understand that you've apparently gotten your heart set on seeing me with her, I . . . ah . . ." Nigel stopped talking because one of Lena's dogs took that moment to climb into his lap.

Lena turned a smile on Poppy. "He's being shy, dear, and because of that, I'll speak for him."

"I'm not being shy," Nigel said, trying to shove the dog off his lap, which only earned him a menacing growl and had him freezing on the spot.

"Of course you are," Lena countered before she caught Poppy's eye. "Nigel's become the son I've never had, which is why I've taken such an interest in his life, and I've decided you're perfect for him."

Poppy pressed a hand against her temple. "This is *really* not the moment for this," she said as her stomach suddenly gave a flip that couldn't be ignored and bile began rising in her throat. "Stop the carriage."

"I'm afraid I can't do that, dear, at least not until you do Nigel the very great honor of agreeing to become his wife."

Feeling quite as if she was missing something vastly important but unable to think about that because she was feeling beyond queasy, Poppy reached for the door. "I'm afraid I can't do that, and you need to stop the carriage before it's too late."

"Stop being difficult," Lena snapped. "You will marry Nigel, and—"

Whatever else Lena said, Poppy didn't catch as she lurched for the door, barely managed to get it open, ignored that one of Lena's dogs had its teeth in the skirt of her gown, and tossed up her accounts.

CHAPTER 27

"What an unmitigated disaster this night has turned out to be."

Barely stirring as Charles strode into the sitting room of Reginald's Fifth Avenue Hotel suite, he watched Charles fling himself into the nearest chair, tug his tie loose, then nod his thanks to Giles, who handed him a glass of wine he'd just poured from a bottle Reginald had opened. "Did Reginald tell you what happened at the ball, Giles?"

Giles inclined his head. "Indeed, and I can't disagree that the ball turned into a disaster for him, what with his secret being exposed to Poppy, which is why he's now turned brooding—a direct result of him realizing he's lost a lady he'd grown to love."

"I never said I was in love with Poppy," Reginald argued, picking up his glass of wine and taking a sip.

"You didn't need to, sir. As a man who has been in your service for years, I knew within a week of you meeting her that she was going to be someone special."

Charles, surprisingly enough, nodded. "I knew that as well."

"You never mentioned a word about me being in love with Poppy. In fact, you encouraged me to continue giving her etiquette lessons."

Charles took a sip of his wine. "Of course I did. What with you always being so adamant that you'll only marry a very proper sort, I knew that you needed time in Poppy's company." He shook his head. "You're different around her—not as stodgy—and not that you apparently noticed this, but you haven't been brooding nearly as much since you met her."

"I thought you wanted me to continue instructing her because you were considering her as a potential bride."

Charles set aside his glass and frowned. "Poppy, even with her impressive dowry, is an unpredictable sort, and I knew after she launched that snail at Mr. Nigel Flaherty's head that she wasn't the lady for me."

"But you thought an unpredictable sort was what I need in a bride?"

"Poppy's exactly what you need, but I'm afraid you've lost her now, what with how your disastrous night unfolded." He slouched down in the chair. "My night was just as disastrous, and I fear both of us will be returning to London exactly as we left it—as bachelors."

Giles strode for the door. "I think this is where I bid both of you good night, since you apparently have much to discuss between you." Walking through the door, then shutting it firmly behind him, Reginald felt the very corners of his mouth lift.

"Do you get the impression Giles has had quite enough of our drama?"

"And I didn't even get to tell him what happened to me at the ball," Charles muttered before he raked a hand through his hair. "I'm sure you were as taken aback by the debacle my announcement made as I was."

Reginald winced. "I'm afraid I never caught your announcement, Charles. I was trying to catch Poppy, but Lena Ridgeway whisked her straightaway. By the time I managed to dodge guests who were hurrying to hear your announcement and get outside, she was long gone. Then, coward that I apparently am, I decided I wasn't up for all the questions I knew everyone at the ball would be dying to ask, so I called for my carriage and returned here."

Charles shook his head. "Just as well you missed it. It was quite embarrassing." He reached for his glass. "There I was, standing in front of everyone, preparing to make my grand announcement, and—"

"You had second thoughts about who you'd decided to propose to?"

"Of course not, Reginald. I may be slightly flighty at times, but I'm not that flighty. Besides"—Charles leaned forward—"I wasn't planning on proposing to anyone tonight. I was merely going to announce that I'd decided to host a masked ball at the end of January, where I was hoping I'd be able to pull off a most spectacular marriage proposal."

"So you have settled on a particular lady."

"Indeed I have."

"And?" Reginald pressed when Charles didn't elaborate.

"Edith Iselin, but I would have thought you'd already know that by now."

"How could I know that, Charles? You've barely talked about the lady, nor did you ever suggest I offer to give her etiquette lessons as a way to uncover her true character."

"Edith's character didn't need to be uncovered. She's possessed of a sincerely kind nature. She's incredibly intelligent but doesn't come across as a bluestocking, and she's the most beautiful lady I've ever seen." Charles sighed. "From the moment I laid eyes on her, I knew she was the one."

"And yet you still had Giles and me spend hours and hours of our time researching twenty other society ladies."

Charles nodded. "Forgive me for that, Reginald, but having you and Giles occupy those ladies with lessons and rides around the city allowed me to spend uninterrupted time with Edith. She, unlike any of the other ladies, except Poppy, wasn't impressed in the least with my title. That intrigued me and made me long to get to know her, which then allowed her to get to know me—the real me, not the me who's now an earl." He smiled rather sadly. "I believe she'd begun to truly care about me, until . . . disaster struck."

"I'm afraid I'm not following. What disaster?"

"It happened right after I told the guests I was about to make my announcement." Charles shuddered. "There I was, in front of the room, oblivious that Lena Ridgeway had just exposed the truth about you, a truth that some of the other guests apparently overheard. But because I was oblivious to that, I continued on with my announcement, telling everyone I had a grand treat for them." He shuddered again. "My speech, however, came to a rapid end when whispers about you reached Edith's ears, and . . . she was livid."

Charles loosened his tie some more. "She marched her way up beside me, demanding to know why I'd withheld your identity. And then, when I sputtered some nonsense because I was taken completely off guard, she stuck her pert nose in the air and declared that I was morally lacking and needed to seek out the counsel of a man of the cloth as soon as possible so that he could explain to me something about how God expects men to live an honest life. . . . It only went downhill from there."

When Charles didn't expound on that, Reginald scooted his chair closer to his cousin, reaching out to give Charles's knee a pat. "What happened next?"

Charles rubbed his hand over his face, his eyes a bit wild. "Well, as I was standing there, with what seemed like the entire New York Four Hundred scowling back at me, a curious, and I must add profound, notion struck—Edith was right. I have behaved in a most unseemly and less-than-moral fashion, and not simply because I'd concealed your title from everyone." He drew in a breath. "I'd carelessly given numerous young ladies improbable hope that they might capture my attention and then capture the role of countess when I, as I mentioned, had already become completely smitten with Edith and had no intention of settling my attention on any other lady."

Leaning forward, Charles blew out a breath. "Before I could beg everyone's pardon for my bad behavior, Adele suddenly stormed up to join me and Edith, told Edith she was ruining my big announcement, then beamed the most terrifying smile at me and urged me to get on with matters."

"How did Edith take that?"

"Not well. She began in a most un-Edith-like fashion to scold Adele, who began shrieking horrible things about Edith always being jealous of her at the top of her lungs, and because I certainly wasn't going to tolerate the love of my life being treated thus, I, ah . . . well . . . I might have proclaimed very loudly that there was obviously some confusion about what I'd been going to announce because I wasn't announcing any plans to marry but rather that I was intending on holding a masked ball. And . . . that's when disaster really occurred."

"I would have thought that announcing a ball instead of an engagement might have diffused the situation."

"Quite," Charles said with a nod. "But you see, after I announced that, Adele yelled that it was completely unacceptable for me to continue keeping all the young ladies on tenterhooks. She then demanded that I announce then and there who I'd chosen to become my countess, and when I hesitated to do so, I soon found myself being approached by every lady who'd participated in the quadrille—a terrifying sight if there ever was one because even with those ladies looking like angels, what with all the white they were wearing, they clearly had murderous intentions in their eyes."

"I imagine that was a terrifying sight."

"Indeed, and because I was flustered at that point, I didn't notice Adele moving closer to me, until she took hold of my arm and practically bellowed out to the guests that she was going to put an end to the suspense because she, and everyone else, knew full well that I'd chosen her."

Reginald blinked. "She didn't."

"She did, which had me, not having a moment to sort through my words, stating emphatically that she was mistaken because I had no intention of marrying her." Charles shuddered. "And then, when Adele started screaming at me, I turned to Edith and told her she was the lady for me, which had the entire ballroom going silent."

Charles caught Reginald's eye. "That's when everyone got to hear Edith tell me that she wouldn't marry me if I was the last man on earth because I'm an idiot and someone who has no idea how to extend a lady a proper proposal of marriage. She then stormed out of the ballroom and that was that." He began pressing fingers against his temples. "I am an idiot and have certainly lost Edith for good, and all that's left for us to do now is repair to England. Once we're there, I'm going to retire to one of my crumbling country estates where I'll seek out the counsel of the local vicar and hope he'll be able to lend me some guidance about what I should do next."

"You do remember that we came to America because you're in desperate need of an heiress, don't you?"

"I'm hardly likely to forget that," Charles muttered. "But because you and I have now experienced what can only be considered a mortifying life lesson, I need to reconsider my approach to life and perhaps think about taking you up on your offer to learn about investing, which . . ." Charles suddenly brightened. "Might provide me with a way to win Edith back."

"Does Edith not possess a fortune of her own?"

"No idea. We never discussed the matter, nor did I ever ask if Giles looked into her finances."

"And I certainly never looked into Edith's finances because I had not the slightest inkling you were interested in her." Reginald sighed. "I'm afraid I let you down there, Charles. It was my one and only job to make certain the lady you set your attention on was in possession of a grand fortune and could withstand the pressures of being a countess. I failed miserably in that regard, quite as I failed Poppy by withholding the truth about me."

"I told you that you shouldn't wait too long before disclosing all."

Swiveling around in his chair, Reginald frowned as George strode through a now-open door, Beatrix Waterbury by his side and Giles trailing after them.

Reginald rose to his feet. "George, what are you doing here? Should you even be out of bed? You look incredibly pale."

George sat down in the first chair he reached. "I'm still slightly under the weather, but feeling much better. Thankfully, whatever illness I caught seems to be a one-day event, and I couldn't very well stay in bed, not when . . ." George suddenly sneezed. As he pulled out a handkerchief and went about blowing his nose, Beatrix stepped forward.

"Poppy never came home," Beatrix finished for him. "George and I were hoping she might have decided to stop here to discuss what happened with you at the ball in private."

Something heavy settled in Reginald's stomach as he pulled out his pocket watch. "Even with Poppy embracing an unconventional attitude, she wouldn't have sought me out in my hotel. I haven't seen her since she left the ball with Lena Ridgeway, although I tried to catch up with her before she left. By the time I made it outside, she was gone." He looked at his watch. "That was over three hours ago."

Beatrix's brows drew together. "Why did Poppy leave with Lena Ridgeway?"

"Lena offered her a ride when Poppy announced she wanted to go home immediately." Reginald blew out a breath. "She was absolutely furious with me and, truth be told, looked rather nauseous after she learned I'm the second son of a duke. She was so put out with me, in fact, that she all but ran out of the ball, and was apparently so anxious to get away from me that she accepted the first ride that was offered to her."

"But Lena never brought her home," Beatrix said slowly. "When I heard what happened, I immediately left the ball and traveled directly to Poppy's house. Mr. Parsons informed me she'd not arrived back yet, so I waited for her in the receiving room, finally having Mr. Parsons wake George up when it became clear that something might be dreadfully amiss."

"I'm quite concerned at this point," George said, accepting the glass of water that Giles had fetched him and sending the man a nod of thanks. "Especially since Poppy definitely seems to have left with Lena Ridgeway."

"Do you know something about Lena the rest of us don't?" Reginald pressed.

"She's an odd woman who used to suffer from occasional bouts of acute melancholy—or at least there were whispers about that years ago. She's also apparently been trying her hand at match-making, at least according to Beatrix." George frowned. "Don't know why she'd believe Nigel Flaherty and Poppy would make a good match or how she was able to uncover the truth about you, Reginald, or why she decided to disclose that truth in the middle of a ball."

"She said she got curious about me after I told her I was escorting Poppy to the ball, and apparently took it upon herself to do some investigating into my background, making inquiries of gentlemen currently in New York who have connections with England."

"Why would she go to so much bother?" Beatrix asked. "Do you believe Nigel could have put her up to it because he fancies Poppy?"

"What could he possibly hope to achieve by having Reginald's title disclosed?" George asked.

Beatrix frowned. "I have no idea. But Nigel has a reputation for turning nasty when events don't go his way, at least according to my good friend, Isadora MacKenzie. And even though he claims to be a changed man . . . what if he isn't?"

Reginald frowned. "Either way, I still don't understand what Nigel and Lena's intentions are when it concerns Poppy. From what I've heard about Nigel, he's not a fortune hunter."

"But what if he is?" Beatrix countered.

Reginald blinked. "Do you think what happened tonight could have been a desperate attempt on his part to convince Poppy, if he believed her to hold affection for me, to turn her back on me and turn to him?"

Beatrix's brows drew together. "If it was, Nigel clearly doesn't understand Poppy, but with that said, there's a chance Poppy might be in very grave straits at the moment, which means—"

"We need to save her," Reginald finished for her and headed for the door.

CHAPTER 28

Over the two days she'd spent as what could only be described as Lena Ridgeway's prisoner, Poppy had come to a few unpleasant conclusions.

The first of which was that Lena's dogs—all seven of them—were incredibly well trained, at least as guard dogs, since when they were not on duty, they got into all sorts of mischief, eating everything from unattended food to pieces of the furniture.

The next conclusion revolved around Nigel, who certainly was to blame, at least a bit, for Poppy being abducted in the first place, but who hadn't seemed to grasp the lengths Lena was willing to go through to get him married off to Poppy. He'd been the one to hold Poppy's head as she'd tossed up her accounts. But when he'd told Lena they needed to get Poppy back to the Van Rensselaer residence, and then began arguing with Lena after she refused his request, he soon found himself on the wrong end of Lena's pistol. She'd then set one of her largest and meanest mutts to guard Nigel as the carriage rumbled into motion, telling Nigel in no uncertain terms that she knew best what he needed, which was apparently marriage to Poppy, and that had been that.

Poppy still had no idea why Lena wanted that marriage to take place. But because it turned out that the illness she'd most likely acquired through contact with her grandparents had been highly contagious, and because Lena and Nigel had both turned violently ill the day after she'd been abducted, Poppy had been forced to cool her heels in the locked room she'd been in ever since Lena had spirited her out of the city.

From what little Poppy had overheard as she'd been carted through the night in a carriage stuffed with dogs, Lena's late husband had kept a cottage somewhere up the Hudson, and that's where Lena had decided to hold Poppy until she came to her senses.

The whole situation was beyond bewildering, but the one conclusion Poppy couldn't deny was this—Lena Ridgeway was mentally unstable, which made her a more than dangerous woman and made it more than urgent for Poppy to figure out a way to escape from the madness that now surrounded her.

A key scraping against the lock suddenly drew her attention. A second later, the door opened, revealing Nigel.

He was looking the worse for wear—dark circles under his eyes, face unusually pale, and stubble on his jaw.

"I've brought you some soup," he said, swallowing as he hurried over to a small table and deposited the tray he was holding, backing away quickly, which gave testimony to the idea he was still feeling queasy.

"You might find it encouraging to hear that you won't be under the weather long," Poppy said, moving to the table and taking a seat. "I feel remarkably well today, and—"

"Shh . . ." Nigel whispered, cutting her off as he looked over his shoulder. "Don't let Lena know that. She's up and about too, apparently having willed herself to get better, and I don't think it'll benefit either of us to let her know you're well. No telling what she's got planned for us next."

He jumped the slightest bit when Brutus, the dog that Lena had set to guard him, padded into the room and immediately began growling. Nigel plopped down in one of the two chairs the room offered, drawing his legs to his chest. "Shoo," he said, which only had Brutus sitting on the floor directly beside the chair, baring his teeth.

Poppy resisted a smile, turning her attention to her soup. She immediately began spooning out chunks of the meat, which she slipped under the table to the two poodles Lena left in Poppy's room every minute of the day.

"I'm truly sorry about this, Poppy. I had no idea Lena was—"

"Insane?"

"Exactly, although I had begun to realize that she wasn't normal and that she was taking an unusual interest in my life, but I never imagined she'd go to these lengths to apparently make me happy." Nigel blew out a breath. "Perhaps it would be easiest if you and I just gave in to Lena's demands and got married."

Poppy looked up. "I'm not marrying you, Nigel, nor do I even want to, and you don't want to marry me either." She looked to the door that Nigel had left open, a rule Lena had made, claiming that such an action would save Poppy's reputation. It clearly showed how muddled Lena's thinking had turned, as a ruined reputation would have certainly given just cause for why a wedding would have to take place—not that Poppy would have agreed to that, but still. After making certain there was no sign of Lena, Poppy lowered her voice and nodded to Nigel. "We're simply going to have to find a way to escape."

When he immediately began shaking his head, Poppy dug another piece of meat out of her soup and threw it to Nigel, who only barely managed to catch it. His face turned slightly green at the sight of it. "Don't think I'm ready for food just yet."

"It's not for you. Give it to Brutus."

"Oh." Lowering his hand ever so slowly, Nigel looked clammier than ever when Brutus went after the meat, swallowing it whole and licking his chops a second later.

"See? He stopped growling at you." She turned back to her bowl, but before she could fish out another piece, Lena strolled into the room. She was wearing an unusual day dress of deepest red, paired with a large matching bow in her hair, and, unfortunately, she was looking remarkably healthy.

"Ah, you're eating, Poppy. Thank goodness. I was afraid you'd waste away to almost nothing, which certainly would leave the dresses you've been wearing of mine hanging from your frame, which wouldn't be a good look for you at all." She nodded to a wardrobe against the wall. "Do feel free to help yourself. As you've evidently noticed, I have a large selection, all of which I'm more than happy to share with you."

Poppy glanced down at the dress she was wearing today, one that was at least twenty years out of date, what with how much fabric was devoted to the skirt.

She frowned. "I'm surprised you'd store so many dresses at your late husband's cottage. Hardly seems as if that was convenient for you."

"This wasn't actually his cottage, dear. He bought it for me, and this"—she turned in a circle, gesturing around the room—"this is where I was kept when he decided I was suffering from bouts of insanity." She stopped turning and caught Poppy's eye. "There's no need to fret that I'm insane, though. I used to suffer from a wee bit of melancholy—acute melancholy, as numerous doctors called it—but that melancholy all but disappeared after my husband died." She began gesturing around the room again. "He died right in this very room."

Poppy's mouth turned dry. "Did you kill him?"

"Of course not. Simply because I've suffered from melancholy frequently over the years doesn't make me bloodthirsty."

"Not even when your husband apparently kept you a prisoner here?"

"Oh, I suppose I did think about harming him, but I never followed through on those thoughts. He died from overexerting himself after I was having a touch of a fit when he wouldn't allow me to add a few more dogs to our family. He decided to throw me over his shoulder to get me back into this room where he was planning on locking me away again. I'm afraid he was far too old at that point to carry me, so he collapsed in the middle of this very floor and . . . that was the end of him." She moved to Nigel and sent a pointed look to the chair he was sitting in.

Nigel slowly lowered his legs, winced when Brutus growled low in his throat, then rose to his feet and moved to stand on the other side of the room, seeming to want to put as much distance as he could between himself, Lena, and her still-growling dog.

Sitting down in the chair Nigel had just abandoned, Lena pulled her ever-handy pistol from a pocket of her dress, placed it on her lap, and smiled pleasantly at Poppy. "Now then, why don't you impress me with what you've learned from *Lord* Blackburn about proper conversations? Better yet, why don't we discuss *Lord* Blackburn's blatant dishonesty with you, which might have you putting those pesky feelings you probably still hold for the man aside. And don't try to convince me you don't have feelings for him. That was all too obvious to me when he interrupted us the other day and said *he* was going to be escorting you to the ball, laying waste to the lovely evening I'd been hoping you'd share with Nigel. Why, your expression after he said all that was downright sappy."

Poppy settled back in the chair and considered Lena for a long moment.

That she'd been furious with Reginald was not in question. It also wasn't in question that she had feelings for the man, and complicated feelings at that. But she was fairly certain he'd taken her parting words to him as a demand for him to never contact her again, even though she'd simply been desperately ill when Lena had disclosed his duplicity and needed to get away from the ball before she'd gotten ill all over the gleaming marble floor.

But even knowing that he'd been less than honest with her, he wasn't a cruel man, which made it hard to believe he'd set out to deliberately make sport of her. He'd also come to her rescue time and time again, and had even taken to looking out for her when it looked like someone was trying to sabotage her Season.

That right there is why she'd decided, as she'd been locked away for almost two days, that if she ever escaped from Lena and her madness, she was going to have to seek Reginald out. She needed to hear from him exactly why he'd withheld his true identity from her. That would hopefully allow the anger she still held over his duplicity to fade even more than it already had, and—

A snap of a finger brought Poppy out of her thoughts, a snap that had come from Lena's direction and had three of her dogs scampering to her side.

"Mooning over the man is not going to help you get over him," Lena said, smoothing a hand over the head of one of her poodles. She nodded to Nigel. "Why don't you tell her something about yourself, dear, something that will impress her."

Nigel arched a brow. "Do you believe it'll impress her, Lena, if I tell her you want me to marry her so I can get the land deeded to her—land that will finally allow me to proceed with a mining venture I've been interested in?"

"Wait, that's why Lena wants you to marry me?" Poppy asked before Lena could do more than scowl Nigel's way. "Because of my land?"

Nigel nodded. "I'm afraid so. There's an enormous coalfield under Garrison Farms, and even though the rumors are true about me being extremely wealthy, I've unfortunately found that money doesn't always get a man what he desires."

"That's where I come in," Lena said, smiling fondly at Nigel even as she wagged a finger at him. "And while I know you're put out with me for taking control of this situation, you must understand that I've only done so because you've become the son my late husband would never allow me to have." Her eyes hardened. "Did I tell the two of you that my parents actually bought my husband for me? Not that I knew it at the time, but that's exactly what they did."

When Nigel merely gaped at Lena, Poppy cleared her throat. "You haven't mentioned that."

Lena ran a finger along the contours of her pistol. "My parents were always concerned about me, coming to believe there was something dreadfully wrong with me because I occasionally had outbursts of temper, quite like I imagine most children do. However, they decided my outbursts were not normal, which had them dragging me to one doctor after another over the years, as well as having me committed to a few asylums." She looked up. "They finally realized, what with how they were getting older, that they weren't going to live forever. My mother, who was actually a dear soul, didn't want to have to commit me to an asylum for the rest of my days. That's when my father approached Frank Ridgeway and extended him an offer he simply couldn't refuse."

She leaned forward and brushed aside the curtain that covered the one window in the room. "I was so delighted to discover there was a gentleman interested in marrying me, and delighted that my parents had decided it was time for me to be presented to society as well. Being presented wasn't an extravagant endeavor back then, mind you. I simply put up my hair and attended a formal dinner my parents held. And because I was well behaved at that dinner, they began allowing Frank to escort me to a few society events, which I enjoyed tremendously."

Lena turned to Poppy. "We were married within three months. I quickly learned, though, that Frank had no intention of sharing a normal marriage with me, nor was he ever going to allow me to have children, not wanting to pass on my . . . *affliction*, as he called it, to anyone else. When I flew into a rage, I soon found myself locked away in this very room, something that happened frequently during the years we were married." Her eyes gleamed. "I also became aware of the disturbing fact that once a woman marries, she has no control over anything—not her money, not her property, and certainly not her life. It was at Frank's complete discretion whether or not to send me off to asylums. He began sending me off more frequently after my parents died and he came into control of all their money."

Lena smiled sweetly—a smile that was, in actuality, downright terrifying. "I found it so liberating after Frank died, realized I was finally free, especially after I learned that the fortune Frank had left behind was mine to spend however I pleased. It was lovely to be able to travel to my many houses whenever I wanted. I readily admit I was becoming rather lonely, though." She nodded to Nigel. "I cannot tell you how delighted I was when you arrived at my home in the city to speak with Frank, having no idea he'd died. You were so considerate, taking the time to explain how Frank had invested in a few of your endeavors, and you were so apologetic about how one endeavor was no longer viable since you'd been unable to acquire the land you needed."

Poppy frowned and turned to Nigel. "You weren't the one who was responsible for the bank trying to foreclose on my parents, were you?"

Nigel winced. "I'm afraid I was. Not that I'm proud of that."

"But how did you manage it?"

"Well, when I was attempting to get control of land in Canonsburg because of the coal discovered there, I was also trying to get my hands on Garrison Farms." He blew out a breath. "I sent a man down there to see if your father was willing to sell, which he wasn't. So, after I looked into your father's finances, I learned he'd taken out a large loan to expand his business into Kentucky. I then made a large deposit in that very bank, which then caused the bank manager to call in your father's loan early when I threatened to pull my money back out."

"That's despicable."

Nigel nodded. "Agreed, but when your grandmother swept in and saved the day, I began to realize that I did need to change my ways, especially after everything went so horribly wrong for me in Pittsburgh." He shook his head. "I was stunned to find myself ostracized from Pittsburgh society after society members there discovered I'd used rather intimidating and unethical tactics in a failed attempt to acquire farmland down in Canonsburg."

"You told me your employee was responsible for that."

Nigel nodded. "Yes, but I only did that because I didn't want to find myself ostracized from New York society as well, not when I'd just entered it, and—"

"To remind you, dear," Lena interrupted, "you only got to mingle with high society because of me."

As Nigel retreated into silence, probably because Lena had gotten a rather wild look on her face, Poppy narrowed her eyes on him.

"I do hope you're not going to disclose next, Nigel, that you somehow managed to trick Lena into getting you into high society."

"He did nothing of the sort," Lena snapped before Nigel could respond. "I told you, he came looking for Frank, and during that visit, I realized that the darling boy might actually need me." Her gaze drifted back to the window again. "No one has ever needed me before, except my dogs of course, but they're not really the same thing." She heaved a sigh. "I've always wanted someone to need me, which is why I asked Nigel if he'd be so kind as to join me for a New York Season." She turned back to Poppy. "I've also always wanted to be known as a lady with an eye for matchmaking, and what perfect way for me to finally embrace that notion than to find Nigel a wife? Why, after you launched that snail at him, I thought it was a sign that you were exactly the type of bride he needed."

"Because I hit him with a snail?"

"No, because you were so charmingly embarrassed afterward, and my Nigel kept smiling at you. That's when I knew you belonged together." She shook her head. "I must admit I might have been pushing a bit too hard when I hired those men to steal your reticule, intending for Nigel to impress you when he raced to your rescue again, but this time not having to share the spotlight with another man."

"You hired men to steal her reticule?" Nigel asked.

"I did, because again, I have only your best interests at heart, darling. But . . ." She grimaced. "They were supposed to ambush you in Central Park, since that's where you told me you were going to take Poppy to ride that day if she was available." She released a dramatic sigh. "Good thing I followed you to the Van Rensselaer home, which allowed me, along with the three hired thugs I had in my carriage with me, to see you depart from the Van Rensselaers' without Poppy."

"I would have thought that circumstance would have caused you to abandon your plan," Nigel said slowly.

Lena waved that aside. "I'm not one who enjoys being thwarted, dear. After you rode off, I nipped in to the Van Rensselaer house on the pretense I was paying Viola a call and learned that Poppy had gone to Rutherford & Company for tea. I then deduced that you were probably heading off for Broadway as well, in the hopes that you'd run into her."

"I wasn't on Broadway because I'd decided to track Poppy down," Nigel argued. "I thought to stop in at my barber since I had some unexpected time on my hands."

"How disappointing," Lena said before she brightened. "But it all worked out well in the end. I positioned myself and the hired men in an alley directly beside Rutherford & Company, then set those men after Poppy when she finally left that store, telling them to wait until they caught sight of you before wrenching Poppy's reticule away from her."

"But I was nowhere to be found," Nigel pointed out.

"I know, but you did manage to stumble onto the scene at just the right moment. You then retrieved Poppy's reticule without hesitation, although I am sorry the man smacked you in the face, which was not well done of him, but it proved to me that I was a brilliant strategist and that I would succeed in seeing you married to Poppy sometime in the near future."

Poppy blinked. "But that was—"

"Brilliant?" Lena finished for her with a nod. "I know."

"That wasn't the word I was going to use, because, if you ask me, since Nigel didn't know about your plan, it was merely a very peculiar circumstance that he just happened to arrive on the scene and give chase to the man who'd stolen my reticule."

"It was a sign, dear, one I took to mean I was to continue with my matchmaking efforts in regard to you and Nigel."

Poppy chanced a glance to Nigel, who was rubbing a hand over his face, clearly at a loss for words.

Poppy couldn't say she blamed him. Shifting in the chair, she stilled when a thought sprang to mind. "Did you hire those men to continue following me? Because one of them tried to abduct me down in Five Points."

Lena raised a hand to her throat. "How concerning, but no. I imagine that was simply one of those peculiar coincidences as well, probably brought about because you'd put up more of a fight with those men than I'd prepared them for. I told them you were a demure and retiring sort."

Poppy frowned. "Were you also responsible for the balcony incident, one where I could have very well lost my life?"

"If I'd wanted you dead, child, I wouldn't have chosen to toss you over a balcony. There would have been no subtlety in that, but no, no one was responsible for that incident except yourself, although it sparked my plan to set Nigel up to save you again."

"What about the musket balls?"

Lena nodded. "That was me. I got the idea after Miss Adele Tooker tripped you up with that cane at Delmonico's. She's a horrid lady, although I can't help but appreciate her determination to take out the competition to achieve what she wants. That's why I took a page out of her book after I noticed Lord Lonsdale being far too friendly toward you at your tea. I needed to make him believe you were a clumsy sort, not suitable to become a countess, and I just happened to have those musket balls in my reticule, which was very fortunate indeed."

"Why would you keep musket balls in your reticule?" Poppy asked.

"One never knows when one might need a musket ball."

Not bothering to point out how ridiculous that answer was, Poppy shook her head. "Poor Adele. There were many people present at my tea who thought she was responsible for that."

"Make no mistake about it, Adele would have had no qualms

about laying you low if she'd had ready access to musket balls," Lena said.

Poppy leaned back in the chair. "I still don't understand how you believe abducting me is going to get that land for Nigel or get me to marry him. You must realize that it's a plan doomed to fail."

"It's not," Lena snapped, sitting forward. "It's brilliant, and it won't fail. You'll marry Nigel, and he'll get the land he desires as well as the wife a man of his station in life deserves."

"But I don't want to marry her," Nigel said, speaking up, even though doing so earned him a growl from Brutus.

Lena frowned. "She's perfect for you. Beautiful, wealthy, and she seems to be enjoying quite the success this Season even with the drama she's experienced. Why, I heard a few ladies whispering that she's actually now considered a diamond of the first water, and that, my darling boy, is exactly what you need in a wife."

"Forgive me, Lena," Nigel began, shooting Poppy an apologetic look, "but I'm afraid Poppy simply doesn't appeal to me. Yes, she's beautiful, but in all honesty, she's exhausting."

Lena blinked and considered Nigel for a very long, very uncomfortable moment before she finally nodded. "Fine. You won't marry her. However"—she leveled her gaze on Poppy—"you will agree here and now to sign over that farm to Nigel. I won't see him deprived of that."

Poppy shook her head. "Even though you apparently eavesdropped on my conversation with Murray when I told him my parents had deeded the farm over to me, that's not accurate information. I insisted my parents change the deed to include my two brothers, so I'm afraid that I wouldn't be able to sign anything over to you even if I wanted to—which I don't, if that's in question."

Fury flashed through Lena's eyes as she sprang to her feet. "Then what good are you to me?" she shrieked right before she raised the pistol, aiming it directly at Poppy's heart.

CHAPTER 29

"That's Lena's carriage, all right," Murray said, passing Reginald the opera glasses he'd been using to get a better look. "It's bright red, and there's not another like it that I've ever seen."

Aiming the opera glasses to the carriage that was parked in front of an impressive cottage, Reginald took a second to look around the yard, finding two dogs lying on the front porch, sleeping.

He lowered the glasses and nodded to Murray. "Remember to thank your mother for me, Murray. Without her remembering that Lena's husband had this cottage, we would have been hard-pressed to find Poppy."

"If she's in there," Murray said before he sent a warm smile to Maisie, who was sitting on a horse beside him. "We have Maisie to thank for bringing my mother into the situation. Truth be told, I would have never thought to ask her."

Maisie returned the smile. "Your mother is a society matron and has spent years listening to all the rumors, so it seemed only logical to me to question her about Lena. Lucky we did since she knew all about Lena's unfortunate past, what with her being prone to melancholy and her husband hiding her in that cottage over there."

"Lena may have an unfortunate past," Viola said as she pulled her horse to a stop next to Reginald, "but that doesn't excuse her from abducting Poppy. I have no idea what could be behind her actions, but—"

"We'll soon find out," George finished for her as he nodded to the cottage. "I'll ride down there first."

"Absolutely not," Reginald argued. "I'll go. You stay here with everyone else."

"She's my granddaughter."

"And I'm hoping she'll be my—" Reginald stopped talking as everyone turned expectant looks his way, Viola sending him an encouraging sort of nod when he didn't say anything else.

Drawing in a breath, he tried to compose a rational response, one that wouldn't take too long to explain.

He'd had more than enough time to think matters through over the two days since Poppy had gone missing, and what he now knew without a doubt was this—he loved her, loved everything about her, even her less-than-strict adherence to the rules and her maddening proclivity to become involved in the most outrageous escapades.

He knew he'd hurt her by withholding his truth, but he was determined, if nothing else, to at least get an opportunity to explain why he'd done that, beg her forgiveness, and hope she'd give him another chance.

"I think you were about to say *wife*," Charles said, edging his horse forward as he peered at the cottage. "Maybe we should all storm the place, take them by surprise."

Edith Iselin, who'd insisted on helping them find Poppy, began shaking her head. "That could very well get someone killed."

Charles frowned. "Would it bother you if I got killed?"

"Don't be ridiculous; of course it would. I may still be furious with you, but I'm not furious enough to want to see you dead."

Charles shot a glance to Reginald. "There might still be hope for me after all."

"What say we put that notion aside, at least until we retrieve Poppy?"

"Right," Charles said with a nod. "We should focus on the situation at hand, figure out how—"

A gunshot suddenly split the air, and Reginald didn't hesitate. Sending his horse into motion, he bent low over the saddle, retrieving the pistol he'd put in his jacket pocket. He jumped from the horse before it came to a complete stop, made it two feet toward the porch, then suddenly found himself set upon by snarling dogs.

"Here, puppies," he heard Beatrix yell, and to his disbelief, the dogs lost all interest in him, scrambling over to Beatrix, who was tossing them pieces of what seemed to be one of the sandwiches Mr. Parsons had packed for everyone before they'd left the house that morning.

"Go," she called. "I'll keep them busy."

He needed no further urging. Racing up the steps, he tore open the front door, barreled into the entranceway, then faltered for the barest second at the sight that met his eyes.

Nigel was running his way, dragging a brute of a dog that was attached to his pant leg, as Poppy ran by his side, two poodles trailing her, although the dogs didn't seem to be trying to attack her. Her eyes widened when she caught sight of him.

"Run, Reginald! She's got a gun!" Poppy yelled right as Lena Ridgeway careened out of a room, a smoking pistol in her hand and a smile on her face that had his blood turning to ice.

Fury soon replaced that ice, though, when Lena stopped running, raised her hand, and aimed at Poppy.

A shot rang out from behind Reginald, one that left Lena shrieking and shaking a hand that no longer held a pistol.

Turning, Reginald found Murray standing behind him, holding a pistol, a look of complete astonishment on his face.

"I told you that your aim was getting better, Murray," Maisie Leggett said, striding forward, her pistol already trained on Lena, who was still shaking her hand as she, oddly enough, plopped down into a dainty chair and crossed her arms over her chest, looking remarkably grumpy.

331

"I wasn't aiming for her pistol," Murray muttered. "I was aiming for over her shoulder, but . . ."

"It's hardly good form for all of you to pay an unannounced call on me," Lena interrupted, releasing a huff. "Why, it's bad manners, no doubt about it. I'm hardly prepared to entertain callers, not with how all of my servants are currently tied up out in the barn, an unpleasant action I was forced to take after they decided I was holding Poppy against her will."

"You were holding Poppy against her will," Reginald said, coming to a stop directly in front of Lena, while Murray hurried to collect the gun he'd shot straight out of Lena's hand. "And to be clear, that's against the law."

Lena waved that aside. "It's not as if anyone is going to cart me off to jail, my dear. I'm rich, filthy rich, and you must know that money can buy a person out of anything." She looked around him and frowned. "But where's Nigel? He was here just a moment ago, as was Poppy."

Reginald frowned. "They fled outside because you were apparently trying to shoot them."

"But not to *kill* them. I was only trying to get them to listen to reason." With that, Lena's gaze suddenly turned vacant as she looked around the room, obviously having retreated to a world Reginald couldn't see.

"You should go see to Poppy," Murray said, nodding toward the door. "Maisie and I will watch over Lena, although I get the distinct feeling she's not a threat to anyone right now. Nigel, however, might be a different story."

"Too right you are," Reginald said, racing for the door. He leapt down the front stairs and took off across the lawn, skidding to a stop when he found Nigel lying in the middle of the lawn, holding a nose that was bleeding while Beatrix stood over him.

"Give me one good reason why I shouldn't shoot you," Beatrix demanded.

"You can't shoot him, Beatrix," Poppy said, striding around the corner of the house, the two poodles still by her side. "He's as much a victim of Lena's madness as I was." She stopped by Beatrix's side, held out a hand to Nigel, then after he got to his feet, thrust what seemed to be a piece of fabric at him.

"Brutus tore that from your trousers," Poppy said. "Might as well use it to staunch the bleeding from your nose."

"What happened to Brutus?" Nigel said, swiveling his head to look over the yard, stilling when he caught sight of Reginald, who narrowed his eyes on Nigel for the merest of seconds before he returned his attention to Poppy.

She was wearing a dress that was made up of yards and yards of fabric and bows, the fabric trailing over the grass behind her. Her hair was pulled back in an untidy tail that streamed down her back, and her face was pale, but she looked more beautiful than she'd ever looked to him.

"Lena apparently commanded Brutus to guard both of us," Poppy said, pulling Reginald from his perusal. "But when he tried to round me up, those two"—she sent a nod to the poodles—"went after him. Last I saw, he was racing over that far hill, and I doubt we'll be seeing him again."

"Can't claim to be upset about that," Nigel said. "I really grew to detest that dog."

"What I'm curious about is why it doesn't appear as if Poppy detests you," Beatrix said, her eyes flashing on Nigel.

"I'm curious about that as well," Reginald said, moving forward as what could only be described as a ruckus sounded from the cottage.

"We need some help in here," Maisie called through the front door, ducking as a book flew over her head.

"Good heavens, I forgot about Lena," Poppy said, lifting up the hem of her skirt as she dashed toward the cottage.

"I've got this, Poppy. Stay out here," Viola yelled, hurrying for the door, sternly shooing away a dog that had begun to growl at her, which had the dog whimpering and dashing away.

"You're not going in there without me," George shouted, racing to join his wife.

Poppy, being Poppy, didn't stop her mad dash toward the house until she suddenly tripped on the skirt of her gown, sprawling in a heap on the ground, the two poodles immediately cavorting around her, as if they thought she was playing some type of game with them.

Striding to join Poppy as Viola called out that everything was in control in the house, Reginald stilled when the poodles stopped yipping and began growling, their growls ceasing the second Poppy sat up and wagged a finger at them. "Stop it. You're being rude." Lifting her head, she caught his eye.

"I'm surprised to see *you* here," she said, shoving aside hair that was falling in front of her face. "Not that I'm complaining, mind you, since you've once again raced to my rescue, but why aren't you back in London?"

"I couldn't very well return to London after I discovered you were missing, nor would I have returned to London even if you hadn't gone missing, not until I had a chance to apologize to you." He held out his hand, which she ignored, but that might have been because one of the poodles was licking her face. "You made it abundantly clear at the ball that you never wanted to see me again, but I'm hoping you'll at least give me a few minutes of your time to explain why I didn't tell you the truth about me."

Poppy peered over the poodle's head. "I'm listening."

Reginald blew out a breath. "I was afraid you'd be furious with me once you discovered I'd been less than honest with you."

"I was furious with you."

He caught her eye. "And now?"

"My time spent locked away allowed my temper to cool."

"Does that mean you're ready to forgive me?"

Poppy pushed the poodle off her lap and lumbered to her feet. "I suppose that depends on that apology you mentioned you wanted to give me."

Reginald glanced to where Nigel and Beatrix were standing, finding both of them watching him closely, Nigel holding the bit of fabric from his trousers against his nose.

"I'm not sure now is the appropriate time to discuss the matter, Poppy," he began. "I'm still woefully confused about what part Nigel had to play in your abduction, or why I shouldn't be considering tearing the man limb from limb."

"Not that I'm an expert in the lady department," Charles suddenly called out, striding across the lawn with Edith at his side, "but I believe you'll have plenty of time to sort out the Nigel business. You might not have much time to sort out the Poppy business if you hesitate to do as she just asked and apologize."

"That means get on with it," Edith said, pulling Charles to a stop a few feet away from Reginald even as she sent him a rather telling arch of a brow.

"She's very forthright, isn't she?" Charles asked with a smile, taking hold of Edith's hand, which she immediately tugged free. "And exactly what I need."

"This isn't your moment, Charles," Edith pointed out, although she did so while returning Charles's smile with a smile of her own.

"Quite right, so . . ." Charles nodded to Reginald. "Have at it. We're listening."

Reginald frowned. "I'm not sure I want all of you listening."

"Too bad," Charles countered. "We're not going anywhere."

Blowing out a breath, Reginald turned to Poppy. "I'm not sure where to begin."

"I believe 'I'm sorry, Poppy, for misleading you' might be a way to start," Poppy suggested. "And then you might move on to begging my forgiveness."

His lips twitched. "Should I repeat everything you just said, or is it sufficient if I just agree with all that and move on from there?"

Her eyes narrowed the slightest bit. "What do you mean, move on from there?"

He took a step toward her, and then another, smiling when she immediately took a step away from him. "I figured that since you got my apology out of the way for me, that I should move on to the next bit."

"The next bit?"

"Indeed," he said, reaching her a second later. Smiling, he pulled her into his arms, ignored that one of the poodles seemed to have sunk its teeth into the leg of his trousers, lowered his head, and . . . kissed her.

Poppy immediately stiffened in his arms for all of a second until she, much to his relief, stole her arms around his neck, leaned into him, and began kissing him back.

As the worry he'd been holding ever since he'd learned she'd gone missing faded away, Reginald knew that no matter what it took he was never letting the lady in his arms slip away from him again.

He loved her. It was as simple as that, even though she was the most exhausting and exasperating lady he'd ever met in his life.

Life would never be dull with Poppy by his side.

"You seem to be getting distracted because, if you didn't realize this, you stopped kissing me," Poppy said, taking a step away from him, her nose wrinkling.

He smiled. "Guilty as charged, but I only became distracted because that remarkable kiss we were sharing had me thinking about other remarkable things."

A touch of color stained her cheeks. "You found our kiss remarkable?"

"I find everything about you remarkable."

And just like that, she was back in his arms, yanking his head toward hers right before she kissed him.

"Not sure I approve of a man kissing my granddaughter like that," Reginald suddenly heard George bluster, which had him ending the kiss and glancing toward the house.

George was standing on the porch, shaking his head, while Viola and Maisie were leading a very docile-looking Lena out the front door, steering her toward the red carriage. Murray walked behind them, pistol at the ready, in case Lena turned wild again.

"Someone might want to let Lena's servants out of the barn," Viola called. "We could use their help as we take Lena back to the city."

"Don't take her to jail," Nigel said, striding over to join them. "She doesn't deserve that because she's obviously not well."

"Where do you suggest we take her?' Viola asked.

Nigel frowned and took hold of Lena's hand, not that she seemed to realize that since she now appeared to be in an almost catatonic state. "I'd welcome any suggestion you may have, Mrs. Van Rensselaer. Perhaps, if you and your husband would be so kind as to ride in the carriage with me, we can determine where best to keep her, hopefully in a more pleasant setting than that of an asylum. She mentioned she doesn't care for those, and it might be worth considering to try and find a place that would allow her to keep her dogs."

"I'm sure, what with the fortune Lena has at her disposal, we'll be able to make arrangements for her that will keep her somewhat happy while keeping society safe from her madness," Viola said, earning a nod from Nigel before he helped Lena into the carriage, her dogs immediately jumping in with her, although the two poodles who'd been licking Poppy gave a few yips good-bye before they joined the pack.

"I'd best give Nigel a hand," Murray said, climbing into the carriage, Maisie squishing herself in after him, a dog immediately climbing into her lap.

A second later, Viola, with George by her side, began advancing rather determinedly toward Reginald.

There was something slightly terrifying about being approached by grandparents after they'd just witnessed their granddaughter being soundly kissed, although Poppy had initiated their last kiss, but still.

"Shall we assume you've accepted Reginald's apology, Poppy?" Viola asked, smiling at her granddaughter, who immediately returned the smile.

"I believe you can assume exactly that," Poppy said.

"And . . . ?" George pressed, arching a brow Reginald's way.

"I've not actually had time to get more than the apology business taken care of," he admitted.

"Seems like you have some time now, what with Lena and Nigel out of the way, although I'm still rather confused about what his role is in all this." George nodded to Poppy. "I thought the man fancied you, which had me thinking he'd stolen you away to force you to marry him."

"The abduction was all Lena's idea," Poppy said. "As for Nigel fancying me, he might have thought he did at first, but he apparently came to the conclusion that I'm exhausting." She turned and caught Reginald's eye. "Something you've remarked upon a time or two as well."

"But I, unlike Nigel, find that completely charming," Reginald said.

Poppy's eyes twinkled. "How delightful."

"Will you also find it delightful if I say that I adore you, love you, and will do whatever it takes to make you my wife?"

She blinked. "Absolutely."

"Good." He leaned closer to her. "And would it also be delightful if I tell you that George and I have been talking about creating a charity in the family name, one that you and I would run, if you're agreeable?"

"That's delightful as well."

"Wonderful." He moved even closer to her. "How about if I tell you I want to live in New York and not England, and—"

She placed a finger over his lips. "There's really no need for you to continue."

"Why not?" he said around her finger.

"Because I love you as well, and I was yours from the moment you called me remarkable."

Unable to argue with that type of logic, Reginald wrapped his arms around her and kissed her again, although it was a rather chaste kiss since George and Viola were looking on. However, as he held Poppy close, he decided there and then that remarkable was a word he would take to using often, especially since he knew that a life with Poppy was certain to be quite remarkable indeed.

EPILOGUE

JUNE 1886

"I've done it now, disappointed my mother again, but this time, instead of banning me from Newport or revoking my credit in all the stores, she's threatening to send me off to stay with a spinster aunt in Chicago."

Looking up from the ledger she'd been working on, one that listed donations she kept track of for those in need, Poppy smiled as Beatrix sailed into the library, looking fashionable as always, although her hair was somewhat of a mess as red curls escaped their pins.

"What did you do?" Poppy asked as Beatrix flung herself into a chair.

"It's not so much what I did—it's what Thomas Hamersley did." Beatrix released a dramatic sigh. "He apparently got up the nerve to tell his mother he was in love with Helene. Mrs. Hamersley then surprised him by giving him her blessing, declaring she'd become fond of Helene and found her to be a most delightful lady. With that blessing in hand, Thomas proposed to Helene, she said yes, and they'll be getting married soon."

"But that's wonderful. Helene adores Thomas."

Beatrix waved that aside. "Yes, yes, of course she does, but

I would have thought they'd have given me a bit of notice. My mother was convinced Thomas and I would wed at some point, an idea that I freely admit I continued to allow her to believe, what with how it spared me any matchmaking attempts on her part." She released another sigh. "Mother's now furious with me, believes I'm destined to remain a spinster, which might be what got her thinking about that spinster aunt in Chicago."

"I've heard Chicago is lovely."

"I'm sure it is, but I've only encountered Aunt Gladys a few times in my life, and from what I can recall of her, she's unpleasant."

"Perhaps if you were to try and behave yourself for the rest of the summer, your mother will reconsider."

"That sounds like a lot of work."

"What sounds like a lot of work?"

Poppy's heart immediately skipped a beat as she looked to the door, knowing she'd find Reginald there, the man she would forevermore call *husband*.

They'd married a mere six weeks after he'd rescued her from Lena, deciding to be married in the small church Poppy had attended since birth. Reverend Thomas Cameron had officiated, and he'd not been able to disguise his delight that Poppy had, indeed, discovered what else the world had to offer after she'd gone to New York. She'd found the man she was meant to spend the rest of her life with as well as a good use for some of the Van Rensselaer fortune. She and Reginald were currently in the process of creating a charity that would lend much-needed assistance to the most vulnerable of New York City.

Reginald's parents, the Duke and Duchess of Sutherland, along with Reginald's sister, and his brother, his brother's wife, and their children, had caused quite the stir when they'd arrived in Poppy's hometown. But while the duke was one of the most important gentlemen in England, he'd hurried to put everyone at ease, insisting on being addressed as Richard, while his wife had done the same, preferring Lizzie over Your Grace.

After Poppy and Reginald had gotten married, and after they'd taken a holiday traveling by private Pullman car back to New York, stopping anywhere that struck their fancy, Viola had given them a large reception, inviting the entire New York Four Hundred. To Poppy's surprise, she was greeted by society with enthusiasm and told numerous times by young ladies and society matrons alike that her debut had been the success of the Season.

After New York, they'd traveled to England with Viola and George, Poppy wanting to see where Reginald had grown up and meet the members of his family who'd not been able to attend their wedding. She'd turned a bit anxious when she'd gotten a look at the homes Reginald had once lived in, but he, apparently realizing her distress, had hurried to reassure her. He claimed he would always love England, but while he'd grown up in country estates that a person could get lost in, surrounded by artwork done by the early masters, nothing had ever been strictly his, since the laws of entitlement demanded everything be passed down to the eldest son.

America was where he wanted to make his mark.

After making a stop in Paris to order fashions from Worth for the upcoming Season, which Poppy was determined to only enjoy in limited amounts, Reginald set about finding them the perfect location on Fifth Avenue to build a house of their own. They'd settled on a lot that wasn't too far away from Viola and George, but just far enough.

That house was not quite finished, which was why Poppy and Reginald were currently still living at her grandparents' house, although Viola and George had repaired not to Newport for the summer, but to Kentucky, both intent on making up for lost time with Elizabeth and Harold as well as with their two grandsons.

"Poppy believes if I behave myself, my mother won't be so put out with me," Beatrix said, pulling Poppy from her thoughts.

Reginald smiled. "Then I take it she heard about Thomas and Helene?"

"Where'd you hear that? I only heard a few hours ago."

"Miss Mabel. I stopped in at Rutherford & Company after I went to check on how progress is going on the Van Rensselaer Charity House down in Five Points. She also told me that Adele Tooker, after her mother whisked her away to take a tour of the continents, is to marry the Earl of Crawford."

Beatrix wrinkled her nose. "That hardly seems right, not with how conniving Adele was with Lord Lonsdale."

Reginald smiled. "The Earl of Crawford lives on an estate far removed from London, and while he does travel back to London to take his place in the House of Lords, he's not a very affable man, which means he and Adele will probably suit each other admirably, spending their lives bickering about one matter after another."

"Oh, well, that's all right then, and at least Mrs. Tooker can take some comfort in the fact her daughter is procuring the family a title, which might soothe some of the embarrassment that poor lady felt at the first Patriarch Ball so many months ago when Lord Lonsdale was trying to make his grand announcement. But, speaking of mothers, I really should return to mine." Beatrix rose to her feet. "I left before we'd finished our conversation because it was turning rather heated, but if I let her stew too long, well, it's never pleasant."

She sent Poppy a wink. "Besides, you're watching Reginald again in a most concerning fashion, one that suggests you'd like to kiss him. And what with me apparently well on my way to becoming a confirmed spinster, I don't believe that's something I want to witness. Might make me turn morose and all." With that, she blew Poppy a kiss, sent Reginald a cheeky grin, then sailed out of the room quite the same way she'd sailed into it.

"I say she'll be married by next Christmas," Reginald said before he smiled a smile that turned Poppy's knees all sorts of wobbly. "But since we are now alone . . ."

He'd barely taken two steps toward her when Murray strode into the room, looking dashing in a custom-made suit. He stopped in his tracks. "I'm not interrupting anything, am I?"

"I was about to kiss my wife."

"Oh, so no, I'm not interrupting anything too important since you can commence with the kissing after I leave." He threw himself into the chair Beatrix had just vacated. "I've been banished from my mother's house."

"You don't live there anymore," Poppy said.

"I know that, and before I forget, Maisie and I have purchased the lot right next to where you're building your house on Fifth Avenue. Thought I should tell you before it's finished in case you don't want to live next to us."

Reginald strode to stand before Murray, holding out his hand. "Don't be an idiot. Of course we'd love to have you and Maisie as neighbors. Congratulations."

Murray grinned and shook Reginald's hand. "That's a relief. Maisie has her heart set on that lot, and I would so hate to disappoint her."

"What are you going to do with the unit you purchased at the Osborne Flats where you're living now?"

"I'm going to make that my art studio." He released a dramatic breath. "My art, though, is exactly why I got banished from Mother's house for the afternoon. She and Maisie are up in the attic, sorting through all the paintings I've done over the years to see if any of them are good enough to display in the art gallery Maisie insisted I open. They didn't seem to appreciate it when I pointed out that some of the pieces are rubbish, so they tossed me out. Having already stopped by my tailor and then taking a stroll through the store where I buy my paints, I was beginning to run out of things to occupy my time. I was riding Wilbur past my new lot on Fifth Avenue, and because it's not far from here, and because Wilbur does adore you, Poppy, I thought I might as well stop and see if you and Reginald were in."

"I should go say hello to Wilbur and take him a carrot as well."

"We'll come with you," Reginald said, and taking hold of her hand, they walked with Murray through the kitchen to get a carrot, then outside into a beautiful sunny day.

"Still intending on building a stable next to the Van Rensselaer

Charity House so you can rescue workhorses that are too weary to work?" Murray asked.

"I am, although Reginald and I are also looking into buying a farm outside the city with pastures, where the horses would have space to roam." She smiled. "Maria Romano's father, Mr. Frank Romano, who has been making quite the name for himself as a master plumber, has an interest in moving his family out of the city. I'm happy to say that he would be willing to live on a horse farm in the future if we find one that would still allow him to continue growing his plumbing business."

"Remarkable how our encounter with Maria that day in the snow managed to improve the entire Romano family's life," Reginald said.

"Remarkable indeed," Poppy agreed, the very word reminding her that she had some pretty remarkable news to tell Reginald and had been trying to think of the perfect—

"Oh, I almost forgot," Murray said, drawing Poppy's attention. "I ran into Nigel at the House of Industry when I was dropping off some clothing Maisie has been collecting for those in need. He'd apparently just returned from a business trip to London where he met with Lord Lonsdale. It turns out there's a vast amount of coal on a few of Charles's estates, and the two men have agreed to work together." He smiled. "From what Nigel told me, it's going to be a lucrative venture and will provide Charles with what sounds like an impressive fortune."

"But Charles has no need of another fortune, not when it turned out Edith Iselin's fortune was larger than any of the other heiresses out last year," Poppy pointed out.

Murray nodded. "True, but Nigel seemed to be of the belief that becoming involved in the coal industry was a way for Charles to prove to Edith that he truly loves her simply for herself and not for her money."

Reginald smiled. "Edith certainly turned out to be exactly what Charles needed. She's a no-nonsense lady who fills the role of countess admirably, and she's even quite proficient at managing

Charles's mother, the dowager countess, making her mother-in-law stick to a strict allowance." Reginald's smile widened. " I have to imagine Edith will insist on working closely with Charles and Nigel as they enter into business together, making certain Nigel stays committed to abandoning his old, and need I say, nefarious, business ways."

Poppy returned the smile. "I think Nigel *has* changed his ways. He makes a point of visiting Lena at the Long Island Home Hotel for Nervous Invalids every week when he's in town, a place she seems most content, what with how they agreed to allow her the company of her dogs. According to Nigel, she's even grown accustomed to the guards who are tasked with watching her every hour of the day and apparently doles out advice when they share their romantic troubles with her."

Murray shook his head. "Not certain how sound that advice could be, but at least she's not been forced to spend the rest of her life in an asylum."

"Which she does have Nigel to thank for, since he is the one who convinced the doctors that even though Lena couldn't live freely among society, she deserved to at least live the rest of her life in some semblance of peace." Poppy smiled. "If that's not proof that Nigel's turned his back on his previous ways, there's also how much of his time he spends at the House of Industry. He told me he enjoys volunteering there and especially enjoys spending time in the company of Reverend Lewis. Reverend Lewis is certainly inspirational, and has, I believe, allowed all of us to realize we have a duty as children of God to take a more active interest in those less fortunate."

"Can't argue with that," Murray said. "I'm sure Reverend Lewis is delighted that members of the New York Four Hundred are beginning to do more than simply send charities a few dollars every now and again. He has you to thank for that, Poppy, what with how you've turned so determined to get all of society involved in philanthropic endeavors."

"She can be determined when she sets her mind to it," Reginald said, smiling as he caught Poppy's eye, the smile leaving her distinctly weak at the knees again.

Murray released a snort. "Honestly, there the two of you go again. I think this is where I take my leave before you embarrass me." Giving Poppy's cheek a kiss, then shaking Reginald's hand, he swung himself up into the saddle, clicked his tongue, then sent them a cheery wave as Wilbur ambled away.

"Do you think we're really alone at last?" Reginald asked, taking hold of Poppy's hand and pulling her back into the house through the kitchen.

"Until someone else arrives at the door."

Reginald looked to Mr. Parsons, who was stirring something in a bowl as Mrs. Hardie poured more flour into it. "Would you tell anyone else who might come to call that Poppy and I aren't receiving visitors this afternoon?"

Mr. Parsons smiled. "Of course. I'm sure it must get a bit tiring being the most sought-after couple in the city."

"You have no idea," Reginald said with a grin, pulling Poppy through the kitchen and then up to the suite of rooms they were using until their house was finished.

"I was thinking we might go to Delmonico's for dinner later," Reginald said, kicking off his shoes before he dropped into a cushy chair in the sitting room attached to their bedchamber.

"That might be nice, although I've been somewhat queasy today, so we'll need to wait and see if my stomach settles down."

Concern immediately flashed through his eyes as he took her hand and pulled her down directly on his lap. "Do you think you're coming down with a cold?"

Poppy considered that for all of a second before she blew out a breath. "I wasn't intending on merely blurting this out, but I'm not coming down with a cold. I'm coming down with something remarkable."

Reginald grew completely still. "What?"

"Remarkable. I'm coming down with—or rather, carrying might be a better way to phrase it—something remarkable."

Reginald shifted her on his lap. "Am I to understand you're expecting?"

Poppy's vision turned a touch blurry. "I am. We'll be increasing our family before the year is out, and if you ask me, life can't get any more remarkable than that."

"I won't argue with you there." With that, Reginald brushed a tear from her face. "Have I told you today how much I love you?"

"At least twenty times."

"I've been a bit negligent then." With that, he told her he loved her again, drew her head toward his, and then . . . he kissed her.

ACKNOWLEDGMENTS

The longer I'm in this unusual world of publishing, the more I understand how much effort in takes on the part of a great many people to get my stories out into the hands of readers. I'd like to take a moment to thank some of those people.

To Raela Schoenherr, my editor who has been with me from my very first book. Your proficiency with story always amazes me, and your suggestions have improved my writing with every book.

To Jennifer Veilleux, a recent, and I must add, wonderful addition to my editing team. Your willingness to chat through plot points is so appreciated, especially when I write myself into corners and have no idea how to get out of those disasters.

To Noelle Chew, my marketing director and friend. Even though you did make me hike to dinner in really hot weather, up an incredibly steep hill, while wearing heels, I always enjoy your company, as well as your expertise in everything publishing related.

To Amy Green, my publicist. You rock. There's really nothing else to add there.

To Rachael Wing, my adoptive daughter. Thanks for taking it upon yourself to decide I needed an assistant. You're a bit bossy, but you were right—I desperately needed your help. So delighted you've found your perfect job at Bethany House. I can't wait to see what the future has in store for you.

To everyone else at Bethany House. You've been amazing to work with all these years. I couldn't do this without you.

To Natasha Kern, my incredible agent. Thanks for all the support and advice. I appreciate you always looking out for me.

To Al and Dom, my guys. I'll just leave it at that because I know it embarrasses both of you when I get mushy.

To The Gilded Gals of Turano Street, my fabulous street team. Thank you for the amazing support you give me, as well as all the ways you go about promoting my work. It's been such a pleasure getting to know all of you.

To all my readers. You're the best part of my job! Thanks for reading my stories.

And to God, who gives me all of my stories and gives me so much more every day of my life.

Jen Turano, a *USA Today* bestselling author, is a graduate of the University of Akron with a degree in clothing and textiles. She is a member of ACFW and RWA. She lives in a suburb of Denver, Colorado. Visit her website at www.jenturano.com.